Redeemed

Redeemed by Pollyanna Porter

Author of *Rectified*, a 2022 Eric Hoffer Book Award da Vinci
Eye Finalist and RECOMMENDED by the US Review of Books

· · · · ·

"This compelling family saga starts with a bang and keeps
exploding like a string of fireworks. We're swept along from
the tranquil confines of a Vermont barn to the sordid
secrets of WW2 Nazis, by way of New York's art world.
There is insightful depth of character and emotion but
never at the expense of suspense, mystery…and just a touch
of the supernatural. "

— Joseph A. Citro, author of *Loose Ends*, *Passing Strange*,
  and *Shadow Child*

· · · · ·

"Told through the points of view of the major characters,
this book moves at a mesmerizing fast pace. David discov-
ers that his grandparents were involved in returning stolen
art from the Nazis to its rightful owners. History buffs are
sure to enjoy the connection to the Monuments Men, and
the author includes historical information about their
endeavors. This moving story follows David and the Dunne
family through upheaval and tragedy. The author hits just
the right balance of fascinating historical details and
romantic intrigue. The characters are well-rounded, and
the dialogue flows smoothly throughout the work. Porter's
novel is exceptionally well-written with beautiful descriptive
language. Her book is a must-read for history buffs and
romantics."

— *US Review of Books*, Book Review by Kat Kennedy

Redeemed

Pollyanna Porter

2022 / *Vermont*

Book Design by Jennifer Payne,
Words by Jen (Branford, CT)

Quote by Angelou, Maya from *What It Takes interview*, American Academy of Achievement, May 2018

Printed in the USA

Library of Congress Control Number: 2022919152

ISBN: 978-0-578-78295-9

Copies of *Redeemed* may be purchased
from online retailers or by visiting:

www.pollyannaporter.com

Dedication

*To my grandchildren — Reese, Brody, Will
and Liv. May your lives be filled with worth
and purpose, health and happiness.*

and

*To the memory of my own grandmother, Dah.
Bertha Thomas Porter (1888-1975)*

*Once, a young girl and an old woman had
all the time in the world for each other,
and the child never forgot.*

"When you know you are of worth, you don't have to raise your voice. You don't have to become rude. You don't have to become vulgar. You just are, and you are like the sky is, as the air is, the same way water is wet. It doesn't have to protest."

— Maya Angelou

1999

David

Emily, yes, I'm trying to pull over. Hold the line. Shit, there are absolutely no fucking shoulders in Vermont. Give me a second."

I slowed down and turned into a small entrance to what looked like a boat launch. I put the rental in park and climbed out. The morning sun was peeking through the trees above, shadows dappling the area. The small lake in front of me was a blue-green and very still.

"Are you ready? The bidding starts in ten, nine, eight..." Emily's voice was breaking up.

I walked over to a large rock near the ramp to the water and held the flip phone up close to me. There was no one on the lake. Across the way was a beach with a swimming rope and, further back, a snack bar and bathrooms. Several paddle boats and canoes were lined up along a small pier. At this time, 8:30 a.m., no one was about. I strained to hear what was going on with Emily.

"David, sorry, this isn't the Baylor painting. I thought it was. It's coming up."

"Okay, Emily, can you hear me better now?"

"Yes, now I can. Stay put. At the start of the call, you were in and out."

I sat on the rock and took in the morning, here off Route 100. I didn't recall the name of the lake. I tried to remember if it was Lake Amherst — or was it something like Woodriff? The area across the water was Plymouth State Park, but the lake wasn't named Plymouth. I was sure of that. I used to come here for end-of-the-year school picnics when I was young, but I had forgotten this whole area. Right now, though, I was greatly annoyed that I was here and not in New York at the auction. But, as the only living relative of my grandfather, it was imperative that I come back to attend his service and meet with the executor of his estate.

I heard a woman's voice and turned to the dock at my right. A small cottage was nestled in the narrow strip of land that bordered the lake. It was brown clapboard with an old gray dock jutting out. I heard the woman call to someone, "Remember what Daddy said — no diving, the water's too shallow. The lake is very low right now."

The woman walked into my view. She was tall and wore blue jean cut-offs with a red tank top. Her hair, a light auburn, was pulled up high in a clip. On her hip was a baby patting her chest, its chubby legs clasped firmly around the woman's waist. The baby wore a yellow bonnet, a little white t-shirt, and a diaper. She was nudging at her mother, clearly wanting her breast.

I watched as the woman moved to a bench on the dock and sat down. She lowered the right side of her tank top, exposing a breast. I looked away, suddenly feeling uneasy — she had no idea she was being watched. But then I turned back, my curiosity getting the better of me. The baby latched onto her nipple with enthusiasm. The woman shifted the baby across her lap and took off its bonnet. As the baby nursed, her little hand reached up and played with a loose tendril of her mother's hair.

There was a boy further down the shoreline, just to the right of the dock. He yelled out, "Watch this cannon ball, Mom!" She turned, cupped her hand over her eyes, and watched.

The boy went barreling down the grassy path and jumped into the lake. It was a perfect cannon ball, and I watched the ripples spread out on the surface of the water. It wasn't officially summer until tomorrow. *The water must be freezing,* I thought, remembering my own swimming hole days. The woman turned back and looked down at the baby, brushing her hand across the baby's back. "Amy is hungry this morning, very, very hungry."

I heard Emily say over the line, "This is taking forever, sorry, David."

I didn't reply, too busy watching the woman. I'd never seen someone nurse so openly before, or a baby so enraptured. The way they were looking at one another had such an intimate quality. I knew I should give them privacy. *I'll leave quickly if she sees me.*

The boy appeared again. This time he was further down from the dock, near a large outcrop of rocks. I looked back at his mother. She was oblivious to the boy, focused only on the baby. I heard her start to hum.

There were natural footholds along the rock face, and the boy was intent on climbing to the top of the ledge. His mother had mentioned the lake's low level, how he shouldn't dive. I could tell it was shallow — the tall lake reeds were exposed all up and down the shoreline. Now the boy stood on the ledge and looked as if he was debating whether or not to jump.

Don't do it kid. There was a flat dip in the rock, a perfect launching spot. I looked back at the woman. She remained intent on the baby in her arms, now switching to the other breast.

"David, here we are…"

Emily's voice was lost to me as I saw the boy look at his mother, hesitate, and then dive. I stood up from my rock, straining to see him come back up to the surface. I waited. Nothing.

A dark, almost crimson-looking stain suddenly appeared, floating up to the top. I threw down my phone and pulled off one shoe and then the other and started to run. I managed to shed my suitcoat as I made my way across the boat launch, down along the water's edge, and into the water. While I ran, I yelled at the woman, "Hey! Hey! Your boy! He's hurt!" The water was cold, and instantly my legs felt heavy, my pants ballooning out with the weight of the water.

I waded out to the area where I thought the kid had landed. I looked down and then back up at the spot where he'd dived from. I moved all around, trying to feel for his body.

I followed the blood and suddenly saw the boy, fully submerged under the water. He was listless, floating near a large log on the bottom of the lake's floor. I dove under and pulled him up. Wrapping my arm across his chest, I started to run for the shore, the water just past my waist.

I saw his mother standing at the water's edge. She was holding the baby and screaming, "Tommy! Oh my God!"

I could see a large gash at the top of the boy's head where his hair parted. He was bleeding profusely.

When I reached the shallow water, I hoisted him up into my arms and heard him gasp. "How far is the nearest emergency room?" I yelled.

"In Langdon!" the woman responded. Then she turned quickly to the boat launch. "I don't have a car, is that yours?"

Carrying the boy up out of the water, I nodded and started running to the black sedan 30 yards or so from the cottage. The woman was right behind me with the baby.

I laid the boy in the backseat, and she climbed in beside him. I quickly moved around to the back of the car and opened up the suitcase in the trunk. I grabbed two of my dress shirts, tearing off the dry-cleaning seals.

"Wrap these around his head," I said. "Can you do that and hold the baby?"

The woman was gripping the baby in her arms and holding the boy's head in her lap.

"Take her, please!" she cried out.

I reached in and grabbed the baby. She started to wail.

"Just keep her facing me," the woman said, "and she should be okay."

I watched her wrap the boy's head with my two white shirts. He was unresponsive, and the blood from the gash was seeping through, staining the fabric immediately. The baby continued to scream.

"How many miles?" I was ready to fly.

"About six, down Route one hundred. Once we get into town, it's right there."

The woman reached for the baby and I passed her over. Just before I closed her door, she asked, "He's breathing, you see it, right?" Her eyes were imploring.

"Yes, he's breathing."

I got into the driver's side, backed the car up, and turned left onto the main road. I started to drive, gaining speed and beeping at the few cars I came upon. Miraculously, every vehicle pulled over and I sped on, down the winding scenic route. Cottages nestled among the trees and the dark, blue-green water whirled by as I drove faster than I'd ever dared before. In the back seat, it was deathly quiet. I didn't turn around — I couldn't.

Rachel

He drove fast and I thought, *We'll all be killed. Amy, no car seat and in my lap, Tommy, bleeding all over.* My heart was racing, my hands shaking as I held on tight to both my babies. I pointed at the road, silently telling the man to take the fork up Vernon Street to the emergency room doors.

The minute he pulled in and stopped, he yelled, "Now! We need help now!" Two people were smoking cigarettes on the grassy bank, and one of them dropped theirs and ran through the doors.

The man, still covered in blood, jumped out and came to the backseat, opening the door wide. He had a panicked look, but then put a hand on his chest and took a deep breath. Bending down and in a much calmer voice, he said, "Tell them that when he dove down he hit a log on the bottom of the lake. And that he wasn't submerged for more than twenty seconds — thirty tops, okay?"

I nodded and started to move Tommy, but he shook his head, "I think they're going to come fast; let them lift him."

Just then two men came rushing out with a gurney and placed Tommy carefully on it.

"What's his blood type?" one of them asked, and then, "Is he on any meds?"

I answered and they sped off. I reached out and handed Amy to the man, right there, standing just outside the door. "Keep her safe, please!" I implored. The man had saved Tommy and gotten us here in one piece — he could stand guard a little longer. I turned and ran after the EMTs into the building. I shuddered as I felt the air conditioning hit me and then followed the gurney through two sets of double doors. I was scared; my hands shaking and splattered in Tommy's blood.

David

I looked down at the baby and watched her lips begin to quiver as she stared at me, winding up, getting ready to cry. Remembering what her mother said earlier, I quickly turned her to face forward, surprised by how heavy she was.

I went into the emergency room like that: barefoot, drenched, with no phone and no identification. It was all back at the boat launch. I stood and watched the nurses behind the glass partition. I finally asked, "Hey, does anyone know the little boy and the woman who just came in?"

One of the younger nurses who had been talking on the phone made her way over to me. "Hey, hi. I'm Donna, a friend of Rachel's." I looked at her blankly.

"You know, Tommy's mother?" She reached down to touch the baby. "And sweet little Amy here."

"Okay, good. So, the boy is Tommy, and the mom is Rachel and this surprising little tanker is Amy. Has anyone called their family? I was driving by and pulled off — right before this all happened."

I shifted the baby. I was leaving a puddle of water where I stood. My toes were dirty; wet lake sand covered them.

"Yes, I just did," Donna said. "Rachel's husband is on his way here, and I believe Susan, Rachel's mother, is very close by and coming as well."

"Good, that's good," I replied. Amy was putting her fingers in her mouth and making all sorts of noises. She didn't seem at all fazed by my wet shirt against her back. "Do we know how the boy's doing yet?"

"I think we will shortly. I do know you saved his life. You know that, right?"

Just then an older woman, maybe about 60, came in through the double doors. She looked frightened, but then smiled when she saw Amy. She walked up to me. "There's our baby girl!"

Amy enthusiastically greeted her, kicking her legs and squirming. The woman reached out to take her.

"Please," I said, handing Amy to her.

The woman saw my blood-stained shirt and, with clear fear in her voice, asked, "Donna, what about Tommy?" The woman looked like an older version of the mother — Rachel — with long gray hair held back in a big clip.

"I know they're working on him now; we'll hear soon," said Donna before she moved away from us.

Susan asked, "Can you tell me what happened?" She motioned to a bank of chairs adjacent to the entrance doors and we sat down. I felt a blast of warm air come through as two people entered.

I explained the boy's dive from the rock ledge and his mother not being aware that he had done it. "He didn't come up. I ran to him and found him under the water." I ended with, "My guess is a concussion and stitches, and probably no swimming for a while."

Susan reached over and took my hand. "Oh my gosh, you saved him. Thank you so much. I don't know what else to say…just thank you." Amy was cooing in her grand-mother's lap but now looked at me and smiled on cue.

Suddenly a big guy came in. His blond hair was cropped short and he wore gray athletic shorts and a maroon Langdon baseball tee. A coach's whistle dangled from around his neck. He held a ball cap in his hands.

"Mom! How's Tommy, what's going on?" He looked at the three of us, clearly in a state of alarm.

Susan gestured to me. "This man here saved Tommy — saw him dive and not come up. He pulled him out of the lake, then drove Rachel, Tommy, and Amy here. We haven't heard anything yet."

I stood up.

"Holy shit, man, thank you." The big guy gave me a bear hug as he spoke. He then took the baby from the woman and raised her up to kiss her head, her face, her belly. The baby, oblivious to the drama unfolding, started laughing.

"Tom — Rachel wants you." The younger nurse from before was standing just outside in the hallway.

"Okay, thanks, really. Mom, can you get his number, please?" The man — Tom — gave the baby to Susan and disappeared through the double doors.

I turned to her. "I should get back to the boat launch and recover my shoes and things, maybe find a place to change." I could feel the tension in my neck and shoulders and rolled my head back and around to try and relieve it. It had been one big adrenaline rush from the moment I ran into the water to racing to the hospital and now here with the family. I needed to decompress. "But I want to know how the boy is. Can you call me? I'll give you my card."

Susan smiled and said, "Of course."

But when I reached for my wallet, I realized I didn't have it. "Ah, I forgot. It's back at the lake. Could you take down my number?"

"Yes, absolutely. Let me get something to write on from the nurses' station."

She returned shortly. "Here you go, again." She handed Amy back to me while she stood poised with pen and paper.

The baby, perhaps growing familiar with my face, reached up and touched my ear. It felt strange, and I moved my head back, away from her reach. Her little hands, my wet pants, and the whole atmosphere of the waiting room was getting to me. But then the baby started to make noises — loud babbling. It was definitely the start of early talking. I couldn't resist and asked her, "Is that so?" She smiled up at me and continued to babble.

"Ready," Susan said, and I told her my cell number and then added my New York number too.

Suddenly Amy stopped her baby talk and dove for her toes, trying to nibble them. "Whoa, where you going?" I said, holding her back up awkwardly. I wasn't used to babies at all.

"And your name?" Susan asked, looking up. I saw her daughter's features on her face.

"David Sumner."

"I'm Susan Blanchard, and this beautiful little girl is Amy Dunne. My daughter is Rachel, and you just met my son-in-law, Tom — her daddy. And Tommy Junior is the boy you saved."

I nodded and replied, "I think your grandson is going to be fine, but please, call me to let me know when you can."

Susan reached for Amy. I patted her bare back as I gave her to her grandmother.

"David, thank you, thank you so much." We hugged awkwardly. I tried to keep my wet clothes from brushing up against her.

I stepped outside and inhaled deeply. I was relieved to be done with the baby; the whole experience had drained me. The rental car was right where I had left it; haphazardly parked at an angle across two spaces. The backseat door was still wide open. I closed it and climbed in behind the wheel. I was terribly thirsty and needed water.

IT WAS EASY TO FIND MY WAY BACK along Route 100 North. I pulled into the boat landing and parked once more. My phone, sunglasses, shoes, and suitcoat — with my wallet in the pocket — were all where I had thrown them, scattered along the way to the water's edge just past the other side of the cottage. I had seven missed calls and three *"What the fuck…"* text messages, all from Emily. The Baylor painting was long gone, and I was going to hear about it.

I stood at the trunk of the rental and opened my suitcase. I reached in and took out clean boxers and a pair of socks. I didn't have any more clean shirts except for a white t-shirt. I grabbed it. From the garment bag, I took out pressed pants.

Closing the trunk with the clothes now in hand, I looked around to see where I could change. I quickly walked over to the passenger side door and took out the rental's paper floor mat.

The small lake had come alive in the hour and a half I'd been gone. It was just past 10:00 a.m. and the beach across the way was filling up with sunbathers and swimmers. There were two paddle boats and a canoe close to this side of the lake. Two girls wearing life jackets were steering one of the paddle boats. I heard one of them say, "We aren't going out far, why do we have to wear these? I can see the bottom of the lake."

The other one responded, "Paddle harder, let's catch up to them."

A couple of SUVs with empty boat trailers were parked where I had been earlier. I walked over to the little brown cottage and went around to the dock where the woman had sat. *Rachel* — now I knew her name. She'd acted on impulse, jumping into my car and trusting me with her kids' lives. *Never ever has that happened to me before,* I thought. And I did it too — got the boy help and kept the baby safe.

I stepped up onto the deck. There was a large sliding door facing the lake. I wondered if I dared open the door so I could change inside. I took a chance.

It was small with a loft, rustic and musty smelling. I moved away, just out of the door's range and quickly changed, placing my wet clothes on the paper mat from my car. It didn't take me long. When I was done, I walked into the kitchen, took down a plastic cup, and filled it with tap water. I drank it all down and filled it again. I then placed it in the sink along with a couple of other dishes.

As I started to leave, I saw a framed photograph on the wall near the woodstove in the corner. I quickly walked to it. It was of the family: mom, dad, boy and baby. It was recent; the baby looked just like she did now. I thought the woman was beautiful. I wanted to remember her like this, relaxed and smiling, rather than the frantic woman covered in her son's blood, asking me if he was breathing.

Before I drove away, I turned off my phone. I had a five-hour drive back to the city, and after this morning, I wanted nothing to do with the auction or work or Emily's wrath.

As I once again pulled out onto the main lake road, my thoughts took over. *I saved a life today. I saved a little boy. I, David Sumner, who has never done anything noteworthy, did something significant this morning.*

I turned off the air conditioning and rolled down my windows. Summer scenes of motorboats slicing through the water, kids diving off rafts, and two women picking berries along the side of the road greeted me. Driving much slower this time and in the white t-shirt with my arm resting outside the window, I felt like a teenager again, living back at the farm, wanting my life to start.

When I got back to my apartment in the city, there was a message on my machine. It was Susan, the grandmother, telling me that the boy was going to be just fine. That I had been right — a concussion, stitches, and no swimming for a while. She also added that her daughter, Rachel, would be calling me in the next few days.

I knew I should shower and change and head to the loft to go over what losing the Baylor painting meant with Emily. But I didn't. Instead, I closed the blinds and turned on my sound machine. I glanced at the alarm clock. It was just past 6:00 p.m. I was exhausted. I needed to sleep before going out later. As I closed my eyes, I replayed my hand reaching down and grabbing hold of the boy's arm as he lay at the bottom of the lake. I had pulled him up, surprised at how light he was. *That was my hand,* I thought. *Mine.* For once, I wasn't an asshole messing things up. I closed my eyes and waited for sleep. My grandfather's memorial service seemed like a lifetime ago.

Rachel

I dialed his number and waited.
He picked up on the third ring.
"Hello?"

"Hi, this is Rachel Dunne. You saved my son at Echo Lake a few days ago."

I took the house phone out onto the porch. I sat in the wicker chair and put my legs up over the arm rest. "I wanted to call and personally thank you. I know that's an understatement, but it's all I can say, really. So, thank you."

His voice was surprisingly clear and strong. "You're welcome. I have to tell you — I've been replaying it over a lot in my mind. It was a huge adrenaline rush for me. I'm trying to get all the pieces in place. Did I yell to you when I hit the water? I think that I did, but I'm not sure."

I moved the cell to my left hand and watched two big robins in the crab apple tree just past the screen. I didn't want to, but I replayed the sequence of events of the near drowning in my mind. I remembered I had turned away from the lake side facing the state park and had looked behind me, wondering what all the commotion was at the water's edge. At first, I couldn't tell what or who was making it. I saw a man starting to run into the lake, fully clothed, yelling something. My first thoughts had been, *Wow. He's really pissed at someone.* But then I understood his words and that they were directed at me.

"Yes, you yelled something like, 'Your boy is hurt!' as you made your way to him. I remember being in a daze and running down from the dock. I was so out of it. I'll never forgive myself. It's like I forgot all about Tommy."

"I think you were pretty focused on the baby." There was a pause and then he continued speaking. "I had pulled over to bid in an auction — a work thing. I heard you tell him not to dive. Then, as I was waiting for this auction to start, I watched him go to the big rock wall and knew you weren't aware that he intended to dive."

Hesitantly, I asked, "Did Tommy's accident mess you up? With your work?"

"Not exactly...Well, just a little, but nothing that couldn't be fixed. In my business anything can be smoothed over if you kiss up enough. Um...I have to tell you, I've never done anything remotely like this, ever, in my entire life. It's huge, you know?"

I let that sit for a second. "Yes." And then, "Thank you so much."

"Again, you're welcome."

"Oh, and your shirts...I'm sorry but they were ruined. He bled so much. The doctor said head wounds bleed more than any other part of the body. My husband and I want to reimburse you, though. And I've worried your backseat may have blood stains. Does it?"

"Don't worry about the shirts; I have two dozen of them, hanging up right in front of me. And as far as the car goes, it was a rental. They never said anything."

"Okay, only if you're sure." I didn't know what else to say. He'd seen me at my worst: neglectful and hysterical. I wasn't going to win Mother of the Year in his eyes, that's for sure. I stood up and walked back into the kitchen. Tom was leaning against the counter. I whispered to him, motioning to the phone, "Do you want to talk?" He nodded and I passed the phone to him.

I quickly ran upstairs and opened Tommy's door. He wasn't supposed to read or watch TV for a few weeks. He was quietly playing with his Legos on a table and the curtains were pulled closed, cutting off the light. His room, the smallest of the three bedrooms, was messy; piles of baseball cards and stuffed animals lined the floor and his bed was too little for him now. *This room needs work,* I thought. *Poor kid.*

He looked up and smiled. His hair was shaved and the staples over the cut looked gross, like Frankenstein. I smiled back and said, "The man who saved you is on the phone. Come down and thank him, okay?"

Downstairs, I caught Tom's attention and pointed to Tommy who was now entering the kitchen. I motioned for Tom to hand him the phone. "Hey, Tommy wants to talk. Do you still have time?" Tom asked David Sumner.

I whispered to Tommy, "Start with a big thank you."

He did me one better. "Hi, my name is Tommy Dunne Junior, and I'm the boy you saved. Thanks a lot." Tommy glanced at me. I gave him a thumbs up and Tom smiled. Our little guy was growing up.

Tommy Jr.

I couldn't ride my bike, play ball, or even swim. It sucked. Mom kept raising her eyebrows at me every time I asked to do anything. I even had to stop playing Madden NFL. About the only thing I could do was sit on the porch and go through my cards, all of them — so long as I didn't read the tiny print. Oh, and I could play Legos. But I was sick of Legos. I did get my cards organized and Mom let me get new binders with new plastic sheets. At least that was good.

I was also getting a bigger bed. "It's about time," Mom said when the man at the department store had me lie down and try out the different ones. The one I really wanted was a bunk bed, but Mom quickly put the kibosh on that. "No, I'm not going to lie awake at night, waiting for the crash."

Grammie came by a lot and each time she brought me something good to eat like Ben & Jerry's Chocolate Fudge Brownie ice cream or mint chocolate chip cookies.

One time, I heard Mom say, "You're spoiling him."

And Grammie said back, "I know, but it can't be fun, cooped up the first three weeks of the summer."

Amy wanted to gum everything. I yelled at her the first time I saw one of my baseball cards in her mouth. "Where

did you get that?" She looked at me with her whole face
puckered up, sad-like, and started to cry, big time. I felt
awful that I made her cry, so I picked her up and took her
out into the yard. I let her touch every leaf hanging from the
branches and all the tree trunks she wanted to; we had three
big maples, two birch, and one crab apple tree. We even ran
after a butterfly, me calling out, "Let's get it, Amy!" That
— me carrying her around the yard, letting her touch stuff,
her little hands holding onto my shirt — became something
we did every day as I got better.

We all took turns talking to the man who saved me.
Mom talked the longest, I think. I guess he lives down in
New York City. He was real nice to me and asked if I liked
the Yankees. I told him I love them but only when they lose
to the Red Sox. He agreed!

He then asked me if I'd like to come to Yankee Stadium
and see them lose to the Red Sox in late August. I couldn't
believe it. I gave the phone back to Dad and I heard them
talking dates, and yep, it's true — we're going! That man
must be rich. We're having a party for him, sometime soon,
like in a week. Dad told me he owed the guy more than he
could ever repay him. But a party, with all our friends and
family, would be a great way to show him how thankful we
were.

My head was healing. The staples were almost ready to
come out. I had 16, can you believe it? And a concussion.
I'm lucky to be alive. I could have drowned — actually I was
drowning when he pulled me out. I didn't remember
anything, except deciding to climb the rock ledge where all
the teenagers dive off. That's it.

Mom felt bad, like really bad. Every night she climbed
into bed with me and told me stories, mostly about when
she was little. It felt kind of lame, but I liked her voice, best
of all, and I'd quickly fall asleep.

Tom Sr.

I woke up at exactly 3:12 a.m. and realized Rachel wasn't in our bed. I moved to her side and leaned way over — looking to see if the bathroom was closed in the hallway and if the light was seeping out from under its door. Nope, nothing.

I got up to check the kids' rooms. She wasn't nursing Amy or lying with Tommy. I tiptoed down into the kitchen. It was dark and quiet.

Opening the screen to the porch, I saw her sitting and taking in the night air, although it wasn't much cooler than the day's heat had been. "Hey, Rach, are you okay?"

She turned to me and I saw that she was crying.

In a broken voice, she uttered, "I almost let him drown. No, I *did* let him drown. David Sumter, I mean Sumner, saved him. But if I'd done nothing, just sat there on the dock, nursing Amy, we would have been going to his funeral. He'd be in the ground, Tom, cold and..."

I moved over to the white rocker closest to her and sat down. I knew this had been festering in her head, knew her emotions were raw. When the nurses let us in to see Tommy, Rachel had wept, like big, wailing weeping. I felt sorry for the family in the next room.

"Rachel, you can't go on beating yourself up like this. What good does it do? My God, remember what your mother said? You were nursing a baby, not shooting up heroin."

She wiped the tears and smiled. "Yeah, Mom did help me see that, but since this whole thing, I've really been questioning myself as a mother. If I can't watch my ten-year-old properly, how the hell am I going to make sure my eight-month-old doesn't choke, or fall, or, I don't know, put her finger in a light socket?"

I reached over and took her hand, pulling her to me. She climbed up onto my lap and I wrapped my arms tightly around her. I was big enough that her long legs looked short next to mine.

Rocking slowly, I whispered, "Here's what I know, Rachel Blanchard. You are the best mother there ever was. I know this because you're the best wife there ever was. Remember the night we made Tommy? Pat and that loser boyfriend of hers left the campground arguing. You and I were just hanging out by the fire and you turned to me and asked, 'We'll never be like that, will we?' Remember what I said back?"

"Yes, kind of…but help me remember, what did you say?"

I ran my hands up and down her arms, feeling how soft and supple she was. I then reached up and wiped away the tears that remained on her face. "I said that we were so far beyond that petty shit, and then you snuggled up to me and asked, 'So far beyond that we're ready to be parents?' And that was that. Nine months later, Tommy arrived."

"It's really more like ten months," Rachel replied as she stood up from the rocker. Her hair was disheveled and her nightie was frayed at the neckline. I could see the little girl she once was and what our baby Amy would grow to look like. My heart swelled.

Leaning against the porch door, she paused and said, "I think these feelings, these worries will go. I just need time."

"Come to bed, baby. Stop feeling so guilty." I got up and held out my hand to her.

She looked at me with my hand extended, then turned to the yard that was cloaked in complete darkness. "Okay," she whispered and took my hand.

At the top of the stairs, she hesitated. "I'll be there in just a minute. Let me peek at the kids."

As I was climbing back into bed, I heard my own mother's voice when I told her I was going to ask Rachel to marry me. *"I wish you'd had a chance to date other girls outside of Langdon — even at college — just to be sure. But I'll never wish you met another woman to be the mother of my grandchildren."*

I needed to make her feel that she was an awesome mother. I needed to reinforce it as much as possible this summer. I heard Tommy's door close and Rachel walk into our bedroom. *I also need to start planning the party for David Sumner,* I thought.

David

S he was doing that, you know, with your hair." Rachel
looked up at me and quickly covered herself and Amy
with a light blanket. It had hearts on it — little pink
ones. The music outside had been turned up and the
cul-de-sac was alive with people coming and going. It turns
out the cottage on the lake wasn't their home — this house
in Langdon was. It was a Victorian, big and rambling, with
a screened-in porch like the others in the circle. Its decora-
tive trim needed a new paint job, and a large crab apple tree
long past its spring bloom framed one whole side of the
house. The party was in full swing. After using the bathroom, I had wandered upstairs. Now I stood in the doorway
of the baby's room.

"Tommy played with my hair the same way." Rachel
smiled briefly at me and looked down at Amy who was
nursing.

I'd made it a priority to come to their home tonight and
toast to Tommy's rescue. I had realized, back in New York,
that I couldn't let go of that morning so easily. It had been
seared into my psyche, and my work at the loft in Chelsea
no longer seemed as important as it once did. I was missing
another auction to be here; Emily went in my place. She was

also meeting potential clients out on the island. I'd given the realtor the 'go ahead' to start the listing process on my grandparents' farm and had told him I could come back to Plymouth as many times as he needed me to in order to get the house ready to sell. I didn't quite understand it, but I craved more time with this family — with this woman.

"Do you mind?" I asked as I nodded to the chair against the wall.

"Of course not, sit, please," she said quietly.

Looking around the room — at the crib, the changing table, and the dresser, I could see there was definitely a theme going on of hearts and pink and white gingham prints. The wall had a set of picture art featuring giraffes and elephants, and near the closet was the same family picture I'd seen at the small cottage on the lake.

I glanced over at Rachel and commented, in a low voice, "I think you're like the first authentic Mom I've ever known." As soon as I said it, I regretted my words. She looked puzzled.

"Authentic? Do you mean real? In the city they don't have real moms, mothers?" She smiled, looking inquisitive.

"I mean, well, the women I know, the young women, all have nannies. I never see their kids at all."

She whispered back, "Wow, that must be sad." She moved her free hand up and down Amy's legs. I remembered how surprisingly heavy Amy had felt when I held her in the waiting room.

"Amy's a pretty healthy baby, isn't she? I mean like big and healthy."

Rachel laughed. "Yes, she is. She's in the ninety-sixth percentile. Let's hope she hasn't inherited her father's size."

I smiled. "She'll be a center in the WNBA."

Rachel looked down at her and said, "I think Amy is going to be, well…" Her words drifted off. But then she looked at me and said, "Between Tommy and Amy, I had several miscarriages. Just when I'd finally accepted, you know, that we'd be a family of three, she came along. My little girl is a miracle baby."

I didn't know what to say in response. She appeared vulnerable, and yet, I knew she was strong — the way she'd jumped in my car, holding onto both kids tight and trying to stay calm for their sake. Her attitude had kept me calm all the way to the emergency room.

We sat for a few minutes in the quiet room. Rachel discreetly moved Amy to the other breast. I turned to give her privacy, but looked at her out of the corner of my eye. "I can go. I don't want to make you uncomfortable, you know, while you're feeding her."

Rachel smiled. "I've nursed this child in the middle of Tommy's field trips and at every high school baseball game this season. I think the question is: are you comfortable?"

I nodded and Amy settled in sleepily. I didn't want to leave.

"What is it you do, exactly?" Rachel looked straight at me now. Her mascara was smudged and her hair was messy, especially around her face. There were beads of perspiration above her lip. The baby's room was warm. The drought had continued and the humidity was high.

"I buy and sell art for rich people."

She nodded and rocked a little bit. "How do you know if it's art they'll like? Do you just know them that well?"

"Most of my clients are buying art for investment or status; rarely does personal pleasure or what they like enter into the transaction. In fact, some of my clients have a percentage of ownership in an art piece that they'll never have in their physical possession. It's kind of a thing."

"Really?" Rachel seemed puzzled. "I thought people bought a painting because it 'spoke to them' or it complimented their color scheme or achieved what they were hoping for in their home décor like in a cabin or...um, a cape on the water."

"Ah, art that's geared toward the middle class is like that. You're absolutely right. The art I deal in, however, is often worth thousands, even millions of dollars. You see, to spend that amount, it becomes an investment." I hoped I didn't sound arrogant and quickly added, "Art should move you, should mean more than a clump of money, definitely."

"Wow, millions of dollars...I paid nineteen-ninety-nine for those two prints." She nodded toward the animal art I'd already noticed. "And I thought it might be a rip off."

I laughed and raised my eyebrows. "Oh, believe me, the art world is full of crooks. Art dealers trying to pass off fake masterpieces, sell stolen paintings, or buy legitimate art with dirty money." I watched Amy's body go limp; she was definitely asleep.

Rachel held up her finger to her mouth in a 'shush' signal and stood up. She moved to the crib and gently laid Amy down on her back. I watched her straighten up as she stared down at the sleeping baby. This complete focus was what I remembered from the morning at the lake. A fleeting thought came to me — *Had my own mother ever looked at me like that before she left?*

Rachel moved to the fan in the window and turned it on low, then motioned for me to follow her. We both left the room. She closed the door but left it slightly ajar, reaching for a doorstop 'iron.' My grandparents' house was full of those old doorstops.

Slightly ahead of her as we walked down the hallway, I stopped and took notice of the baby pictures on the wall. I could hear two women talking downstairs. One was asking if the deviled eggs had made it out to the tables. The screen door banged shut. A dog was barking outside. It sounded like it was coming from the back of the house.

Rachel stopped and pointed to the first few pictures. "Tommy when he was three months. Here he is at two."

I smiled and glanced at her. "He looks like Tom, while Amy's more like you."

Unexpectedly, Rachel's eyes swelled and she started to cry. She quickly brought her hands to her face, brushing away the tears. "Sorry, there I go again. I've been a wreck these last few weeks. I can't ever imagine losing him, and I almost did. If you hadn't been there, he would have…" She didn't finish.

"I was there, though," I said softly, standing next to her. "And he's right outside now. Everyone is toasting him tonight." It felt strange being so close and witnessing such raw emotion like this. I didn't know what else to say. I watched her try to compose herself. I wasn't used to a woman so genuine — without any pretenses or hidden agendas.

"No, actually, they're toasting you, David, and we should join them." She suddenly hugged me tightly. "Thank you." She smelled like soap and Amy; a scent I'd smelled for the first time outside the doors of the ER when I was holding the baby. Rachel let go and smiled. I couldn't ever remember being this moved by a woman in tears before.

We made our way down the stairs and into the kitchen.

"I drink a beer or two a week, and right now I'm parched. You?" she asked as she gathered her hair up into a ponytail. She moved to a small mirror hanging on the wall beside the refrigerator and wiped under her eyes. The kitchen's ceiling light and fan were on. I watched the hair around her face move in the air's circulation.

It was warm all the way around. In the city, air conditioning units would be blasting, with everyone walking about in cashmere, cold and cut off from the summer's heat.

I nodded, agreeing to a beer. Rachel grabbed a couple of bottles from the fridge and uncapped them on the opener near the door. It had a Red Sox decal. Again, I was reminded of the house in Plymouth. We had one just like that. I used to uncap a bottle of root beer on the way out to work in the cherry orchard. I thought of the farmhouse, now vacant, my mother long gone, and both grandparents now dead. I couldn't help but compare it to this old house, alive and bursting at its seams with all the people outside.

I opened the kitchen door. Colored lights were strung along the outside of the screened in porch and across the yard to a pole. Cars and trucks were parked around the cul-de-sac and Credence Clear Water Revival was playing loudly on someone's car system. Tiki lanterns were lit at the neighbor's house next door. The party was definitely spilling over into their yard too.

Young Tom, sitting in the back bed of someone's pick-up truck, was watching two boys on skateboards circle the loop. A few older kids, teenagers, were throwing a football across the grassy median.

Big Tom, stationed at two grills, towered over everyone. He turned to us, and, in a voice deep and booming — definitely a coach's voice — called out, "Hey everybody, here's the man of the hour right now, the guy who saved our kid!"

I drank too much, and Rachel wouldn't let me drive to the farm. I spent the night in Tommy's room. The party broke up around midnight, but a few of us moved to the porch and continued to drink, Tom pouring shots of tequila.

I had forgotten how beautiful a summer night in Vermont could be. The stars were incredible. I woke up to the sound of Tom snorting at Amy in her highchair and her belly laughter. I left before Rachel woke up. I thought it best to; I had dreamed of her.

Rachel

I woke up in a panic, then remembered it was Sunday, Tom's morning with Amy. He had a lot to drink last night; he must have one heck of a hangover. I stretched out, debating if I should grab another hour in bed. Then it hit me — David was here. He'd been in no condition to drive last night. Thank God we got Tommy that new bed, or else I'd be terribly embarrassed.

I quickly got up and washed my face and brushed my teeth. I ran my fingers through my hair. I pulled on a pair of cut-offs and a t-shirt and made my way out to the second-floor landing. But I hesitated and went back into the bathroom. I put on a touch of mascara and started to leave. Then I went back and reached for my lip gloss. *Just a little*, I thought.

My mother and Meg, who lived next door, were drinking coffee at the kitchen table. I looked at them and asked, "Is everything okay?"

Meg looked at Mom. "She looks just like we did: disappointed that the man of the hour already left."

"Morning, Rach," Mom said. "David left fairly early. That man, why he could park his shoes under my bed any day of the week!"

Meg burst out laughing and hit the table. Mom smiled at her, then added, "You're wearing lip gloss, I have my best fuchsia blouse on, and Meg…"

"I wore my special eau de parfum this morning!"

My face reddened. "You ladies are too much."

Meg spoke, "I can't decide if he's better looking than George Clooney. He's definitely just as handsome. Susan, remember *One Fine Day*? We drove down to Peddan to see it. Afterwards we ate at that little restaurant, oh I can't think of its name but you liked the scrod in that lemony sauce. I loved that movie!"

Just then I heard Tom and Tommy Jr. talking as they came down our walkway. Amy was in the stroller. "It's been three weeks today, Dad, so I think that's good. I can start to do stuff, right?"

I opened the screen door and stepped out. My baby girl smiled at me. "Handsome, handsome, handsome!" I heard my mother sing out as I let the door swing closed. I *was* disappointed that I'd missed David. I wanted to apologize once more for crying like I had.

Tom heard the ladies from inside and looked up at me, smiling. "Are they still at it?"

I nodded. "Guess so. Imagine them back in high school together. They must have been some duo." I came down off the steps and started to pick up Amy. I gave Tommy a quick hug and looked over at Tom. He looked awful. "How you feelin'?"

"Shots of tequila then baby duty…What was I thinking?"

I grinned and replied, "Apparently you weren't."

I was unbuckling Amy and talking way too fast. "Tom couldn't come today. He's filling in to coach the south part of the north-south baseball game. It was last minute. Of course, he's thrilled. I hope you're okay that it's just me and the kids, and Tommy's buddy, Karl."

David smiled and said, "No, yes, I mean that's great, I'm glad you still came. I think we've got a beautiful day ahead of us."

He looked more casual than I'd see him yet. He still wore a tailored shirt but his pants were blue jeans and he had leather sandals on his feet. They looked expensive.

He helped me unload the car and we carried everything up onto the porch of the old farmhouse. Tommy and Karl were itching to go off, explore the place. I told them to hold on. Turning to David, I asked, "Is there anywhere they shouldn't go, or you know, get into?"

David scanned the barn, the fields, the orchard, and shook his head. "No, I don't think there's any place they need to avoid."

It was peaceful up here, and the road was distant enough not to be a worry.

"There's no well we should know about?" I asked. "That the boys could fall down? I've been traumatized about wells ever since Baby Jessica fell into one. It happened right before Tommy was born."

David looked a little baffled. "Um, no, there's no well, I can assure you. Just a brook that's shallow and fun to wade in, even fish in." As he set down Amy's diaper bag, he said, "I vaguely remember the Baby Jessica thing."

I turned to the kids. "OK, boys — you're free to go, but come back if either of us calls for you, got it?"

Tommy smiled and grabbed Karl's arm. Off they ran towards the barn.

It was nice to see Tommy fully recovered and able to play without restrictions. The hair where they'd shaved his head for the stitches still looked a little funny, but I assured him that by the time school rolled around, no one would notice the scar. I hoped I was right.

Tom had told him that he was welcome to tell his new classmates about the near drowning. "It'd be good for other kids to know that they should heed the warning of adults." It was still a sore subject that Tommy had done what he'd done despite our warnings. But both Tom and I knew that in the bigger scheme of things, the fact that he was saved was what we should hold dear above everything else. That's why we'd accepted David's invitation to come out to his grandparents' farm. It was another opportunity to show him our gratitude. I thought our visit would be short and sweet since Tom wasn't with me. After all, we had nothing in common.

I looked over at the large cottonwood with the Adirondack chairs scattered underneath and said, "We could spread the quilt I brought for Amy over there, right between the chairs. She'll have some shade and today's temp is perfect. Does that work?"

David replied, "Yes, let me help."

WHEN WE WERE FINALLY SETTLED and Amy was comfortable on the quilt with some of her squishy toys, I looked at the view. It was beautiful. The farm sat on a knoll, and from this spot we could see the road and hear the cars and trucks, though the highway noise was muffled by the lilac trees all along the bottom of the property. The biggest silver maple I'd ever seen was to the left, almost at the foot of the driveway. It was swaying in the light breeze, its leaves like bits of silver tinsel. Across the road, fields of different colors made a patchwork, all the way up to a large working farm. Cows, goats, and a couple of horses were in the distance, small but still discernible.

The house itself was old and needed work; its white clapboards were broken here and there, and its roof, especially over the long porch, needed to be replaced. But I imagined hearing my father's voice: "It's got good lines, good bones. See the way it's positioned — bank of windows facing east for the morning sun, porch to the west, watching the sunsets. Someone knew what they were doing when they built it."

I looked at David who was looking at me. His sunglasses were on the top of his head, and his legs were crossed. *He crosses his legs in a way Tom never does — or can't because of his size*, I thought. He seemed comfortable yet expectant, maybe waiting for me to start the conversation. I didn't know what to say. Suddenly, I wished Tom was here. The two of them would already be talking. I heard my mother's voice again, *"Handsome, handsome, handsome,"* and smiled. He was definitely better looking than George Clooney.

"So, um, did you notice Tommy's hair coming along, even better than at the house party?" I asked, wishing I had something more stimulating or witty to start with.

"I did, and I think there'll be a time when no one can tell. He probably won't be self-conscious about the scar. What do you think?"

Nodding, I replied, "I think you're right." I gazed out over the little valley. "Are you sad to sell the farm?"

He seemed perplexed and said, "No, why would I be?"

"I don't know, David, honestly this, right here, is what I hope heaven is like." I moved my hand, taking in the view before us and then turned behind me to the back meadows, the barn, and the start of the orchard.

We sat again in silence, watching Amy. She had started to scoot on her tummy, not quite crawling but she could get places. She was doing that now.

David asked, "Should I point her back to the center of the blanket?"

I nodded and he picked her up, gently repositioning her.

"Thanks," I said. "When she starts to finally crawl, life will get more complicated."

"Hey, refresh my memory on Baby Jessica. She survived, right?" He smiled at me and I thought, *You must make a lot of women swoon.*

"Yes, over fifty hours. It was a miracle."

I FELT AMY'S BARE FEET and her chubby hands, making sure she wasn't cold. The breeze was ruffling her little curls. I wished I'd brought my camera to take a few pictures of her, of here, of this day.

I reached for the cloth diaper to wipe her chin. She didn't like that and made a face. David laughed out loud and I looked up at him.

"She's already a character, isn't she?" he asked.

I sat back in my chair and nodded in agreement.

David began to talk, and I settled in to listen. He had a crisp way of speaking, each of his sentences delivered in a confident, assured voice.

"I never knew my mother really. She left me here to be raised by my grandparents. It wasn't ever clear to me why she did that. My grandparents were probably clueless about her reasons too. It was boring here; I couldn't wait to leave, see what was out there. I did about two months of college but couldn't hack it. The goal of getting a degree was lost on me. I was ready to be 'doing stuff,' not studying so I could eventually be 'doing stuff.' I headed to New York and I've been there ever since."

"Do you like New York?" I watched him turn from me and take in the view. I waited; the boys were off exploring, Amy was content, and the day's weather was a gift.

Turning back to me, he answered, "Yes, most of the time. It's the proverbial rat race and pressure cooker, but it suits me. Although nothing I've done in the city — not since I first got there in nineteen seventy-seven — has ever been as important as saving Tommy. Nothing."

I instantly teared up. A strong desire to move to him came over me. I didn't, but I wanted to. Other than when I first met Tom, I'd never felt this way before. It was fleeting, but powerful.

He continued talking. "I never knew my father's name. My mother took that with her when she split in sixty-five, maybe sixty-six. I think this place has been a constant reminder that I was left behind. So, to answer your question — no I'm not sad to sell it."

I lowered myself down on the blanket near Amy. She was teething and her drool was once again noticeable. I gently wiped her chin, and she yawned. I thought she was ready for her morning nap. If I nursed her, I knew she'd fall right to sleep.

Moving my legs up under me, I turned to David. "I work at the Children's Center, down in town. I've been there a while. Sometimes we see cases of children left with their grandparents. Probably, most of the time, the children are better off and in a more stable environment. I'm not saying that's the case in your situation, though." Then hesitantly I asked, "Have you ever seen your mom again?"

He looked thoughtful. "No, never. But when my grandfather died, I found her death certificate in his desk still in an envelope postmarked five years ago from Portland, Oregon. Funny thing was, it hadn't been opened — at least not until I opened it just last month."

"Maybe your grandfather was saving it for you, wanting you to be the one to open it."

"I thought about that, but, well, I haven't been back here in a very long time. When I got the call that he'd had an accident and died, it was my first trip back in a while."

"What kind of accident was it?" I reached over and placed the ring of teething keys in Amy's hands.

"His tractor rolled over onto him, crushing his chest." David pointed down the slope of the yard. "About halfway down the driveway. He must have stopped to do something. This incline can be a pain — about a dozen balls are down in the gully along the lilacs, toys I never bothered to get as a boy."

I stood up and looked towards the barn, then bent over and picked up Amy. I asked David if he would reach into the diaper bag near him and grab the little blanket stowed there.

She and I settled in, me carefully covering both of us.

David stood up and said, "Why don't I go check on the boys, okay?"

I smiled up at him and he surprised me by touching my shoulder. It was subtle, and nice, but surprising all the same.

AFTER DAVID RETURNED and Amy was settled on the quilt to nap, we quietly talked about lots of things. I told him about my own father's sudden death out on the golf course and how my mom was handling it. How my older sister from California had flown in and run the show, taking a lot of my mother's wishes and modifying them to fit her own.

"She — my sister's name is Heather — moved Tom up into the top spot at my father's fencing business. Did Tom want it? To Heather, it was a given, but I don't know. I think

Tom was in over his head and has been ever since. He's an action kind of guy; he'd rather be installing fencing than looking at numbers and spreadsheets. And Mom, she kind of let Heather handle it all, like she always has in the past. My sister is in corporate…What's it called? Corporate America? She's rich, married to another corporate kind of guy with kids from his previous marriage, and none of her own. I think she wants it like that — you know, a once-a-month stepmom kind of thing."

I was surprised at how bitter I sounded. I don't think I'd ever conveyed this much of my real feelings about Heather before, even to Tom.

David took in all I said and replied, "You're a mother through and through, aren't you?"

I smiled and then said, "Your turn."

He told me about his grandmother's death in 1981, and I detected some feelings, possibly of regret, surrounding it. "I never got a chance to come back after I left. Just to sit at her kitchen table and enjoy her cooking, the way she'd talk about the weather, like we had all the time in the world."

He looked out at the fields across the highway. "But, to be totally truthful, that's not the way it ever was with me. I was usually bored stiff sitting in the kitchen, listening to her ramble on and on. My time was always ticking away, I felt, here on the farm. I'm sure she detected that in me. I wish, Rachel, for just one afternoon before she died, that I had sat and, well, you know, just sat…"

I looked at him and could see his sadness, and, perhaps, a touch of loneliness.

"Have you ever been married?" I asked.

"No, and at the ripe old age of almost forty, I don't think I ever will be."

"Ah, you're just a late bloomer!" I laughed and so did he.

"Can I ask you your age," he said, "or is that a faux pas with women?"

"Nope it's okay, because, Mr. Sumner, I am a whole four years younger than you!"

That lightened our mood and we got silly, comparing my art 'experiences' to his; hand and foot prints, macaroni art, leaves pressed with the iron, and the steadfast puppets on popsicle sticks. I described each art project's process, ending with the magnificent masterpieces my preschool toddlers created. David's eyes were lit up and it seemed as if he was amused.

When it was his turn, he described his years as an art handler and then a little about his career as an art dealer. But he didn't make it funny like I had, because of course it wasn't funny. I think he made a lot of money and was kind of downplaying it for me.

DAVID YELLED FOR THE BOYS TO COME. They started running from the barn. Standing at the sink, in his grandparents' house, I looked out at the chairs under the cottonwood. Amy had woken up from her nap and had been her usual smiley self. After I'd changed her, David had said he'd watch her while I went in to get our lunch. He had moved to the blanket and was making funny faces and noises for her. Everyone was hungry; I was glad I'd made a lot to eat.

Reaching for the picnic basket, I opened the screen door and stepped off the porch stairs. I felt incredibly happy; my babies were safe and close by, David was charming, and my feeling of awkwardness was completely gone.

Tommy Jr.

I watched the gigantic spider move in its web. I thought for a second about grabbing one of the old, empty milk bottles on the shelf and nudging it inside. Karl would want to see it. Instead, I moved the other bottles around, trying to see if there was an even bigger spider hiding. I could see pretty good because at the other end of the space was a small window, like in the oldest part of our cellar at home — what Dad called our cistern.

Behind one of the last milk bottles, I saw something wedged in the wall that looked kind of shiny in the light. I reached in, took hold, and pulled out an old, dusty book. I opened it and thumbed through the pages. Names and addresses with lots of numbers were written down.

Suddenly, I heard Karl up above, looking for me. We were playing a game of hide and seek, but I knew he'd never find me down here in this little room because I'd closed the door above.

I stayed silent, pretending I was Indiana Jones and Karl was a Nazi officer coming to try and capture me. I looked down at the book and turned to the last page of writing. I quickly looked over the names and addresses written there: *"Berenson-Hemlock…Arenberg-Lockwood-Chestnut Hill…*

Jacob Geller-Walpole. They were all spies like me! I recited their names and addresses one last time, trying to memorize them before I was grabbed and thrown in front of a firing squad.

Karl's voice sounded far away. "Come out, come out wherever you are!" Then, a few minutes later, "Tommy, it's time to go eat, your mom's friend is calling us."

I put the book back and rearranged the bottles as they had been. I climbed up the ladder and just before I closed the hatch, I pushed the ladder away so no Germans could climb down. I heard it fall to the floor. I spread the straw back over the little opening and scooted toward the barn's big doors. Karl jumped out from behind the stacked hay bales, scaring the 'you know what' out of me.

"Let's go fishing after we eat!" I said as Karl hit me and yelled, "You're it!" We ran back to Amy's blanket and met Mom and David there. I was starved; we all were. And Amy had her first taste of a big dill pickle! She loved it. Even when she made funny faces, she kept leaning over to me for more. I thought, *This could end up being the best day of the summer.*

Rachel

Amy fell asleep again — her second nap of the day — while David walked with her in his arms. He was showing me the property. We were down in the middle of the orchard. The cherries were too gone to pick, hanging shriveled up on their stems. "All this needs to be weeded out, mowed, and the trees pruned," David was saying.

He then turned towards the rolling meadows. "I once got a puppy, a chocolate lab, for Christmas. I named him 'Dash.' He'd run from one end of the farm to the other, falling down, getting back up — 'dashing through the snow.'"

I smiled and said it was a cute name.

He nodded and continued talking. "When he was a little over two years old, a tractor trailer leveled him. My grandfather found him and wrapped him in a blanket before he told me. I was twelve and thought the world sucked. Basically, I've thought that most of my life."

"I'm sorry." I could see the boys, really just the tops of their heads, as they fished in the little brook, excited to possibly catch something. "I think I personally would have liked living here. I grew up in a development where all the houses looked the same. I knew who lived in every house, who rode what bike, and later — I'm embarrassed to say — which parents had easy liquor cabinets to get into."

David feigned being shocked and said, "Didn't figure you for a wino, Rachel. No, not at all."

I hit his arm and replied, "I'm not, but oh, I had my fair share. Though it was mostly rum and coke, sometimes tequila. My friends and I played hard, but we were good kids."

"What kind of a childhood did you have?" he asked, seemingly interested.

"As I said, I grew up closer to downtown Langdon. My father had that fencing company. My mom was a stay-at-home mom, always there. Really, I'm boring, and I already covered most of it back there, under the tree."

"Well, did you go to college?"

"I got an associate degree in early childhood. I've been debating going back to get my bachelor's, but the timing has never been right. I love my job; the pay is poor, way too low, but I love the little ones."

"When you say low, like, what are you talking, if you don't mind me asking?"

David shifted Amy to his other arm. Her sweet little head was resting on his shoulder. I worried about the spot of drool on his shirt, near his neck. I reached up and wiped her chin, then touched the clean part of the cloth diaper to his shirt. I could smell his aftershave and noticed two small moles below his ear. Our height difference was barely discernible. I suddenly registered how close I was to him and stepped back. "Let's just say low, okay?" I started walking again.

He caught up quickly and moved alongside me. I tried to make sure I didn't bump into him as I skirted around the trees. He glanced at me and asked, "When did you and Tom hook up?"

Some of the cherry tree branches were overgrown and almost touching the ground in front of us. I ducked under one and then turned and held it back, waiting for David to pass before I answered him. "Our junior year, so we were about sixteen or seventeen."

He stopped. "And you've been together ever since?" His voice held some disbelief in it.

I looked at Amy, sound asleep in his arms. "Yes. You make it sound like that's a huge feat, but yes, we've been together ever since. So have many other couples."

"Then he's the only guy you've ever..." David stopped. He looked puzzled or maybe embarrassed, I couldn't tell which.

Suddenly, I wasn't quite so sure it was a good idea to be here without Tom. It wasn't that I didn't trust David. It was something else. Like we were sharing way too much personal stuff, moving into a familiarity with each other that was undeserved. *Maybe I shouldn't be letting him carry Amy so casually either.*

I reached up and took Amy from his arms. "Let's go see if the boys caught anything." I walked ahead of him, out from under the old cherry trees.

DAVID HANDED ME THE CUP of black coffee he'd made for my drive home, and I thanked him. It was almost dinnertime and the kids were already in the car, buckled in safely. Amy, in her car seat between the boys, was smiling at Karl. He was clearly enjoying her attention.

"Thank you, this was such a great day," I said. "Really. Hey boys..." I looked in the rear view mirror and caught Tommy's eye with a look that said, *"What do you say?"*

He picked up on it immediately. "We had a blast and I'm really glad you let Karl come."

Tommy hit Karl's arm and Karl piped up, "Yeah, thanks a lot. Even though we didn't catch any fish, finding that bullfrog was cool."

Leaning into my window a bit, David looked into the back seat. "Remember, we're going to Yankee Stadium soon to see those Red Sox win!"

I looked up at David and smiled. "Take care."

He reached in and gently placed his fingers around a few loose strands of my hair and lifted them up, tucking them behind my ear. Then he tapped the top of the car and said, "You too." He stood back as I drove down the drive.

The intimacy of his gesture was alarming. I blushed and looked in the rear view mirror to see if Tommy had seen it. He was making a face at Amy and I could hear her laughter. "Well, that wasn't cool," I said out loud as I turned onto the main road.

"What, Mom?" Tommy asked.

"Nothing." But to myself I whispered, "Nope, not cool." *We'd become way too comfortable with each other*, I thought. *How did that happen?*

T he very next week, I stepped out of the convenience store in the center of Langdon with a large Italian grinder, a bag of chips, a bottle of water, and a root beer. My plan was to eat about a third of the sandwich for lunch and save the rest for Tommy before he went to his fifth-sixth grade football practice later that day. The middle school's lunch period started at 10:40 — a crazy time for kids to eat. By 3:00 they were famished, and then Tommy had a 90-minute practice. I didn't particularly like the grinders there, but he did, and I had a good amount of time off for lunch so had decided to head over.

As I was walking past the gas pumps, I heard someone call out my name. I turned back and there was David, standing beside an old, rusty truck, screwing on the gas cap. "Hey, Rachel."

He was smiling at me, looking like he belonged on a magazine cover: the sophisticated modern man juxtaposed against the dilapidated blue Ford.

I came back around. My car was parked at the Center where I worked, just a ten-minute walk from there to here.

"What's going on, Mister City Slicker?" I asked. I felt my face redden slightly as I remembered how he'd said goodbye to me at the farm. The late August day was overcast and the wind was kicking up. Dust and dirt from the parking lot swirled about in little cyclones.

"Nothing other than realtor stuff. Hey, hop in. I'll give you a lift."

I turned towards the Center and then looked back at him. Suddenly, I felt carefree and bold. "I've got lunch. Have you eaten?" I immediately thought about rescinding my offer; it was Tommy's food after all, but I didn't. I knew I could come back to get another sandwich later. And for some reason, I really wanted to spend the next hour or so with him. I knew it was a contradiction to how I'd felt leaving the farm, but I didn't care.

David leaned against the back tailgate, looking at me. I quickly added, "But if you've got stuff you need to do, I understand."

He stood up. "No, I'd love to eat. Let's find a place to sit down. I've got time."

He opened the passenger side door. The springs in the bench seat creaked when I sat down. He glanced my way and raised his eyebrows as he started the truck. "Let's hope this clunker doesn't die today."

I directed him to the little league park just on the east side of town, about a five-minute drive. We got out of the truck and walked to the nearest picnic table. I waved to Walter, the groundskeeper of the fields, who was emptying the barrels of trash by the bleachers.

As I took out everything from the brown paper bag, David sat watching me. I didn't want to think too much about it, but I was excited to be here. We had opened up so much last time and I had found myself craving that companionship again. I thought maybe he felt the same way.

I placed the root beer, chips, and half the grinder in front of him. I uncapped the water bottle and took a sip. It was breezy and looked like it might rain. We needed rain, lots of rain.

"I've spent several years of my life here as a kid and now as a mother," I said as I looked out over the ball fields.

David nodded, then glanced down at the food. "This is great, thank you. I haven't had a root beer in, well, forever."

He took a few bites of the grinder and wiped his mouth as he chewed. Looking out beyond the fence, he said, "I remember playing here lots of times when I was in Babe Ruth. It was a nice ballpark. My grandfather used to…"

Just then a gust of wind came through and the whole sheet of what was left of his portion of the grinder blew up and away from the table. Shredded lettuce and bits of tomato took flight as David jumped up fast, mouth full, and ran to pick up the grinder paper. He returned triumphantly.

I clapped. "Just like a fly ball, huh? Chasing it down…"

Sitting again, he replied, "Mind you, I'm forty years old — today actually — and out of shape."

I smiled and replied, "Nah, you still got it." I cut him another piece of the sub and said, "Happy Birthday."

"You sure?" he asked, then added, "I've got plans back in the city later tonight, but this is my first birthday celebration of the day, so thank you."

I glanced up at him quickly. "And here you are, slumming it with me."

"No, I'm actually upping my game right here, right now." He flashed me that lady-killer smile.

His comment was smooth. *A little too smooth,* I thought. But it pleased me more than I wanted to admit, and I couldn't help but smile back at him.

We sat for a little bit longer, eating and making small talk. He told me the farmhouse needed some major work according to a local builder he'd paid to come out and inspect it. David wasn't sure he wanted to spend the money but shrugged and said, "I guess I'll have to in order to sell it."

He asked about the kids and Tom and was curious if the south won the game Tom had coached. I answered him, now holding onto my hair because the wind was crazy. "No, they hardly ever do. The north has bigger schools, more Division One players to draw from. But according to Tom it was a respectful showing."

"Is Amy crawling yet?" David took a sip of the root beer. *He must find me and my life totally mundane,* I thought. But I answered, "She's crawling a little more each day. Soon my beautiful baby girl will be the terror of the cul-de-sac."

WHEN WE FINISHED EATING, I walked our trash bag over to Walter as he came around the nearest side of the playground. He'd been the groundskeeper for as long as I could remember.

He smiled and waved to David. *He probably thinks it's Tom,* I thought, suddenly feeling a pang of quilt. When I returned, David stood up and brushed his pants off. A piece of tomato was stuck to his right pant leg, just above his knee. I laughed as he flicked it off.

"For the crows," he said. Then he turned and pointed to the dugouts.

"My grandfather used to stand just to the right of that dugout and watch me when I played down here. He never missed a game. I remember it so clearly, yet it was what — at least twenty-five years ago?"

I now stood and replied, "I think flashes of our childhood are always just below the surface, ready when we want them. See this?" I turned sideways and lifted my chin, pointing to a scar on my neck. "Fell off that slide — " I motioned to an old metal slide on the playground — "one winter when I was here. I hit a piece of ice. Every time I'm here I see the 'great fall' as if it happened yesterday."

David smiled and looked back at me. "I'm positive that your kids will have wonderful memories of their childhood."

I was touched by his sentiment and replied, "I hope so."

As we walked back to the truck, he suddenly grabbed my hand and held it up. "You're a nail biter. See? Just like me. We're kindred spirits."

I quickly looked at his fingernails and saw that ours were similar. I looked up at him and held his hand for a moment longer, then quickly let it go. I didn't say anything until I was back in the truck. Again, his ease at touching me — like with my hair before — gave me pause. *But I'm not pulling away from him, am I?* I thought. *And I had asked him to come to lunch. Am I that bored and desperate for this man's attention?*

But I wasn't bored. And I loved my husband. Still, something I couldn't explain was drawing me to him. Maybe it was because I'd never met anyone like him before.

"Why do you bite yours, do you know?" I asked.

He shook his head. "I don't know why — maybe I'm nervous, a worry wart, who knows. You?"

David started up the truck. It rattled as we pulled out onto the main road.

"I've always been a biter. My mom used to put awful tasting stuff on each nail, but I still bit them. You may think this is crazy, but kids who are nail-biters are deep thinkers. My father used to ask, 'You fixing all the problems of the world?' as I nibbled away."

I gave him directions to the Children's Center. I was returning with a few minutes to spare from my hour-long lunch. As I started to thank him for the ride, David interrupted me.

"Rachel, I've never been a deep thinker. Lots of times I don't think — I don't think things all the way through. I just act or react."

I hesitated and looked over at him. "When you saved my son, thank God you weren't a deep thinker, thinking away at the boat landing on that rock. Tommy wouldn't have made it. Besides, deep thinkers are overrated."

I started to get out, but then turned and added, "I used to watch reruns of this show, *Dobie Gillis*, with my father when I was a little girl. I remember a statue of the deep thinker in each episode. Imagine if you'd been like that statue when you were at the lake waiting to take your phone call? You'd never have seen Tommy dive in."

David burst out laughing. "That statue is a bronze cast of Rodin's The Thinker. It's famous and worth a lot of money. There are several casts of it throughout the world."

I nodded. "That's cool." I closed the truck's door. "But I like you just the way you are, worry warts and all."

David didn't say anything in return; he just sat, looking at me.

I pushed my hair back. "What, have I got two heads, or do I look like Medusa with all this wild wind?"

He grew serious. "No one has ever said that to me before — liking me just the way I am. That's all."

"Well, maybe you've *never* given anyone the chance." I moved away from the passenger door and turned towards the Center.

He called out after me, "The grinder was delicious, the company even better."

I waved goodbye as I walked across the street and through the gate to the Center. Unlike the day at the farm, I felt like I'd had the upper hand with him today. But as I walked up the steps an uneasy feeling started to take hold. I'd fallen right back into flirting with him — again. *Time to stay away from David Sumner*, I thought.

David

She leaned into me, and I could smell her breath. Darcy was a heavy smoker, and she reeked. I tried to move away, but I had no place to go in the booth. We were packed in like sardines around the large round top in the corner of the bar. I started to inhale and hold it before exhaling through my mouth to minimize her cigarette smoke. It didn't work.

We were in a dive bar on the West Side. It was our third stop of the night in this 'birthday entourage' of mine as Emily was calling it.

Darcy, Chelsea's hottest art dealer at the moment, was in the middle of a story. "So, I see Ian slam the back door out to the alley behind the gallery and then Derek looks over at me and says, 'This is not okay.' He gets up and follows Ian."

Darcy's new shipping coordinator, Laura, was on my other side. I felt her leg press against mine, up along my thigh. I gave her a quick glance, and she practically fell into me. She was definitely three sheets to the wind. She placed her hand on my thigh. I moved it away. She put it there again. This time I held on to her right hand with mine. If I needed to, I'd put down my drink and hold on with both hands for however long it took me to get the hell out of here.

What a shit show of a birthday party. I glanced around, trying to find Emily.

Darcy continued, "The boys started to yell at each other, 'All you do is use her!' And then Derek yelled back, 'The fuck I do — we're in love!' It was so sweet, David. My up-and-coming artists fighting over me in a back alley!"

I smiled at Darcy. I had to be careful not to offend her by seeming disinterested. Her influence in Chelsea was significant, and I needed her.

Suddenly, I felt Laura's hand again. She was even more aggressive, placing it on my crotch. *What the fuck! Did she plan on giving me a hand job right there under the table?* I abruptly batted her hand away and tried to stand up. But the round top was too close and I was trapped. Several of the glasses wobbled, but I didn't care. I needed to get out from around the table. I raised my voice, "Let me the fuck out now!"

Darcey and the others, including Laura, looked surprised and then confused. I didn't care if I was hurting people as I climbed over them. I needed to get out.

Once free of the table, I walked up to the bar. Some chick, dark haired and good looking, swiveled around to me and said, "So, you're the birthday boy, the big four-oh?" I looked again for Emily and saw her sitting on the last stool of the bar, talking on her phone. She looked worried. I didn't give a shit — this fucking party was all her idea and it was a disaster.

The woman next to me moved her legs, definitely crossing them in a suggestive way. She wasn't bad looking, probably been around the bars a lot like I had.

"Yeah, I'm fucking forty today. Whoop-de-do." I twirled my index finger around and then asked, "What are you drinking?"

SOMETIME, ABOUT 7 A.M., I made my way into the kitchen. I hovered over the sink and spat, turning the water on to watch as it swirled down the drain. I sat at the island and ran my hand over the quartz countertop and looked at the high-end dual fuel range. I'd never once cooked on it except for the one time I'd bought Jiffy Pop popcorn. It had set off my fire alarm, and I'd had to disable it quickly so the other tenants in the building wouldn't have to evacuate.

The cleaning lady had been here yesterday. Everything glistened. There was a large bouquet of flowers and several cards along the credenza. I tried to remember where I'd left the box of Havana cigars and the bottle of cognac I'd received as gifts last night. *Actually,* I thought, *I don't really care.*

The sun was starting to come up over the nearby roof tops. I tried to remember what this hour had looked like back in Plymouth the morning I'd left the farm and headed toward the lake on my way back to the city. I wanted to go over all the details of the rescue again. But when I closed my eyes, that's not what came to me. Instead, I watched the paper flying off the picnic table and saw Rachel's face when I brought it back. I heard her say, "Nah, you still got it."

Enough of this bullshit, I thought, *I'm going after Miss Vermont.* I smiled at that, my new nickname for her. I stood up and moved back to the sink. I bent down and took a drink from the faucet. The woman at the bar was in my bedroom. It had been such a lousy birthday party. I burped, then hiccuped. I was still slightly drunk.

I knew I was attracted to Rachel, but I'd been trying to be good and keep it light. Feel her out. Not make any big moves. But for what? This was my reality — the girl in my bed, the hangover spreading through me — and maybe I deserved something a little sweeter this time. Someone I didn't meet in a bar at 2 a.m.

Yesterday's surprise lunch in Langdon had been a game changer. Rachel had given me just enough to let me know she was open to something more. *Shit, it'd be nice, for once, to be around a woman who was both genuine and possibly a challenge too.* That's what I wanted for my birthday — Rachel. Miss Vermont.

The cleaning lady had left the coffee machine ready for me. I hit the 'on' button and turned back towards the bedroom. Once the Yankee-Red Sox game was over with Tom and the boy, I'd make my move. Timing was everything.

Emily

Sometimes he was just mean, but oblivious to it. The first time I interviewed with him, he'd looked at me and said, "You could work out. You definitely have the right credentials, and you're plain enough. That's good."

What a dickhead, I thought, but I needed a job and had overlooked the comment. Now, I know it was because he'd screw anything that was half-way attractive, even at the cost of doing harm.

He'd been pissed at me about his birthday party last week. How was I to know that Darcy's new art handler was so lecherous? God, the girl was from Kansas; she looked like she could be Dorothy's little sister. The whole night had gone south fast, especially my three, no, four calls with my two brothers. It was official — my mother's dementia was a result of Huntington's disease.

"We need to plan accordingly," Jason had said.

"What does 'plan accordingly' mean?" I'd asked. We'd already gotten her a spot at a top-notch care facility.

It was his reply during the next call that gave me chills. "We all need to get tested, it's genetic."

Much of the rest of the night had been a blur after that. My last call to Willis, my other brother, had been at 2 a.m. in the bar David had disappeared from. I'd asked Willis if he was going to get tested, and if Macie knew about Mom's diagnosis yet? His wife was expecting and was having a difficult pregnancy as it was. He hadn't told her, and he wasn't sure about being tested himself. "I don't know if I want to know."

I WAS BROUGHT BACK TO DAVID pacing the loft when he said, "I want a dozen roses sent to Rachel Dunne's Langdon house. Today."

This rankled me. David did a lot of harm to a lot of women through his 'liaisons.' *But not this time,* I thought.

"For God's sake, David, no! She's not one of your rich bitches, okay? Sending her roses is totally inappropriate. Send the family a big basket of fruit, like from Harry & David. I'll order it right now. Kids love fruit and I guarantee she does too. Then move on and let her be."

He didn't acknowledge what I just said and left the room.

I looked out over our workstation and realized we had a whole lot of shit pending. It wasn't like David to be so preoccupied with something other than 'business.' I knew he'd been affected by saving the boy, and that he wanted to keep that relationship 'alive,' but honestly, the Dunnes of Vermont were as far from the art scene of New York as could be. It was up to me to point this out, in as many ways as possible. I had hoped, after the ball game, that they all, especially Mrs. Dunne, would just fade away.

Also, he had some important social engagements coming up and he needed to be at his best. Our future rested on his ability to make connections with all the people associated with producing, buying and selling art — and Mom's care wasn't going to be cheap. The thing with David, though, was that he blended too much socializing with his 'dick wagging' business style more than anyone I knew. It was a formula for disaster a lot of the time. Other times, it actually sealed the deal. My friend, Calista, told me I was — more than anything — 'David Sumner's fixer.' I knew exactly what she meant.

"There he goes again," I said as he cupped the phone up to his ear in the next room. It wasn't a business call, I could tell. It was personal, and I suspected that meant he was calling Mrs. Dunne. I knocked on the window, and David quickly gave me the middle finger and turned away.

"Fuck you," I said out loud to my boss. "You're an asshole."

Rachel

We were dancing to Barney's song, *It's Nice Just to be Me,* when Pat came into the room and motioned to me.

"Kaitlyn, I'll be right back," I said.

Pat handed me the phone and said, "I think it's David." She had come to our party, had a great time, even stayed after it broke up. "Too much tequila," she'd moaned to me the following Monday.

"Oh wow, I'd better take it." I walked out the front doors and stood on the porch. The air was cooler; fall was coming. "David, hi. I didn't expect you to call."

"Hello, Rachel. Hey, I was thinking maybe we could get together."

His voice sounded different. Less open and warm — sharper somehow.

"You come down to the city," he continued. "Spend a weekend. I could show you around."

I was a little baffled. Tom and Tommy had just returned from the Yankee-Red Sox game with him a couple of days ago.

"Oh, that doesn't quite work for us right now. Tommy has football practice almost every night and then the games are starting on the weekends. Amy's cutting two more teeth and isn't sleeping well."

There was a long pause, and I wondered if I'd lost him. "Are you there?"

"Yes, I am. I actually had just you in mind, Rachel. You know, you coming for the weekend."

I turned back to the door. I could still see and hear the children singing and dancing. I wanted to get off the phone; he was making me uncomfortable. I wasn't sure if I was reading him right, but then I thought, *No, I am.* It was clear I'd gone too far with what I'd seen as innocent flirting.

"David, I can't do that. It would be really inappropriate." I quickly added, "And it's not practical, either. I can't leave Amy, and you know why."

"I'm sure you'd be able to come up with some plan, some way to make it happen. I really want to see you again, Rachel."

I moved along the side of the Children's Center building, past the office windows. I looked in, hoping none of the ladies in bookkeeping or records were watching me. I needed to nip this right here, right now.

"Whatever you think is going on, David, or what you hope will go on between us is not going to happen. It's just not. Now, I'm at work, I'm outside, and I'm not doing my job." I hung up and walked back to the pre-k room quickly. I was rattled, but also kicking myself. *If I had just cut it off after that day at the farm…*

I reached for the phone and picked up. "Hello?" I was out of breath. No one spoke. "Hello?" I said again, with a hint of annoyance.

"It's me, David. Can you talk?"

I immediately tensed up at the sound of his voice. I looked out at Tommy as he attempted to tie a balloon. I was helping him fill water balloons for a couple of friends who were coming over in an hour. We were experiencing a wonderful summer -like Saturday, and Amy was down for a nap.

"Yes, I have a quick minute." I turned away from the kitchen window and moved into the den, wondering if he was going to take back what he'd said about coming to New York.

"I wanted to apologize for my call before. I'm sorry."

"Okay, David." This was awkward, but I was glad we were finishing this.

"It's just that I really feel we connected and that…there's something between us."

I took a deep breath, realizing he still didn't get it. Quietly, and with more patience than I'd had with him in our earlier call, I began to explain. "Listen…" I leaned up against the staircase and glanced upstairs. Amy had just settled down. "If I gave you reason to believe that I was or that I could be interested in something more with you, then I'm sorry. I know that I flirted with you…But there's nothing between us. I'm not single, I'm not available. My family is…"

He interrupted me, "We can make this work. I know how, it's not impossible."

"No!" I said, alarmed. I moved across the room, back towards the kitchen. "My God, you sound like you do this kind of thing all the time." I held the phone and waited, looking through the kitchen door at Tommy again.

He didn't reply.

"Yeah. This isn't new to you, is it?" My tone had definitely changed. I was pissed.

"I just think if I drove up, we could meet and talk."

"No!" I abruptly hung up. I stood there, practically shaking. I just went from zero to ninety in about three seconds.

I needed to get back to Tommy; he was calling for me.

LATER, AS I SAT WITH AMY out in the yard, I combed over the day we spent on David's grandfather's farm and then the brief lunch we'd shared at the field. The farm day had been wonderful, there was no denying that. He'd been charming, treating me and the kids like royalty. He was interesting and I liked his smooth, polished manner. Then running into him like that outside the convenience store and having a few minutes together had felt natural at the time — even if a part of me knew it might have been a mistake.

But none of it was as simple as that, was it? I thought. There'd been something between us as soon as I'd stepped out of the car at the farmhouse porch. Maybe even before. We'd been thrust into such a shockingly intimate experience by Tommy's near drowning that we'd already established a bond. Maybe that's why we had shared a lot about our past; he about his mother, and me on my resentment towards my sister.

I'd acted in ways I wouldn't have ever acted if Tom had been right there beside me. Like when I hit David's arm about the 'wino' comment or tried to wipe his collar. And the way I went off on describing my projects with the kids, trying so hard to be entertaining. I was embarrassed by it now. And if Tom had been sitting in the passenger seat, David never would have touched my hair like that. Grabbing my hand to see my nails — that wouldn't have happened either.

I wasn't going to tell Tom about David's phone calls or my foolish behavior in all of this, because it definitely wouldn't sit well with him. But I also didn't want to spoil his or Tommy's regard for David. They'd come back from the ball game in New York and had talked non-stop about it and him.

Later that evening, I was starting dinner while Tom rocked Amy on the porch. I stopped making the hamburger patties and looked out the kitchen window. Should I even mention my brief lunch with David to Tom? And then the bigger question — what had I been thinking? If I was being absolutely honest with myself, I knew I'd been flattered that a man like David — polished and worldly — could be so attentive to me.

I turned on the faucet and started to wash my hands. I saw David's puzzled look again when he asked if Tom was the only man I'd ever been with. "Enough," I whispered as I dried my hands. *Whatever happens moving forward, I have to keep my distance.*

There's that guy again…parked over next to the green little Honda." Kaitlyn nodded past the playground fence to the row of cars along the street.

"What do you mean?" I asked, nonchalantly turning to where she meant.

The day was beautiful, with sunshine and fall colors. My group, the Red Poppies, were just starting to play after having had lunch in the classroom.

One of the 4-year-old boys yelled, "Watch me, Miss Rachel!" as he roared down the slide. I gave him a big smile and a thumbs up. I turned my body a little more sideways so I didn't appear to be gawking at the car, but I could see it as I did a panoramic view of the play structures and the street.

"It's the second time I've seen him around here,"
Kaitlyn said. "Parked and just, I don't know, watching us."

She glanced at me and then called out to a little girl,
Haley, who had just come outside after using the bathroom.
"Go on, Haley, join Ava and Blair!"

"Maybe he's on his lunch hour and likes to hear kids
playing," I offered.

"He's cute, you know, in a real sexy way. I would say
dark and steamy."

I grew serious. "Really, you're sure it's the same guy?"

She started to move away from me, heading to the
sandbox where two little boys were arguing over the big
dump truck. "Yeah, like I said, he's cute, so, you know, I
noticed him."

I called to her that I would be right back and then
headed to the gate, opened it, and let a car pass by. I made
my way to the dark sedan. It had New York plates. I walked
straight up to the car. I knew it would be David, and it was.
Her description of him was spot on.

Shaking my head, I asked, "What's going on here,
David? What are you doing?"

He looked embarrassed but said nothing as I stood at the
side of the car, my arms crossed.

"Listen, this is not cool, okay? You have to stop."

He wouldn't look at me. I bent down at his window.
"You saved my child, my Tommy. I will forever be grateful
to you, and I mean that." I was pleading now. "But I
don't…I don't owe you anything else, okay? Yes, we had an
amazing day at the farm. We really talked, about big,
personal stuff. And then running into each other on your
birthday was fun. But it's just friendship, David, that's all."

"You know it could be more than that," he replied
harshly as he looked up at me.

I shook my head, and in a determined voice said, "No, I don't want it to be more than that. I shouldn't have led you to believe that I wanted more, because I don't. I'm a married woman, a *happily* married woman. I have a family. I can't, I won't, take this — you and me — any further." I quickly glanced back at the playground. I needed to get back.

When he looked back up at me again, I thought I saw a depth of sadness pass over his face. It was only for a split second before he sat up and started the car. In that clear, assured voice of his, he said, "Then I'm sorry, Rachel. This is it. I won't bother you anymore. I want the best for you and your family."

The parking spot in front of him was empty. He pulled up and out and never looked back. I watched the car disappear down the street. *I hope that's the end of it*, I thought as I scooted back to the Center. I was sorry too if I had led him on at all.

David

The Manhattan penthouse was impressive and near Times Square. I wondered what the asking price was on it. I watched everyone around me, especially the girl I was with. I couldn't remember if her name was Alisa or Aleesha. She was a beauty: wavy, long, blond hair, tall and thin with big emerald eyes. Her black dress was molded to her, and the tear drop earrings she wore glistened in the soft lighting. She looked classy. For a minute, I forgot how much she was costing me; the escort service was outrageous.

EMILY HAD STOOD AND STARED AT ME when I'd told her I didn't have a date for New Year's Eve.

"Are you kidding me? You, who have…" She hadn't finished her sentence; instead she'd looked at the floor and then turned away from me.

That day, we didn't say another word to each other until she'd scooted by me to leave. She'd quickly stood on her toes and kissed my cheek. "Happy New Year, David. I'll see you on Tuesday."

"Yep, Em, unless, of course, the clocks don't work, the subways can't run, and my building's security system is shot to hell."

"It's all hype — the computers will turn and keep working..." She'd closed the loft's door.

She and I had both known that I didn't have a date because all the women I was 'involved' with were with their husbands and families. Christmas and New Year was a long stretch for me, but my cell would be ringing next week for sure, and then I'd hear how 'awful' it was without me — blah, blah, blah.

DALE NEWCOMB, A BUSINESS ASSOCIATE, came by and cocked his head towards me while looking at the girl. He was impressed. I barely looked at him, my mood suddenly taking a nosedive. I wanted everything to stop: the music, the champagne, the chatter. I wanted it all to come crashing down. Nineteen-ninety-nine to 2000: I secretly hoped the world's computers, banks, stock market, all of it would implode. *Why not?* I thought. *This world sucks.*

I had tried to put the whole Rachel shit behind me but I still thought about her. Not as Miss Vermont — that seemed disrespectful to who she actually was. She'd gotten in under my skin, and no matter what I did, I couldn't quite shake her. The thing was I really thought there had been something between us. But I'd sworn to stop pursuing her that day outside of her work. It was clear she wasn't interested and unlike some women I'd known, it wasn't a game to her. Sometimes, though, I imagined her and me out and about in the city, even with her kids — like we'd all been that day on the farm.

As soon as we'd listed it, I'd gotten an offer on my grandparents' place. I hadn't followed through on any of the renovations since somebody had quickly put in a bid with plans to tear down the house and barn. Basically, they'd only wanted the 27 acres of land. I'd given the realtor the green light, glad I didn't have to drive up any more except for a final clean out. But about three days after receiving the offer from a man named Robert Snell, it had hit me that he was the guy who owned the junkyard further down Old County Road. His torn fencing exposed hundreds of broken-down vehicles and discarded farm equipment, an eyesore coming up over the rise just past our turn. Many times, I'd heard my grandmother lament, "That man is the epitome of blight." I couldn't do that to the memory of her, so I'd stopped the sale immediately. Then I'd gotten a call out of the blue from the farmer across the way. He and his sons were interested in leasing the orchard, getting it back in shape, and selling the cherries. I'd asked him, "Including the little house out back bordering it?" Since he said no, I'd told him the cost would be minimal. I felt good about the plan and had had my grandfather's lawyer draw up a simple lease. I could coast for a while before I'd have to list it again. And it would give me more time to either do the renovations or figure out what I wanted to do with the property.

I turned back to look at the ball dropping on the big screen in front of us. Here I was, on New Year's Eve, with a beautiful woman beside me, and I was thinking about Rachel Dunne and Vermont. A familiar feeling of longing came over me, and I hated it.

"Fuck Vermont," I whispered to myself as the countdown reached three, two, one…Alisa/Aleesha wrapped her arms around me and started to kiss me.

I'll never go back there.

2001

David

I hung up my cell and looked at the television once again. My God, the inferno — people jumping from the buildings, fleeing in dust-covered, terrified faces, and the constant replay of the planes hitting the towers was making me nauseous. The news was unfolding, breaking developments every few minutes, it seemed. I got up and headed into the kitchen. I could still hear sirens and wondered if more shit was happening elsewhere in the city.

Emily had brought a friend, Jimmy, to my place, and they were glued to the set. Jimmy was holding Emily's hand while she sat, crying. I was glad he was here for her. I thought about Tom Dunne calling me, just seconds ago, and how appreciative I felt. *What if it had been Rachel, though, instead?* I didn't carry the thought any further. I had made a decision about her, and I was sticking to it.

A large, unopened pizza box was on the island, along with two bottles of wine and some imported beer. We hadn't touched any of it. I grabbed a bottle of water from the refrigerator and thought of Tom's call again. *"Hey, good to hear your voice. I'm just calling to make sure you're safe — and you are."* I looked out at the skyline as the sun was setting. Lights were coming on and I could see pockets of people standing on their balconies. I called to Emily that she and Jimmy were welcome to spend the night even though the subway was running again. I didn't hear her reply.

AS THE HOURS TICKED BY, the city remained in shambles and nothing could go on or get done. It was enough to check in with one another, make sure we had what we needed, and comfort those directly affected.

In the wee hours of the third morning, I acknowledged the fact that if I'd been in the Twin Towers, no one would be posting a large print of my picture looking for me, as many people were doing close to the site — what they were calling, 'Ground Zero.' It was the first time I really understood that, since my grandfather's death two years ago, everyone in my family was gone.

More than once, I wished I could hear my grandmother's reassuring voice that everything would be okay. Instead, I listened to Rudy Giuliani's, the Mayor of New York.

I touched base with a few patrons and a couple of their significant others. They were subdued and yet needy, too. Later in the week, I met one woman near my place in Chelsea. She cried to me about how she felt her husband, one of my biggest clients, wouldn't have cared if she'd been on the floors that burned. It was a distant possibility since it was where their financial planner's office at Cantor Fitzgerald was. "He'd see it as a great misfortune," she said. "A terrible tragedy for our family and our friends, but then I know he'd see it secretly as a windfall. His chance to be free of me." I tried to reassure her that wasn't the case, but honestly, my energy level was low, almost non-existent.

I went back to Tom's simple check in: *"Just making sure you're safe."* Had Rachel been by the phone when he called? *Does she hate me?* I wondered, then quickly remembered to put all my thoughts of her away, closed up tight.

Eventually, the city started to breathe again. But none of us who lived here thought we'd ever be the same. Giuliani basically said those exact words in a press conference. But he vowed we'd be strong and recover. I hoped so.

Rachel

I sat stunned, watching the news. Meg had come over right after dinner and we'd talked quietly, sitting on the porch until we both felt we were ready to see more on the TV. Amy had fallen asleep in Meg's lap and I'd taken her right up to her crib — she'd missed her afternoon nap. It'd been a beautiful day in Vermont with temperatures hovering around 68 degrees and lots of sunshine. I'd telephoned Mom, but she'd decided to stay put and continue to watch the news at her house. It was all shocking.

When Pat got the call, mid-morning at work, she'd walked in and had quietly motioned for Kaitlyn and me to come over. She'd explained the planes and the towers and that more planes had possibly gone missing. It seemed surreal. We'd hugged each other, and shortly after, parents began to filter in to sign out their children. I'd hugged a mother whose brother worked in one of the towers. "Please, please, Rachel, pray that we hear from him soon."

Pat and I locked up the building after the last child went home. Tom had sent his staff home early from the fencing company and had picked up both Amy and Tommy. He'd kissed me on the Center's porch and had whispered, "It's going to be okay."

I'd leaned into him, my big guy, and said, "I need to hear that."

NOW I SAT ON THE COUCH and, like all of America, listened and flipped the channels to the different networks as the news coverage was endless. All flights had been suspended and there was heightened security in case of other attacks.

Tom came down from upstairs. "Tommy's fallen asleep. I think he'll be fine, but let's keep talking to him about it." I nodded in agreement and stood up. Tom looked tired and was definitely subdued.

He followed me into the kitchen. I began to load the dishwasher as he helped clear the table. "Hey baby, I'm gonna call David Sumner and make sure he's okay. I think the towers were in the financial sector, but you never know."

This surprised me. "Really?" I turned and looked at him. It was dusk; the last bit of the evening light fell on the crab apple tree just outside the window. "You're going to call him out of the blue? Won't that be weird? I mean — kind of awkward for you?"

Tom seemed pensive. "Nah. We've messaged about the Red Sox recently. They're trailing the Yankees in the American League right now. We're both bummed." He ducked out to the porch and returned, holding his cell. "I want to do this real quick."

I leaned against the counter and watched as he made the call. The conversation was short. I heard David's brief reply, "I'm okay, thanks for the check-in. It's crazy. You guys take care." He sounded sincere and appreciative.

When Tom hung up, he glanced at me and said, 'I'm glad I did that. I'm heading back to the den."

I called out after him, "I don't know if I can watch much more, but I'll come in a minute." I walked over to Amy's highchair and released the tray. I carried it to the sink and turned on the water, waiting for it to become hot. I poured dish soap on the cloth and then looked out the window. It was now dark and my reflection stared back at me. I had immediately thought of David when the mother mentioned her brother being in one of the towers. Hearing his voice just moments ago brought me back to the last time we spoke. I had been blunt with him and he had responded coldly, barely looking at me.

I scrubbed the tray, then set it aside on a towel to dry. I started the dishwasher. *I'm sure he hates me,* I thought, as the hum of the dishwasher filled the kitchen. *How could he not?* I turned the kitchen light off and walked into the den just in time to see the replay of the second plane hit. *All those people…gone in an instant.*

2004

Tom Sr.

I watched Rachel walk back into the gymnasium with Amy on her hip. Amy was almost getting too big for her to carry. But I understood why she held her — tonight's game had a huge turnout. Our boys' basketball team needed to win to advance to the semi-finals. Rachel stood just inside the doorway, watching both teams shoot baskets. It was close to the end of halftime. I knew all the players; many of them would make up my varsity baseball team roster in the spring.

Sometimes, like now, I was blown away by how much I loved her. Like how beautiful she was and why she'd chosen me out of all the people placed in her path. I watched her, forgetting about the kids on the court, until the buzzer went off.

Rachel started to walk towards our spot in the stands, smiling at people she passed, even reaching out and touching the head of a little guy who'd run up to her. *Probably a kid in her class,* I thought, as she started to climb the bleachers. When she finally made it to me, I took Amy from her arms and set her down between us. I leaned over and kissed Rachel quickly.

"What's that for?" she asked, smiling.

"Oh, you, just being you." I felt incredibly lucky.

"Sweetie, give Daddy his lollipop."

Amy held up one of three tootsie roll pops she'd bought at the concession stand. They were all orange — our favorite flavor.

As we sucked on our pops, we watched the start of the third quarter. The score didn't look so good for us; we were down by twelve points. Tommy was going in, and we both sat up straighter as we watched the players gather up, getting ready for the jump ball. At over six two, Tommy, a freshman, had been pulled up to the varsity team for play-offs. He told me, confidentially, that he was nervous and hoped he wouldn't screw up.

"You'll do just great, Tommy — give it all you got," I said to him when he came home to tell me Coach Barrett had called him out of Algebra II class to tell him.

Now he was in and playing for the first time at this level. He tipped the ball to one of the Langdon players then raced down to cover the basket for the rebound.

Though Langdon closed the gap a bit, we still lost by seven. Tommy played decent defense, and I couldn't wait to tell him so.

"I'll swing you home and then come back for him, okay?" I said to Rachel.

"He's going to be bummed, isn't he?"

I was carrying Amy now as the crowd dispersed to the parking lot. A whole lot of people had come despite the freezing temperatures this last week of February. I saw headlights come on, cars pulling out and driving down to the school's entrance.

"Oh, he might be, but I don't think so, not really. He played great for a freshman, and the rest of the team fought hard. The other team was just too good; their offense had those two guys who didn't miss the three pointers."

Rachel took my hand and we walked down the bank to our car. *I'm the luckiest guy in the world,* I thought for the second time as both Amy and Rachel held on to me.

Emily

I came in and dropped the newspaper down in front of David. He was at his workspace already, the area relatively neat. That was something I admired — he kept his shit orderly. It must have been a quiet night last night. He usually didn't appear until the early afternoon.

Every morning I was happy to come to work. I poured myself a black coffee and sat at an angle to David. Sneaking glances his way, I thought about being here, having this job. I'd come from the Andy Warhol Foundation as an editorial assistant. While that place held a certain aura, it was a mess as far as the drama of the staff and the in-fighting and back-stabbing. Before that, I was a full-time unpaid intern who basically answered the phones and ran errands at one of the better-known galleries. To get anywhere there, I'd needed to know someone personally. I didn't, so I'd started looking.

Accepting the position with David had been a huge risk. At first, I hadn't recognized just how much a step up it was until I realized he thought I knew a lot more than I really did. He valued my Art History degree from Barnard more than I did, I could tell. He just about ate up my transcript, reading aloud from it: *"Cultural Studies, Economics and Advanced French."* He also knew I'd taken several fine arts classes, like painting and drawing.

It wasn't until the third week that I learned he had no formal degree or background in art other than experience working as an art handler in Soho for a decade. It was during the fourth month that I discovered just how much people wanted to be in his orbit: artists, serious art collectors, and investors. He could see art, read its trajectory up or down and anticipate what was coming. And rich women were drawn to him — the looks and the charm were as much a part of his business acumen as his art knowledge and experience behind the scenes.

I began to sit at the table beside him during the complicated loan negotiations he was involved in when it came to acquiring pieces, and I traveled with him often. We were several years apart, but he treated me, many times, as his equal. When his calendar was too full, he'd say, with utmost confidence, "Em, I defer to you; you prioritize what I should attend and what you can just as easily cover." He hadn't blinked when I'd asked for my own budget line for clothing.

I had no idea who his assistant had been before me. I couldn't imagine anyone else in my shoes. David was hard to navigate in and around, yet, I'd never felt more alive or a part of something this exhilarating in my entire thirty-years of life.

By the end of my first year, I realized David had his demons. It was hard to characterize but I'd say, basically, that he didn't like himself. Like the time the English couple, the Cushings, came to Darcy's gallery hoping to meet him. He had helped with the Damien Hirst Show and it was a wild success. David could hardly tolerate their accolades and had come off as rude. And then there was that dinner with my brother, Jason. David had joined us and when Jason had shared that he'd finally tested for the disease my mother had died from and that it was negative, David had responded sarcastically. He'd asked why Jason had bothered, said if it had been him, he would have enjoyed the game of Russian Roulette. He'd mimed an imaginary gun to his temple and fired. Neither my brother nor I thought it was funny.

DAVID'S BITTERNESS TOWARD HIMSELF was alarming. This morning he looked like he'd had a visit from one of his demons.

I pointed at the newspaper. "Read the article down on the far right. It's incredible."

I watched as he stopped answering an email and looked down at the paper. Before long, he was standing up and pacing the room while reading the news story.

Riding in on the subway earlier this morning, I'd been shocked to read that a bronze cast of Rodin's 'The Thinker' had been found in the rubble of one of the World Trade Center towers. Apparently, the Cantor Fitzgerald bond trading firm had several pieces from B. Gerald Cantor's collection. But the thing was, according to the article, a firefighter had found the cast — about 28 inches in size, intact — and even posed for a picture with it. Then it had gone missing. Speculation was that it had been stolen. This had happened almost three years ago.

When I surmised that David had finished reading the whole article, I piped up, "Remember that weird call from Dale Newcomb? I screened it for you about, I don't know, maybe four months ago? He was asking if you had anyone interested in Rodin pieces? This may be why. Was he trying to move it?"

David glanced my way and said, "Who the fuck gives a shit, Emily, really? Art is stolen all the time. Dale Newcomb is a sleaze ball."

I was taken aback; I was not expecting that reaction. Looking at him, I tried to figure out where this was coming from.

Sensing my surprise, David added, "It's old news. I've been hearing about this since it supposedly went missing. Besides, I hate Rodin. He's overrated. Get me the Christie's East inventory — what we highlighted — so I can spend as little time as possible with the asshole Finley family today."

I didn't respond.

"Please," he said as he returned to his email.

I stood up and went to get the print-out. There was only so much I could do for him. Psychoanalysis was not in my job description. Besides, I had my own issues. Jimmy and I wanted a child. Unlike my younger brother, Jason, Willis and his wife had opted not to have him get tested for Huntington's disease. Their kid was beautiful and they were settled in, raising him. "We're going to enjoy our lives; it's the here and now for us, Emily," Willis had said. Jimmy agreed with their stance. But I couldn't quite see beyond my mother's last years, incapable of speech or movement. She'd died in the care facility not knowing who I was. *Do I want that for my child? To remember me like that?* I thought. *Of course, I don't.*

Rachel

Mrs. Stevens' class was visiting, performing community service. We were all outside at recess, except for the babies who were being fed and rocked for their afternoon naps.

There was one middle school girl, in particular, who seemed especially engaged with my Red Poppies. She talked to each one of them in an animated voice. I asked Mrs. Stevens who she was.

"Believe it or not, she's one of my toughies — misses a lot of school, tells off the staff. But then look at her today; she's in her element, she's shining. Her name is Katie."

I definitely agreed.

Amy was riding the big tricycle around the playground. It had a red wagon attached and another little girl, Ivy, was in the back. She was determined to paddle Ivy around and, with her head bent, she almost made it. But there was a slight incline, up around the slide to the covered porch.

I watched her struggle. Then Katie came and put her foot on the back of the tricycle Amy was riding and pushed her up the last bit of the incline. When Amy 'parked the tricycle,' she leaned over to Katie and whispered something.

I couldn't tell what she said, but Katie looked puzzled. Just before Mrs. Stevens's group of middle schoolers boarded the bus, I asked Katie what the little dark-haired girl had whispered to her.

Leaning out the bus window, Kate responded, "I'm not quite sure, but it was like, 'My rickshaw,' or something like that, 'needs to stay here.' But again, I'm not positive."

"Rickshaw?"

Katie nodded and disappeared from the bus window.

I knew a rickshaw was a large cart used in Asian countries to move people around in heavily populated areas. How had Amy ever heard of the word, let alone used it in that correct way? She was only 4 years old.

It reminded me of the time we went to Fort at No. 4 to see the open-air museum displays of colonial life. We watched women baking bread and churning butter. Amy had clapped her hands together and proclaimed, "Mommy, I did this before!" I'd tried to get her to explain what she'd meant on the way home, but her thoughts were on to something else and she'd soon fallen asleep in her car seat.

I made a mental note to tell Tom about today's exchange with the older girl. It was odd. Amy said things at times that none of us — my mother included — could figure out. But, like the other incidences, I looked at her sweet, happy face and let it go.

David

M r. Michaels, David Sumner is here to see you. He's early but said he'll wait."

I mouthed to his gorgeous secretary, "Tell him to take his time."

She nodded and opened his door once more. "And Mr. Sumner says to take your time." Closing the door, she looked back at me and then returned to her desk. Ellen was a classic beauty, a natural blond. I didn't mind stealing a glance.

Within moments, Mrs. Michaels, a statuesque older woman with dark red hair piled high in a twist, walked into the office. She was wearing a navy-blue suit with a soft, pink silk blouse. On her arm she carried a Gucci purse in the exact same shade of pink. It'd been a while since I'd seen her and our parting had not been under the best of terms. She smiled at me and said to Ellen, "I'm just going to go freshen up, don't call into him yet."

As his secretary swiveled in her chair until she was facing away from the both of us, Mrs. Michaels motioned for me to come. I got up quietly and said, "I'm going to just step out to make a few calls."

I followed Mrs. Michaels out the door and down the hall. She ducked into the ladies' room and a second later opened the door and whispered, "Come in, come in." I didn't want to, but a lot was riding on this meeting with her husband. I couldn't chance upsetting 'the apple cart.'

She lit into me, asking why I hadn't responded to her text messages. I lied and told her I had a new phone. She said, "Bullshit," and took out her own, quickly dialing my number. My cell, in my suitcoat breast pocket, immediately started to ring.

Just then we heard two people approach the ladies' room. I looked around, and, seeing Mrs. Michaels' smug look, ran to the last stall and quickly closed it. I debated standing up on the toilet seat but didn't, realizing I would tower over the top. I sat on the toilet and braced my feet up against the door. I prayed no one would come to this stall.

"Oh, Mrs. Michaels, your husband is free right now. He wants you to know he has someone else coming in shortly." It was Ellen's voice, the gorgeous secretary.

I heard the door open and shut. I hoped it was Mrs. Michaels leaving.

A second woman spoke. "Did I see the infamous David Sumner go through your office door a few minutes ago?"

"Yep, he's waiting to see Mr. Michaels. All he does is buy old men the art they want and then fucks their wives."

The second woman replied, "I wondered if all that was true."

"It is. I think all the old, rich guys look the other way because they're banging the even younger ones now. It's kind of a symbiotic relationship and Sumner feeds off all of them."

"Well, he's starting to look like he plays a little bit too hard, know what I mean?" There was a pause. "I'm going to the Cape for Thanksgiving, what about you guys?"

"Sticking around. Mathew has to work. Do you like this color lipstick on me?"

"Yes. I couldn't wear it though, too much orange for my skin tone."

They left. I came out of the stall and walked up to the mirror. The bright lights weren't flattering; my skin had a sallow cast and my eyes looked tired with a tinge of redness. I quickly took out the 'lumify' drops from my pocket and applied one to each eye, tilting my head way back. *I need to drink more water*, I thought, and left the women's room.

As I entered Mr. Michaels' office once more, Ellen turned to me and said, "Perfect timing, you can go in."

I walked out not more than 15 minutes later. Mr. Michaels wanted the percentage of ownership I had left in the Dali painting. He was my last investor, and now I could broker the deal. There was a good size commission in it for me. I gave the secretary a huge smile, but Ellen never turned to look up. I knew what she thought of me.

Going down the elevator, I replayed what the women had said. I'd be lying if I didn't admit it bothered me. My own take on a lot of the shit I did was that I was a parasite. If I spent too much time thinking on it, though, I'd drink and do more blow than I already did.

AT LEAST I'M NOT A SWINDLER, I told myself as I opened the door to my place. I was a legitimate art dealer of contemporary art, delivering authentic pieces to my clients each and every time. I thoroughly vetted the new artists, as well as the 'recently uncovered or discovered' work from established artists whenever such pieces were brought to my attention. Records of all transactions, including the bill of sale and detailed description of the art — title, medium, dimensions, and copyright — were first reviewed and then filed meticulously by me and Emily.

I knew stories, true incidences of dealers trafficking in stolen art and fake pieces with falsified documentation. My name was never associated with any of them. I'd seen how quickly those assholes fell when their cover was blown or how easily they were manipulated by powerful people calling the shots behind the scenes. I'd worked too hard and for too long to see everything go up in smoke. Besides, my grandfather had always impressed upon me the need to follow the rules — whether in a game of checkers or getting my car inspected. "Those are the rules, Davy." I just wasn't always thrilled about following them.

No, my shit was wrapped up in dealing with a number of rich folks who had a whole lot of unhappiness. My sexual liaisons with needy spouses were a by-product of doing business — or so I told myself.

I read my emails, then I quickly figured out the commission I'd make on the Dali. It was sweet, and Emily would be happy. I'd be sure to bump up the percentage for her year-end bonus. She worked hard and was always loyal to me.

My cell rang and I looked at it: Mrs. Michaels' number. I quickly declined the call. Maybe it was fucking time to actually get a new phone and number. I'd run it by Emily tomorrow.

I reread the text messages I'd exchanged with Tom Dunne last week. The curse was finally broken — the Red Sox had won the World Series. It was incredible! I wanted to remember his very last text, a joke about the Yankees blowing game seven at home.

I changed and got ready to go out. I hadn't thought of Rachel once when Tom and I had our back-and-forth messages. Not until now…but I quickly suppressed the urge and glanced at the clock; It was barely 11 p.m. The night was young.

2006

David

I felt the boy's weight as he leaned over, tugging at the woman beside me. "Rosa, I'm hungry, I want my cereal."

I opened my eyes and saw a small child sitting near the woman, up by her pillow. My mouth was dry and my eyes hurt as the morning sun streamed in through the French doors that were left open last night. I could see the pool water glistening outside and heard the sound of a weed-whacker, its high-pitched starting and stopping, starting and stopping.

I glanced over at the woman beside me. She was completely out of it, her rich black hair covering most of her face on the pillow. I could hear her making little muffled breathing noises, but she didn't move at all. A moan came from further down, near the foot of the bed. There was a second woman, blond and older, her hand and arm stretched up over her head. Gold bracelets, loose on her thin, tanned arms, clinked as she turned her head away and moved her arms to under the sheet.

The boy remained intent on waking the girl beside me. "Rosa, wake up." His voice was quietly persistent. He ran his hand over her hair, fanning it further out on the pillow, and then he looked at me. He wore pajamas with cartoon characters on them.

"I'm going to get up, close your eyes," I whispered and waited until he did. I moved quickly out of the bed.

I was naked and covered myself with my hands. I thought the women in the huge bed were also probably naked.

I saw my clothes on the parquet floor and quickly grabbed them as I made my way to the bathroom. My mind skidded over the circumstances of why I was here and where here was. I'd drank way too much and snorted coke until the wee hours of the morning. It was a party, out in the Hamptons.

My back ached and I almost fell trying to put on my briefs and then my pants. I looked at myself in the mirror above one of the sinks. I looked like shit and felt even worse. *I need to get out of here fast,* I thought. *Where's my cell?*

It hurt to pee — too much sex and I was sure it had been unprotected. I splashed water on my face, then I cupped it, drinking thirstily. I put on my shirt, even though it reeked of booze and had a stain down the front. I came out of the bathroom. The boy was still there, now with his head on the same pillow as the sleeping girl.

I remembered she was the nanny for the blond woman at the foot of the bed who was the wife of one of my patrons, Miguel Rinaldo. The nanny had come to tell Mrs. Rinaldo something and then never left. We had a party after the party — the three of us stumbling into the guest bedroom off the pool house. Something about the girl was nagging at me, though. I felt my bowels shift and wondered if I was going to need to use the toilet.

The boy sat up and asked me, louder this time, "Can you get me my cereal?"

I ignored him and grabbed my cell and wallet, quickly glancing to make sure my credit cards were still there. I put my loafers on and walked to the open door. Just before I stepped out into the brilliant sunshine, I heard Mrs. Rinaldo say, "For Christ's sake, Anthony, get your own fucking cereal." I looked back at the boy. He appeared resigned to having to wait longer.

I walked around the immaculate in-ground pool and glanced at the back of the big house. Wine glasses were scattered on the ornate patio tables and a large floral arrangement was shedding its petals.

I heard a truck start up out front and walked hurriedly through a latticed-covered garden. The bees near the roses were loud, and it was already warm outside.

"Hey, hold up! Any chance I can catch a ride with you?" I asked. The old truck's bed was outfitted with assorted rakes and garden equipment.

The heavy-set man behind the wheel called out, "Sure, hop in."

I climbed up and in, feeling like I'd die if I didn't get away from here. The boy had followed me out and was standing in the circular driveway.

As I looked in the side mirror and watched the kid grow smaller and smaller, I heard his mother's voice again: *"For Christ's sake, Anthony, get your own fucking cereal."* I rolled down the window and looked out at the other perfectly landscaped homes we were passing.

I hadn't heard my own mother's voice in years. I closed my eyes and saw her lying on a couch with a man, their arms and legs intertwined. I was about that kid's age. I'd wanted something — what? I couldn't remember. She had thrown a pillow at me, yelling, "Leave me the fuck alone."

I held up my left hand and looked at it. It was shaking.

"Rough night, uh?" the gardener asked.

I ignored his comment and pulled down the visor. I didn't have my sunglasses. I must have left them back there. My head was pounding and my stomach growled. I hoped I wasn't going to be sick.

Again, that nagging feeling…What was it? And then it hit me. I had been trying to figure out if the nanny was of age. She kept telling me she was 20. I remembered her Hispanic accent and the way she moved her body, her beautiful body. Mrs. Rinaldo was passed out, and we kept at it. Even as fucked up as I was, I'd thought she was too young. But I chose not to care.

I felt the bile coming up and quickly told the gardener to pull over. He veered to the shoulder and I stumbled out of the cab and bent over. I threw up, hearing my own retching sounds. I closed my eyes. *This has got to stop.*

I FLED THE CITY THAT EVENING and drove up to Vermont, to the farm. When I passed the boat landing, I stopped and climbed out. Standing at the edge of the water, I wondered how broken a man could get before it was time to end it. *I'll find out,* I thought as I watched the moon above the lake, its stillness deafening.

But I didn't end it — that night or the next or the next. The farm took me in, quietly but assuredly, whispering to me, *"This is where you're supposed to be."*

I drove down Route 100, making up a grocery list as I went. I had to stop going to the convenience store for one meal (grinder) at a time. And, I admitted, a hopeful chance encounter with Rachel. Since I was back in the area, I knew we might run into one another. My vow to leave her alone still held firm, though — I wasn't going to do anything to sour my return to the farm. It was all I had now, I realized. I passed the boat landing and thought about how down and out I'd been the last time I'd seen it. That was already three weeks ago.

Town was busy, the start of the long Labor Day weekend. I knew I needed to call Emily, tell her I was done with New York and to pay September's rent, already late, and then no more. I dreaded the call, but was kind of surprised by how sure I was about making it.

I'd tell her to take over the business; she was more than capable. Any outstanding decisions were now hers to make. She could frame my departure in any way she felt comfortable. I trusted her. I would also tell her to take any and all of the furniture she wanted, but to make sure my clothes went down to the Salvation Army on 8th Ave. I wanted that. There was something poetic about my Armani tailored shirts and casual dress pants on some poor bloke. *Hell, I'd been down and out in a different way,* I thought. *Maybe someone else would have better luck.*

On the way out of the grocery store, I quickly turned into a bagel shop across the street. I hadn't picked up any breakfast items other than coffee. The door jingled as I went in. It was quiet and I smelled cookies baking. A woman about my age, with short spikey brown hair and several earrings on each of her earlobes, looked up at me from behind the counter. Her arms were impressive, her biceps clearly having seen a gym and the sun. She wore a black tank top and around her neck were a couple of silver necklaces with gemstones dangling from them.

I took off my sunglasses and commented that I came in to buy bagels but would definitely be leaving with cookies, too. She smiled, but it was reserved, and I thought, *That's enough of my small talk.*

With much deliberation, I picked out a half dozen assorted bagels and three oatmeal cookies. I also bought a lemon-drop bar. As she cut it, I quickly said, "Make it two, please, and sorry I took so long."

When she was ringing me up, she paused and said, "David Sumner, right?" Before I could answer, she added, "Do you need cream cheese for your bagels? We've got assorted individual packets if you want some."

I stared at her and hesitantly replied, "Um, packets would be great, thank you. I wish I could recall who you are, but I'm sorry, I don't. What's your name?"

She didn't smile but gave me a sideways look. "I don't think you'd remember my name if I said it, but you and I went to high school together. Graduated class of seventy-seven. We actually screwed in the bed of your grandfather's Ford, oh, I'd say about thirty years ago."

I stood there, completely at a loss and feeling terribly embarrassed or ashamed. I couldn't decide, thinking it was probably both.

She crossed her arms. "Actually, you were a bit of an asshole in high school, you know — arrogant, the guy who got all the action. That, I bet, you do remember."

Now wanting to get out of there, I asked her, "What do I owe you?"

She reached into a refrigerated cooler behind her and grabbed some cream cheese packets. She then tallied the amount at the register and handed me the bag and slip. I extended my card to her and she rang it through.

She returned it, and I thanked her. When I got to the door, I turned and said, "Just so you know, I grew into an even bigger asshole when I left Plymouth."

She paused before saying, "Well, if it's any comfort, I wasn't so sure it *was* you because I thought you were kind of nice a few minutes ago. And really, our lustful foray — it kind of set me straight, because that's when I discovered I wasn't straight." She smiled.

I returned to the counter and held out my hand. "Hi, my name *is* David Sumner who's working on not being an asshole."

She shook my hand in return. "I'm Julie Decklin, and this is my shop. My partner, Hélène, has a little studio-gallery out back; she's quite a good artist."

"I'd like to check it out sometime." I held up the bagel bag and said, "Thank you."

"You're welcome, David." Then she turned to greet new customers coming in.

On my next trip to the market, about two and a half weeks later, I decided to stop at the bagel shop first. I thought the way Julie and I had ended it was cordial, and I wanted more bagels. When I walked in, Julie and an older woman were sitting at one of the café tables talking. No one else was there. I hesitantly asked, "You open?"

"Hi, David, yes, we are." Julie stood and walked my way. "We just finished the morning rush; now we're taking a break."

"Loved your bagels — I'm back for more." I moved towards the counter.

The older woman spoke up. "I'm Hélène, Julie's partner. I should probably thank you for the significant role you played in her, um…formative years, no?"

She had an accent, maybe French, but I wasn't sure. Her smile was lovely, and I went over to the table and extended my hand.

"Not exactly my claim to fame, but…"

She was maybe in her late 50s and just the opposite of Julie with long graying hair and a full figure. She wore a colorful, flowing dress and silver bangles on each of her wrists.

"We actually googled you," she said. "You're an art dealer, very impressive. Stay and sit."

I liked her immediately; she was warm and welcoming. I sat down and wanted to clarify my new thing, which wasn't anything at all.

"Ah, I'm no longer an art dealer. I kind of had an epiphany not too long ago and left."

Hélène smiled and then reached over and covered my hand. "It's become a dirty business; no one I know now is buying for the love of art. It's all about status and investment. Is that what you think?"

I was truthful and replied, "I, more than anyone, was in it for exactly that. Blue chip art for the rich, and a few of the famous. What other commodity outperforms the S&P 500, gold even? When the market dips there's no connection. Art, the lowest rate loss there is." I looked over at Julie and quickly added, "And, honestly, it's a stressful existence. Always aware of who owed me favors, and who I owed favors too, and the women…" I didn't finish.

"I think, David, you and I may have some similar experiences, n'est-ce pas?" Hélène patted the table, clearly anxious to talk.

"Hey, Julie, would it be okay if I have a bagel and a cup of coffee here?" I asked.

MY EYES GREW BIG when Hélène described her years in Soho in the '80s, exactly how I remembered my own in the time before I got established.

"Loved those cast-iron buildings with big, cheap, vacant lofts for rent," she said. "All the young artists — some fresh out of art school, others up from the subway, doing their magic, and money pouring in from all over. Lots of young performance artists too, the hip hop, gibberish: Jean Michael Basquiat, Keith Haring, Jeff Koons. The minimalism — the way it was all about the materials and experience, and the industrial places being used, taken over. Artist performances on Mercer, Crosby, Houston, Spring Street, along West Broadway, popping up and provocative, always provocative, making you think.

"It was like jazz — impromptu, you didn't know what you were going to see. Less academic and more in the moment, along with the social commentaries. You saw and felt their cynicism, our own cynicism. C'etait la vie, non?"

She paused and waited for me to respond.

I glanced out the bagel shop's window and was transported back to those days. I remembered Kevin Paul, a great kid over at the gallery of Tony Shafrazi. We used to meet in the afternoon for coffee. He was a street artist who was finding his niche and pissing off the artists who were not so naturally gifted, who had put in more time and money to be noticed, considered.

I smiled at her and started to speak. "It was by accident that I ended up in Soho — I dropped out of college, the University of New Hampshire, and made my way to the city. I was looking at ads and a guy, Puerto Rican and pretty, said, 'Soho is where it's happening.'"

Hélène seemed genuinely interested so I continued. "I became an art handler for a few galleries, mostly Martin Lawrence: wrapping art, moving it from one place to another, always in awe of the value of whatever piece I was responsible for. We called ourselves 'the bomb squad.' Had to move Warhol, Miro, Dali, and lesser-known artists, all with precision and incredible care. I did that for almost ten years. It's where I learned the business, the inside scoop, and made connections."

I stood up with my empty cup. "You need a refill?"

Hélène shook her head. I walked over to the carafes of fresh coffee, pumped the Pecan Roast into my cup, and returned to the table. A couple of people were in the shop now, but Hélène still sat, waiting patiently for me.

"I was living with a young sculptor, fresh out of Pratt. She wouldn't leave her rented loft for days, so her rich daddy — some hedge fund bigwig she never mentioned to all her starving artist friends — had all these food places give her credit and he'd pay at the end of each month. She had the restaurants on speed dial. We never ate so good, sometimes ordering eight, nine dinners a night as her loft filled up most evenings.

"Her name was Ashley. I have no idea what happened to her; after I made my first connection with some big money, I left. I didn't worry about her, though. Her father's pockets ran deep. But I never saw her work anywhere. I wondered if she finally gave up, married her own hedge fund manager, and, you know, moved out to Westchester County for the big house, couple of kids, a nanny."

"And hopefully a little studio out near the garden where she could enjoy some solitude," Hélène added and started to get up. I realized we hadn't even broached the subject of her own art gallery, here, right behind the shop.

"I'd really like to know about your work, see your gallery. Can I make an appointment to come back?" I asked as I stood and followed Hélène, placing my plate and cup in the bin for dirty dishes.

"Tell you what, let's not make it so formal. Come by during the weekday when it's much quieter."

"That sounds good, thank you."

She started walking towards a back door just past a display of gourmet coffee and travel mugs for sale.

"For what it's worth, David, I also left after my own epiphany. It had to do with scotch, a whole lot of scotch — top shelf, bottom shelf, it didn't matter."

Julie motioned to me and I came up to the counter. She held out a bag. "Same ones you got your first time, plus the cream cheese. I added a couple of lemon bars, made fresh this morning — those are on the house."

WHEN I GOT BACK TO THE FARM and unloaded the groceries, I sat at the kitchen table. I thought about those early days in Soho, almost thirty years ago when I was young and eager. I wasn't a hungry artist, but I liked the energy of everyone around me.

The first time I slept with a wealthy, older woman, she'd passed me three crisp one-hundred-dollar bills right along with a bottle of Perrier to go. I'd spent a couple of hours in the afternoon with her at some hotel in the Lower East Side. She had commissioned me on the spot to represent her son, an up-and-coming artist. I'd written out a contract on the back of the room service menu. He'd done okay, I'd gotten him noticed. *Why did I only see the money as the end game, even then?*

I stood and walked into the living room and looked at the thermostat. I turned it completely off. Just yesterday I'd gone in to tell the oil company that since I had moved back the number of gallons budgeted for the house could be lowered some. I'd already switched the setting to manual instead of automatic. The woman running the office had kind of looked like Rachel — tall, long auburn hair, and a big smile. I looked at her name tag: Janelle. Funny how I'd chosen to return here over all the places I could have gone. And that the one day here on the farm and the afternoon at the ball field with Rachel had been the highlight of my last seven years. I couldn't decide if that was truly pathetic or possibly remarkable. *Whatever it is, get over it*, I thought and I walked out the kitchen door.

I stood on the landing, just down from the bagel shop, and looked in through the studio's front door. Hélène was moving between four adults: three women and one man, as they sat on stools at easels with paints and brushes out. A woman was standing at the front of the room and speaking to the group. One easel was vacant. *That's mine*, I thought.

Hélène had invited me to try a class in oil painting at her studio. I'd been impressed with her oil paintings and had told her so. To fill some empty hours at the farm, now three months since I'd moved back, I'd started to dabble in painting again — something I hadn't done since high school. I'd gone so far as picking up some canvases, paints, and oils from Hélène's supplier.

I spent several weeks trying it out, painting what I could. But I needed more instruction, and Hélène had mentioned that a woman named Claire Waite would be teaching this class.

The early December night was cold, and I was glad I'd worn my grandfather's old wool coat. I recognized this woman, Mrs. Waite, at the front of the room. She had been my art teacher when I was in high school in Plymouth. She'd been a good teacher, only about four or five years older than the senior class. A lot of the guys had crushes on her. Like usual, I had been a real shithead in Art.

One day, as we were 'exploring' painting with watercolors, Miss Piper — which must have been her maiden name — had come up beside me. I'd been painting the farm, the way the slope of the yard fell down on the big Maple, and the house up to its right. She'd stood for a few seconds and then said, "David, this is excellent. The proportions are correct. I love your use of lighting and choice of colors too."

Any praise from my teachers in school was rare. I'd smiled, really pleased that she'd thought my attempt was decent. She'd pointed to the driveway and said, "You might want to give it more contrast, the texture of how gravel is, some gray, some black." I'd understood what she'd meant and nodded. She'd moved on.

A couple of asshole friends of mine were smirking at what had just transpired between us. One of them had mimed a blowjob, bringing his hand up to his mouth, making a circle, then moving it back and forth. I decided to 'one up him' and leaned back, looking down the row of tables. I'd brought up my fingers, splaying them in a V with my tongue in and out. Both boys had cracked up. I'd quickly turned to find Miss Piper looking directly at me.

When Advance Drawing was offered the next semester, I'd gone into the art room to ask her to sign my course request sheet. She'd been washing brushes at the back sink. I had noticed that all the chairs were put up for the day, making it easier for the custodians to sweep.

I'd smiled and held up the sheet. "Would you sign for Advance Drawing? It needs your permission if you think I'm good enough."

Miss Piper had turned and wiped her hands on her paint-splattered apron. She was pretty, nothing spectacular, but nice.

"David, you're good, like really good. Those watercolors of yours are the best I've seen this year, maybe in the whole time I've been teaching at Plymouth. Actually, they're better than most of the Vermont scenes for sale in the tourist shops."

"Thanks. I gave them to my grandmother for Christmas. She really likes them."

I held up the sheet with a pen.

"But I'm not going to sign the add sheet yet. Not until you promise me there will be no sexual innuendos, gestures, or comments directed at me or anyone else. That will never be tolerated in my classroom, ever. The Advance Drawing class has six girls and your buddy, Keith. I've told him the same thing. No sexual comments or gestures, and he assures me that he understands."

She'd paused and looked at me. I knew what she wanted me to do, same as Keith had: give my assurance that I wouldn't be doing the sexual crap she'd seen me do before. I wasn't about to grovel; I never did. So I'd given her nothing and kept quiet. Finally, I'd turned, and on the way out, hit one of the chairs off its table. I'd heard it fall as I walked out the door.

NOW, I FELT LIKE I WAS ONCE AGAIN outside her classroom, wanting to come in. I turned and went to the truck. I sat for a moment before starting it up. *When will all my fuck-ups stop fucking things up?* I asked myself.

By the time I got back to the farm, I had worked myself into a fury. I wanted to take the class, hoping to learn how to use the paints, the oils, the whole oil-painting process in order to make something halfway decent.

Walking into the house, I moved to the two canvases I'd painted. I grabbed them and the matches off the windowsill. I flew out the front porch, down the stairs, and crossed the driveway. I punched the truck's passenger side door with my free hand. It instantly hurt. I opened the shed's door and started throwing things around and up against its walls, looking for some gasoline. I finally found a red, five-gallon can, half full. Picking it up, I unscrewed the cap.

"This gas is probably twenty fucking years old," I said aloud.

I brought it outside and went to the burn barrel. I wedged the two canvases in, poured the gasoline over them, and lit it up, throwing the whole book of matches in.

"Pissed off and fucked up," I said as the paintings burned.

It's what a woman in Chelsea had yelled at me, the night before the Hampton party where I'd screwed the nanny and Mrs. Rinaldo. I had called the woman's husband when she'd refused to leave my apartment until we'd 'talked.'

As soon as I'd heard his voice on the line, I'd impatiently said, "Your wife is here, and I'm tired of her." She'd glared at me and then ran down the stairs, instead of taking the elevator. In between her sobs, she'd yelled, "Why are you so pissed off and fucked up?" It had reverberated up the stairwell.

I stared at the flames now reaching up and out of the barrel, the sparks leaping to the sky. "Pissed off and fucked up." That was me. I turned to go back inside the house.

BEFORE SUNRISE, I got back in the truck. The living room had taken the brunt of my anger. I'd thrown the chairs out the porch door and picked up the dining room table in a fit of self-pity. I'd broken the table into several pieces, using my feet to stomp on them. Now one foot hurt like hell.

I drove to Hélène's studio and parked. There were lights on in the bagel shop. She and Julie were moving about. I knocked on the door and Julie motioned for me to come in.

"David, it's okay," Hélène said, looking at me expectantly. "I saw you last night, just outside the studio. I can show you the process, how the paints stay open and wet, how to wipe it down, make changes. We can do a few lessons — just us. It'll suit you better, d'accord?"

I moved to the window and glanced out. I rubbed my face and ran my fingers through my hair. Turning back, I replied in a hoarse voice, "I knew the woman teaching, Hélène. It wasn't going to work out. Another case of me being a real asshole from, well…before."

Julie spoke up, "There's a great counseling outfit in Windsor. I went for a bit, it was helpful. I think they've got a fairly new person on board. Can't hurt to talk about the past, David. It can be helpful to push through some things."

Hélène smiled at me and replied, "A certain amount of retrospection is good for the soul; the past should never stop you from moving forward. Tu vois?"

Amy

I was 8 and a half and I knew he was sick. It was a strange and scary feeling I had in the bottom of my tummy. Every time he'd swallow, he'd look a little hurt, just a tiny bit, and turn his head to the side. When Jelly Beanie stopped sitting on Daddy's lap, I suspected she could smell it. We read in our Scholastic magazine at school about dogs being able to smell or sniff out sickness, diseases, and she was a beagle so…Mom, Tommy and everybody else didn't see anything, couldn't see what I saw.

One night when Daddy came to tuck me in, I'd put my arms around his neck as he leaned in to kiss me. I'd whispered, "Oh Daddy, I know it hurts."

He had looked at me with a weird expression and then kissed me goodnight. He'd walked to my door, then came back and straightened one of the pictures on my wall: a calico cat with big, big eyes. My room was full of Margaret Keane prints, all in colorful frames. I was allergic to cats, but wanted one real bad. Grammie had given me my first poster when I was 5 and said, "You can have all the kitties you want." I even had little kitty figurines on my dresser and nightstand and my bedspread was all kittens.

When he left my room, I thought, *My eyes are probably that big, like the kitties, looking back at him.* This thinking of mine, that something wasn't quite right, became our special bond, our 'knowing' deep in that place where I kept my sad thoughts.

I wondered if I should tell Mommy about his hurting. There were lots of times Daddy went out of his way to make sure nobody noticed. He wanted ice cream almost every day after supper. Mommy laughed whenever he'd call out, "Is it Butter Pecan or French Vanilla tonight?" She'd pat his belly and hand him his dish, but I didn't smile or laugh. I knew the ice cream made his throat feel better. When I'd eat mine, I'd sneak little looks at him. A few times he caught me. He'd turn back to the TV or to Mommy or Tommy real fast and say something funny. He didn't want me to bring it up again, I could tell. So, I didn't. I stopped liking ice cream as much.

2007

Tom Sr.

Well, that's bullshit," I said as I glanced at Rachel. "There's no way that little thing, that tumor-growth, whatever you call it, is going to take me down."

The doctor looked at me, and we both turned to Rachel. She looked pale and her breathing was suddenly irregular, like she was taking big gulps of air but nothing was going down.

Doc James got up and came to her. "Tom, stay right next to her."

He pulled up a chair and sat in front of Rachel. "Let's focus on breathing, okay? In and out slowly. Look at Tom here, see how he's breathing — in and out."

He picked up her wrist and checked her pulse. "You've heard some scary news, I know, but there are treatments and many options available for throat cancer that you and Tom and I will discuss. You're here now with Tom. See him, he's fine, sitting right beside you." His voice was soothing, like a father to a child.

Rachel didn't turn to me; she remained looking straight at Dr. James. He continued to talk, now in a nice, easy-going manner. "I remember the time you and Sylvie played ball; you hit a line drive so hard it almost took out the shortstop. Remember that game? You girls won, and I let you take the convertible out after."

Rachel's breathing started to slow down and Doctor James smiled as he continued. "I probably don't want to know where you went or what you did, but it was fun seeing you girls drive off. Did you know Sylvie is expecting a little girl, just like Amy?"

Rachel nodded and then glanced at me.

Moments later, she was holding my hand and appeared to be better, her breathing even.

"Honestly, Doctor James, how can…Hell, I'm six four, I weigh two seventy and can bench press the same amount. How can that thing — " I squinted at the x-ray — "that blur I can hardly make out bring me down? Can't you treat it like tonsils and just take it out?"

Rachel squeezed my hand and looked expectantly at Dr. James.

"We have lots to discuss," he said. "The benefits and risks of your options, and of course, your personal preferences all have to be considered. I'm not going anywhere, guys, I'm in this with you."

Dr. James walked over to us again. "You're a big guy, Tom. You're a fighter."

I WAS SITTING UP IN OUR BED, waiting for her to come over. "Want to fool around?" I asked as she put on her flannel nightie.

She moved the throw pillows to the chair beside our dresser and shook her head. "Really, Tom? After the day we've had?"

"Okay, that's a no I guess." I pulled back the down quilt and the top sheet. She climbed into the bed.

"I think we need to make a list of questions, things we need to know in order to make the best decisions moving forward." She glanced up at me.

"Yep, agreed. Rach, we talked about all this in the car. And Dr. James said that lots of people, now more than ever, survive cancer. I'm gonna be just fine." I moved my arm around her and she snuggled in, adjusting to remove her hair that was caught between our arms.

"I also think we need a better plan on how and when to tell the kids," she said.

I hesitated. "Amy may know already. She's got a sixth sense about weird stuff, remember?"

Rachel sat up and looked over at me. "Why do you think that she may know?"

I did a quick weigh in. Should I tell her the truth about what Amy said to me over a year ago? But then I'd be admitting that the sore throat had been around longer than anyone knew. Or should I keep it vague?

I chose to keep it vague. "Oh, just a feeling." I reached for Rachel, and we once again held each other. I was feeling guilty, though, and my thoughts drifted to us as kids.

"Remember that dance in school, where things started between us?" I asked.

"Yes, I do. Why?"

"I've never told you this, Rach. When I went to the back of the gym, out the side doors, I was going to meet Pat. She had come up to me and asked me to meet her out back, in like five minutes. And I went. Seeing you come across the parking lot was, well, it was what I really wanted. But I went out there initially to meet up with Pat."

I looked down at the top of her head and turned her face gently up towards mine. "I've wanted to tell you that for some time."

"Well, I guess so, since it's been almost twenty years."

She wasn't fazed at all, and it made me feel better about withholding the truth of my throat hurting and Amy's comment.

I was tired and pulled her closer as I moved down under the sheets and turned on my side.

Rachel whispered, "Since you came clean, I guess I will too…Pat asked you to come out back because I asked her to ask you if you were interested in me. Then Johnny Mitchell asked her to dance so I said, "Screw it, I'll go myself.""

"Really? You two were scheming back then, uh?"

"Yep." She turned her head up to me and asked, "Have you been thinking, all this time, that Pat had like, a thing for you?" Her eyes were mischievous and she was smirking.

"No, not really…But, well, kind of."

Rachel started laughing. The only way to shut her up was to kiss her. We did end up fooling around, after all.

David

He was a kid, no older than mid-20s. I almost didn't sit down because I was so unnerved by his age. But I did go to the green chair he nodded at and sat. For a few, painfully quiet minutes, I weighed what to do: keep on keeping it all in, or finally give it air.

Looking at him, I asked, "How long have you been at this practice?"

He smiled. "Oh, I'm in my fourth year, and I'm actually thirty-three years old. I know how young I look. I let all my new patients, including their parents, know my age. It seems to help them settle in better. I mainly treat adolescents, boys mostly, around issues of loss, anger, and things they can't name or identify. Or control," he added.

It hit me then, right there, as I heard the trucks zoom by out on Route 5, that this kid might be exactly who I needed. A memory of me as a drop-out college know-it-all came to mind. I saw my grandfather in my bedroom.

"Davy, take some time, think about this," he'd said. "Lots of freshman grow into loving college, make best buddies, and even fall in love. Hell, guys my age all go back to their alma mater with their wives, cause that's where they met 'em."

But I'd had enough after six weeks at the University of New Hampshire, and I wanted out. I'd looked up at him and said, so full of arrogance, "Yeah, well, I'm not going back, I'm heading someplace where there's stuff going on, things to see, shit to do. I am out of this crapola place."

He'd stepped aside as I'd gone into my closet.

Nana had been standing in the hallway. "Alex, let him go," she'd said. It was the last time I'd ever heard her voice. Or slept in my bedroom until my grandfather died years later.

NOW I NODDED AT EVERETT and said, "Oh, I fall right in there — an asshole at sixteen and still an asshole at forty-eight. There's not much growth there, believe me."

Everett smiled. "Ah, but is juvenile court suggesting you come? Are you slated for therapeutic interventions as part of a court order and a parenting plan?"

I crossed my legs and responded, "I probably should have been referred way back when. My grandparents were in over their heads raising me. I never did anything too illegal, though. They were very law-abiding and instilled that in me. I'm terrified of breaking laws, you know, the ones with hefty fines and jail sentences."

"Seems to me that's not a bad thing. It's kind of a welcome relief for me to hear after some of the clients I listen to. And coming here at your age and of your own volition...Pat yourself on the back. That's another good thing."

Strange, I didn't feel as awkward here as I first thought I would. Maybe his age was going to be a plus. I left his office after our initial meeting in a good place. It was a start.

During our second session, I told Everett — I referred to him as the boy shrink in my mind — that unlike the kids he saw, I knew what my problem was. I was angry all the time, mad at the world, always had been. But now it was getting worse, especially when I'd burned the canvases.

"Okay that's good, David. That's good that you've identified this emotion that you feel is dominating your life. Now, I want you to think about what's behind it. Our emotions are generated by what we think of things, how we interpret things in our life. Do you know what's prompting these feelings of anger? What need of yours could be behind this?"

I sat and thought, trying to remember a time when I wasn't mad, when I felt okay about things. A memory of fishing popped up, down at the brook behind the root cellar. I was little, maybe 8. Then the time Rachel and the kids came to spend the day — that magical day.

"I know there are a few times I can specifically remember when I wasn't mad. One day in particular that well, it changed my life. I guess in big ways."

"Okay, we can start there: When you weren't mad. Tell me about that one day, David."

I briefly told him about the morning I'd saved Tommy in the lake and how we'd raced to the emergency room. Everett jotted a few things down, and at one point I stopped talking.

He looked up. "So, this day, the summer day you saved the child — that changed you profoundly. I can certainly understand why."

I shifted in the chair. "No, I mean, this event *did* for sure affect me, but that's not the day I meant where I wasn't angry. That came later in the same summer."

"Ah, got it. Why don't you describe that later day? And David, I'm taking notes just so I can remember the points you make, so I can review them later and get an idea of where to go from here. I don't want you thinking I'm judging you in anyway."

I nodded and started to speak. "Rachel, the mom of the little boy I saved, and her family came to spend the day at my grandfather's farm. Kind of a thank you again for, you know, saving Tommy. But something came up for Rachel's husband and he couldn't make it.

"That day, all day, I watched Rachel, this beautiful woman, taking care of her baby, Amy. She brought a big blanket and we spread it out on the grass between the Adirondack chairs. I helped Rachel, grabbing the toys out of the diaper bag, especially those little things, um… colorful plastic keys that babies put in their mouth. Amy was teething, Rachel said. At one point, she took out a cloth diaper and wiped Amy's chin because it was all drool.

"We sat and talked about everything and watched the baby while Tommy and his friend played. After a little bit, I checked in on the boys and they were in the barn, up in the hay loft.

"The weather was one of those days in Vermont where there's a slight breeze keeping the bugs at bay and the sun and clouds took turns. I remember Rachel went into the house to get the basket she had brought for our lunch. I took off my shoes and moved onto the blanket to play with Amy. She was laughing as I made faces: funny ones and noises, like a cow, a dog, I don't know, just having fun seeing her reaction. I wiped her chin with the cloth Rachel had used. Except for when I brought Tommy to the hospital, I'd never been that close to a baby, ever. Amy was chubby and had wispy tufts of hair, really just a few dark curls on top of her head. She was beautiful.

"We just sat taking in the day, the beauty of it, and each other's company. Rachel had moved her arm in a wide arc, taking it all in. 'This is heaven, David, or what I hope heaven is,' she'd said.

"The boys asked if they could go fishing and I went to the shed and got the poles and some very old lures. I pointed to the root cellar, a grass hump down in the east meadow. We were in a drought, so I didn't think they'd have any luck with the brookies."

I stopped talking and looked at Everett. "Is this too much?"

"No, David, not at all." He smiled.

"Okay, I'm just going to stand up and move around." I continued as I paced in his office. "I've thought a lot about that day. It's kind of a memory I go over and over. I never sold the farm, instead I just leased out part of the land. I left the city and moved back last fall. Things were falling apart for me in New York. And I've kind of settled into living back here. I think I might have come back because of Rachel. I could have relocated, gone anywhere, but I didn't. I came back to where I'd been the happiest, even for just that short time." I hesitated, then added, "That's probably why I never put the farm back on the market either."

Everett asked me to think more about this day for our next session. Two weeks later, I walked in and started talking before I even sat down.

"I think I saw Rachel and her baby and boy as this perfect family, the family I never had, as either a child or a grown man. Like I said, that day her husband, Tom, wasn't there, and you know, I felt like I was him or could be him. I felt this incredible peace. And I was in awe of Rachel." I stopped and sat down. "You know Angela Nettles?" I looked at Everett intently.

"The actress? Sure, who doesn't?" he replied, curiously.

"I fucked her in an elevator on Fifth Avenue, in Midtown. What man doesn't want to do that?"

"Well, I'm gay, so not me actually."

"Ah, gotcha. Well, my point is that I wasn't in awe of her, but Rachel…Rachel, I was. She made me feel good, made me feel worthy for saving her son, like I was a good person who was never broken. And like I said, she was beautiful."

"David, the canvases you burned, were they of her?"

"Yes, the first ones. But I've started trying to paint again. I thought seeing someone, you know, to talk to, might help me work things through so I could paint them right."

"Paint them right…What do you mean by that?" he asked.

I turned and stared out the window. "Paint them without all the anger."

"Okay, this is a start, a really good start."

"I think, Everett, I'm tired of the anger."

He nodded.

I added, "It's exhausting."

Our fourth session was in the late afternoon on a Friday. I was kind of excited to get in and start talking.

"I think I get it now, Everett," I said as soon as I stepped into the room. "You were on to something when you suggested that Rachel might have represented the ideal mother for me. But she was also an attractive woman who I was, well…attracted to."

I stopped talking and looked at him. "Are you in a relationship?"

He smiled. "Yes, early stages."

"Good." I sat and stretched out my legs. I tried to articulate what I had been thinking about in between our sessions. "It was all so new to me, that day on the farm. I'd never been around a woman and her kids like that before. For the first time, I saw a whole new set of circumstances — possibilities around the way I could live that were so different than how I'd been living."

"I can see that," Everett replied.

We both sat for a moment, comfortable in our silence.

"David, if Rachel was in New York City and at a place you frequented, like your favorite haunt, would you have regarded her in the same way? Would you have been as attracted to her?"

I thought for a minute. "No, probably not. Part of her attraction was that she and her kids were like the total package, but also..." I tried to get to the essence of my memory of her. I glanced out the window. The sky was growing dark, and the weather was changing. I stood up and walked to the window. There were storm clouds on Mount Ascutney.

Turning back to Everett, I continued, "She accepted me exactly as I was. That was a totally new way of being looked at for me."

I sat back down. "She also seemed so unconcerned with her own looks, or at least how she looked in front of me. My opinion of her didn't matter. I think it was because her life was so full already. Rachel didn't have that hungry look a lot of people in the city have. You know, people trying to make their mark, find their fortune, get their break, make it big, be discovered."

"And what about you?" he asked.

"What about me?

"Did you have that hungry look?"

I sat and answered, "Yes. For sure."

"What were you hungry for?" he asked, staring at me.

I had no reply. He wrote something down, stood, and placed the writing pad on his desk. "Think about that question and let's pick up there next time."

He usually left me with something to mull over. I liked this tactic, getting me to further process stuff even when we weren't together.

I walked out to my grandfather's truck, got in, and started it up. I'd forgotten how cold and bleak it could be in late February. I pulled in at the Quick Stop before leaving Windsor. A tall French Roast coffee was a dollar eighty-nine on special. I poured two.

I drove home to the farm as it started to spit snow. I had finished two paintings, and I was okay with them. I was tempted to show them to Hélène to see what she thought, but I didn't. Her tutorials were helpful, and I had adopted many of her techniques. But I didn't think I was ready for her critique or anyone else's for that matter.

AS THE SNOW SWIRLED around in the headlights, I went back to that farm day and remembered Rachel stepping off the stairs with the picnic basket. That moment, that look she gave Amy who was laughing at my silliness, was filled with so much love. Could I paint that moment?

A young, gangly kid came out of Everett's office. His mother looked at me apologetically as she stood and followed him out into the vestibule. Everett passed by too, smiled, and said, "I'm running to the men's room, but go on in."

On the back of an envelope of the oil bill, I had written down Everett's question: 'What was I hungry for?' For two weeks, I'd thought about his question, jotting down a few answers in response. But then I circled the last one. It read: 'I was hungry for self-worth.'

When Everett came in, I handed him the envelope before he even sat down. He smiled and said, "Got to tell you, David, you get high marks for homework every time. Most of my clients need to be reminded of what I asked them to do. That review takes up the first half hour with teenage boys."

I smiled too. "Well, I want to get the biggest bang for my buck, and I'm trying hard to figure things out."

Everett glanced down at the envelope, and I said, "I was hungry for self-worth, but I didn't feel I had any. Saving the kid gave me worth, I thought, and in Rachel's eyes too. I was open with her, more than any woman I've ever been with. But then she rejected me and, well, you know the rest."

Everett furled his eyebrows and said, "No, I don't know how she rejected you, David. You haven't told me this."

I did my usual: got up and started pacing. I was embarrassed to tell him, but full disclosure was necessary here. "I tried to start an affair with her, but she wasn't having any part of it. Told me to leave her alone and I did. And I've left her alone ever since."

Everett nodded but remained quiet. After some silence, I sat back down and looked over at him.

"David, I'm going to ask you a couple of big questions, and they aren't meant to be answered immediately. So, think for a bit before you try to answer, okay?"

"Fire away." I leaned back in the green chair and stretched out my legs.

"Do you feel that your mother left you at the farm because you weren't worthy of her love?"

My eyes must have conveyed my surprise, because Everett looked down at his notes. "And the second question — did you have sexual encounters with the many women you've spoken about as a way to maybe gain some of that worth?"

"No," I answered immediately, sitting up. "I had sex so much because I hated myself. It was an act of self-loathing."

"Why did you hate yourself?"

I whispered, "Because my mother stopped loving me."

"And, why do you think she did that, David?"

"Because I wasn't good enough."

Everett stood up, something he rarely did in the middle of our sessions, and wrote something down, tore off the paper, and handed it to me. "David, please read back what I just wrote out loud." He leaned against his desk and looked at me.

I cleared my throat and read, "What should a six-year-old child do to make his mother love him?"

I looked up at him. Everett said, "Please read it once more."

"No, it's a stupid question, I'm not going to reread it."

"Precisely David, because a six-year-old child shouldn't have to do anything to get their mother's love. Not good enough? You were a child who deserved unconditional love. You had nothing to do with your mother leaving."

I crumpled the paper up into a ball. I was going to toss it into the trash can, but I didn't. Instead, I smoothed the paper back out on my leg and read it again. "Damn," I whispered.

Rachel

Tom was coming back home after a neck dissection. They'd discover that his throat cancer had moved to the lymph nodes in his neck. As we were standing at the elevator to leave, a young nurse came up to us. "Mr. Dunne, I have a wheelchair here for you." She wheeled it right up to him.

I looked down at it and then up to her and said, "Oh no, he won't get in it, he's too stubborn."

Tom looked at me and smiled. He was pale and his weight loss was becoming significant. The Langdon athletic jacket hung on him, and the pants he wore looked two sizes too big. He was also tired. It was past 8:00 p.m. and late for a discharge. But he wanted to come home and the doctor had said yes.

"No, Rach, I want the chair. I'm really beat, okay?" He reached out and the young nurse steadied him as he sat. I could hear him sigh and watched her pick up his legs and gently place them on the footrest.

The elevator door opened. A man wearing a Saint Patrick's Day hat stepped off. I stood and watched him walk down the corridor. I hadn't bought anything green or special to eat for Amy at home. The nurse looked over at me questioningly. She started to push Tom onto the elevator while managing to also gently touch my arm and say, "Mrs. Dunne?"

"Here, I've got him," I replied and she smiled at me. It was a tender, sad smile.

It was already dark and overcast as we made our way to the car. Tom held his head back slightly and said, "It smells like rain or snow, which?" I was glad he couldn't see my tears falling. I wiped them away before we reached the car.

"Yes, it feels like something for sure, baby," I said as I glanced up at the mountains, their silhouette dark against the sky.

Amy

Mr. Chase, my 4th grade teacher, walked over to my desk, bent down, and quietly said, "Amy, your mom's signing you out. She's in the office." His eyes looked sad. *He knows,* I thought. I had a feeling it's what all the teachers did during their long meetings: talk about the sad situations their students were in. It made me kind of mad that I was one of their topics now.

I put my set of neon pens into their case and then into my desk. I walked over to the alcove and picked up my backpack. I quickly remembered my reading book and went back to my desk. Mr. Chase smiled at me and nodded because we always had reading for homework.

I gave Bella a little wave and quietly closed the door. The hallway was empty, my sneakers on the floor the only sound I could hear.

Mom smiled as she held open the school office door for another mother coming in, then we walked out together. I saw Dad in the front seat. It was still weird that he didn't drive anymore. He couldn't; it hurt him to turn his head because of his neck.

"We have a surprise for you," Mom said in a sing song voice.

I shrugged, "Okay."

She put her hand behind my shoulder, resting lightly on my back. What I really wanted to say to her was, "Dad's dying, it's hard to get excited about anything," but I didn't.

When we reached the car, Tommy popped up in the backseat and made a funny face. I burst out laughing and climbed in. He ran his knuckles across my head, his 'knuckle head sandwich' and hugged me, pulling me across his lap. Having him home was a game changer.

It was late May and the lilacs along the school's avenue were pretty shades of lavender and purple. I could smell them as Mom drove past. She actually stopped the car and rolled down all our windows.

Tommy, taking in a deep, exaggerated breath, remarked, "Now, are these hydrangeas or lilacs?" For a 20-year- old, sometimes he wasn't too smart.

All three of us chimed in, "Lilacs!"

Mom shook her head and continued driving.

Dad called out, "Where to, Amos?" It was a running joke in my family. Ever since I was 4 and we went to Splash Town in York Beach, Maine, I'd made it my battle cry for any family outing. I had outgrown the chant, but because it was Dad who asked, I replied, "Ha, ha, Splash Town, York Beach, Maine."

Mom replied, "Got it! Swimsuits and towels are packed, lobster tonight!"

I looked over at Tommy and he smiled. "Are we really going? Really?"

Dad turned in his seat, his head slightly tilted my way. "Opening Day tomorrow. We'll be the first ones at the gate!"

I reached as far as the seatbelt would allow and hugged my father gently from behind.

My mother was looking at me in the rear view mirror. I gave Tommy a high five and said, "Yes!"

I waved to him as he sat on a bench by the pool. Despite it being the first opening day, the lines weren't bad at all. We'd been at it since 10:00 a.m. We'd done the Leap of Faith, the Typhoon Lagoon, the Million-mile Water Chute, and Mom had joined us in the giant wave pool. I'd told Dad that now I just wanted to float in the regular old pool while Tommy and Mom went to get something to eat. He'd smiled and said, "Okay, show me the way."

THE POOL WAS MOSTLY FILLED with little kids with swimmies on their arms or vests around their chests. I didn't mind; I was on my back floating in the deep end and resting. I liked hearing the little ones call out to their parents to watch them 'jump in,' 'swim under,' 'dive,' and my favorite, 'catch me!'

I closed my eyes and tried to picture Dad and me here when I was 4, before his sickness, when he was big and strong. I know I had a pink and white two-piece Hawaiian flowered bathing suit. But I wasn't sure if I really remembered it or just remembered it from a picture.

A little boy with bright orange swimmies paddled up to me and asked if I could throw him. I was happy he saw me as a big kid capable of doing that.

"I can try," I said and turned to swim to the part of the pool where I could touch. But before I had a chance, he wrapped his arms around my neck and started to climb on me, pushing down on my shoulders. I couldn't stay up. I went under, working hard at trying to get him off of me. I came up for air, but he was still there, hanging on.

"Throw me, throw me," he demanded. I went under again, struggling to catch my breath.

Suddenly, I felt a big churning in the water and saw long legs next to mine.

I was lifted up to the surface and heard my father's voice near my ear. "I've got you, Amy." He was holding me up above the water as he swam, me pressed close to his side.

When we reached the ladder, he released me. I climbed up and out. I was crying, sputtering and spitting out water. He told me to sit and I did, my arms wrapped tightly around my waist.

Talking to me in a calm voice, he said, "You're okay, Amos, you're okay." I calmed down and looked at him as he held onto the ladder.

I nodded and reached for his hand to help him climb up and out of the pool. He shook his head and, looking totally gray, said, "I think you should ask that man lounging over there to help me out, okay? And he might need to get a second guy. Then have the park page Mommy."

WHEN WE GOT BACK TO THE MOTEL ROOM, Dad went right to sleep. Mom said the day had been wonderful for him, but he was exhausted. Neither of us shared what had happened in the pool except to say that a little boy was annoying and wouldn't leave me alone.

Tommy and I walked to a Dairy Queen close by and had big Peanut Buster Parfaits for dinner. Then he decided to have their Triple Chocolate Brownie too. I took a few bites, but I was full and really tired from all the sun. I got a piggyback ride almost the whole way back.

A little while later, the TV was on low and Mom was reading. Tommy was out by the motel's pool talking to some teenage girl from Canada. She was, what Mom would say, 'a real looker.' I was ready for sleep. When I bent down to give Dad a kiss goodnight, I was surprised to see he was awake.

He reached for my hand and held it. "I'll always be with you, Amy, for the bad, scary times like in the pool, but for the happiest of times too. I need you to know that."

I nodded and whispered, "Okay, Daddy." I kissed his cheek and he held my hand tightly. I didn't let go — instead I laid down beside him.

He was still my superhero.

Tommy decided to leave Keene State for the following year, his junior one, and come home. Mom didn't seem to object too much. I think she was actually relieved. Dad needed more care to stay at home. Tommy said he couldn't see anyone else lifting, bathing, or feeding him but family.

We all settled in. Sometimes I imagined us closed off to the rest of the world where only Mom, me, Tommy, and Grammie were allowed in. Like it was our own little treehouse in the Berenstain Bears woods and you needed a password to get in.

Mom and I left for work and school every day while Tommy and Grammie took care of Dad. Then at night Mommy and I took over; Tommy would often go out, meeting up with high school friends who had stayed around instead of going off to college. I don't think Mom ever slept those nights until she heard Tommy back in the house again. The fall became the winter, and the snow made me feel like we really were in hibernation.

ONE EVENING, when Mom was at Parent's Night for her preschool, I heard Tommy on his cell, out on the porch. His voice was different than I was used to. He was pissed off, big time, and I heard him say, "That piece of shit's alive while my father's practically dead."

I stood in the kitchen and watched him open up the porch door angrily and then slam it as he moved down our sidewalk. It was cold outside. He was in Nike shorts despite the snow on the ground. *None of this is fair, none of it,* I thought as I unwrapped the dinner Mom had left out for me.

Tommy Jr.

I was drinking too much, down at the Tavern. The bartender didn't care that I was underage — he knew my id was clearly fake. Seedy old guys were always there along with the usual losers. I guess I counted myself as one too. Here I was — hanging out and playing pool most nights. I started to get good at it, and the older guys around my father's age began putting money down. One guy, who sat at the bar practically every night, was always watching me. I didn't like him at all and told him that after too many cheap beers. He didn't say anything back, just kept watching me.

Then one night the roads were really bad — black ice, power lines on the verge of snapping, and the wind was howling. This guy left the Tavern and hit a guard rail; he spun out, totaling the shit box of a truck he was driving. I couldn't believe he lived through it, and here was my father…upstairs, wasting away to nothing but bones. Jarod Wade was the asshole's name. It took me two days to remember where I'd heard it before.

ABOUT THREE YEARS EARLIER, Dad and me were in line at the grocery store, waiting for the cashier to finish with the woman ahead of us. I was impatient and wanted to get home to eat. Our practice had gone over 'cause our infield sucked that day. Dad made us run the bases like ten times. I still had homework to do.

The guy in the next line was getting agitated. I heard him say, "Run it through again."

He had a shitload of groceries and a little girl in the grocery cart. Our cashier rang up our few items — bread, milk, and two boxes of cereal. I grabbed a bag of cheesy crackers and Dad nodded okay. Then I put in a pack of sugarless gum for Amy and a dark chocolate ball thing in a bright red foil for Mom. Dad grabbed cherry-flavored cough drops.

"'Member what Mom says, cough drops aren't candy."

Dad laughed. "I got a little tickle in my throat."

"Too much yelling at us in practice." We both smiled at each other.

"I said run it again, now." The guy was louder, and Dad looked over into that aisle. He nodded at the guy, and said, "Hey, Jarod, can I help out?"

The guy barely looked at Dad; I could tell he was embarrassed. The little girl looked scared.

"What's the problem?" Dad asked again. Jarod looked up at him and said, "Always something, Tom. The damn check didn't hit my account and my debit card won't go through."

The cashier turned her light on and said to him, "We'll return the items."

Dad walked through our check- out line and went around to where the guy was. He looked at the cashier and said, "I'll cover this, just put it on my card." Dad fished out his wallet and handed her his MasterCard.

"Okay, that's works." She turned off her light.

Jarod said, "I'll swing by practice tomorrow, Coach. Thanks for spottin' me."

The next day after practice I got into Dad's truck and said, "Hey, that guy, Jarod, never came by, did he?"

Dad didn't answer me. We started to leave the field's parking lot.

"He ripped you off, didn't he, Dad? He just said that, right? That he'd pay you back but he didn't."

Dad pulled down his visor and asked, "You see what was in the cart? Food, Tommy, it was food for probably the next two, three weeks. He has four kids and not much work. I think he's probably way behind on rent, maybe even his gas and electric bill. We bought him a little breathing room, that's all." He glanced my way as we stopped at the entrance to the fields. Two girls on bikes were turning in. A few kids were on skateboards calling out to them. We pulled out once it was clear. "I'll tell you, though, when we were in high school, he was one hell of a second baseman. We played Lyndon and he made three double plays in that game — three! We lost at States that year but it sure as hell wasn't because of Jarod Wade. I actually struck out in the bottom of the ninth, man on first and second. Jarod sat with me on the bus. I felt like crying. Pretty soon he tells me a joke, then another one, and I start to feel better. Bailing him out yesterday was the least I could do for a great player and a good friend when I needed one."

We pulled up to the house, and I carried the grocery bag in. Amy's eyes lit up when I gave her the pack of gum. "Don't swallow any of the pieces, okay?" She was like 6 and a doll — wrapping her arms around my waist. When I threw Mom her little dark chocolate thing, she smiled.

I leaned into Dad as he was microwaving the homemade mac and cheese that Mom had made us. "You're a good guy, aren't you, Dad?" I was almost as tall as him at 16. He put his arm around me and kissed my forehead.

"Always feel for those less fortunate, Tommy, always."

IT MADE NO SENSE TO ME that Wade could drive drunk, have a spin out, and end up fine while my dad, who always looked out for everybody, was curled up in a fetal position, dying. *Where's the justice in that?* I wanted to shout. *Where?*

I hated Jarod Wade, hated his fucking guts.

2008

Rachel

On a scale of one to ten?"
He barely held up
four fingers.

That's bullshit, I thought and turned to the hospice nurse. "Add about three more fingers so it's really a seven."

She nodded and reached for the morphine. I leaned down, next to his ear, and whispered, "Baby, this is no time to be Superman." He closed his eyes, and I moved to Tommy and whispered, "We need to get Amy and Grammie." Tommy looked quickly back at me. He got up quietly and left our bedroom.

I tried to stave off sleep. I got some ice chips from downstairs for Tom, but he wasn't responding. The chips melted, and soon it was a bowl of water. Mom gently rubbed my shoulders and spoke quietly about the time I first brought Tom around, and then, of all the times she knew he was the one for me. I tried to smile, but I watched Amy and Tommy in the room. *She's taking care of me, but I need to take care of them,* I thought.

On the morning of the third day, the hospice worker told me she needed to go home quickly to tend to her cat. Mom left to go downstairs to make banana bread and a new pot of coffee. She kissed the top of my head. It felt like I was little again, but I welcomed it. I reached up and squeezed her hand.

Tommy was on the floor, combing through pages of baseball cards that were spread out before him. It'd been years since I'd seen him do this. Amy was sound asleep in the chair beside our dresser.

I got up and bent down to touch Tommy's shoulder. I whispered, "It's okay, sweetie, to catch a little sleep…"

He looked up at me. "How will he let us know when it's time?"

"I don't know, but I'll move my chair closer and keep watch. I promise I'll wake you." I watched Tommy lay his head down on the plastic sheeting of his cards, up against my hope chest. I edged the easy chair up and sat down once more, reaching for the afghan. I leaned my head back and watched Tom.

Amy

I woke up and looked around the room. Mom and Tommy were asleep. I didn't know where Grammie was — probably in the kitchen since I smelled something baking.

The hospice lady, Thea, wasn't here either. She was a strange lady until she started to speak. Her voice was like the voice we all needed in our heads, soft and rolling with words that were comforting. I liked her a lot, and so did Mom, I could tell.

My neck was sore. I'd had it at a bad angle for a while. I massaged it, then moved over to Daddy's bed. His breathing was kind of different, maybe a little harder than what it had been, but I wasn't sure. *Should I wake Mommy?* I wondered. I climbed up onto his bed to check.

Tom Sr.

I felt her breath up near my face — it smelled faintly of spearmint. She touched my eyelids lightly with her fingers like butterfly kisses. I'd been waiting for her, the pain intolerable.

"Daddy, it's okay, you can stop fighting if you want. I'll see you on the other side, we all will."

I opened my eyes, the effort demanding much of me. Rachel was sleeping, her legs draped over the arm of the chair; the afghan around her had fallen to the floor. She looked exhausted, and so much older. Tommy was stretched out on the carpet, his head up against the hope chest, sound asleep.

Amy, lying next to me in the bed, was stroking my cheek. She moved closer, the weight of her bringing me peace. I felt myself lifting. There was no more pain, none. *Oh my God,* I thought, *you've taken all the pain.*

I was whole again; the big strapping man that I had been, that Tommy was now. I wanted to see Rachel's eyes, wanted her to see me as I once was, as I was now, above her. But I needed to go, I wanted to go. The other side was beckoning me. I heard my father's distant voice calling. I floated up and out.

2008

Rachel

I sat on the floor after locking the door. My black skirt was twisted, and my pantyhose had two runs already starting, just past my big toe on my left foot. *Cheap* — but actually they'd been fairly expensive at Rite Aid. I got up and turned on the water and washed my face. It was red and blotchy, and my eyes were swollen. I replayed my sister, Heather, telling me, "Touch up your face."

I wanted to punch her, right there in front of all the people filling up the house. Lay her out flat and shut her the hell up.

There was a light knock on the door. "Someone's in here," I answered.

My mother, just outside called out, "Rachel, open up. I want in."

I opened the door and she came in, locking the door right behind her. She sat on the edge of the tub. I sat back down on the floor.

"I wished she'd shut the fuck up, Mom, she's driving me crazy," I said.

"Oh, sweetheart, I'd say she means well, but actually, I wished she'd shut the fuck up too."

I quickly looked up at her; my mother never swore.

"Pat heard her say that, and I think she's telling that sister of yours to put an effin' sock in it." Mom raised her eyebrows and then readjusted her own black dress over her knees.

"Good! Pat's the one to do it, too." I remembered once, during field hockey, how Pat lit into one of the girls on the opposing team as we were leaving for the bus. She'd said a racial slur to Karen Bobar during the game. Pat wasn't going to let it go.

"Where does she get off swooping in here and telling you what you're going to do with the family business? Or what I need to do with my face and how to arrange the frickin' food on the dining room table?" I looked at her imploringly.

My mother reached down and touched my shoulder. "I think it's what she does in California, but I'm sick of it too. Listen Rach — I'm selling the business, it's what I want to do."

She paused, then smiled and said, "With the money we'll go to the south of France with the kids and rent a villa for a month, or take a cruise up out of Juneau to see the whales."

I joined in, "How about we buy a river boat and mosey on down the Mississippi…"

"Or the Florida intercoastal?" she suggested, still smiling.

"Better yet…" I reached over and grabbed some toilet paper off the roll. "We could sell the business, sell both our houses, and buy a place up in the Northeast Kingdom on one of the lakes. I'll homeschool Amy, you take up quilting." I blew my nose loudly.

"Or, we could spend it all — and buy an inn on the Cape with ocean views!"

We quietly sat some more and I smoothed out my skirt. Mom looked out the window and then down at me. "I'll put the proceeds in a college fund for both kids. Tommy's going back to Keene and our Amy has big things ahead of her, I just know it."

I nodded, reached out, and threw the toilet paper in the small trash basket.

We both stood up and turned to the door. But I couldn't open it. I couldn't bring my hand up to turn the doorknob.

I looked back at her. "Mom, my Tom is gone, my Tom is dead."

I crumbled into her, folding myself onto the floor again. She held me and whispered, "I know, sweetheart, I know."

David

I saw the silver Jeep with the 'for sale' sign and turned onto the badly-rutted road up to the old house. And I thought the farmhouse needed work — this place looked abandoned and uninhabitable. Its windows were all shut tight and the discolored gray blinds were drawn down, a few torn. Two of the attic windows were broken, shards of glass still visible. The chimney was crumbling, its bricks disintegrating in various spots. There was no grass growing in the yard. Bits of knotweed and crabgrass had taken over the area leading up to the house. An old gas pump stood next to a collapsed shed. A tree growing up through the shed's roof gave the area to the left some shade. One lone straight-back chair, a dull red, was turned upside down on the porch.

I was surprised when the door opened right away and a man stepped out. He was on the rough side, wearing a dirty, long-sleeved undershirt and pants that were too short. He was barefoot. A mangy cat followed him, skinny as all get out.

"You interested?" he asked, pointing to the Jeep parked at the edge of the road.

"Might be. What can you tell me?" I heard myself sounding like my grandfather as he used to barter, bicker, and converse with the local farmers.

"It's got fifty-six thousand miles, give or take a few. Been recently serviced down in Langdon at Bensons. It's reliable, but I'm not driving too many places these days, know what I mean?"

He looked older, about 70, but there was something going on with his eyes. I wasn't sure what, but it looked like cataracts: one eye was definitely cloudy.

"Can I take it for a spin, see how it feels?" The day was rainy and I felt my shoulders getting wet.

"Now, what kind of a fuckin' fool do you think I am, letting you drive off my property in it and leaving me that heap of scrap?" He pointed to the pickup truck.

"Maybe you knew my grandfather — Alex Sumner? I'm his grandson, David. Been back a while."

"That why I see the lights on sometimes when I walk the lower fields? You in there?"

"Yes, sir."

He gave me a pensive look. "So, um, your Jenny's boy? Your age is about right."

"You knew my mother?" The rain started to come down harder. The old man pointed for me to step up onto his porch. I moved to it. The roof was tin, and the rain was making a racket.

He leaned back against the door. "Your mother was the prettiest thing around. Sure, I know her. I count Jenny Sumner as a goddamn best friend."

"She's dead. Died in nineteen ninety-four, near Portland, Oregon," I said this with a bit of sarcasm, thinking, *Best friend, my ass.*

The old man grew quiet as we stood there with the rain pouring down his eaves, the orange tiger lilies taking the brunt of the runoff.

"We used to have bonfires up past Snell's junkyard in the field out back," he said. "It dips down in back, can't see a thing from the road. Roaring fires — we'd all bring beer and wood and somebody to cozy on up to." He took a can of chew out of his back pocket, opened it, and took a pinch, placing it up under the side of his cheek. He held out the can. I could read the flavor — wintergreen — but shook my head. "Had to bring wood else you were a freeloader. Jenny and I had some of our best times up there." The old man looked hard at the Ford. "My eyesight ain't what it used to be. She drove her daddy's red Ford back then. Your momma loved those fires, hell, we all did. We were young and full of it."

I asked, suddenly realizing this may be the closest to the knowledge that I would ever get, "You know who my father is?"

He looked me squarely in the eyes and replied, "You don't want to go there, boy, you hear?"

The whole business about buying the silver Jeep was now gone. I was in this and said, arrogant as all hell, "Why, is it you...?"

He stood there, looking at me. Old as he was, he still seemed formidable, like he could pin me in a moment. But I didn't back down.

"Tell me, are you my old man?"

He looked out at the rain, reached down, and picked up the cat. In a steady, but strangely compassionate voice, he said, "Son, any one of us farmers along this valley could be your daddy...Sorry, but that's the truth. Your mother was the best-looking girl for miles around, and she knew it and knew all of us, up and down Old County Road."

Like mother, like son. Fuck the car. I decided to leave, turning towards the truck.

He reached out and grabbed my arm. "You leaving with a bad taste in your mouth about your mother? Know this, boy…any one of us, then or now, would beat the living daylights out of any bastard who tried to hurt her." He paused, then said, "And each one of us would have counted ourselves lucky to have been your father."

The next day, I drove back down and told him, "I want the Jeep."

He replied, "Cash and its yours." Then he walked up real close to me and said, "You look just like her, dark and pretty. I'm sorry you never knew."

"Knew what?" I asked.

"That your mother was loved."

TWO MORNINGS LATER, I walked down Old County Road with an envelope of cash. The old man was cordial and handed me the keys. He didn't count the money, which surprised me.

I drove into Bridgewater to a car wash. The grime on the Jeep's windshield and front hood washed away in dirty streaks as the soap spray and heavy-duty brushes did their thing. I pulled over to the island where the large vacuum hoses were. I put in two bucks, grabbed the hose, and then lifted up the tailgate. I saw that the old man had left a few newspapers and empty beer cans in the back of the Jeep. I reached in to grab an armload of paper to put in the trash bin when one section fell away, onto the pavement.

I bent down and picked it up. Immediately, I saw a picture of Tom Dunne. At first, I didn't understand — the picture was on the *Obituaries* page. The date at the top was February 9, 2008, just about five months ago. The vacuum hose coiled up and fell to the ground, its high-pitched sucking noise deafening. I leaned against the Jeep and began to read the obituary, glancing at his picture several times. I couldn't wrap my head around it. He'd died at home surrounded by loved ones. He was only 45 years old. *"In lieu of flowers, please consider a donation to the Langdon Athletic Association."* The picture looked like it had been taken out on the ball field. Tom's hair was cut short and he wore a coach's whistle around his neck. He was squinting in the sun and smiling. I reread it again, still in disbelief. I tried to remember the last time we'd messaged one another. It'd been a while, definitely before I left the city.

I didn't finish cleaning the Jeep. All my thoughts swirled around as I took in the news. *No one had called me.* Then I thought, *Why would she?*

I left the car wash and headed back to the farm. But I didn't get too far before I pulled over into a turn-off for the brook that ran alongside the road. I turned off the Jeep and sat. I still couldn't believe that Tom Dunne had died. I'd always seen him as the luckiest man alive — having a woman like Rachel who loved him and a couple of beautiful kids he so clearly adored. I picked up the folded paper and reread it all. I went back to the part 'In lieu of flowers.' I'd send a donation; a big one in his name. I thought of Rachel and how devastated she must be. That bothered me, thinking how hard this must be for her. I decided to get a certified bank check for the donation to keep it anonymous. She wouldn't want to see my name.

I saw the jelly woman again, standing beside the store with the back of her white SUV up. The folding table was set up, covered with assorted jellies. She was speaking to another woman, handing her change. I slowed down, passing the Tyson Store. I turned the Jeep into the inn's parking lot and sat and watched her.

She was about my age, with a head full of curly gray hair, that soft, rich gray some people my age are lucky to have. Her face and arms were tanned, and she wore a baggy, white hippie blouse over some torn blue jeans. A money bag — or was it called a fanny pack? — was around her waist. Her eyes were dark, and she had a small stud in her straight, even nose. I couldn't see it from this distance, but I had noticed it the last time I'd bought jelly from her, parked on the other side of the lake. She wasn't very tall, maybe five four, tops. The sandals on her feet were brown, clunky Birkenstocks.

A sign dangling from the table read, 'The Jelly Lady,' and a big pitcher of fresh wildflowers was placed in the middle of the table. The back of her car was full of baskets with the different jellies and preserves she made. She painted stained-glass windows too; she'd told me the last time I bought two jars. She was also a member of the local artisan co-op down in Peddan.

I mentioned that I had started to paint a little bit and we chatted some. We didn't share any more personal information, but I liked her way, her quick smile, and, I guess, her jelly and jams.

I asked Hélène about her one day in the studio. She opened the door between the gallery and the bagel shop and called out to Julie, "Hey, is the Jelly Lady single?"

I just about died, but Hélène said, "Mais oui, c'est bon, you are showing interest in someone. That is nothing but good for you, David."

Julie came to the door and said, smiling, "One of the customers says she's divorced and lives up Hawk Mountain."

I about died again, but not completely, because here I was.

I got out of the car and crossed Route 100. She saw me coming and smiled. "You need more jelly? So soon?"

"No, not really…" I waited until I was right up to her table. "I need your phone number."

She brought her hand up to her chin and gave me a thoughtful look. "How about you give me your number, instead, and we'll just see."

"That works, and I'll take another two jars — this time the mint."

She wrote down my number and then wrapped the jars in butcher paper. "My name's Annie, by the way."

I took the change she gave me and said, "I'm David Sumner, but please don't google me."

Already approaching her table of goods was a younger woman in her early 30s, holding on to the hand of a boy about 8. "I hope Michael and I aren't interrupting anything, Annie," the woman said, looking at us both and smiling.

"No, no, Sara, it's all good!" As I started to cross the road, Annie yelled out, "Of course, now you know I'm going to…google you, that is."

WE STARTED OUT SLOWLY, first coffee and a bagel down at Julie's. Hélène did know Annie from the artisan co-op; she just didn't know she was also the Jelly Lady. The three of us enjoyed ourselves, even though Julie kept shooting Hélène the evil eye to get her to leave us alone. But Hélène's easy, welcoming manner put us both at ease. Hélène managed to mention a lot of my 'art dealer' accomplishments, like who I had represented, what artists I had 'discovered.' Annie said, smiling, "I googled him too."

I looked at her with surprise. "But I'm not in all that now."

Hélène nodded, adding, "We both had enough."

Dinners out and at her place became our norm. She was a good cook, and I loved her small studio just off the modest mountain home she lived in. The stained-glass windows she made were unique and beautiful. She had started to sell them online through something called *Etsy*, heading to the post office a couple of times a week. Her divorce had been ugly and still stung. I stayed clear of mentioning my past with women. It was nothing I was proud of.

I met her friends from around Bridgewater and Woodstock. She already knew mine, the sum total of Julie and Hélène. We went to some dinner parties and I enjoyed myself, but mostly I enjoyed seeing Annie in different settings, enjoying herself.

She was vivacious but not in a glaring way. Her artist friends were, in many respects, similar to me — leaving the city and rat race and finding a piece of satisfaction out here, in the middle of nowhere. Sometimes, at the parties, Annie would come up beside me and gently place her hand in mine and listen to my conversations. She'd add to it or simply drift away and I'd watch her engage with someone else.

I painted during the day and then we'd meet up three or four nights a week. I sometimes stayed over — she was easy going in bed and that was nice too.

It was probably the best relationship I'd ever had; one that was based on respect and an even give and take. For once, I didn't need anything from the woman I was with and I didn't have to maneuver in and around other people, making sure I didn't fuck things up. Plus, we laughed a lot, neither one of us ever too serious. I loved this coasting along of ours. I thought, one night coming home, *I could go on like this forever.*

One winter day, mid-morning, Annie pulled up to the farmhouse. She'd been to the farm before, but never unannounced. I was surprised and came down off the porch, smiling.

"Hey, what's up?"

I watched her get out of her car and come around to me. "Oh David, I'm so embarrassed but I have to use your bathroom…I feel sick. I'm coming back from Peddan, and I don't think I can make it to my house."

Her face was pale, and I quickly walked ahead of her into the kitchen. She'd never actually been inside the farmhouse before — we always spent our time at her place. I thought she'd be more comfortable using the larger bathroom upstairs so I directed her to the stairs. "Second door on the right. Do you need a bucket too?"

"Yes, I think I do." She kicked off her boots, and I heard her run up the stairs.

I set out the bucket for her before sitting at the kitchen table to wait. I called to her twice, then went upstairs. The bucket was gone.

At one point, I brought her a fresh towel and washcloth and asked, outside the door, "Annie, can I come in and see how you are?"

I heard a weak, "Okay." I opened up and there she was, slumped on the floor, holding the bucket. "I think it's a fast-moving bug — don't get near me, David. I just feel so tired."

I got her to my bedroom and into bed. I covered her up. I think she was already half asleep.

I DIDN'T HEAR HER COME DOWN into the living room. I was fully engrossed in painting. It was a smaller canvas of Amy as she lay sleeping on the blanket, her hand in her mouth, her little body in perfect proportion. A few other paintings were scattered about. I'd finish the one of Rachel stepping off the porch steps, but it wasn't completely dry. It was leaning against the sideboard in the dining room.

"Wow, David." I turned to see Annie standing there.

"Oh, hey, you feeling better?" She wasn't as pale as she had been a few hours earlier.

"Yes, a little. These are incredible, and this one…" But she didn't finish her sentence as she moved into the dining room and stood in front of the sideboard.

I looked around and said, in a self-deprecating voice, "Oh, just some painting I've been doing, but thanks."

Four days later, I finally called Annie because I hadn't heard a thing.

"You good?"

She was brief and to the point. "Thanks for calling me. Yes, I'm much better, thank you so much. Listen, um, David, I've had a lot of fun with you for what — the last five, six months, but I think I'm going to, well, I think we need to move on."

I was surprised, but played it low-key. "Okay. Is there something I did that offended you or turned you off?"

Annie let out a deep sigh and then replied, "I could really, really like you, David. All right, that's bullshit, let me be honest here. I could really, really love you. But you aren't ever going to be available emotionally for me. I know that now, especially after seeing your paintings."

I didn't know what to say, so stayed quiet. She ended the call.

Now I had no reason to stop painting, get washed up, or head out — there was no more social life, no one to take to dinner, to go out with, to sleep with. I lost track of time, barely even seeing Hélène and Julie. I painted.

Amy

S orry about your dad. That must suck." The girl was
standing in front of the mirror, putting on eyeliner. I
didn't know her name.

She and her friends came just about every day after
school, like me. I waited at the town's public library for
Mom to get done at the Children's Center. It was lonely
going home to an empty house.

A friend in my class, Jackson Larson, walked halfway to
the library with me each day. He'd been kicked off the bus
and his mother worked at the Dollar Store. Sometimes he'd
run out quick and hand me a pack of gum or lifesavers from
her counter. I never knew if he stole them or paid. Lots of
kids thought he was mean, but I liked him and liked walking with him.

I MOVED TO THE SINK in the library's bathroom. The
girl was reapplying dark, almost black lipstick. She was
taller than me, by a lot. She stopped and glanced at me
through the mirror. "My mom worked with your dad at the
fencing place. She went to his funeral."

I nodded and turned on the water faucet. Her hair was
dyed a deep blue-black, cut short, and kind of spikey.

"What's your name?" she asked.

I replied, "Amy."

She turned to me and said, real nice, "I'm Ellie. See you around," and then she left.

The next week in school, after my music class, she passed me in the hallway. She was walking with two other girls who looked like her: hoodies, skinny jeans, eyeliner. I guessed they were eighth graders.

She didn't say anything as I passed her, but then I heard, "Hey, Amy! See you at the library!"

When I walked through the front door that afternoon, I saw them, already there on the leather couches in the periodical section. Their textbooks were open, and it looked like they were doing homework. I knew they did that first, then shared headphones as they listened to music on their iPods.

I walked slowly by, faking like I was looking for something. Again, Ellie called out after me. "Amy, over here!"

The woman at the circulation desk said, in a nice, low voice, "Girls, not so loud."

"Sorry, Ms. Winter," Ellie said, then asked me, "Got any homework?"

THEY WELCOMED ME into their group. I think I became kind of like their little sister, or what is it called — a mascot? They never asked me anything about my father directly, but told me I could share memories of him if I wanted to. And that I could opt out of saying anything to them on days I didn't feel like talking at all. When I didn't remember how to do improper fractions, Liz helped me out; she was a math whiz. Ellie liked to write, and I asked her to read some of my first drafts — what Mrs. Silverman, my 5th grade teacher, called our sloppy copies. Ellie was kind and encouraging, telling me to use all my senses when I wrote.

"Make it pop on the page!" She'd put her finger up into her mouth and make one big popping noise. I always looked over to the circulation desk to see if Ms. Winter was mad.

All of them started to bring me t-shirts they'd outgrown, and sometimes jeans. I bought a hoodie like them and I started to wear it all the time. They showed me how to do eyeliner in the library's bathroom. I was getting good at it.

Mom saw the girls sitting with me one night on the library steps. She was late in coming and very apologetic. The girls stood up, waved, and turned to walk down the street.

When I got in the car, Mom asked, "Those are the new friends you've been talking about?" I could tell she was more than just curious.

"You don't like them, do you? Is that why you gave them that look?" I was defensive and ready to pounce on her.

But Mom didn't say anything back and we drove home in silence.

MRS. SILVERMAN MOTIONED for me to come up to her desk one day right after dismissal. Jackson was standing outside the classroom window, waiting for me and looking cold.

"Amy, your mom called and asked how you're doing in my class. I told her the truth."

I was nervous and asked, "The truth?"

"Yes. That in the last couple of months your homework completion has improved greatly and, while you're still too quiet in class, I feel you're more focused in understanding the concepts. I think you're heading for honors if you keep this up."

That weekend Mom reluctantly let me get a fake nose ring. I wanted a new hoodie, but I didn't push it.

2009

Rachel

I didn't know what to do — put my foot down about the older girls, the nose ring, the dark makeup, and now the bits of blue hair, or act like it was no big deal. There was a lot of inaction on my part these days, so, as of yet I hadn't done anything. Meg and my mother were my sounding board. Neither of them seemed to have a clear-cut position either. Tommy was overwhelmed with his course work back at school. He was determined to make up for the year he'd missed, so I didn't ask him to weigh in.

Mom finally said, "These new friends are filling a void and we should let her be. Right now, let's all just be there for her. And as far as counseling, you both will know when you're ready. It took me some time before I wanted to go, and then I got a lot out of it."

One late January afternoon, Amy was at Ellie's house for a surprise birthday party for one of the other girls. On the way to pick her up, I mulled over what Tom would think of Amy's new look. Would he be mad at me for allowing her to do this? Or would he 'go with the flow' like my mother suggested. "What should I do, baby?" I asked out loud. But no one answered.

I pulled into Ellie's driveway and honked the horn. I turned the heat up in the car and waited. The front door opened. It was Ellie's mother wearing an oversized man's winter coat and she was carrying a brown paper bag. I knew her from the fencing company but for the life of me, I couldn't remember her first name. As she approached the car, I smiled and rolled down my window. She was young. I wondered if she'd had Ellie as a teenager.

"Hi Mrs. Dunne. Amy will be right out. They had fun." Her face grew serious and she shivered. I could see her breath. "I have something for you. I got it just yesterday, and I knew I'd see you today." She paused and seemed to search my face.

"What is it?" I asked, suddenly nervous. Had Amy done something, gotten a hold of something she shouldn't have?

"One of the new owners found a sweatshirt of Tom's — it was some place in the warehouse. They've moved a whole bunch of shit around and, well, they were going to throw it out but I wouldn't let them."

She handed the bag over and I opened it. I reached in and pulled out his old, gray sweatshirt, one of two he sometimes brought home to wash when he was installing fencing. It had the Blanchard Fencing logo on the back and Tom's name on the front. There was a tear in one of the sleeves. Without thinking, I brought the sweatshirt up to my nose and inhaled deeply. Tears came, and I buried my face in the soft, worn cotton material. It smelled strongly of him, his smell before he was sick.

Just then Amy ran up to the passenger side door. "What's going on? Mom?" She was carrying her coat and looked from me to Ellie's mom and back at me again. I couldn't speak, overwhelmed with the magnitude of losing Tom.

I heard Ellie's mother say, "Sweetie, give your mom a minute, okay? Run back in and grab a piece of cake to bring home. And for goodness' sake, put your coat on!"

"Thank you," I finally whispered. "This was kind of you, Denise."

"It's Deneen," she replied as she cupped her hands up to her mouth. My car registered 18 degrees outside. "He was such a good guy. We've all missed him this past year."

I nodded but didn't say anything else. She turned and ran back inside her house.

When I was backing out of the driveway with Amy finally in the car, I accidentally went up over the side of the snowbank to the right of their culvert. I was disoriented and drained from my exchange with Deneen. I heard the car's tires crunch on the frozen, hard-packed surface. Amy looked over at me, clearly worried. "Mom, what happened?"

I hesitated and stopped the car. I reached over the back seat and grabbed the brown paper bag. "Ellie's mom gave me a sweatshirt of Daddy's. It was still at his work." I watched as Amy took the bag. "I was crying because it smelled so much like him." Amy didn't move. "All of this is so hard, I know, baby. If you want, you can open it."

She set the bag down between her feet on the car's floor mat. "Nah, I'm good." She stared straight ahead. I reached over to take her hand but she moved it to her lap. "Really, I'm fine."

We drove the rest of the way home in silence. I heard my mother's voice, "Just be there for her." I wasn't sure that was enough — for either of us.

Sidney

The big guy came in and moved to sit in the front of the classroom. I wondered if anyone sitting behind him could see. Maybe with the chairs in this fishbowl set up it wouldn't matter. Maybe that was the whole purpose of the fishbowl design, after all. I dimmed the lights and started my slideshow.

I ended right on time and the lights came on. "Read chapters one through three and read the two articles posted in Canvas, please. I'll be discussing Hitler's early steps to confiscate the property of the Jews on Thursday. For those of you who have not purchased the book yet, please do so. Most of our readings will be from it, as well as supplemental articles that I'll provide. Thank you."

I brought a syllabus over to the big guy since he'd entered late and had missed when I'd passed it out. "Are you a freshman?" I asked. He looked older.

"Nah, but I needed to take an elective. This one sounded okay." He was mellow, probably hungover.

"What happened? You flunk out and daddy got you back in? Or wait, you're on the basketball team and they needed you to take an easy freshman class you knew you could pass." I was snide, standing in front of him.

He looked up at me, and his faced changed. He grew serious. It seemed like he was weighing what to say back to me. He slowly straightened up and cleared his throat. "My father got sick and died. I took some time off, you know, to be with him, and then to make sure my mother and sister were okay."

I felt horrible as I scrutinized him. His face was handsome, in a kind of big jock way. His eyes were kind.

He added quickly, "Don't feel bad — I wasn't doing so great, and my GPA sucked before I left. But, well, shit happens as they say, and I'm back. It's pretty sobering to have a parent die. Makes you realize you can't be a kid anymore."

I repeated that the book was available in the bookstore. As he was just about to go through the door, I called out, "Hey, thank you for that last comment you gave me about your GPA. That was charitable of you. I'm sorry for your loss."

He waved and walked out. I looked down at my roster and noticed the two names that weren't checked off after I took attendance at the start of class. "You must be Thomas Dunne," I said out loud. "I can see you're not Tatum McBride."

Tom Jr.

After that first class, I was determined to ace it since she thought I was nothing but a dumb jock. And honestly, that's what I was. But I could tell she really disliked dumb jocks. What she didn't know, like everybody else, was that I could perfectly recall the slideshow she'd just given, in exactly the same order with the precise captions. I'd done it with my sports cards, done it with all the stats of my favorite teams since I was all of 8, 9 years old. It was my hidden talent, and I was hoping to score big for working at ESPN or the new Bleacher Report. I knew my days playing sports were numbered, and I didn't want to be a coach. I wanted to report sports, use my memory to my advantage.

So I took the course very seriously, and I think that surprised her. I started to linger after class, always asking her more in-depth questions about the content. I was flirting, for sure, but also very interested too. I'd gotten into World War II planes as a kid with my dad. We'd comb over big, colored photographs and descriptions of the planes on both sides in books I'd gotten for Christmas. I'd watched all the war movies with my grandfather, like *The Bridge over*

River Kwai and my all-time favorite, Steve McQueen in *The Great Escape.*

ONE AFTERNOON I was, as usual, the last to leave class. Ms. Hoffman — 'Sidney', as most of us called her — was standing up front. We could call her by her first name, I think, because she was young; my bet was around 26 or 27. She was gathering up her things, lifting the screen, unplugging her laptop, putting assignments into her book bag. That day we'd touched upon the Battle of the Bulge, the last major offensive Hitler mounted against the Allies. Rolling up my papers like a megaphone, I brought it to my mouth and, in a very solemn voice, I recited Winston Churchill's famous 'Battle of the Bulge' quote: "This is undoubtedly the greatest American battle of the war and will, I believe, be regarded as an ever-famous American victory."

She looked up, smiling as I came down the aisle. "So, Mr. Dunne, when do you graduate?"

"I'm officially done next month, on May seventeenth. I doubled up some this past year and I took classes last summer." I hesitated then added, "I'm staying in Keene for a while. Are you, um…" I stopped. All my confidence in what I wanted to ask her had left me.

She looked directly at me. "That's good to know. Maybe you and I could see what the summer brings?" Then she turned back and continued to gather up her things. I was being dismissed. But I wanted to make sure I understood what she'd meant, so I didn't move away. Instead, with more courage than I actually felt, I replied, "I hope that means what I think it does."

She stopped and leaned against the table she often sat at during class. "I could get fired if I had a relationship with you now. Student-teacher dynamics and imbalance of power are all at play here."

"I understand." I glanced back at both of the doors leading into the lecture hall. "I would never ever do anything to jeopardize your position. Please know that."

Sidney nodded at me but didn't say anything more. It was enough. I walked away feeling like I was on cloud nine.

A few days later, I saw two girls from my World War II class sitting next to the window of the bar with their pizza and cokes. It was Monday night and we had class tomorrow, where we were expected to give a brief overview of what we were writing our term papers on. I knew mine, had decided it a full week ago.

One of the girls caught my attention and called out, "Hey, if you're alone and want to join us, we're brainstorming our topics for Sidney's class."

I nodded and thought, *Why not?* I ordered a large meatball sub and a draft. I had to show my id. I liked being able to drink legally.

When I reached their table, they moved an open course book and a sheet of paper with topics scribbled on it over so I'd have some room. They were young, freshmen and cute, not in the 'looks' way but in the 'young' way. The girl who had called out to me was April, the other one was Maddy. I nodded and said, "I'm Tom." Both of them said, in unison, "We know."

Maddy had an idea for her paper and asked, "Can I bounce it off you two? I think it's good, but will Sidney like it?"

"Go for it," I said, giving her a smile of encouragement. I quickly thought, *These two were finishing up eighth grade when I graduated high school.*

"Great, okay, I want to do my paper on Eva Braun and how she daydreamed her days away during the Third Reich. I want to really make her come alive with all sorts of anecdotes, that, well, that really give you a good idea of what she was like."

April shot me a quick, questioning glance, and I smiled and replied, "I'm not sure what Ms. Hoffman will think, but it's definitely worth a try. And I know I'd be interested in reading it."

Maddy smiled and took a bite of her pizza. I looked at April and said, "I've had my topic nailed down for a while. I'm doing it on the Monuments Men: the soldiers who spent their time tracking down the stolen art, the masterpieces that Hitler had confiscated. They were heroes in their own right."

April gave me a thumbs up and Maddy jumped in. "Maybe my topic is too far removed from what we've been studying?"

Suddenly, I saw who just entered the pizza joint. April's mouth dropped open, and I laughed. It was Sidney. She waved and held up her finger, as in, 'Just one minute.'

She maneuvered around the tables, holding a pizza box to go. "Hey guys, how are you?"

I wanted to appear somewhat indifferent, so I shrugged my shoulders and simply said, "Okay, you?"

Sidney quickly acknowledged me and then turned her focus to the two girls. "Looks like maybe you're deciding on your research topics?" She looked down at the paper the girls had written on. "I know you've both tossed around some ideas. And Tom, are you sticking with yours?"

"I am," I replied. Sidney gave me a quick smile, but her focus returned to April who shrugged her shoulders, appearing to be at a loss.

Sidney asked tentatively, "Can I give you a couple of suggestions to maybe help you out?"

April nodded. "Yes, please!"

"Great, let me start by pointing out that there's so much out there about Hitler and his drive to confiscate as much as he could. Military units, the 'Kunstschutz,' took gold, silver, cultural items, paintings, books, and religious artifacts from the Jews. He wanted to obliterate Jewish culture from the face of the earth. But for him to be the ruler he envisioned himself to be, he had to show how mighty he was. He needed more money for the war effort, so gave permission for certain art to be sold. Other art was confiscated too, and not just from Jews. For instance, the Nazis disliked any works of Modernism."

We were interrupted by a rowdy bunch of guys marching past us with a half dozen extra-large pizzas. I nodded at them; I knew them from the athletic complex.

Once they left, Sidney started to speak to us again, "They — the Nazi Party — also hated 'degenerate art', or art they deemed offensive to the Third Reich's principles. A handful of specifically designated art dealers sold these art pieces with many buyers from around the world interested in acquiring pieces from this confiscated art trove. The money from the sale of these pieces was funneled back into the Nazi war machine coffers."

Now Sidney smiled and said, "You could look into all this; art that wasn't allowed by the Reich and then what happened to that art. Or, actually, you could research the many places Hitler had art stashed, hidden in salt mines, on train cars — the repositories numbered close to a thousand. You could even write on what the Nazis did to advance Hitler's wishes for a huge museum in his name."

April nodded and Maddy hesitantly asked, "Is research-ing Eva Braun way off topic?"

Sidney seemed pensive, then answered, "No, I'll allow it, Madison, *if* you find legitimate research and focus on how she was instrumental in Hitler's quest to do what he did. Hitler was a man who did incredibly awful things. It's important that we understand all the forces at play that made him do what he did. So yes, it's a go if you really delve into Eva Braun's influence."

April, now more at ease, said, "One of the things I found really interesting that you covered in class is how staff at different museums at the time of the Nazi occupation reacted, especially like Rose Valland."

Sidney's whole face changed. "She's an incredible figure to do a paper on!"

I suddenly decided to ask Sidney if she'd ever heard of a local man named Jacob Geller. I'd come across his name when I'd googled my topic, and something about it was bugging me.

"Jacob Geller? No, can't say that I have. Why?" Sidney asked, looking at me.

"It stands out to me, but I don't know why. It's probably nothing," I replied.

As she started to leave, she called out, "Hope I didn't bore you guys too much outside of class." We watched her go.

"She's so great," April said.

I added, "Yeah, her class is good."

We finished our food and the girls walked back to their dorms. I started to walk towards my place, wondering again why that name — Jacob Geller — nagged at me. But then I moved on, imagining me and Sidney together. I had no doubt that once I graduated, we'd see if there was something there between us. It just seemed like forever to wait.

As the class got up and started to disperse on the last day, I watched Sidney. She was speaking to a couple of students and something she said made them laugh. I waited. I was patient. "Dinner, now?" I asked as the girls left and I walked down the aisle of the fishbowl.

"No. We have to wait for grades to close to make sure I'm not influencing you in any way, you know, into a relationship." She waved to Maddy and April who were leaving the classroom up in the back. April called out, "Can't wait to take another class with you!" Sidney's smile was beautiful, breaking her seriousness into little bits and pieces.

I frowned. "Oh yeah, that imbalance of power thing again." I didn't laugh, knowing it was worth it.

THE AFTERNOON MY FINAL COLLEGE GRADE slip arrived and the semester was officially closed, I walked to her apartment. She opened the door before my second knock and pulled me in. We definitely stopped talking about World War II. We didn't eat dinner till almost midnight. She had Chinese takeout boxes in the fridge, leftover from the night before. It wasn't nearly enough, but then I discovered she had a whole cupboard of ramen noodles and cheesy crackers. I was in love. My summer had never looked so promising.

Sidney

A re you embarrassed to go in?" he asked me. I looked up and shook my head.

"Okay then, Ms. Hoffman, let's get to it." He held the door open for me.

We were at a country club not far from Keene. It was a 'going away party' for one of the adjunct professors I'd befriended. It was also our first public outing since Tom had graduated.

The two other couples were already at the table out on the covered deck overlooking the 18th hole. We moved towards them.

"Sid, so glad you could make it!" Kimberly, who was leaving to teach at Williams College, called out.

"Hey, hi everybody!" I made the introductions and Tom and I sat down.

Just then the server approached us and asked if we wanted a cocktail. I smiled and said, "Yes, please, a merlot."

Tom reached into his back pocket and took out his wallet. Handing his license to the server, he said, "I'll have a pint of your local IPA, please." He then turned to the rest of us, leaned in, and said, "Sid has no idea what a cougar she is — you should see who I had to fight off outside."

I hit his arm and rolled my eyes. My friends laughed and I relaxed. Throughout the evening, I watched as Tom held his own. At one point he walked off the deck with the other two guys to the edge of the green. I had no idea where they found putters or golf balls, but soon they were practicing their putting.

When we got back to my apartment, I asked him if he'd had a good time. He replied, "Sid, the more important question is, *did you?*"

Tom Jr.

A re you embarrassed to go in?"
she asked me. I looked down
and shook my head.

We were home in Langdon, standing outside the Tavern. I wanted Sid to meet a few friends of mine, and our favorite bar was closed due to a leaky ceiling. We'd made a quick decision to meet here in this rat hole instead.

I opened the door and in we walked. I hadn't been here in a long time, not since Dad was sick. I scanned the bar and then looked over at the biggest table near the two pool tables. My buddies were there, along with some girls we used to hang with.

Things were a little sketchy for a while. Sid was quiet and the girls from home weren't all that friendly. I was drinking fast, starting to think this might have been a huge mistake. Someone put a Black-Eyed Peas song on the jukebox and my friend, Chris, stood up. "I'll challenge anybody to a game at the table. Who's in?"

Sidney, clear as day, called out, "I am!" and scooted out past me to the pool sticks up on the wall. No one kind of knew what to do. She came by me and whispered, "Bet on me, all your money, every game."

I looked up at her and laughed. All I saw was that brilliant woman in front of the class at Keene. She was fearless.

She whooped everybody's ass, including my own, and I was good. Sid had a way of just decimating the table and then standing back, looking totally innocent.

The girls were in awe and told her they loved her 'kicking ass.' The guys, well, I guess the best word for them was 'intrigued.'

We drank way too much and walked home to the cul-de-sac. I asked Sid where she'd learned to play pool like that.

"My grandparents had a pool table instead of a dining room table. As soon as I didn't need a highchair anymore, I played pool. They were my babysitters — my parents had careers and worked long hours. I got good."

I smiled. "That's an understatement, Sid."

L et me see your teeth," she said as she turned to me.
"Why?" I asked, amused.

"Because that's something my father will do, subtly, you know. He'll evaluate your mouth, like whether you have an overbite or an underbite. Orthodontists do that to everybody they meet, at least my father does."

I turned and opened my mouth, my teeth on full display.

"Go on, bite down now, please."

I did. "Will I pass?"

"Yeah, your bite's good. That's a relief."

We got back in her Toyota and pulled out of the last rest stop on the Mass Pike. We were driving to her parents' home in Wellesley for this beautiful fall weekend.

Sid had shared with me that although her family was Jewish, her parents were not very religious. "We only celebrated a few of the major Jewish holidays. Education and activism, you know, causes are big with my parents. My mother's career as a labor union lawyer is kind of a Jewish cultural value. 'Actions speak louder than words,' so get involved. Does any of this make sense to you?"

I nodded and asked what her parents thought about her post graduate degree on lost Jewish artifacts and art and her being a lecturer at Keene State.

"They paid for my education, and this job is a solid start and it's for a just cause, so they're supportive. But if I was working with migrants in Santa Cruz, trying to get them better pay and working conditions, they'd be equally supportive."

The house was a large, two-story, red brick Colonial with an ornate portico. We pulled in and parked in front of the three-car garage. I got out and stood, taking it all in. *Pretty ritzy,* I thought, wondering what Sidney must have thought of my modest old house in Vermont. It was a third of this size and paled in comparison.

I turned and watched a woman come out a set of French doors onto the back patio. It was all landscaped; a bank of fall mums in ornate urns lined the walkway as it curved around to us. Someone had left a rake leaning against the trunk of a red maple, its leaves still very much on the tree. The woman waved and smiled as she walked up to us.

She was as small and as beautiful as Sidney. I whispered to Sid, "Now I know what my wife will look like in thirty years." Sidney gave me a puzzled expression and then smiled.

I gave Mrs. Hoffman a big hug.

"Welcome, Tom, welcome to our home." When we pulled a part, she still held onto both my hands and looked at her daughter with affection.

"Hey, Mom, it's great to be home." We all turned to the house.

Amy

Grammie was trying so hard to be cheerful. I watched her light the candles and turn towards us at the table. It was my 11th birthday and no one came. I actually had only invited Tommy and his girlfriend. Mom said I could have Ellie and a couple of the older girls over, but I figured she didn't really want that so I never bothered. She kept looking up at the clock and glancing out the kitchen window. Grammie said, after we ate dinner, "Let's get this show on the road, Amos — let's have cake and open gifts!"

We were getting dumped on; a lot of snow was falling and I figured Tommy wouldn't drive here because of it. He wasn't answering his cell, which made Mom even more worried. The weather on my birthday — always close to Thanksgiving — was a wild card. Snow or rain, sun or clouds, you never knew. But I was disappointed, and I couldn't hide it.

I blew out the candles and looked over at Mom. She was smiling, and while I knew it was a smile of love, she was kind of annoying me. Here we were, a whole year and a half out from Dad dying, and she was still trying to act like everything was normal. But it wasn't, especially for her. I noticed how most of the things Dad used to do now fell on her. And she'd lost all that attention — nobody reached out to hug her or call her beautiful or say, "Hey, baby, what do you think?" Just last night, I watched her on the couch doing nothing at all. No TV, no book, nothing, just sitting. I'd skipped down to get dinner and there she was. It was sad, but a little annoying at the same time.

The cake was my favorite, chocolate on chocolate with vanilla ice cream. I opened my presents and couldn't believe I got a brand-new iPod. That was a surprise. I also liked the new flannel pajamas and the three books I'd asked for.

We went our separate ways — me upstairs and Mom and Grammie talking in the kitchen. I couldn't wait to chill in my room. I moved to the window and looked out. The cul-de-sac was cloaked in white fluff, the streetlights glowing against the big snowflakes as they fell. The radiator along my wall clanked and I knew it'd clank again, even louder. I could feel the cold air seeping through my window. Our house was old, but on nights like this it felt big and strong. That reminded me of how Daddy used to be. I walked back to my bed and laid down. I wondered if, at this exact moment, he was thinking of me wherever he was. I wanted to think that was so.

SOMETIME LATER, I heard the plow sweep past our house, it's yellow blinking lights casting my room in a strange glow. A couple of minutes later, I heard some commotion downstairs. It was Tommy and Sidney. He'd made it home after all. I could hear the cupboards open and close and plates being put out on the kitchen table. Grammie was laughing, and before I knew it, Tommy was standing outside my bedroom door.

"Wake up, birthday girl. We're going out to play in all this white stuff as soon as we eat cake!" I thought his cheery self was a little more convincing than Grammie's. I stood up and he looked in at me. "Hey, maybe we'll get lucky and wash that blue hair out!"

I scrunched up my face and said, "Haha, aren't you funny."

I came down into the kitchen. Everyone looked up at me. I nodded and moved to the closet off the kitchen in search of snow pants. I was 11 now, maybe too old to play in the snow. But I didn't say that to anybody. I tucked my hair up into the first hat I found.

Rachel

"How does it feel to be someone's muse *and* subject?" she asked me. Her gaze was disconcerting. I looked down at the children, all holding on to the rope as we waited for the gift certificate from the bagel shop lady.

The woman spoke with a strong accent. I thought she may be the owner of the gallery further down the landing, but I wasn't positive. I didn't understand what she was asking me. I turned towards Kaitlyn, wondering if that's who she was speaking to. But Kaitlyn shrugged her shoulders.

It was cold out, and we were all in snow gear. It had been a spur of the moment decision of ours to stop on the way and get the last remaining item for our winter raffle. We were en route to the hill at the elementary school. Our sleds were already there waiting for us; Pat dropped them off in her car earlier. She also had a big thermos filled with hot chocolate and marshmallows ready for the little ones.

The woman came down off the landing toward me and stopped. I had my dark gray wool scarf wrapped tightly around my neck and my big, furry Cossack hat on. It was my '*Doctor Zhivago*' hat — what Mom called it when she'd ordered it for me.

The woman moved closer. She was dressed in a long, cable knit sweater over leggings, but she wore no coat. She was in clogs, standing on the icy pavement. Her hair was gorgeous, thick and long, a silver gray. *My God, it's 20 degrees out, she must be freezing.*

"Je vous trouve belle aussi" she exclaimed and turned abruptly, walking back up the stairs and into the gallery. Kaitlyn was speaking to the bagel shop owner, thanking her for the donation. We readied the children to continue our walk to the school, each of them holding the rope as we moved together.

Just before we crossed the parking lot, I glanced back. There, in her gallery's window, was an oil painting on an easel. It was of an orchard; its trees bare and twisted and the winter sun slicing the snow in shadows. Other works were displayed, but none as prominently as that one. A placard under it read, '*Student work, lessons available.*' As we moved away from the shops, I had the strangest feeling: *I've been there, I've stood under those trees.*

ONCE AT THE HILL, Kaitlyn waddled over to me. We were bundled up in coats and scarves, snow pants and boots. "Who *was* that woman and what did she say to you?"

I shook my head. "I have no idea. But we're all set now for the raffle. That's good."

Kaitlyn replied, "Honestly, Rach, you do look kind of foreign, kind of old world in your scarf and that hat. She's probably Russian and you reminded her of the 'motherland.'"

We both started to laugh until we saw one of the little girls, Mari, fall off her sled. "Can she get up on her own?" Kaitlyn wondered aloud.

I wasn't so sure and started to walk down the hill to her.

The woman had spoken French, that much I knew. But I'd taken Spanish in high school and didn't understand a thing she'd said or what she'd meant before that.

The hill was slippery, and I turned sideways as I made my way down. I remembered a time that Tom and I had come here when Amy was in kindergarten. It had been really slick and Tom had given her a push off in her saucer. As soon as she'd left us at the top, he'd called out, "Wow, that's way too fast." He flew down after her — slipping and sliding. I could hear the ringing of her laughter all the way to the bottom. *When was the last time I heard Amy laugh?* I couldn't remember.

I was trying hard to keep it together every minute of every day. I suddenly felt sorry for myself and began to cry. I brought my mittens up to wipe my tears — the rough wool was scratchy and I took a deep breath. I kept walking.

I reached Mari and helped her stand, brushing off the back of her colorful snowsuit. Her cheeks were rosy and her curly brown hair, covered in a hot pink hat, framed her face. She took my hand and we made our way back to the top of the hill. I placed her on the big toboggan sled and climbed in behind her. I held on to her extra tight as Kaitlyn pushed us off.

When the toboggan finally stopped, I didn't move. The painting of the orchard had affected me. Its starkness and the knotty, gnarly branches spoke of loss and of longing. *I'll never have what I once had with Tom*, I thought. Mari leaned over and scooped a handful of snow to bring to her mouth, but she hesitated and offered it to me first. I blinked through my tears and took a cold bite.

2010

Emily

I got into the rental and turned it on, then latched my seatbelt. Shawn, my assistant, was babbling. I quieted my racing thoughts just long enough to hear him say, "Yeah, my God, he really has gone down the proverbial tubes, hasn't he? Do you think it's drugs? I mean his clothes were dirty, his hair was covered in paint, and he hasn't seen a barber in months! I'm glad I didn't go inside the house. Gross — just like him. It's probably a meth lab!"

I looked in the rear view mirror as I started down the driveway. David was leaning on the railing of the old farmhouse porch, watching us leave. I put out my hand and waved. There was no response.

What I just saw, what he just showed me, was extraordinary. It went beyond anything I'd ever seen at any gallery in the fourteen years I'd been in the business. His studio was the living room and dining room with all the furniture pushed back up against the walls. The windows were open, and along this side of the porch I could see two chairs out at the end — thrown haphazardly. They must have been, at one time, the living room chairs. I imagined, in his creative fervor, he'd tossed them out. The dining room table was nowhere to be seen; that too was probably outside.

Sawhorses were set up in two different spots, with pieces of plywood serving to hold the paints, brushes, rags, and oils. Painted canvases stretched from one end of the house to the other, all different sizes, leaning against the built-in bookshelves, along the back of the couch, near the fireplace, and suspended across the tops of chairs leaning against the faded floral wallpaper. Two paintings were even in the friggin' pantry beneath the canned soups, pickles, and boxes of saltines.

I had been bombarded by vibrant, magnificently bold colors and vivid detail. And David, standing there, not sure what to do as I walked from one incredible painting to the next. The painting of the baby on the blanket — that's when I started to lose it. I turned around and thought, *I'm in his head, no, it's his heart. I'm in his heart.* There was no other way to describe it.

"Well?" he asked as I wiped my eyes.

"Do you have a Kleenex?"

He reached down and tore off a paper towel from a roll on the floor near one of his easels.

I reached for it and blew my nose. "I also need a glass of water."

When he returned with the glass, I asked, "Are there any more? And have you shown them to anyone else?"

He looked at me and smiled. I think he was embarrassed. "Yes, along the steps of the stairs to the second floor." He pointed to the hallway off the living room. "And a painter friend of mine down in Langdon came out and saw them this winter."

I climbed the stairs and studied each one. He didn't come up with me. I think he'd gone out onto the porch to talk with Shawn. Four years of painting, four years of being totally immersed.

I knew he'd dabbled in painting in his adolescence; he'd told me he had. But these, all of these, were beyond dabbling. "These are some of the best oil paintings I've ever fucking seen," I said out loud.

The three subjects were of the family he'd become involved with, what ten, eleven years ago: a woman named Rachel, and her son, the boy he'd saved. She had a baby then too.

I quickly went back to the largest painting that was leaning up against the couch. It was of the mother, sitting and nursing the baby — the baby's hand reaching up to grab a tendril of the mother's hair, and behind them, water glistening. "This is the day he saved the boy, the first time he saw her," I whispered.

I quickly took out my iPhone and snapped photos of everything before me. Then I heard the screen open and David's footsteps. I put the cell away.

"David, you know these are incredible, don't you?"

He looked down at the old wooden floor and then back up at me. "I think they're good. The biggest one is in here, in my grandfather's study."

I opened the door. Lying on top of a big wooden oak desk was the best one yet. It was of Rachel, the mother, stepping off the stairs to the porch, right outside here, carrying a picnic basket. She wore cut-off blue jeans and a pale-yellow shirt with the sleeves rolled up and her collar askew. The expression on her face was one of pure joy, as if she couldn't wait to get to where she was going.

I suspected it was from that day he'd kept talking to me about — when I'd told him roses were way inappropriate. I moved a straight-back chair over and stood up on it to get a better view.

I turned to him, still perched above the painting. "Good? My God, they're extraordinary and will be the talk of, well, what gallery are you thinking?" I stepped down off the chair and looked at him.

"That's it, Emily, I don't want them anywhere near the city. New York ate me up; I can't go back."

"But, David, these have to be seen, have to be experienced." We stood looking at each other, and then I heard Shawn yell, "Hey, we got to get going. Once it gets dark it's no man's land out here!"

NOW, DEEP IN THOUGHT at the end of the driveway, I hesitated before turning onto the main road. I stopped the car, put it in park, and jumped out.

I heard Shawn yell, "What the fuck?"

I started to run back up the hill to the farmhouse, yelling to David.

He came back down off the porch. I stood, panting, hands on my knees. "I'm so bloody hell out of shape," I whispered, then straightened up.

"A gallery outside the city, then, or one around here. That's what we'll do. Let me do some research. I'll call you. But David, for Christ's sake, use the landline! Your cell reception is shit," I said, finally catching my breath.

"Now you're talking, Em." He turned and went into the house.

By the time I got back to the car, I'd thought of two, possibly three, gallery owners from the city I was calling in the morning. *If he won't go to them, I'll get them to come to him.*

Tom Jr.

Sidney, where's the guy who did all this?" I didn't feel good, like my legs were starting to buckle.

Sidney replied patiently, "Tom, he's not a guy, he's a painter and this is his opening. His name is David Sumner and I believe it's that man, over there, under the painting of the mother and baby."

She stood there now watching me. I recognized the name immediately. I thought I might throw up.

I stared down at her. "Look at them, all of them. What do you see?"

She turned all the way around, taking in the paintings; of the woman nursing a baby, a boy poised to dive from a rock ledge, a different angle of the same woman and baby, and then a series of paintings of the woman, the baby and the boy on a blanket, near a brook, fishing pole in hand and a close up of a baby with a drooling chin. The largest one was of the woman stepping off a porch with a picnic basket. She was smiling, looking further out, and her happy expression was palpable. The paintings were remarkable, and the buzz in the room was growing.

"There's something going on here, Tom, isn't there?" Sidney asked, looking at me, already beginning to know what that something was.

"These paintings are of me and Mom and Amy. And that guy — I mean painter — he's the guy who saved me. He's the guy who…" My voice trailed off. I was overcome by the paintings; the intimacy of them and their remarkable beauty. I had to sit down, but not here.

"I need to leave," I told Sidney. She grabbed my hand, steering me to the door.

We drove straight back to Keene. She called her friend, Kimberly, and told her I wasn't feeling well. I felt bad that I had spoiled a visit with her professor friend who now worked at Williams. Sidney responded, "Don't worry, darling, she and I can get together anytime — we aren't far from each other."

I didn't talk much on the way back. I didn't feel like it.

Emily

I was sitting on the granite steps outside the gallery. It was getting dark and the lights inside lit up the paintings in a fantastic glow. Bursts of colors and images flooded the senses. Students and parents were huddled in small groups, moving to each new canvas.

The gallery had done an excellent job getting the word out. Graduation weekend at Williams College meant another opportunity to socialize in this small, quaint New England college town. Jonathan Taylor, the gallery owner, had paired the momentous day of graduation with the opening as a way 'To Honor the Love of Family.' It had definitely hit its mark.

Where was he? I checked my phone again — 8:05. He said he'd make sure to stop by, see David's work.

Two college kids were coming out, down the steps. I looked up at the kid — he didn't look good. The girl beside him saw my face. "He's suddenly not feeling so hot." She held his hand. *Sweet, young love,* I thought. As she went by me, she smiled.

"Hey, what do you think of the paintings?" I asked, quickly turning to her. The young man kept walking, but she held back.

"Really just incredible. I can't explain what they evoked in me; memories of myself as a child, but also…he captured the essence of the connection between mother and child. Again, just incredible."

I watched her run to catch up with her guy. She had articulated exactly what I had felt the first time I'd seen the paintings on the farm. Like all the moments of family life were, when separated, equal to the momentous moments that we thought marked our lives. David's paintings had been the impetus for me to open up the discussion again with Jimmy about having a baby. Maybe we *could* have the kind of moments he had painted and be happy for however long we had. Jimmy was convinced we could.

David shot down three of my gallery suggestions before I'd stumbled on this one. I'd suggested it because I knew Dick Rickert's daughter was graduating here this weekend and he'd be more apt to come to see David's paintings than in another far-out-of-New York setting. I also knew Jonathan Taylor, knew his style, his penchant for detail and presentation.

David had mulled over the idea of having the opening here for about three minutes before replying, "That works, Em, thanks."

Dick Rickert's gallery in Chelsea was definitely one of the best places for David's work. It was prestigious on a scale that could get his art out there. But Dick was also practical and fair, and not an art dealer who was high maintenance. I knew David needed a firm footing if and when he returned to New York. Dick Rickert was exactly that. In other words, he was not typical of some of the New York art dealers who David had known and had actually become himself at a point.

I'd written an artist bio for him, developed a social media profile, taken photos of all the paintings, and worked with him on developing his artist story. I'd spoken to him about the importance of staying genuine, of scanning the crowd to weed out the first-time art buyers from the serious collectors. In this crowd, I doubted we had many, if any, collectors. That's why getting the paintings to New York was imperative.

We'd also invited some art critics from Boston — I couldn't tell for sure by the guest book if they were present. Sometimes they used pseudonyms to fly under the radar. I also didn't know any of them by sight. This wasn't New York, my stomping ground.

At one point, David had said, "Emily, everything you've ever heard me say, you just regurgitated back to me." I'd thought that was probably true, but the two of us couldn't be more apart in how we operated around clients. I'd wanted to say to him, "You're right, but I don't need a fixer, do I?" Instead, I'd smiled, satisfied that this was coming to fruition.

My last comment to him on the eve of the opening had been to get cleaned up, to come looking like a million dollars. David had laughed and said, "I'll come looking my best." And he had.

Jonathan Taylor came out onto the steps and smiled. He lit up a cigarette and tucked the match under a potted plant. "It's going well, although I've heard two different people ask David if they could commission him to paint their family — had you thought of this? That people would love the paintings but want their own family members in them?"

Just then a dark Mercedes pulled up and Dick Rickert rolled down the window. "Hey Emily, are there any drinks and hors d'oeuvres? I'm sorry but my wife and daughter are starved and I promised them I'd take them to dinner after… They just need something to hold them over."

"Absolutely!" I replied and turned to go in. I needed to make sure Dick Rickert and his family had everything they needed, and to tell David the big kahuna had arrived.

Tom Jr.

I wrote down the three names and addresses exactly as I remembered them. I hadn't yet told Sidney that I could do this — you know, memorize stats and images and recall them exactly as they appeared.

Seeing David Sumner and the paintings last night had blown me away. But after that, in the middle of the night, the names and addresses had come to me. I'd gotten up, grabbed a notebook from my backpack, and gone into Sid's bathroom. That name — Jacob Geller — the one that had been nagging at me since I'd come across it while doing research in Sidney's class, was what I wrote down, along with two others. I'd read about his family's masterpieces being confiscated during the Nazi occupation. An article in the local *Valley News* covered the Geller family's attempts to track down their lost art and heirlooms. Now I understood why I'd had that nagging feeling. I'd come across his name and address before somewhere — it *must* have been as a kid since David Sumner was the trigger. While I couldn't pin down the specifics surrounding their names, I was confident it was only a matter of time before I remembered.

"TOM, WHAT'S THIS HERE?" Sidney asked as she picked up my notebook. I was on her tiny deck, drinking a very big glass of chocolate milk. I came into the kitchen.

"Names and addresses I memorized as a kid. I wrote them down last night. There's some connection to David Sumner, I just don't know how exactly. And this one here — Jacob Geller? I've read about him for your class. He survived the Holocaust but lost everyone and everything. It's been bugging me because I knew I recognized his name. It's from this list I found when I was a kid."

Sidney sat down at the kitchen table and tapped the notebook. "All the names appear to be Jewish, you know that, right? They're Ashkenazi Jews' surnames from Eastern Europe. Jewish last names often, but not always, are an indication of what region they're originally from."

She pointed to the first name and address written. "Like Hannah Berenson; Hannah is an old Biblical name, and Berenson means 'son of bear.' Jacob Geller — that's Yiddish. The last names here — Adam and Elisabeth Arenberg — Berg means 'mountain.' Yep, they're Jewish." She took a sip of her espresso and then looked at the notebook again. "And they all have New England addresses."

I put my hands on Sidney's shoulders and said, "There you go, showing off that big, beautiful brain of yours."

"But wait…you said you memorized them when you were little? What's that all about?" Turning in her chair, she looked up at me. I sat down at the table.

"Sid, I aced your class because, well, I took the time to read everything and I had a fantastic professor, but also because I have kind of a photographic memory for things I want to remember. Maybe my parents know about it, but not really anyone else. I know a lot of sports facts, but this here — " I moved the notebook back to me and looked down at the names again. "This was something I wanted to remember, for some reason. It's hard to explain."

"That's impressive, Mr. Dunne. And you think David Sumner, or at least just seeing David Sumner, is connected to this memory?"

"I know so."

Toward the end of the week, I decided to take a run. I left Sid's apartment, and instead of heading to the campus, I took the rural route out of town. I wanted to clear my head and try to remember anything I could about the names. I headed south, running a few miles out towards Swanzey. The road wound its way through the countryside. My pace was steady as I mentally reviewed the circumstances surrounding our family and David Sumner. The early spring rains and melting snow had left large pools of standing water in many of the fields. The air smelled sweet until I came upon a small farm. I slowed down and began to walk, placing my hands on my hips as I caught my breath. A farmer, on an old tractor, was spreading manure. The row of windows on the side of the barn facing me reflected the afternoon sun. It was then that I had a flash of the small cellar in the barn on Sumner's farm.

I stood for a couple of minutes, replaying the memory of climbing down the ladder and finding the book. I remembered that I was alone and hiding. I turned back towards Sidney's and began to run again. I adjusted my pace, knowing I'd burn out if I kept going so fast. An uneasy feeling started to take hold of me. I knew that Jacob Geller's past had been filled with hardship and loss. *Did the other names on my list have similar experiences?*

Once back, I paced the apartment until I heard the door open. Sid came in carrying a grocery bag. I didn't even wait for her to set it down.

"I was in a cellar and those names and addresses were in a book with even more names and addresses. It was on David Sumner's farm. My mom was there too — not in the cellar but there for the day. Karl was with me, the kid I used to hang with in elementary school. We were playing hide and seek." I stopped talking and took a deep breath. I looked at her expectantly.

Sid asked, "How important is this to you?"

"I want to…" I moved and looked out Sid's slider to the deck and the street below. I wasn't sure myself why this was so important to me. I knew of the horrible circumstances surrounding Jacob Geller's life during the Holocaust — the article made that very clear. But there was more to it. I turned back to Sidney. "I want to know why a man, a Jewish man who survived the horror of Germany during the Holocaust, is in a ledger in an old barn in Plymouth, Vermont. A ledger hidden, like really hidden. Could it have something to do…Jesus, Sid, I know this sounds crazy, but could it be connected to the stolen art?" I walked over to the notebook, still opened to the names I'd written down. "It makes me wonder if there's some dark shit surrounding this."

"Let's not get ahead of ourselves, okay, Tom? I have David Sumner's card from the art opening. Do you want to contact him? He may still be in Williamstown for all we know." Sidney went to the little bulletin board above her phone and took the card down.

I reached for it and walked to the phone. "I can call him, it's faster."

Sidney looked concerned. "Wait, Tom, please. Shouldn't you think first about what you want to say? This is all out of the blue for him too, just like it is for you. And he might not know a thing about this ledger."

"It's okay. I'm not going to mention the Jacob Geller connection or what I know, not at this point. I'll keep it low-key, I promise, really." I picked up the phone and dialed.

Immediately the conversation began. Sid stood, just around the corner, listening.

"Hey, Mr. Sumner, this is Tom Dunne, from Langdon. You saved me when I was a kid. I was actually at your opening last week."

After a few kind words from him, I responded, "Well that's nice of you to say. My father's death was pretty hard for all of us." I paused and looked at Sidney before adding, "I thought your paintings were awesome, but I'm calling about a whole different thing, okay?"

I moved to the kitchen chair and sat down. "This may sound totally weird, but here I go. After your opening, I remembered something that happened that day at your house, on your farm. While you and Mom and Amy were in the yard, Karl, my buddy, and I explored the barn, even went fishing. At some point, we started playing hide and seek. While I was hiding, I found a book with names and addresses in it…" I looked over at Sidney. She was making a brake motion, telling me to slow down. I nodded, paused, and then continued, slower this time. "I was wondering what that was all about. It was in the cellar, not the house cellar — we never went inside the farmhouse. The crazy thing is, I memorized those names and, well, it'll drive me crazy if I can't find out, you know, what it's all about and put it to rest." I looked at Sid questioningly. She gave me a thumbs up.

Mr. Sumner replied, "I have no idea about the book, but I could head to the cellar and let you know what I find, okay?"

"If you can, I'd really appreciate it."

LATER THAT NIGHT, in bed, I wrapped my arms around Sidney. I moved my head close to hers and said, "I really want to know what that cellar and book are all about, don't you?"

She ran her hand up and down my arm, pulling me as close to her as possible. "Maybe there's something to this. I think we have to tread carefully though, Tom."

"Let me ask you this — could art confiscated from Jews end up over here? Could Jacob Geller's stolen art be in the States?"

Sidney turned and looked up at me. "Oh, I'm sure there are plenty of missing pieces in the US. German art dealers sold a lot of confiscated stuff to buyers all around the world with and without Hitler's knowledge."

I leaned down, lifted her hair, and kissed her neck.

She whispered, "Now, love of my life, let's stop talking,"

The very next morning, we were up early; Sid had an appointment and I needed to go to the sports complex on campus. Since graduation, I was working as one of two assistants to the sports manager. I pressed the fruit smoothie setting on the blender and turned towards Sidney. She was reading the Jacob Geller article on her laptop. I turned the blender off.

"Interesting stuff, isn't it?" I asked as I poured the banana-strawberry smoothie into two glasses.

"Yes. I wished I'd read it sooner. I could have referenced it during class, even posted it for an assignment. I'll remember next time I teach the course." She reached for the glass of smoothie and took a sip. "Can I ask you, sweetheart — aside from this strange development with the list of names, how do you feel about the opening, about David Sumner's paintings? With you and your family being his subjects?"

I moved to the sink, ran the glass part of the blender under the tap, and rinsed it out. Turning back to Sidney, I replied, "If I remember right, it was such a scary, close call to drowning — my drowning — that we were all affected by it. All our emotions were running high that summer. David was at the center of me surviving, that I clearly recall."

I moved to the bedroom door with the smoothie and added, "If he wants to paint about it, it's okay with me. He saved me. He's entitled to it." I stuck my head out a moment later. "And they were beautiful paintings, especially of my mom."

Rachel

The phone startled me. I'd been so involved in spreading out the month's bills that I jumped. A woman identified herself as Mrs. Anders and asked if we could speak. *Mrs. Anders, Mrs. Anders…How do I know that name?* I thought.

"I'm the school counselor at Langdon. I have Amy right here beside me."

I glanced up at the kitchen clock; it was barely 9:30 a.m. "Yes, of course. Is Amy all right?" I asked, my voice tinged with concern.

"To be perfectly honest, Amy has had a rough morning and I'm not sure she can get on with her day. I attempted a mediation between her and a classmate. It didn't go so well. Amy remains quite defiant and her language has been… Well, it's language that doesn't meet our expectations."

I stood up and turned around, looking for the car keys. "I'll be there in five minutes. Let her know I'm coming."

MRS. ANDERS OPENED HER OFFICE DOOR and quickly stepped out. "I've never seen her this way. She's pretty rooted in justifying what she did. I think, Mrs.

Dunne, there's a lot going on inside her head and with her emotions lately."

"What, um, did she do exactly?" I could see Amy through the window of the office. She was sitting slumped in the chair, looking totally bored. But her hands told a different story. She was gripping the edge of the straight chair, her knuckles white.

"Your daughter pushed a classmate in the hallway. It wasn't necessarily hard, but the other girl dropped an art project and it shattered. She wasn't hurt and she didn't need to go to the nurse. Amy yelled at her, called her, and I quote, "A fucking twat.""

Mrs. Anders saw the shock on my face.

"Amy wanted me to tell you what happened out here before the three of us meet in there. I think she's experiencing grief, and today it turned into anger. I want to offer Amy some support. Do you remember that we spoke about it a few months back? I think she needs it, even though there's just six weeks left of school. It'd be good for her to learn some coping strategies before the summer."

I nodded, and Mrs. Anders opened the office door. Amy looked up at us. Her look of disdain for me stung. I was embarrassed and hurt. *When had my baby girl grown to detest me?*

Mrs. Anders didn't miss a beat and began talking. "I've briefed your mom like you wanted me to. You're not being suspended today, Amy. The student is okay." We both sat down and Mrs. Anders continued, "Since you didn't speak during the mediation I attempted, I'll try again…What did Bella do to make you so angry?"

I gasped. "Bella? Amy, I don't get it! Bella has been one of your best friends since third grade. What could she possibly have done for you to do this?"

Amy sat up and turned to me. Her hair was dyed a fresh blue again — this time at the tips — and the t-shirt she wore featured what I thought was a Goth rock band. In a voice full of contempt, she responded, "Oh, oh, precious Bella who never stops smiling or sucking up. Yeah, I pushed her. She deserved it. She's such a fake!"

I could hear her voice breaking and see her lips starting to tremble. Mrs. Anders leaned forward and said, "Thank you, Amy, for telling us."

Just then classes started to change and we could hear the hallways filling up with students. Someone yelled out, "There's a sub in Science!" Inside the office, we sat quietly. I continued to watch Amy, trying to understand her motive. It made no sense. She wiped away tears falling down her cheek, smearing her eyeliner. I handed her a Kleenex and she took it without acknowledging me.

Mrs. Anders reached behind her desk and grabbed an unopened bottle of water on a shelf. She walked over to Amy and handed it to her. Amy took it and whispered, "Thanks." The hallway noise settled down. Amy took a sip of water.

I wanted to tell her that pushing Bella or anyone else was never going to be okay, but I waited for Mrs. Anders to speak. She glanced at me and then asked Amy, in a very direct way, "Are you angry with Bella because she has no idea how you feel, how awful it is to lose someone like you lost your father?"

Amy didn't respond. She was shutting down just as she often did at home, up in her bedroom. She shifted in her chair, turning away from us.

Mrs. Anders pressed on, "I can't imagine how hard it must be. I want you to know that you're not the only one in the middle school who's experiencing a huge loss of someone close to them. There's actually a support group for students a lot like you. They meet each week during seventh period on Wednesdays. I reached out to you a little while back about it, remember?"

I interrupted and said, "Now I wish I'd been more insistent that you join."

Amy quickly glanced over, long enough to shoot me daggers with her eyes.

Mrs. Anders continued speaking, "We gather in the small conference room off the library. Mr. Schott and I run it."

Amy didn't acknowledge Mrs. Anders' comments. I was about to reprimand her for being rude when Mrs. Anders added, "I know you'd miss a core academic class, but it's an excused absence. And we often have popcorn or freeze pops."

"Who's in it?" Amy turned and asked.

"You can check it out this Wednesday. I'll catch you first thing in the morning to give you a pass. Let me just see what class you'll be absent from." Mrs. Anders moved the mouse on her desktop computer and said, "It's Math. Is that okay?"

For the first time since I'd arrived, Amy turned fully toward us. "Yeah, okay."

I smiled at her and started to stand. I was nervous about saying anything that could jeopardize her decision to attend the group. I tentatively asked, "So, are you coming home with me now? Or staying?"

Amy shook her head and replied, "If we're talking about who needs a support group, it's you. You're totally depressed."

For a second time, I was terribly embarrassed. Mrs. Anders gave me a sympathetic look.

"Loss affects us all differently depending on where we are in the process. I think, Amy, if you feel you're in a better, calmer place, your mother could go home without you, okay?"

Amy nodded, and I put my hand on the doorknob. "I love you, baby girl," I said and lightly touched her shoulder as I left Mrs. Ander's room. I walked past the main office but didn't stop to sign out. I couldn't. I was too emotional.

When I got home, I sat again at the kitchen table. The bills were as I had left them, along with my scribbling of checkbook balances. *Amy's pissed, I'm depressed, and Tommy's in love,* I thought, and continued to write out the checks.

THAT NIGHT, AFTER DINNER, I walked by Amy's bedroom door. I opened it. She was on her bed, headphones in and reading. She quickly looked up and asked, "What?"

"Just wondering what you're up to, that's all." I didn't know how to tell her that losing Daddy was bigger than anything I could ever have imagined. That it was swallowing me up whole. I closed her door and walked down the hallway. I stopped and looked at the baby pictures, remembering the night we had the party for David. None of us could have fathomed that Tommy's near-drowning would one day be eclipsed by something this enormous.

I turned on the TV above my dresser and started to fold laundry. *Our world's been shattered, but everyone else's is moving on.*

David

The second review in the *Boston Globe* was even better than the first. It gave me praise for reviving the art of 'what is joyful in the human condition.'

What Sumner has accomplished through his intense use of color, light, and movement is that all moments are worthy of capture; that the love of family is front and center, always beautiful, even in the mundane. His ability to evoke our need for connection is profound. After viewing the paintings at his opening at the Jonathan Taylor Gallery in Williamstown, it made me want to, once again, tiptoe into my son's bedroom and stand in awe. That son is now thirty-seven and I'd forgotten the feeling of amazement of being a parent. Sumner brought me back to it like a warm, wet, summer rain drenching me completely in familial love.

Emily had called me twice. She was ecstatic that Dick Rickert wanted to meet. He had potential backers and was ready to make some big things happen for me.

I reread the two reviews in the Globe and then walked out onto the porch. I leaned on the railing.

I thought about how Everett, my therapist, and Hélène and Julie had shown up at the opening and made it that much better. Afterwards, the four of us had driven to a brick oven pizza place and chatted until they closed. Then we'd all gone back to my hotel room and drank some more, except for Hélène. She said, more than once, "I'm so damn proud of you, mon cher garçon."

Finally, Julie turned to Everett and said, "Will you break the news to my love that she's only, what, six years older than David, so she can't be his mother."

Everett told me that while Hélène was proud of me, he was happy that I'd found 'my place.' It was nearly two years since I'd last met with him as a client and I remembered telling him then that I felt I had finally found 'my place.' The anger no longer consumed me, instead I was feeling this incredible need to create, painting daily. He had cautioned me about becoming too isolated, but I had done just that, shutting myself off. Now I was here and clearly ready to engage again.

As I'd walked them out to their car the night of the opening, Hélène had assured me she could drive back. It was nearing 2 a.m. and thousands of stars were out, glistening in the skies of western Massachusetts. Hélène had leaned into me and whispered, "You know, I've seen her, your beauty. She's every bit as lovely in person as she is in your paintings. Elle vivra eternellement, David. You've given her the ultimate gift."

I'd stood in the silence and watched them drive off. I had held on until the very last minute, waiting for Rachel to appear at the gallery. When Jonathan had turned off the bank of lights, casting it in complete darkness, I'd finally accepted it was not going to happen.

Before the opening, Emily and I had talked a bit about how we should approach my paintings with Rachel. "Are we asking or informing her, Emily?"

"We're informing her. There's no need to ask. As an artist your paintings are entitled to the full protection of the

First Amendment. It's not like you're mass-producing their images for commercial gain. If someone had painted my mother like this and me with her, they'd be my most cherished possessions. We could have high quality photographs taken of the paintings and professionally framed for her. Should I make that offer?"

"Yes," I had replied and added, "Write a good letter, okay? As kind as possible."

"Of course, and I'll send it certified, along with the publicity about the opening."

Rachel had clearly rejected Emily's offer and by extension, me again.

NOW, ON THE PORCH, I concentrated on the success of the opening. I thought about how far I'd come as an artist. For the past four years, I'd been consumed, frequently upping the quality of my supplies, spending a bundle on pigments, linen canvases, linseed oil, and different brushes. I was constantly experimenting with the best grade solvents and pigment blends. Hélène had shown me how to mix the oils and pigments together for the best consistency. And the colors, the perfect colors to get the rich realism I sought. I kept remembering Tommy's willowy arms and child's torso as he'd dived, the curve of Rachel's long legs as she'd stepped down from the porch and her bright, expectant eyes, and Amy's chubby hands and dark curls lifting with the gentle breeze. The images filled my mornings as the natural light streamed into the bottom rooms of the old farmhouse.

When each painting was complete, I'd wait to make sure it was the best I could do. Once I was satisfied and it was totally dry, I'd varnish it to further enrich the colors and give it durability. Of all the art styles, oil painting created the quality I sought. Where I'd go from here as an artist, I wasn't quite so sure. I knew Hélène could help me figure it out.

I looked out across the fields on the other side of the road. There was no doubt that the gallery opening had validated all my time, investment, and focus.

I liked Dick Rickert, his wife, and daughter. They'd been extremely complimentary about what they'd seen. Overall, I'd felt I connected with a lot of people that night, both parents and students. They'd appeared to be sincere in their appreciation of my work. Two art students, both young men, had asked me lots of questions on the process, the paints, oils, canvas, even the cost of the materials. Emily had come by feeling she needed to rescue me, but I'd shaken my head and said, "I'm fine, this is great."

It was different this time as the painter and in this setting. The money, the hustle, the games and the glitz weren't there. Instead, it was people actually seeing my work with eyes wide open. I'd met other artists and local folks who were interested and complimentary during the days following my opening night.

There was one remark from an older woman who'd seemed a little standoffish that I'd found disconcerting. She'd walked up to me and motioned to the paintings before us. "Your family is beautiful."

I'd quickly replied, "Oh, no I'm not…They're not my family."

She had looked at me strangely and I'd watched her move to another painting before glancing back at me. I'd turned away from her and searched for Emily.

Jonathan Taylor had seen the exchange with the woman and my puzzled expression.

"That's Louanne Holmes. Very eccentric, but she has a knack for seeing things others tend to miss. It's hard to describe. She writes for the local paper here and I'm sure she'll do your art justice."

TOWARDS SUNSET, I made my way across the meadow to the root cellar. I reviewed the mind-blowing phone call — completely out of the blue — from Tommy Dunne. His quandary on the ledger was certainly odd but I definitely wanted to help him out.

We'd had a rainy spring, and I heard the brook's bubble — what Nana used to call it when she'd sit and mend our socks while I fished as a little boy. "Listen to the brook bubbling by, beautiful boy," she'd said once and I'd giggled, "Nana, I'm not a beautiful boy!"

"It's alliteration, Davy," she'd replied, giggling too. I realized this memory was one of the few times I'd told Everett I hadn't been mad at the world.

The root cellar's door was stuck so I came back to the shed to get a shovel. If I dug around the bottom of the frame, I was sure it would open. Again, it hit me how strange Tommy's request was, but I wanted to do a thorough search for the kid.

Tommy Dunne — I couldn't believe I'd spoken with him. His deep voice didn't quite match the boy of my paintings. I thought about Rachel raising the kids on her own, unless, of course, she'd met someone else. *A woman like that could have her pick,* I thought. Carrying the shovel, I walked back down through the meadow, remembering what she'd said about the farm — that she could have been happy here.

Sidney

As I was prepping for a seminar on my laptop the following afternoon, Tom came out of the bathroom carrying his cell. He looked at me and said, "Mr. Sumner checked; there's no ledger with names."

"Well, I guess that ends that, right?"

He surprised me by saying, "No, it's there, I'm sure of it. I think we need to check for ourselves. Plymouth is only an hour and a half north. Let's plan on going sometime soon."

That night I made popcorn, and we settled in to watch a movie. A commercial began, showing the release for the upcoming film, *Toy Story 3*. In the commercial, the iconic castle of Walt Disney pictures came on.

I glanced over at Tom and asked, "Did you know that the Disney castle right there is based on the Neuschwanstein Castle in Germany? That's where Hitler stashed a whole lot of artwork during the war. It was up to the Monuments Men to get in and retrieve it. They found room after room filled with Hitler's loot — what he took from the Jews and museums across Europe and a lot of other places the Nazis ransacked."

Reaching for more popcorn, Tom replied, "I have read about that. I believe it was suggested reading from my all-time favorite teacher."

David

I saw one, now two flashlights come up over the hill, heading across to the barn. "Who the hell is that?" I said aloud. It was just past midnight. I quickly put on my jeans and grabbed a sweatshirt. My slip-on mud boots were by the kitchen door on a tray. I opened the door and yelled, "Hey!" from the porch.

The motion detector lights came on. I got to the barn doors just as the flashlight wielding people did. One was very tall while one was quite small. They were dressed in black from their skull caps down to their shoes. *They look like they're in a fucking play*, I thought. It was cold for a May night. We were under a frost warning. I could see their breaths.

I was incredulous and angrily asked, "What do you think you're doing?"

The tall guy whipped off his hat and said, "Mr. Sumner, it's me, Tom Dunne, and this is my girlfriend, Sidney."

She surprised me by extending her hand. I shook it.

"We came because, well, I'm convinced that the ledger is still here. And it's important to me. Those names mean something," he said this apologetically. "I want to figure it out, that's all."

I calmed down and looked at them. *They're just kids.* Tommy had certainly grown up. He resembled his father even more. I looked for the scar. *Yep, it's there.* It was barely discernible, but I knew where to look.

"Call me David, please. You said the cellar that wasn't in the house, so I assumed you meant the root cellar down in the meadow, near the brook. That's where I went to look. I never went inside the barn to search because there's no cellar in there."

Tom glanced at Sidney and said, "There's still a good chance then." Turning back to me, he asked, "David, can I check in the barn?"

"I'm telling you, there's no cellar in there."

Sidney jumped in and countered my comment with, "Lots of old barns had milk cellars to keep the milk separate from the cows and other barn stuff until consumption. Fresh milk had to be kept in a clean, out of the way place, usually down in a cold storage area. Tom remembers a place like that in here."

I shook my head. "Well, I have my doubts, but we'll check. Let me get the lights, a few of the bulbs still work."

I opened the doors and felt for the bank of lights to my left. The barn's smell was pungent, a mix of old hay, cow manure, and earth. I thought I could also detect the smell of an animal or two decaying. A few barn swallows were disturbed and fluttered about as we walked in.

Tom stood just inside the door and glanced all around. He said to Sidney, "Boy, I'm glad you're a runt 'cause that's what we're gonna need." He put his black cap back on, pulling it down tight.

We moved further into the barn, following the glow of the lights that worked. I couldn't remember the last time I had gone this far in.

Tom swung his flashlight up and along the wall to the right, stepping under a few big spider webs, over some two-by-fours, and around the bales of hay. A long concrete water trough ran parallel to us, its dirty water long evaporated but now filled with all sorts of shit, I imagined.

Twice, Tom reached out to take Sidney's hand, telling her to watch her step. I worried about nails sticking up and rodents scuttering over our feet. We could hear them. It was clear the barn had a host of nighttime creatures.

I had the second flashlight now and followed behind, keeping it pointed ahead, lighting up the way. I scanned to the left and to the right a few times, catching small eyes staring back at us. A few feral cats slunk in under the barn's broken boards and its foundation.

Tom stopped and turned around, scanning the floor of the barn not far from the base of the hay loft. The ladder to the loft was broken and clearly no longer safe to climb.

"There's a little latch on the floor, and like a trap door that goes below," he said. "I remember it being about here, I think."

I thought he was crazy; never did I remember such a door in all the years I'd spent on the farm.

We both turned our flashlights to the floor, while Sidney knelt down and wiped away bits of hay and dirt. "Here it is, I think…Yes, I feel it. Shine the light right here," she said.

Sure enough, there was a latch. Tom pulled up on it. A small opening, no more than three feet by four, appeared. I shone the light down. We all stood, looking down at the hard-packed dirt floor below.

"There doesn't appear to be any water down there, so that's good," Sidney said.

Tom nodded. "Sid, I'm gonna lower you down with my arms, and what you want to do is move your flashlight. Wait, give me a sec."

Tom stood and turned the way Sidney would be entering the opening in the floor. I watched him position his body, replaying what he recalled from that day. Part of me thought it was incredible that he remembered it to this degree. *But I do too*, I thought. *Like it was yesterday.* I had a sudden flash of Rachel smiling as she held back a low hanging branch for me as I carried Amy. I quickly turned my attention back to what was going on in the darkness of the barn.

"When I lower you, Sid, shine your light to your left. Once you're on the floor, there will be shelves with old milk bottles. The ledger is in a crack in the wall, its binding kind of brown-green but with a goldish thread. Count about seven milk bottles over, move that one and it should be about there."

"Okay, let's do it," she replied. "And if I scream…Well, I hope I don't."

Tom lowered her slowly down while I knelt on the floor, shining the light through the opening.

"I think I'm pissing off some critters," Sidney called up, her voice sounding further away than she was. "Definitely hard to see, and I just stepped on a second ladder; it's broken like the one up there." Her voice was echoing.

"Come on, Sid, count the bottles — let's get you back up here," Tom called down, looking concerned.

"It's here," she yelled up. "Just like you said."

As soon as Tom pulled Sidney back up and out, he wiped the cobwebs off her cap and brushed her pants. She held the ledger up against her chest, smiling.

"So, it's clear I've been proven wrong." I glanced at them both.

Tom looked over at me apologetically. "Like I told you on the phone, I was playing hide and seek with my buddy that day we came to visit you. I found the latch when I jumped off the hay loft. He never found me down there, but I got bored waiting and started to snoop around. The ledger was wedged in the stone wall. The goldish thread caught my eye. I pulled it out thinking I was like Indiana Jones. I pretended I had to memorize the names before the Nazis came. I concentrated on the ones that weren't crossed off yet on the last page." He ended with, "I kind of have a good memory."

I shook my head. "I'll say…Let's start a pot of coffee and see what this ledger is all about, okay?"

Still clutching it to her chest, Sidney replied, "Perfect, thanks."

Turning to go back through the barn, I thought that my grandparents could never have climbed down into that opening, only a kid could. But I'd never known of its existence.

Just as I was closing the barn door, my flashlight lit up the opposite wall. The old canvas pouches we used for picking cherries were hanging from hooks. Suddenly, I got a flash of Joe, the handyman on the farm who came for the warmer months to run the orchard. He was a little man; he'd been a horse jockey down in the Carolinas. I hadn't thought of him or his kindness in years, decades possibly. Joe was small and agile and could fit through that opening easily.

We sat in the kitchen, warming up and talking. Sidney said, looking down at the ledger, that the rest of the names in it appeared to be similar to the three Tom had memorized.

She explained her belief that they were all Ashkenazi Jews from Eastern Europe.

"Many emigrated to Western Europe for lots of reasons, you know, with religious persecution being one. The

Ashkenazi Jews peaked in population around the nineteen thirties, comprising about eighty percent of the Jewish population worldwide. These names may very well be of Jews who were once living in Germany, France, the Netherlands. I've got to believe, David, that this ledger is tied to World War II."

"And the Holocaust," Tom added, his long legs stretched out on the linoleum.

Sidney nodded and answered, "Yes, probably. Tom, why don't you tell David what you know about this name." She pointed to Jacob Geller, the very last entry in the ledger.

I shifted in my seat, looked down at the name, and then up again. The overhead kitchen light was too bright, and it was annoying me.

Tommy sat up and cleared his throat. "Why I wanted to find this ledger is because I came across Jacob Geller's name in an article about his family trying to locate their lost art — masterpieces of theirs from the time they were under Nazi occupation. I knew I'd seen his name and Walpole address before. After seeing you at the opening, I eventually realized it was from here, in your barn."

Sidney hesitantly said, "We're wondering if the other people in this ledger share a commonality with Geller. Maybe their valuable personal property was also stolen by the Nazis." She stood up and walked over to the sink. My eyes followed her, trying to figure out where she was going with this. "I wonder if your grandfather had something to do with…well, any of this?"

I didn't know what to say. I took a sip of the strong, black coffee and looked at each of them. I felt blindsided by the question, but the way they both looked back at me seemed earnest and sincere. I sat dumbfounded with the possibility.

Tom asked if I knew much about my grandfather. I was embarrassed but honest and replied, "I wasn't a great kid. I had a big, big chip on my shoulder and felt stuck on the farm. I couldn't wait to leave. I don't think I ever took any interest in my grandfather's past. My grandmother died of a cerebral aneurysm when I was twenty-two. I never really came back until the summer of ninety-nine when he died."

"Oh yeah, let's not forget that summer, otherwise I wouldn't be here," Tom said, smiling.

I glanced at Sidney. She seemed subdued, taking us both in.

Sidney wanted to google the rest of the names and addresses to find out what she could. Both of the kids were respectful, and more than once, Tom said, "Only if you're okay with this."

I didn't know why I wouldn't be. I was just as curious now as they were. The hard-cover ledger was hidden in a place no one would ever have stumbled on. That alone raised a whole lot of questions. And the handwriting appeared to be my grandfather's. I had gone into his office in the old oak desk and found some of his writing to compare. All of us agreed that it was the same, although the handwriting became shaky with the latter names. No dates were noted anywhere. There were, however, several numbers after each name and address. We couldn't tell what they meant.

The kids never went into his office or they would have seen the shelf of his wartime souvenirs; a German Luger, a bayonet, and the insignias and patches torn from a German soldier's uniform.

"Take the ledger, Sidney. See what you can find out." I hesitated, then asked reluctantly, "Could my grandfather have been a Nazi sympathizer, an anti-Semite?"

Sidney and Tom exchanged a glance. My question hung in the early morning air.

It was a good two weeks after finding the ledger when Tom contacted me and said that Sidney had some information and asked if we could meet. They were down in Keene. We met at the Mexican restaurant, Margaritas. I was on my second bottle of beer when they came in. I moved from the bar to a table, and Sidney got right down to business.

"I'm feeling pretty confident that this ledger contains the names and addresses of Jews who lost most everything. And that…" She quickly glanced at Tom. "And that your grandfather may have trafficked in their lost possessions, at least the things that had value."

I sat stunned. I took a swig of my beer and looked around. Finally, I asked her, "How did you arrive at that?"

"When I googled the names, I was able to ascertain that seven out of eighteen of the people listed in the ledger were in some sort of publication stating that they emigrated to the United States sometime between nineteen thirty-three and nineteen forty-four. Three people mentioned that they paid a 'Departure Tax' to Nazi officials. This was actually a bribe, a chance to get travel visas and leave. The payment was in the form of valued art in exchange for their freedom. And they fled, leaving everything they owned. After the war, they were never able to locate the rest of their property. Like others, though, they felt incredibly fortunate to have escaped the gas chambers. They were the lucky ones."

Sidney pulled out three printed articles from the ledger and moved the pages across the table to me. I scanned them slowly, taking in as much as I could.

One of the articles she had copied was from *The Boston Globe*, dated June 17, 1972. It featured a prominent dance instructor named Hannah Berenson. I knew she was one of the names Tom had memorized and written down. There was a picture of her; she was beautiful and svelte, her hair up in an intricate bun. Ms. Berenson was standing against a curtain, in a classic ballet pose. Her dance studio in Cambridge was well regarded. The title of the article read, *"Hannah Berenson Escapes Europe's Nightmare to Create Beauty."* She'd emigrated early but had learned, after the war, that her whole family was killed. Ms. Berenson stated, *"My life before has been erased. Everyone — my parents and sisters — and everything, including my family's religious artifacts, are all gone."*

A second article focused on the Friedman brothers of Fowler Cove, Maine. A large fire had burned down two whole city blocks in the main part of town, and the family was donating a ton of money to rebuild. The Friedmans were prominent business owners of a shoe and handbag factory that specialized in high-end imported Italian leather. As I read, I thought, *I probably owned their shoes at one time.*

The title was, *"The Friedman Brothers Give Us Hope."* It was the feature story on the front page of the *Fowler Sentinel,* dated February 20, 1969. In the article, the brothers described how they had escaped the Nazis by navigating, with guides, secret and dangerous routes over the central Pyrenees into northern Spain in the spring of 1944. They were 20 and 22 years old at the time. A young woman, also escaping the Vichy French, had married the older Friedman brother.

Fowler Cove had been the hometown of yet another man who made the mountainous trek with them — an American airman who had parachuted into occupied territory. His name was Daniel Merritt. All of them recalled the harrowing ordeal of the cold, the danger of the German patrols, their ultimate journey to the States, and then the welcome they received from the people of Fowler as Daniel brought them to his beloved hometown. *"We give back to this community what was so generously given to us nearly a quarter of a century ago; the chance to begin again. The Friedmans have not forgotten,"* Gideon Friedman was quoted saying at the time.

I tapped the last article after quickly glancing at it. It was the one on Jacob Geller. I'd already read it the morning after the kids had left the farmhouse. "These are dated from some time ago. I was still on the farm, yet I have no recollection of anything remotely art related except for my own little bit of watercolors."

Sidney frowned. "Also, David, in combing over the ledger again, I found a key to what the numbers after each name mean. The key was typed on a long, narrow strip of paper wedged up close to the binding, easily missed. Look where it was."

I watched as Sidney turned to the very end of the ledger and then, out loud, counted back six pages. She then counted up eleven lines and bent the book's binding back as far as she possibly dared without damaging it. She pulled out a strip of paper. "See, here it is."

I chimed in, "Six as in six pages from the back and eleven lines up. Did you know that the farm's address is six-eleven Old County Road?"

Tom stood up and asked if I wanted another beer. I declined and focused in on Sidney's reaction.

"That makes sense, then, doesn't it?" She looked down at the strip of paper, handling it carefully. "The key is spelled out here." She read: "Oh-one-nine means 'art retrieved,' two-one-eight means 'at farm,' two-one-nine means 'at Zeke's,' two-two-oh means 'at Hubberd's,' eight-three-one means 'art delivered,' four-two means 'closed,' five-nine means 'open.'

"Now, if you look at the numbers after each name, they all begin with the 'oh-one-nine,' which I think means that the artwork was retrieved from someone or some entity. Then the destination of the work was one of the three places I mentioned. 'Delivered' could frankly mean anything, but might be to the new buyer. And then the transaction was either 'closed,' or still 'open.' Not sure if that meant there were more art pieces coming for this particular buyer. Again, just my own speculation."

I turned the strip of paper so I could see it without picking it up. An old typewriter used to sit on the stand behind my grandfather's desk. It was a Remington. I wondered if he had typed this key out on it.

Tom returned and piped up, "Look, the last three names, the ones I memorized, have the key numbers 'art retrieved' and 'at farm,' but no other numbers down. Does that mean the stuff is still at the farm? Hidden like the ledger?"

Sidney was looking at me, then shrugged her shoulders and said, "I think that could be a possible conclusion." She carefully put the key back in the exact place she had pulled it from. She closed the ledger and placed her hand protectively across it.

I kept quiet about the significance of the numbers. Right off I knew Nana's birthday was January 9th, my mother's birthday was February 18th, and mine, in August, was on the 31st. My mother had been born in 1942 and my birth year was 1959. The connections seemed plausible, but I didn't share any of these thoughts.

I took the last sip of my beer and said, "There's someone who could maybe give us more information. His name is Joe, and he lived in the little house out behind the main house, down by the cherry orchard. I know my grandfather's lawyer has his current address — he's somewhere in Connecticut now. He mentioned that Joe got a little cash from the estate. Why don't I contact the lawyer tomorrow and then call Joe to find a time we could meet?"

"I'd be on board with going with you, David," Tom replied.

Sidney gathered up the articles and the ledger and asked, "Do you mind if I keep these a little longer, see what else might be in there?"

I wanted to reply, "Sure, go ahead. Let's find out even more on my fucking law-abiding hypocrite of a grandfather." But I didn't. Instead, I shook my head and told her that I didn't mind at all. I felt numb as I left the restaurant and wondered what other skeletons were hidden on the Nazi loving, art thief's farm.

Not long after, Joe and I sat in the living room of his granddaughter's house in Darien, Connecticut, where he'd been living for some time.

"I think you saw your grandfather as just a farmer, but, Davy, Alex Sumner was an interesting man," Joe said. "You could call him a man of many secrets, that's for sure. I wanted him to tell you, but he wouldn't."

"Tell me what?" I asked. My voice was low but persistent. I braced myself for the worst.

Just then, Tom came in from parking the car. His size always took me by surprise. "Tom, this is Joe, um — Joe, I don't even know your whole name."

"Why, it's Joseph Malcom Whittenback." The old man sat up straight in the chair as he said this.

"Good to meet you, sir." Tom reached over and shook his hand. The exchange was nice and formal. Joe pointed to the chair opposite me.

I leaned in. "So, here's the thing, Joe. Did you know that my grandfather may have sold stolen art out of his barn?

Maybe, possibly, art stolen during the Nazis occupation? Art that found its way to the States?"

"What are you talking about, Davy?" Joe asked.

I moved closer, bringing my chair within arm's reach of him. "Tom and his girlfriend found a ledger in the milk cellar of the barn. It's got names and addresses of Jewish families living in the Northeast. It's conjecture on our part, but we think my grandfather sold their lost art pieces and family heirlooms to people on the black market. He used his farm to traffic in it." I leaned back and waited for the old man to say something, but he didn't and I pressed on. "And honestly, Joe, I kind of remember some strangers coming and going once in a while. The ledger we found has a list of crossed off names, but a few of them aren't marked. Do you know what any of this means?"

The old man looked out the window and adjusted the afghan covering his legs. Moving the straw closer to his mouth, he took a sip from a water glass. He was small, the dark skin on his hands paper thin, but his eyes were lively when he smiled. It creased his whole face. He was missing a front tooth, but he didn't seem to mind. "That grandfather of yours did traffic in stolen art, you're right about that."

I glanced quickly at Tom. The dread I had felt seeping in for the past few weeks now flooded through me. My years in New York had been all about circumnavigating this dirty, ugly side of the art world. But it'd been right under my nose and in my own family. Tom was leaning forward too, his whole body covering the straight-back chair.

"But you got it all wrong, son, that's for sure. Your grandfather…" Joe hesitated, inhaled, and wet his lips, seeming to like the suspense he was creating. "He was a member of the Ninth Army Group at the front, near the German city of Aachen. He was a driver for Captain Walter Huchthausen. Do you know who that was?"

Tom whistled and responded, "Holy shit, one of the Monuments Men. Sorry, sir, for swearing." Tom's complete focus told me this was significant.

"Here's what you and this big guy need to know. Your papa was there in the Rhineland, aiding in the recovery of artwork looted by the Nazis. He was the captain's driver, once or twice driving George Stout too. Know that name?"

Tom piped up, "Yes, one of the experts in the Monuments Men, in charge of most of Western Europe's recovery. Let's see — that covered France, the Netherlands, Germany, and Austria. They were trying to save art, cultural treasures, and religious artifacts before the Nazis destroyed it all as they retreated."

Joe smiled. "This kid knows his history. The one time Alex wasn't driving Captain Hutch, the captain was killed by enemy fire. Alex never forgave himself. When he got back to the states, he found the captain's family somewhere down in Massachusetts."

Joe leaned back, clearly tired from talking. I waited, not wanting to over-tax him but still not grasping the meaning of the ledger. Tom had his cell out and was texting someone. I was positive it was Sidney.

"I want you to understand this, Davy," Joe said. "Your grandfather was a firsthand witness to all the pillaging the Nazis had done. When he came back here, to civilian life, he settled into the farm. But about a dozen years later, he was contacted by a network of service men and women who worked on this side of the pond. Their goal was to return stolen art to its rightful owners in the US. The network was farmers, bankers, teachers. Hell, to make it work, some were even insurance bigwigs who knew the real score.

"He did steal art from people, you're right, but he stole it from people in the States who bought looted art, some who even knew that the masterpieces they purchased were confiscated from the Jews during Hitler's reign. He didn't steal to make a profit; he stole to get it back to the Jewish families, the rightful heirs."

I stared at Joe before glancing at Tom. The apprehension I'd felt seconds ago wasn't going anywhere. This was all hard to believe.

Joe reached for my hand and gripped it.

"Alex and his wartime buddies knew that rich folks were insuring certain pieces of their art collection with sketchy histories. Whenever they verified art as looted, they'd make a plan to get it back to the farm. Couple of folks in neighboring states — New Hampshire and Maine, I think — also had the balls to hide it. And 'cause the pieces had questionable ownership in the first place, those rich folks didn't even report it stolen. Would've opened up a can of worms for them.

"Other peoples' jobs in the network were to match up the pieces with the Jewish families they belonged to. People who reported the pieces missing or never returned. Then your papa and his service friends would deliver the art once they had a name and an address.

"Like clockwork, on the thirtieth of every June, the guys would meet up at the farm, get their plans made, and, well, I don't exactly know the rest — I wasn't supposed to. I was focused on the cherry season. It's short. Last week of June through July, I was pretty busy. You remember the cherry season, don't you, Davy? We'd drive over to Colton, get 'em weighed? You rode shotgun for years, my right-hand man." He let go of my hand and shifted in his chair.

Tom asked, "Can you give us an idea of how it would happen? How they recovered the art? I mean they didn't hold up people in their houses, did they?"

I quickly looked back at Joe. "I'm having a hard time with all of this, envisioning my grandfather in these clandestine outings…capers…whatever the fuck you call them."

He frowned. "Now, Davy, watch the mouth. I never knew the details, ever. Your nana never did either, at least I don't think so."

Tom and I exchanged bewildered glances. Again, I wondered how all of this could be true. I hoped it was but it seemed too far-fetched. My grandfather had been quiet and unassuming, not a Sean Connery — daring kind of a guy.

Just then, Joe's granddaughter came in. His face lit up and he said to her, "There's my darlin' coming to check on me."

The woman smiled back. "Are these men tiring you out, Granddaddy? We still gonna dance tonight?"

Joe started to laugh and cough at the same time. She quickly reached over and held up his water with the straw.

"You remember my little Latara?" Joe asked after taking a sip. "She came up to the farm a few of those summers. You guys fished and played, even slept out on the porch till the 'skitters got 'cha."

Latara turned to me and said, "Course he doesn't remember me, Granddaddy, we were little, no more than eight and nine." She smiled. Her face was radiant; she looked at least ten years younger than me.

A long-ago memory came of a skinny, agile girl climbing the big silver maple at the end of the driveway with me down below, praying Nana better not be seeing this. Then a flash of her hand, dark against mine, holding on as we raced through the fields, daring the other to fall first, laughing breathlessly.

"You weren't afraid of heights, were you?" I asked, smiling.

"No, Davy, I wasn't. That's for sure. And you, you could run like the wind."

"We're the same age, but wow, you look so much younger," I commented, still smiling.

"Well, you know what they say — moisturizer goes a long way!" she chuckled and left us to talk some more.

After Joe finished another drink of water and settled back into his chair, Tommy asked, "Mr. Whittenback, as far as you know, is there more art still hidden on the farm?"

The old man seemed pensive and then said, "I can't say, but you got some names not checked off, right? I bet Alex planned on delivering their stuff, but then got run over by his John Deere before he could."

We all stood, Tommy taking a hold of Joe's arm. I picked up the afghan and folded it back into his chair. I wanted to tell Joe that he'd restored my vision of my grandfather today but had added qualities I'd never known about him like bravery and justice. But I didn't because Joe and Tommy were already shuffling through to the back of the house. I paused before I followed, thinking what an asshole I'd been for most of my life — thinking I knew everything.

When I joined them, Joe was showing Tom his backyard bird feeders full of chickadees, finches, and a pair of cardinals. The male cardinal was a deep red. We stood and admired his set up. Right before we stepped out of his granddaughter's front door, I asked, "Joe, where did my grandfather hide the stuff? Out in the barn? Behind walls, under the floorboards? Like I said, I never remember seeing any unusual art around."

"My part was just hiding that ledger, Davy, but if I had to speculate, I'd say in plain sight, right under your nose." We walked down the sidewalk to the Jeep.

Suddenly I turned and trotted back up to the old man as he stood on the top step of the outside stairs. He was holding onto the railing. "Hey Joe, thanks for all the time you spent with me. You were kind and I wasn't the easiest kid."

He nodded and gazed out across the street. "You were always pining for your mother to come back." He looked down at me and added, "Nobody could compete with her. God knows, we all tried."

IN THE CAR ON THE WAY HOME, Tom put Sidney on his cell's speaker. I pulled over into a K-Mart parking lot not far from Joe's granddaughter's house so we could talk to her.

"This is a very interesting development, guys. Do you mind if I try and make sense of what Tom texted me?" Sidney asked.

"By all means, Sidney, start," I answered and leaned back in the driver's seat.

"Okay, thanks. I've been thinking about the Monuments Men. It's so cool that your grandfather was a driver during this incredible recovery effort."

Tom quickly piped in, "Unreal!"

I reached up and pulled down the visor. "Believe me, if all this is true, no one would be more relieved than me to learn my grandfather wasn't this horrible human being."

Sidney continued, "There's a bit to digest here, so let's start. The Monuments Men gave all the pieces they recovered back to Germany, Austria, France, depending on where it was found, with the understanding that it all, or as much as possible, would be returned to the Jewish families or their heirs. But it really wasn't until like the mid-nineteen eighties that Europe started to earnestly return the looted art to its rightful, original families. You see, some works were placed in museums instead of given back. I think, in many cases, that was easier than doing all the legwork to find out the true ownership. And, of course, many museums wanted these masterpieces.

"Then in nineteen ninety-eight, The Washington Conference took place. It brought about a renewed effort to learn the provenance — which is the history of ownership, in this case — of questionable art pieces, and it established a public database of all the unclaimed art and the Jewish families who were still waiting for their stolen pieces to be returned." She paused, then asked, "Are you guys still there?"

Tom looked at me and I nodded. A mother with a small child in a shopping cart walked past my side and opened the car door next to us. I watched her unload her shopping bags.

"We're still with you, Sid," Tom replied.

"Good. Then, just last year the Terezin Declaration happened. This brought more countries into the agreement, and now it includes looted art in the hands of public and private collections, meaning museums, municipalities, and wealthy citizens' personal collections. Remember I spoke about a 'Departure Tax?' The Terezin Declaration included art 'sold' for the sole purpose of fleeing the Nazis. You know that the families never received the true value of the art; it was just exchanged for travel visas so they could leave quickly.

"If what Joe says is all true, Alex and his buddies were in a network way before any of these measures occurred. And this network definitely took a more aggressive approach to right the many wrongs done by Hitler's looting."

I interrupted Sid and said, "So these guys, my grandfather and his associates, were following the basic rule of... common decency, I guess. Taking what somebody else has that isn't theirs and returning it to whomever it belonged in the first place."

Sid replied, "Like Robin Hood."

"Hold on," Tom interjected. "A woman's backing out next to us and it's hard to hear you."

The car left and I spoke up, "We're good now."

Sidney picked up right where she had left off. "Here's the thing, guys — I have no doubt there were ample opportunities for Jewish-owned art pieces to make it into the market here in the US. Some of those designated art dealers in Germany held back pieces they were given to sell for the Reich, entering into secret sales no one knew about. Also, there's documentation that Nazi officials stole valuable objects for their own profit instead of shipping them to Hitler's repositories. They then sold these pieces through art dealers who were complicit in the thefts."

Sidney paused, started to say something more, but then stopped.

"What?" Tommy asked. "What else should we know?"

"If I'm going to be very frank, there's evidence that some of our own American soldiers were accused of looting during the liberation."

"Like taking weapons off soldiers?" I asked. I pictured the Luger and bayonet on the shelf in my grandfather's office. I remembered how carefully he handled them whenever I asked to see the 'German stuff.'

"No, taking weapons off enemy combat soldiers generally falls under 'the spoils of war' and has been common practice 'to the victor' since the beginning of well, time. No, some service men also took valuables out of private homes.

"I know I sound like I'm in a lecture hall," she said, "but here's what your biggest takeaway should be: Currently, confiscated art during the Nazi occupation is dealt with through the principles set forth in the Washington Conference. But you still read about art being found and kept hidden from detection or litigation between museums and family heirs when there's a dispute, some cases taking years to settle. And honestly, there's still an overall lackluster effort to get the art back to its rightful owners by many nations. A network like Alex's — well, I understand why they did it."

I chimed in, "I know in my dealings with Sotheby's and Christy's they're vehement about having accurate records for any piece they move. They won't be involved in dubious sales. They have full-time staff whose only purpose is to research the provenance of a piece."

Tommy, trying to suppress a yawn, interjected, "So not everybody's a crook in the art world, eh?"

Sidney voice grew lighter, much less serious. "Good trip, guys! When you get back, we'll look at everything in a new light and decide where to go, especially about the names not checked off in the ledger." She quickly added, "What an incredible grandfather you had, David."

I looked over at Tom as he put his cell in his pocket. "We got a whole lot to think on, don't we? The three hours back will give us time, for sure." I was relieved about what Joe had told us about my grandfather's role, provided it was all true. *Now's the hard part — how we prove it*, I thought.

Tom moved the passenger seat all the way back and replied, "I'm going to catch some shuteye, hope you don't mind."

AS I DROVE OUT OF CONNECTICUT and into Massachusetts, I thought about my grandfather again. *Was he a hero? Did I really believe everything that Joe had told us?* He had been a quiet, reserved man. I remembered him reading to me — the Swiss Family Robinson series and classics like *Where the Red Fern Grows*. When I got into high school and was reading *To Kill a Mockingbird,* he'd declared, "Best book ever written."

I remembered Nana in the kitchen, making a Tunnel of Fudge cake and me calling out, "Extra fudge!" and Papa saying, "Extra fudge, please, Nana." He had been a tall, thin man with stooped shoulders. He'd taught me how to drive standard and was patient as I stopped and started, clutch in, clutch out, bucking up and down the long driveway. I'd bought my own VW bug the summer I turned 16, after making money from working the cherry orchard. Papa and Joe had stood outside the barn as I'd driven down the hill, not sure where I was going for my first solo spin.

He had never been one to draw attention or to start a conversation about himself. A few times he'd told me to quiet down, to stop making myself the center of the world. I had been arrogant to his humility.

Nana was more direct with me and had said a few times, "The girls won't like you, oh they'll want you, but they won't like you." Funny how both of them had me pegged, even way back then.

I thought about Rachel standing outside the rental car the very last time I'd seen her. She'd said she didn't owe me anything more than a 'thank you' for saving Tom. I looked over at him, a big boy, now a young man. He was kind and polite, and he had treated Joe and me with the utmost respect. *I was a prick at his age,* I thought, remembering a few times I'd almost gotten my ass whipped for moving in on someone else's girl.

Joe had mentioned that I was always pining for my mother to come back. That I didn't know what a brave man my grandfather had been. I didn't know shit about him, until today.

Tom Jr.

I slowly woke up. It took a minute for me to remember that I was with David, on the way back from Connecticut.

I straightened up and brought my seat forward. Somewhere in my subconscious there was a thought bubbling up. I took a few moments to let it come to the surface. I shot a look at David driving. We were somewhere on 91 North, not too far from Keene.

Then it came to me and I asked, "Did you ever think saving me wasn't all there was to our connection, our story?" I looked out the passenger side window and then turned back to him. "Like what if it's all meant to be — you leaving New York and keeping the farm, becoming a painter. Me meeting Sidney in a class she's teaching about World War II and stolen art. Then going to your opening by chance, and just a couple of hours ago, finding out that your grandfather could be a key player in all of this?"

David glanced at me, raised his eyebrows, and said, "I haven't thought it all through yet. But I think I see what you're saying."

"And you know, how you feel about my mother?"

He shot me another quick look. "How I feel about your mother?"

"Well, I mean, your opening, those paintings — they're beautiful. But even me, who has no appreciation for art, could see how much you're in love with her…" My voice trailed off. This was awkward. Maybe I shouldn't have said what I just said.

We didn't talk any more until we passed a sign that read *Food, Gas, and Lodging* at the next exit.

"You hungry?" David asked. "Your stomach's been growling ever since we left Darien."

"I could, as they say, eat a horse. You?"

"Sure, I'm always up for something."

As we pulled into the Cracker Barrel parking lot, David remarked, "Tommy, I think I admire your mom for the mother she is, definitely the mother I saw her to be that summer."

We parked and I climbed out of the Jeep and stretched. "I get that, David, about my mother. Now, let's eat and I'll tell you how awesome those Monuments Men were."

As we entered the restaurant, I still believed there were more feelings behind his paintings of her, but I kept silent. I thought about my mom — she was way too young to go through life alone without ever loving someone again. Meeting Sidney and feeling the way I did about her had helped me move on. And even though I still ached for my dad, sometimes so hard it stopped me in my tracks, I was happy. I wanted my mom to be happy again when she was ready.

Rachel

I slammed her door, furious with her for refusing to go out and water the perennials.

"Hey, why don't you slam it again?" Amy yelled out.

I opened the door, glared at her, and then slammed it even harder.

"Oh, that's just great, Mom! I hear the bats in the attic and look…The plaster's cracking above my dresser."

"Good!" I yelled. "Let the whole house fall down!"

I could hear her footsteps coming to the door. Finally, I'd gotten her to move and come to her senses.

She opened it up. "Right now is not a good time for the stupid flowers. Since you're pissed off at me and I'm this close to losing it with you…" She held up both hands, about two inches apart. "Let's stop! I'm on the last chapter of my book and — " Amy grabbed her backpack on the chair and reached in. She held up a second book, *Catching Fire,* in her hand. "This is the next one in the series. I might *never* come out of this room!" She slammed the door in my face.

TWENTY MINUTES LATER, I stood at the end of our driveway next to Meg, fuming.

"She won't come out. Her head is buried in one book after another. I swear she's getting harder and harder to deal with."

Meg reached for my hand and squeezed it. "I heard you two yelling. There's a lot going on with the both of you. It takes time. All the stages of grief, right? But what do I know? Your mother's the expert. She's gone through it and she's been helping out Carolyn for years now."

I looked back at the house, up at Amy's bedroom window.

"Hey, before I forget, how's Tommy? Still with the older woman?" Meg asked.

I looked over at her and smiled. "Is that how we're referring to Sidney? As the older woman?"

"That's how your mother prefaces her." Meg imitated my mother's voice. "'You know, Tommy spent some time down in Wellesley with that older woman, Sidney...' How much older is she, do you know?"

I looked out past the cul-de-sac. We were waiting for my mother to come pick us both up. Tonight, I was actually joining her at her grief group. She helped run it with the same counselor who she'd first started seeing after my father's death, almost thirteen years ago. Mom downplayed her role, telling me she mostly got the snacks ready, made sure to quietly check-in with those who hardly ever shared, and 'facilitated networking between members,' which meant typing up a spreadsheet of names and phone numbers.

Amy had asked me why she had to go to a support group when I still didn't. I didn't know if she even liked her group on Wednesdays — she never spoke about it, but she still went. I couldn't figure out if it was because she liked missing Math once a week or she was actually getting something from it. *Probably a little bit of both*, I thought.

Meg always went to the group with my mother for support and sat in the foyer knitting. Sometimes they'd have dinner at one of their favorite restaurants after.

I answered her question about Sidney, "The 'older woman' is, I believe, six years older."

Meg's mouth dropped open. "That's all? My goodness, I'm practically four years older than Brian. That's nothing!"

Just then my mother arrived. We both started to get in her car, but she quickly unfastened her seatbelt and hopped out. She had a small, brown paper bag in her hands.

"I'm going to run these up to Amy, I'll be right back out!"

I figured it was cookies or her favorite candy bars. I wanted to tell my mother that Amy didn't deserve any treats. She'd been rude to me and wouldn't even come out to water the flowers. Rain was in the forecast, but I wanted her to get out of her room.

When my mother came back to the car, she was breathless. I looked at her. She was going to be 72 in one week. I thought about how well she was aging, how fit she still seemed to be. I couldn't imagine life without her. I wanted her to live to at least 100.

As we pulled away from the house, I said, "You know Amy was just a little shithead to me. She won't even water the perennials and then you swoop in and give her goodies. Really, Mom."

I was sitting in the back seat behind her. I watched Meg glance at my mother.

"Rach, those were tampons in the bag. You bought the wrong kind and she didn't want to tell you. It's just her third time, and, you know, she's figuring it all out. I got her the brand she likes so far."

"Oh…wasn't that nice of Amy?" Meg asked, turning back to face me. "Not wanting to mention that you screwed up to spare your feelings."

I shook my head, annoyed. "No, Meg, that's not it at all. And Mom, you know that too. Right now, she can't stand me. She'd rather inconvenience you than to ask me anything."

I leaned back and looked out the window. Amy was being hurtful. Whether it was on purpose or not, I was hurt. And she'd brought up the question of my own need for counseling by telling me *she* was not the answer to my depression. I'd asked her to explain that and she'd responded with, "Deal with your own feelings before you come after mine." She was 11 years old and had spoken like Dr. Phil. Her words had hit me hard. I guess I shouldn't be the one to complain about her not leaving her room; I hardly ever left the house after coming home from work. We both had no social life.

ONCE WE ARRIVED AND PARKED at the Peddan Community Center, we all walked in. Meg took up her seat in the main entrance area. I gave her a little wave. "Come out if it's not what you want," she said.

My mother reached for my arm and we went further down the hallway. I kept my sweater on; it was drafty in the big old meeting room. Soon my mother was introducing me around and getting things ready. There were two older gentlemen in attendance. For some reason, I was surprised by that. At one point, I watched my mother speak to Carolyn privately. I thought she was probably explaining that I was strictly here on a trial basis and didn't want any kind of attention. I saw Carolyn nod and then turn to someone who was waiting to speak to her.

Glancing around the gathering, I realized that I was definitely an outlier: the average age of this group was more like early 60s. For the most part, everyone appeared to be happy. I watched one of the men, Frank, flirt with two of the women standing next to him. He was unwrapping two loaves of date-nut bread he'd made, and when he came to hand them to my mother, he smiled and shamelessly said, "Susan, you're every bit as beautiful as this youngster beside you." I thought my mother must be cringing inside, but when I glanced at her she was smiling and clearly at ease.

Carolyn began to call everyone to the circle. I watched as they took their seats while still talking, leaning into each other, asking about travel plans, grandkids and other news. I sat down by a lovely woman who patted the seat cushion next to her.

The counselor asked her first question — "Who has used our number one coping strategy this week?" — and the meeting got underway. I watched as most people raised their hand.

"Good, that's good. Our number one strategy, remember, is to give ourselves and others permission to feel those feelings of grief, whether it's sadness or rage. And any other emotions you may be experiencing. Remember to resist the belief that expressing these emotions is wrong, because how we feel is never wrong."

Carolyn nodded to a small, demure-looking woman sitting directly across the circle from me. The woman lowered her hand and said, "I screamed at the moon last Friday night. The neighbor's dogs started to bark and guess what? My screaming turned into howling." Many around the group smiled. One woman brought her hands up to her chest and nodded vigorously.

The second man, whose name I didn't know, spoke next. "I sat down on a crate, in the back of Shaw's near the expired bread stand, and sobbed on Tuesday morning. My Eunice would comb over the week's offerings like she was panning for gold, and now I'm there alone. I cried for about half an hour. A grocery clerk came by and offered to call somebody for me. That got me crying even harder, because there's no one left to call."

Some of the members responded, "You can call me."

"Or me, Eddie."

"Just please, call one of us. We can be there."

It was endearing, and the man smiled. "Okay, I'll get your numbers. I'll call…I promise."

I thought of Amy at school last month when she'd pushed Bella. My first reaction had been to tell her how wrong she was. But hearing this now, I better understood what was happening. She was coping through rage and took it out on Bella whose life was at it should be at her age — smooth sailing and secure. And me, just before leaving the house tonight and slamming the door to Amy's room? I had been furious at her. But it wasn't just about her and the flowers, was it? It was me railing against my whole shitty life without Tom.

Two more people shared their coping strategy experiences of the week before my mother announced it was break time. I looked at the clock. I was surprised that a break had come so soon. The woman next to me leaned over and said, "We like to eat and socialize. It's good for us."

I made my way to the table and picked up a cookie. My mother was speaking to another woman I'd met before at her house. I couldn't remember her name. I came up behind them.

My mother was saying, "I lost my husband, as you know, years ago. I've been feeling — for a while now, that it's time to begin again. Not forget by any means, just time to move on. I think my emotion may be hopeful, even optimistic."

I came to stand beside her. She glanced at me quickly and smiled, then turned her attention back to her friend. I slowly walked away, realizing she hadn't shared any of those thoughts and feelings with me. Why would she? Here I was — doom and gloom, stuck in a depressing, unemotional vacuum. I heard the friend respond in a positive tone of voice. As I walked around the room toward the door to the main lobby, I thought, *I'm stuck…fuck, I'm stuck.*

I went out the door and walked up to Meg. "Am I, are we — Amy and me — holding Mom back? Does she want to get out there, you know, meet a man, have more of a social life? Is she too worried about me to do that?"

Meg moved to see around me and then picked up her knitting yarn and dropped it to the other side of the bench seat. "Sit," she said. I sat down.

"Susan's reconnected with an old friend from school. A man whose wife died some time ago. Your mom and dad palled around with him and his wife back in the day."

I nodded. "That's really great. I'm happy for her. I'll ease up, Amy too, on needing her. She should be free to do anything she wants."

I stood and turned to rejoin the group, but Meg took hold of my hand. "The gentleman lives in Port Saint Lucie, honey. That's in Florida."

I felt this sudden rush and sat back down. I shivered and then swallowed, feeling my throat start to tighten. I pictured my mom under a big palm tree drinking a Bloody Mary. I looked at Meg's concerned face and started to breathe slowly. Having a panic attack here and now was not going to happen. I took another deep breath. It was time for me to learn how to live on my own.

David

The following Saturday morning, the kids came into the kitchen. They'd spent the night before in Joe's little house out behind the barn, further down the orchard lane. The brothers working the orchard had helped me haul away most of the old furniture in it and I'd swept it clean this spring. I'd found sleeping bags and an air mattress for the kids to be somewhat comfortable on. We'd started a fire in the fire pit and Sidney had gone into Bridgewater to pick up a couple of pizzas and a six-pack.

It was fun talking with them, our conversation drifting over into their personal lives. They both liked Keene — Tom had just finished up a degree in Communications and Broadcasting and was now working on campus. Sidney was a lecturer in Modern European and Jewish History and told me one day she hoped to teach full time on the West Coast.

I made sure to stay clear of asking any questions about Rachel. I didn't want Tom to think I was snooping, especially after him mentioning my paintings and how I must feel about her. Actually, I wasn't so sure myself anymore. Sometimes I thought she had become an enigma to me; a woman I once fell in love with a long time ago who now represented the perfect mother in my mind. *Certainly, the mother I never had.* But other times I saw Rachel as the great love of my life and I, like many artists, was channeling my heartbreak of unrequited love into my art. I drifted back and forth between the two theories, trying to figure it out. Then I'd get really pissed at myself for thinking about her at all and stop.

Tom and I spoke a little more about his father's death. It was hard to grasp that a man so big and good to the core could die the way Tom described. I wanted to ask how his mother was handling it, but again I held back.

I promised them a full breakfast before we ransacked the house and barn looking for art pieces. I cracked the eggs, drained the bacon, and buttered the toast. I was sure I'd have enough for the kids to have seconds.

Sidney came up to the kitchen counter and asked, "What can I help you with, David?"

I smiled at her. She was tiny, cute, and something fierce. I could see why Tom was attracted to her. "Oh, I think there's some homemade jelly in the pantry. Lady I knew made it."

Sidney placed a raspberry jelly jar on the table and took the salt and pepper shakers, a hen and rooster, off the ancient electric range. The Formica table was old and chipped. I suddenly remembered my grandmother's tablecloths and said, "Wait, I'll be right back."

I went into her sewing room and moved to the built-in drawers behind the sewing machine. The room hadn't changed in thirty years; my wall art as a kid was still up and the series of watercolors I'd done of the farm were framed and hanging on the wall opposite her machine. She'd told me once that she loved to sit and sew, then take a break and look at my paintings.

I reached in and thumbed through some tablecloths, deciding on which one. As I was leaving the room, I reached for the handle to close the door. *Funny,* I thought, it wasn't actually on the frame; instead the door was leaning up against the wall just inside the sewing room. Odd that in my four years back, I hadn't noticed it.

Breakfast was good, and the coffee was strong. Sidney thought it made sense to divide the house and the barn up and then switch and have a different set of eyes comb over it again. That made perfect sense to me, too.

Tom stood up and said, "Do we even know what we're looking for? I mean, I get that it's going to be something like out of place or the usual isn't quite the usual, but still..."

I looked up at him and then over to Sidney as she was putting dishes in the sink. My mind was churning. Something he just said was trying to find its target in my mind.

"Hey guys, wait. Sit back down, Tom. Sidney, come back over, please. Let me have a minute or two, of just out loud, free-flow talk, okay?"

Sidney said, "Yes, of course."

"Thanks." I reached over and picked up the salt and pepper shakers. I started to move them around on top of the tablecloth.

"The lawyer who handled my grandfather's estate and gave me Joe's current address said that Alex had actually come in three months earlier, before the tractor accident. He said he was there to finally sign his estate documents. Hell, he was eighty-three, and it was about time.

"The lawyer mentioned that my grandfather's biggest concern during this meeting was to make sure that he had enough in savings to keep the heat on in the house, no matter what, and to contact someone at a telephone number he gave him and tell them of his passing.

"I didn't think anything of it, because people in these parts do that — keep the heat going in unoccupied houses so the pipes don't freeze and the floors don't buckle. The lawyer said that Alex was adamant about the heat as well as contacting this person. After the accident, he called that number for several days but never got anyone. It just rang and rang. The heat stayed on, and then I showed up."

Sidney was watching me closely, thinking hard on what I was saying. She got up and moved around the table. "Art has to be stored in a certain range of temperatures or it'll break down. It's best in cool, not freezing, temperatures, in a dark and dry place with low humidity. The Nazis knew this and used different mines and structures across Germany and Austria to store looted art, gold, jewelry, and currency. Is this what you're thinking about, David? That your grandfather's request has something to do with keeping art safe?"

I nodded. "I'm still free-flowing these thoughts, but yes, maybe."

I stood up and walked through to the living room. It was still my studio, still a mess, but I looked down at the floors. "Alex was really concerned, I think, with more than frozen pipes and water damage on these floors. Let's get real, this house needs major repairs."

I looked towards the sewing room and then back to the kids at the table. "I came home sick from school once. I remember Nana in the kitchen putting on soup and me going into her sewing room to get another quilt for the couch. But she stopped me. I told her I was still cold, that I needed a second quilt. She steered me out, away from the room, and said something like, 'No snooping in there. I'll get you the perfect blanket.'

"I had this thing for never wanting anything of my mother's, what she may have had as a little girl living here. I was mad at her for leaving me. 'Make sure,' I'd say. That was the phrase I'd say to both my grandparents about not using anything of hers. That day I said my usual, 'Make sure, Nana,' and she said something like, 'Well, stay out of that room then, David.' That was enough to sour me from wanting anything in there ever again.

"Just now, going in to get a tablecloth, I realized the door to the room was off its hinges. I've never noticed that before."

I smiled, but I was uncomfortable. I'd just shared some of my hang ups from the past, more than I ever intended.

Tom brought me back and said, "If there's no door then no one could accidentally close it, cutting the room off from the heat in the rest of the house."

"Yes." I nodded and looked to Sidney for what to do next. Her eyes were lit up.

"Okay, we start there, in your grandmother's sewing room."

Tom Jr.

S idney said, "It's kind of like those Highlight magazines my father used to get in his office — he probably still does. You know, where you try to find the objects in the picture, hidden in 'plain sight.'"

David quickly looked over at me and smiled. 'Plain sight' had been Joe's phrase. I moved away from them as they stood studying the sewing room. It wasn't big enough for all three of us, so I went back into the kitchen and started to wash the dishes from breakfast.

The window above the sink was open a crack, its screen a little warped along the sill. Looking out, I could see the slope of the yard, the long driveway, and a side of the barn. The farm's setting was beautiful, even if the house needed work.

I finished the dishes and turned to the table, taking in the living room and dining room — David's studio.

I thought about him and my mom again, how they were both single now and it might be nice to get them together. But I could never broach the subject with her, ever. Mom wasn't okay, and it worried me. And because she wasn't okay, Amy wasn't okay either. The cancer took Dad, but all the months — two years actually — leading up to his final days, and the two years since had taken their toll on her. It was like it sucked all her energy out. I thought about how Amy had withdrawn, becoming this hard-to-reach little person. I had been so consumed with Sidney and school and now this that I wasn't sure I was doing enough for either of them. Maybe I needed to visit more, at least.

"Holy shit!" Sidney shouted. She was usually so reserved that it startled the hell out of me. I practically tripped over the paint stuff as I headed for the sewing room.

David

With conflicting emotions, I started to search the sewing room with Sidney. I'd never poked around in here, ever, because, as I told the kids, Nana had implied my mother's things were in here. But behind that, I felt guilt: guilt that I'd never once come back to see my grandmother after I left the University of New Hampshire. She'd dropped dead four years later, blowing any chance I had. *I probably held that against her, too,* I thought, in that 'me, me' brain of mine.

My grandfather had sent me a letter telling me she was gone. He'd had no other way to contact me, since I never even had the decency to give him a phone number for where I could be reached. I'd read the letter in Ashley's loft with the music blasting and about six artist friends chowing down on spaghetti carbonara and Italian bread. We'd already eaten the huge antipasto salad the restaurant had delivered. I'd decided to scoot into Ashley's bedroom to read the letter between dinner courses.

That night I got totally shitfaced and moved in on a girl, kind of cute, who lived down the stairs with an artist buddy of ours. Ashley didn't seem to mind. Both of us couples ended up mixing it up more than once. I tucked the letter away like I did with everything else related to the farm.

NOW, I CLOSED THE BANK OF small drawers that my grandmother had organized, full of bobbins, threads, needles, tape measure, pin cushions, scissors, tailor's chalk, and marking wheels. I watched Sidney get on the floor and scoot under the sewing table, then the cutting table. She crawled back out and glanced at me, shaking her head. There was nothing.

Most of my grandmother's fabrics were neatly folded, stashed in open shelves along one whole wall. Plastic bins were arranged above the fabrics on shelves that reached to the ceiling. These bins contained patterns she'd used, with notes written in her distinct handwriting on almost each one.

I turned to the garment rack used for hanging her heavier fabrics. They were hanging from clip hangers along the pole. I ran my hand along the fabrics and then turned to open the ironing board closet. But something made me turn back to the rack.

Slower this time, I moved each clip hanger with its heavier fabric to the left, feeling both sides of the fabric by running my fingers up and down it. About at the midway point in the rack, I stopped and looked at the fabric. It was weighty and substantial, like the material you'd find in heavy stage curtains from a movie theatre or a performance stage. It was a deep, dark red velour: two clip hangers worth. I ran my fingers down it again, pressing firmly in and feeling a slight edge…of something. I picked up both clip hangers. They were heavy.

"Sidney, come help, please, and grab the good scissors from the bank of drawers."

I placed one of the hangers with the heavy material on the cutting table and felt the edges again. They were more pronounced. "There's something sewn into this material, Sid. I'm going to cut it away."

Sidney quickly moved the arm of a light mounted to the wall over the cutting table. She turned it on.

The sewing scissors weren't as sharp as I'd hoped. I cut slowly into the fabric, making my way down the first clip hanger of dark red fabric. The slit I cut was about 40 centimeters in length. I reached down and in and felt around. I lifted out a corner of a painting in a gilded gold wooden frame. I pulled it further out and laid it carefully on top of the velour fabric.

"Holy shit!" Sid called out. I heard Tommy move in the living room.

I read the artist's signature. It was a Jan Both oil painting. I knew that not too long ago, one of his paintings had sold for around two million dollars. This one was of the countryside, and like with many of his paintings, a golden glow lit up the scenery. There were figures in the upper right corner: men walking with mules. It appeared to be authentic, an original.

"Holy shit," Sidney whispered again, definitely in awe. "Jan Both — wasn't he a Dutch Baroque painter from, um…what century? The eighteenth?"

"The seventeenth actually. Look at the tag, Sid." Like a garage sale item, she picked up the tag dangling from the back wire. It read, '*Deliver to Jacob Geller — 6 Whiting Ave, Walpole, NH.*' We both recognized my grandfather's handwriting. *It's true,* I thought. *All the shit Joe told us was true.* I looked at Sidney and felt a weight lift off of me. *My grandfather — taking risks to follow the rules, to do the decent thing.* I gave Sid a huge smile. I was so relieved I wanted to hug her. Tommy, standing in the doorway, mirrored our excitement.

"Let's do the second hanging fabric, okay?" she asked. I cut again, and this time Sidney felt inside and picked it up and out. Another Jan Both painting, same dimensions, same gilded gold frame. This painting was of a thoroughfare in the countryside. The figures were in the forefront: one man resting against a tree, another man leaning up against a primitive fence. The sky and mountains were bathed in light. It was beautiful and, like the first one, appeared to be legitimate.

Tommy asked, "Do you guys want me to take the two paintings and give you more room?"

We both nodded and said, in unison, "Be careful!"

WITH SLOW AND DETERMINED FOCUS, we found several more 'pieces.' None as impressive as the Both paintings we uncovered first, but still pieces of significance.

Along the windowsill of the sewing room were several items — in particular, a statue of a dachshund holding knickknacks on its long back, and a large vase of dried cattails. Sidney was able to confidently identify one of the boxes on the dog's back as an antique Jewish silver filigree spice box, maybe dating to the mid 1800s. She explained that the spice box was a ritual item that marked the end of Sabbath. In the Jewish tradition, the spice box held wonderful aromatic spices that 'provided comfort' for the return to the workweek.

In the large vase, under the cattails and buried in packing popcorn, was a pair of smaller Chinese blue and white baluster-formed vases with covers. They were decorated with lotus flowers and vines. Sidney googled them and thought they were very old, belonging to the Qing Dynasty.

Hidden behind the iron in the ironing board closet was a copper pitcher worth a good sum of money. It was substantial — hammered and riveted with a silver finish, now worn. "This pitcher could be part of the Shiva tradition where Jews, after returning from the burial of a loved one, would wash their hands outside the home before entering." Sidney was a wealth of information.

She looked at a similar pitcher on the internet; it belonged to the Ottoman Empire, a region of Turkey, where Jews once lived and fled because of persecution.

The very last discovery in the sewing room was a small, ornate silver item found just inside the last plastic box above my grandmother's fabrics, in the farthest corner of the room. We'd missed it the first time we were combing through the bins.

"Look, it's a mezuzah. This is placed outside, on the right side of the doorposts of Jewish homes. It signifies that all in this house are protected under God's watchful eyes." Sidney carefully held it while explaining its purpose.

All of the items had hanging tags like in a second-hand store. The names of Hannah Berenson, Adam and Elisabeth Arenberg, and Jacob Geller dangled there, along with their New England addresses. The names all matched the last three names in the ledger that hadn't been checked off.

I watched Sidney put them on the table in the kitchen. "I think it's imperative we go through the whole house, guys, don't you?"

Tom added, "And the barn and Joe's little house where we stayed last night."

I nodded.

Years and years ago, I stood at the top of the driveway in front of the old barn as my grandfather said, "Davy you need to do the right thing here. Make the call." I gave him a petulant look. I'd backed into a teacher's car at school; the blue paint was on my back right bumper. The old man had zeroed in on it when he'd come in from the barn.

I kept quiet, giving him more of my evil eye, then said, "What will it cost?"

"More than you think; it always does."

I looked at the spot and tried to wipe it off, but it was on there good. I knew I was fucked. Mr. Benton would comb over the parking lot until he found the car, my car, showing a clear mark that it had been me. I shook my head, and said, snotty like, "Well, she shouldn't have parked so close to me, you know."

Just then my grandmother came and walked over to where we stood. She looked at the Beetles' back bumper, the blue paint, and then at Papa and me. "In ten minutes, I'm calling Mr. Benton. David Sumner, you deciding to do the right thing may take forever, me deciding will not." As she walked away, she looked back at my grandfather. He'd given me another chance to prove myself a better kid, and I'd blown it.

WE STOOD IN THE KITCHEN, looking at the art on the table. I didn't mention to Sidney what Tom had found an hour earlier in the closet of my grandparents' bedroom. Tucked between the wool blankets and two feather-filled down pillows was a dark purple diary belonging to my mother. Tom interrupted me as I was going through the sideboard in the dining room. He bent down and said, almost apologetically, "I think this is something you may want to have." I'd quickly dropped it in the junk drawer in the kitchen.

Now, like an archaeologist, Sidney separated the art pieces and the religious objects. She'd made her own cross-referenced list to compare to the ledger: three different names were on the items and everything was marked clearly. We hadn't discovered any new items, even though we'd spent hours at it.

It was Tom who looked up at me and said, "We need to do the right thing here. We need to make the calls."

I thought of the blue paint on my bug, my grandfather's disapproving stare. I looked over at Tom, and in a resounding voice, said, "Yes, we need to make some calls."

Sidney chimed in, "It'll take me a little time to track down phone numbers and what kind of living situations we're dealing with, but that's the wonder of people-search websites like *Spokeo* or using *Google Street View*. What's good is the older generation still very much uses landlines."

We hid the stuff back in the sewing room and decided to meet up again at the end of the month. The kids were excited, and while I was committed to what I'd said about getting it all back to the families, I was growing concerned.

AS I LAID IN BED THAT NIGHT, I wondered if there would be a lot of questions about the pieces, especially surrounding the Both paintings — questions that we couldn't answer. And if we couldn't answer those questions, was suspicion next?

I'd been an art dealer for years. Would people find out and think I was involved in nefarious art transactions all along? Would my reputation be tarnished?

I sat up and turned on the bedside lamp. I had moved into my grandparents' room; their bed was bigger, and the exposure on the east side of the house often gave me beautiful sunrises. It also helped keep my internal clock — early to bed, early to rise — in place. The natural light along the windows in my studio below was the best light to paint in, too. My years in the city had been just the opposite: late to bed, rising at noon, breakfast at 2 p.m.

Who was I kidding? I thought. *My reputation was shit after my hasty departure and even before that.*

But I'd started a new art world of my own out here on the farm. The gallery opening had been successful beyond my expectations. Did I have a chance to re-enter it all and establish a new reputation? This time as a different kind of player, one based on merit, not bullshit and sex? Could getting involved in returning the pieces to their rightful owners jeopardize that?

Much later, I woke up and moved down the upstairs hallway. I went into the bathroom and peed and then cupped a drink of water from the faucet. I hadn't had hard liquor or any drugs beyond an occasional joint in over four years. Dating Annie had been a joy. We'd actually had some good times. I walked back to the bedroom and sat down on the edge of the bed.

Was returning the stuff to the families worth what might come? I lay back down and crossed my arms behind my head. *I've had a lifetime of actions that have been less than admirable, honorable, or honest,* I thought. This move, getting involved with Tom and Sidney and returning the pieces, was maybe me gaining back ground I'd lost. *Wait, I can't gain back what I never had in the first place.*

I turned on my side, bringing my pillow down to my chest. Just before I dozed off, I saw my grandparents standing next to one another, their hands touching. I fell back to sleep.

Rachel

Pat made me a strong Kahlúa and cream, topping it off with club soda. Like a bartender, she cupped the shaker over her shoulder and shook the glass back and forth. Setting it down in front of me she said, "This is called a Smith and Kearns. It's like a milkshake, you'll like it."

I took a sip; she was right.

"Ah, it's very good, thank you." I reached over and grabbed a straw.

We were at her parents' lake house, just outside of Langdon on the first of the three lakes. She'd inherited it like us, but in order for her to be able to pay the taxes on it, she rented it out during the summer months. She and I did the spring cleaning in late May, then closed it down the beginning of each October. But her renters for the month of July had called in a panic. One of their grown children had been in a car accident and they needed to leave. We had come out in the mid-afternoon to clean and ready it for the second half of July and the new people Pat had found to rent it.

Tom and I had ended up selling his parents' little place down from the boat landing for an outrageous sum of money. I still had some of the proceeds in my savings account. Once Tom's cancer spread, he'd told me to stop spending any more of it — which really meant no more treatments. The leftover money made him feel better, knowing it would be there for us when he was gone.

Right before we closed on the sale of the cottage, I'd driven us out to it one last time. The lake was quiet, the couple of shanties out on the thick ice sitting empty. I'd helped Tom walk to the dock. We'd sat for a bit on the bench holding hands. He had been cold, so I'd quickly ran back to the car to fetch a blanket. A flashback of me running to a different car, panicked, with Amy in my arms, had come to me. *Tommy was saved, but you aren't going to be,* I remember thinking at the time, my heart breaking.

We'd passed the Echo Lake Inn on the way home. We'd been married there, at their wishing well, twenty-two years earlier. I'd wondered what wish I'd made back then. I'd glanced at Tom to see if he'd noticed the inn, but his eyes were closed, the blanket still around him.

IT WAS KIND OF A TRADITION for Pat and me to spend the night at her lake house on each end of the rental season. A chance to catch up and relax, even though we saw each other at the Children's Center every week. "Let's do the same tonight, Rach!" she said after we finished cleaning. "We've earned it."

Tommy was home for the weekend with his girlfriend, Sidney. "Have fun with Pat! We'll keep an eye on Amy," he'd said earlier. Amy and I needed a break from each other, even if it was just for one night. I hoped she would be cordial to them and come out from her room at least once.

Now Pat and I sat in front of the big picture window watching the raindrops hit the silver lake — little plops everywhere we looked. It was gray and overcast this late afternoon. The distant mountains were a blur.

"Doesn't feel much like July, does it? And especially after our long winter," Pat said.

I touched her hand. "I know, but things are getting a little better, at least for me."

She knew I had gone to my mother's grief group a few times. I told her I thought it was starting to help.

"It ain't easy girlfriend, is it?" She looked at me with compassion.

I wanted to tell her that Tom's long and difficult passing *was* receding, a little more each day, and that the ache was starting to grow duller. On some days, I could go until I was done with work and opening the kitchen door before I thought of him. This shocked me. He'd been my guy since I was a teenager.

"Honestly, Pat, I feel disloyal when I don't think about him. I can go the whole day — at work, in the store, picking up Amy from camp — before it hits me that he's gone. And then I feel guilty."

Pat stood up and walked behind me to the bar. "I think what's happening, Rach, is that you're in the living world and you're going about living. Tom would want you to move on; he'd be glad to hear this. If you're starting to climb up and out of that dark place you've been in, well, that's a good thing, not a bad thing."

I turned and stretched my arms across the back of the couch. "I think from the moment I heard his diagnosis I went into mourning. Like all our dreams of seeing Tommy and Amy graduate high school, go off to college, get married, start a family of their own, all that stopped in Doctor James's office."

"So..." Pat came back around with a second drink for herself. "So maybe now's the time to start imagining those dreams again, Rachel. They're still there, right? Tommy and Amy are moving along, it's just that Tom can't be with you in the 'living' sense."

I smiled and took a big, straw-slurping last sip of the Smith and Kearns. It was delicious. We'd worked hard today, and Amy and Tommy were spending a little quality time together — I was entitled to a little fun.

Pat read my mood and asked, "Hey, you want to do a shot or two of tequila? Play some Jewel, Dido? I'd add Sarah McLachlan, but she'll make me cry."

Lucy, Pat's 14-year-old golden retriever, had to be put down a week ago. Those Sara McLachlan animal rescue commercials always made us both tear up.

I stood up and said, "Hell yeah! Where's the CD player?"

We sat at the bar once more, and Pat poured us two shots of tequila. *Foolish Games* by Jewel was on and we knew the words by heart, singing them loudly.

Suddenly Pat stopped and exclaimed, "Oh my God, remember David? The guy who saved Tommy? I got so shitfaced the night of your party on tequila that I threw myself at him. Poor guy, some country bumpkin wanting to 'butter his roll,' so to speak!"

I started to laugh, then downed the shot. It burned, and I made a face. "My mother wanted a roll with him, and Meg too…" We both screeched, and I imitated what I remembered one of them saying: "He can park his shoes next to mine any day of the week!"

In front of the window, as the rain came down harder, I felt young, and silly. Jewel's classic *You Were Meant for Me* came on and Pat quickly got up to move the CD to the next song.

"No, don't. This is my favorite one. It's okay, really." I patted the couch cushion next to me and Pat returned.

Holding our drinks, heads touching, we once again belted out the words, knowing them all by heart. When it was over, Pat raised her glass and I followed. "To my sweet Lucy and your dear Tom."

LATER, AS I GATHERED UP our glasses and took them into the little kitchen, I thought about Pat, years ago, on our porch with David Sumner. I pictured his glamorous life in New York — surrounded by gorgeous, young women in opulent settings showcasing the world's most expensive art. I started to fill the sink up with sudsy water. Here I was, in sweats, ready for bed. It was barely 9:00 p.m. and I considered *this* a night out. I sighed and turned off the water. David's life couldn't be any further from mine.

Sidney

"We need a cute kid about nine," I said. "Someone who can win over the front desk person, because we sure didn't. Maybe even cry on cue if they need to."

"My sister could do it, she used to be cute." Tom motioned with his eyes to the back stairs in the kitchen that led up to the second floor.

A couple minutes later, I knocked on Amy's bedroom door. We really hadn't talked since I came back to Langdon this weekend.

"Yeah?"

"Hey Amy, can I come in?" No response. "Amy, it's Sidney. Can we talk?"

"Okay, I suppose," she called out reluctantly.

I walked into a room that was surprisingly void of what you'd associate with an 11-year-old girl. It looked like a room that no one slept in; the walls were almost bare except for a blue dream catcher dangling from the ceiling light above the bed. The bedspread was a plain cream color and there was not one stuffed animal in sight. There were, however, piles of books along one wall, reaching to just below the bank of windows. They looked mostly like Young

Adult fiction but it'd been so long since I was Amy's age, I didn't recognize any at a glance. She watched me as I looked all around.

"Do you mind if I sit down?" I didn't wait for her to answer and crossed her room to sit in the straight-back chair near her dresser.

Amy was stretched out on her bed, headphones on and attached to her iPod. A book lay opened near her. She sat up and brought her feet over the side of the bed. There was a look of annoyance on her face. She said nothing, not trying to hide her displeasure at seeing me.

Her long dark hair was wet. A big bath towel lay in a clump on the bedroom floor. I thought her nose ring must be fake. Who lets their kid get a nose ring at 11? She wore a black tee and black skinny pants. Her eyes were dark, and the black eyeliner she wore was expertly applied. That was impressive.

She was physically small for her age. *That's good*, I thought, and smiled.

"I could never do that, listen to music and read at the same time. You can, uh?"

Amy looked at me and said, "Sometimes I can, other times I can't. But I always keep them on."

I nodded. "Your brother and I could use you for something. It involves a little play acting."

She stood up and walked to her dresser, pulling off her headphones and placing the iPod on top of it. "Oh no, definitely no way. I'm not doing anything like that. I can't even raise my hand in class. I hate attention."

"Um, this isn't like that. Can I tell you what we need you for, then you can decide? But here's the deal: you can't tell anyone, not even your mother, about this. Absolutely no one, got it?"

I thought I saw a spark of interest, but Amy covered it up quickly with a look of indifference. I waited.

"I'm listening," she replied and sat back down on her bed.

I began to tell her what my graduate thesis was about: the stolen art pieces during World War II, and how Hitler wanted a 'Fuhrer Museum' planned for a place called Linz, in Austria. That there were over a thousand places in Germany and Austria filled with the looted property. How it was a real disgrace that the family heirlooms of the Jews had been seized and that, even when the Axis lost and the Allies recovered the art, some people still bought the art, knowing it wasn't right. That this was still going on in the art world right now in the US and other countries despite worldwide recognition that the art should be returned to the rightful heirs. She was looking straight at me, but I couldn't tell what she was thinking.

I went on to explain, "Now here's a strange coincidence. Really, Amy, this has to stay quiet. I need you to know that Tom and I haven't shared this with anyone."

I leaned towards her. "We are in possession of some of that stolen art and family religious heirlooms, and we have a chance to return them to their rightful owners — the people it was stolen from.

"Here's where you come in. We need a girl to play, well, possibly a younger girl than you are now, in order to return a religious object to Hannah Berenson at the Sunrise Terrace Nursing Home in Greenwich, Connecticut. We need you to pretend that you're her granddaughter bringing her a plant or a cake, whatever. We still have to figure that out. But you'll really be bringing her something of her family's that was taken from them a long, long time ago. The play acting has got to be as genuine as possible because you may have to cry if they tell you, 'No, you can't see your grandmother.' We tried to talk to someone on the phone, then went there in person, but we bombed — they wouldn't let us in to see her." I waited for her reaction.

"I'd have to be her great-granddaughter for it to be realistic," Amy replied, looking over at her dresser. "And we have Girl Scout cookies frozen in our big freezer. I think I still have my uniform."

She got up and grabbed the headphones again. She was dismissing me. I stood and looked at her. "Great! We'll get our act together on our end and let you know when we're heading to Connecticut. And thanks, Amy, really."

"No problem," she said, lying back down on her bed, shifting her body away from me, and reaching for the book again.

Amy

Sidney left my room. She had no idea that we read *Number the Stars* in Mrs. Allen's class last fall and the play, *The Diary of Anne Frank,* right before April break. Not long ago, when I spent a night at Grammie's, we'd started to watch an old movie called *Schindler's List*. But we both agreed it was too graphic and sad. Right now, Ms. Winter had *The Devil's Arithmetic* on hold for me at the public library.

I knew all about the Holocaust but not anything about the stolen art stuff. Ms. Winter could help me out with that.

When Sidney asked me if I could cry, like, on demand, I wanted to tell her, "I've been crying this whole life of mine."

Ellie and the rest of the older girls had moved on to the high school and hadn't gone to the library hardly at all this spring. I missed them; it had been boring in school, after school, and especially now that summer had started. I had no friends. Mom suggested I call Bella to see if she'd want to spend some time with me. I told her what a colossally dumb idea that was. Bella and I didn't have much in common now, and besides, I knew she didn't like me anymore. Who could blame her? I'd pushed her and broken her statue.

I got up off the bed and started to open the drawers to my dresser. I knew my old uniform was in one of them.

You almost done?" I asked Sidney. She was braiding my hair into two braids, reaching down to the middle of my back. The nose ring and eyeliner were in the top drawer of my dresser at home. I'd trimmed off the blue ends of my hair. I also let out the hem of my skirt on my Girl Scout uniform. While I was still short, I *had* grown a little bit since fourth grade.

"Yes, almost. Are two little bows over kill?" Sidney asked.

"Depends, what color are they?"

"White, it's all I had."

"That's okay."

I got out of her car and waved quickly to her and Tommy. I adjusted my sash and looked down at my shoes. My feet had grown too, and my shoes hurt.

We'd found the nursing home in Greenwich easily enough since it was their second time here. They were going to stay parked around the circle, waiting for me to return. I carried a brown bag — a sturdy Shaw's one — with four boxes of Girl Scout cookies in it. The third box down, the sugar ones, held the mezuzah. It was sterling silver and very ornate. I was told by Sidney that it belonged on the door of a Jewish home, even sometimes on all the doors inside too.

Sidney thought this mezuzah was dated sometime between 1850 and 1900. She said it was to remind the Jewish family members of God and their heritage. That it was a symbol of God's care and protection.

The nursing home was a sprawling tan brick building, all one level with white marble floors and dark mahogany walls, at least in this front part. When I entered the double doors, chimes went off. I stopped just inside, and the doors automatically closed behind me. Big blue urns with plants were spread out between floral couches and matching chairs. I thought it looked more like an expensive hotel in a movie than a nursing home.

A woman sat behind a big receptionist's desk, in a leather chair that swiveled. I thought Ms. Winter, at the library, would love a chair like that. Blazoned across the front of the desk was a rising sun, with *Sunrise Terrace* written below it in fancy letters. This woman didn't look that old, maybe my mother's age. Her name tag read 'Judith Nudy.' I wondered if she ever got teased for being 'Judy Nudy' as a kid in middle school. Or maybe she married Mr. Nudy and then became Mrs. Judy Nudy.

I was prepared to be a pain in the ass. I figured I'd keep talking and talking until she couldn't wait to be rid of me. Then if that didn't work, I'd turn on the water works.

She started smiling at me as I made my way across the marble floor. That was good.

"Hello, I'm Hannah Berenson's great-granddaughter and I'm here to bring her this year's cookies." I held up my bag, reached in, and took out a box.

"Well, good morning young lady." Judith Nudy was a smiler. "Did someone call to let us know so we could ask Ms. Berenson if a visitor was all right today?"

I screwed up my face in contemplation and answered, "I'm with my father this week. He might not know the rules. My great nana is on my mother's side. My cookies came early. I'm sure my mother *would* have called if it was her week."

"Where's your father right now? He should be accompanying you." Mrs. Nudy looked toward the door, scanning the circle.

I thought, *it's time.* I took a deep breath and let it rip.

"Oh no, that wouldn't be a good idea. My father is in the car yelling at his financial advisor. Then he's gonna call his friend and place a very, very big bet. But hey, I'm here to see my great-grandmother. It's a joy that she's with us for yet another year, isn't it? In fact, I can't think of another thing, besides my grandmother's clean bill of health, that makes my mother so happy, can you? And isn't this weather just something? I still got all my softball games in; my coach says it's very unusual for a whole season to go by without one canceled game. Do you have kids, and if so, what are their names? I bet you have one my age who's just finishing up the fourth grade and boy we had a lot of word problems in math this year — having to decide what operation to choose. 'Is' means equal, and 'of' means times, 'decreased by' is subtraction. It's confusing, you know? My teacher, Mr. Chase, never got a handle on a good seating chart for our class. At first, he let me and Olivia and Bella sit in a group, then he had to move us 'cause, well, we talked too much. His next arrangement didn't work out so good, either. Riley and Ryan got into fights, stopping the whole class more than a couple of times. So, can I see my great-grandmother and bring her the cookies she ordered?"

Mrs. Nudy, no longer smiling, looked confused and replied, "Yes, please, head right down. I'll sign you in."

I smiled and took a big breath — ready to go again. "Now, it's been a little while since I've been here, you know, with all the year-end stuff going on, concerts plus ball games, and now we're in the full swing of summer camps. Oh boy, lots to choose from, I never know if I should pick something like pottery or swim, depending on..."

Mrs. Nudy interrupted me and said, "You need her room number?"

"Ah, just what I was gonna ask, funny how…"

She cut me off, "It's Room one-thirty-two, down this hallway on the left."

I smiled, even bowed my head and said, ever so sweetly, "Well, aren't you nice, Mrs. Nudy! I'll make sure to tell my great nanny that." I scooted down the hallway, stopping just long enough to take a long sip of water from the water fountain. My mouth was dry.

The hallway looked more like a nursing home. I visited the one in Langdon every year, singing in the school's choir. There was the smell of antiseptic, like in Daddy's room at home after the visiting nurse came. A man passed me going down toward the receptionist's desk. I was prepared to smile, but he didn't bother to look my way. That was rude, but good too.

Room 132 was further down the hallway than I wanted it to be. Finally, I stood in the doorway of the room. I could see the back of a woman's head as she sat in a chair. She was facing the front of the building, overlooking the yard. I could see Sidney's white Toyota in the circle, waiting.

It was very quiet and I didn't want to scare her. I knocked on the side of the door frame and walked in. She turned to me as I walked up behind her chair and then around it. She was old, like probably the oldest person I'd ever seen up close and in person. Her hair was silver and long, with sections of it parted so I could see her scalp. Her face was small, and her eyes looked milky. Then she smiled at me, and it made her face not so old anymore.

"Hi Mrs. Berenson. I brought you some Girl Scout cookies and, well, something you had a long time ago." There was a small table on wheels that moved. It was already positioned near her with a drink and a straw in it.

"Do you mind if I move this, your drink, just for a minute?" I held it up but she didn't answer so I moved it to the dresser. I thought that was okay.

I got right in front of her, bent down, and said again, "I've got cookies and something else for you, okay?"

She wasn't smiling anymore and replied, "I'm not deaf child, blind — yes. I can hear you perfectly. And I'm not a missus, I never married."

I nodded, reached into the bag, and started pulling out the cookies. As I piled the boxes on top of one another on the table, I announced, in a much lower voice, "There's Thin Mints, Tagalongs, and my personal favorite, Samoas." I kept the sugar ones, the Do-si-dos, in my hand.

"Mrs. Berenson, I mean Ms. Berenson, I'm going to hand you something now that was taken from your home a long time ago. We wanted to make sure you got it back. Could you hold out your hands, please?"

She seemed to hesitate, but then did as I asked. Mr. Sumner had packed it carefully inside the cookie box. I unwrapped the cloth and placed the mezuzah case in her hand. I watched her run her fingers over it once, and then for a second time. Her eyes were vacant, but her voice held disbelief as she said, "Child, this is my family's mezuzah. I'd know it anywhere. I touched it every day as I went through our door. How, how did you get it?"

"I'm not sure, Ms. Berenson, but we wanted to make sure it got returned to you."

Suddenly, she reached over and grabbed my arm at my wrist and held on. Startled, I looked at her. But who I saw was not this old woman; instead, I saw a girl with long dark hair, head held back and laughing. She was wearing a yellow star on a gray wool coat. Then, like a wave, I felt a profound sense of fear and sadness wash over me.

"Is it you, little sister? Come closer, let me touch your face."

Just then a very large woman with a black beehive hairdo came into the room, her white uniform stretched to its limits. "Ms. Berenson doesn't have ANY grandchildren, let alone a great-granddaughter." She didn't look pleased, in fact she looked really pissed. "What are you doing?" she asked me harshly.

I panicked and abruptly pulled away from Ms. Berenson, scooting quickly past Sasquatch and then out the door. I heard her yell, "Stop that Brownie!"

I turned back and yelled, even louder, "It's a Girl Scout uniform, anybody can see that!"

I saw an exit sign and pushed open the door. An alarm immediately sounded. I was outside, on the side of the building facing the main road. I ran around to the front and saw Sidney's car start to move. Just as I started to sprint for it, I tripped on a sprinkler head and fell, my shin stinging. I got up.

Suddenly, a series of sprinklers went off and I criss-crossed through them, trying to avoid a total soaking. I reached the rear passenger's side door, opened it, and yelled, "Go, Bigfoot is coming!"

Tommy stepped on it, and we sailed out onto the street as Sidney called out, "Did you get it to her, Amy? Did you?"

I nodded and gave her a thumbs up. I was drenched, my feet were sore from the too small shoes, and my sash was in disarray. I looked down at my wrist. I could see a red mark forming where Hannah Berenson had grabbed me. I closed my eyes. I wanted more of the dark-haired girl but nothing came. The feelings were gone too, though that was a good thing.

I wondered if touching something from your past could be as powerful as seeing something from your past. *I think it could be.* And what about smell? Mom had cried over Dad's sweatshirt. It had been powerful for her and sad for me to see her like that. I tried to make the 'popping' noise like Ellie did when she'd tell me to write using all my senses. More than anything, I hoped the mezuzah would protect Ms. Berenson from here on out.

Emily

I watched David listen as Dick Rickert told him and the potential backers, a very wealthy-looking middle- aged couple from Slovakia, how he could catapult David's career and make his own gallery top tier at the same time. I would not characterize David's expression as excited or even interested. He appeared disengaged, bordering on rude. I tried to get his attention, to remind him that there was a lot riding on this meeting. Tapping my pen didn't do it, so I abruptly said, "Excuse me, I need to speak to David privately. How about a ten-minute break?"

Dick Rickert looked relieved. He too had noticed David's lack of enthusiasm. We walked down the hall, to a small sitting area overlooking the harbor. It was pretty, with blue skies and the bay full of boats. The meeting spot we were using in Stamford was attractive even though it had clearly been hit by the recession; two of its spacious offices along this side were dark, definitely unoccupied.

"David, these investors have come out here from the city because you wouldn't go to them. Dick wants to represent you and they're willing to put up the money to get prime space in Chelsea for your work. This isn't a normal thing, you know this. Dealers, with new promising artists, are chomping at the bit to pitch to them. Two years ago, the art world crashed, got tossed on its head just like everything else did in the recession. No one is moving much, but you, you have a chance here."

I didn't dare tell him I suspected the couple was looking to launder money and that Dick's proposal was just what they had in mind. I knew David was no dummy and may have already suspected this too.

He stood up and put his hands in his pocket. He looked out over the bay. It struck me that in the four years we weren't in contact, he had changed. Older for sure, but he was also calmer, more at peace.

"I don't want any of this, Em. Big, dirty money sucks, you know?" He paused, then continued, "Hell, I'd be out on my ass if I'd stayed. I couldn't have survived this downturn, except for putting myself out there to the usual patrons."

He sat back down. Looking at me intently, he spoke slowly. "Those patrons — who you know I screwed literally and a few too many times — couldn't hold me up now financially anyway." He sat back in his chair. "If I'm going to be honest, that's what I was doing in the best of times: screwing everybody."

I reached out and touched his knee. "David, don't be so hard on yourself. You never did anything illegal or bought and sold them anything they didn't want."

He crossed his legs and ran his fingers through his graying hair. He'd cleaned himself up a bit since the first visit to the farm. He smiled at me.

"I painted my way up and out of the black hole I was in. It makes no sense for me to climb right back down into it, does it? My paintings — I don't think I could sell even one of them, Emily. Not one. They mean too much to me. They'll stay at the farm."

I sighed. "Then why, David, did I even set up this meeting out here in the first place?"

"I'm sorry. I think I got caught up in the opening, how well the paintings were received, and me at the center of all that attention. I didn't know how I really felt until now, listening in there. I appreciate all you've done, really. But I'm okay. This isn't what I want."

He glanced at me and continued talking. "I think I'd like to do a series of paintings on mothers and their children as I find them out in the real world. Like I did with Rachel — a bit of Americana. I have a friend who owns a small gallery in the ski town south of Plymouth. I think I'd like to head in that direction."

"But that doesn't necessarily pay the rent, does it?" I shifted in my seat and added, "We can wait for Dick to find backers who are known to us — you know, transparent and respected. It may take some time, some more rebound in the financial markets first."

"Listen, Em…The farm's paid for. The taxes are about eight grand a year and the utilities maybe another two thousand. I've got money saved. I did get a call from a stockbroker down in Boston, wondering if I'd do a portrait of his daughter and two grandsons. Who knows, maybe I'll do portraits on the side. Could help out, money wise."

I contemplated what he'd just said for a minute before responding, "I should be upset or mad at you, but I'm not."

He reached over and touched my hand. "You've been a good, honest friend for many years. I'll make sure you're compensated for all this time you've spent on me."

We both stood up. "Will you let them know?" He motioned to the conference room. "I've got some kids I'm having lunch with."

"Yes, I'll let them know." I hesitated, unsure how to say what I wanted to say.

"What is it?" he asked.

"I'm pregnant. It's very early — just a couple of weeks, and a lot can happen. Jimmy and I aren't telling anyone yet, at least not for a while. It was your paintings, David, that helped change my mind about having a baby. You made me see that it's our journey…not our ending that defines our lives."

He reached over and pulled me to him. We hugged, and as we moved apart, he smiled and said, "Congratulations. You'll be a terrific mother." He turned toward the elevators.

Without planning to, I called out, "You loved her. I see that now."

He stopped walking for just a moment. I thought he was going to turn back around and say something, but he didn't. He continued down the hall between offices. He reminded me of Don Draper in *Mad Men*, my new favorite show. If David was of that era, the 1950s, and was wearing a hat, I could see him tipping it to every woman he passed as they all looked up and smiled at him.

I turned to go back to the New York people.

Amy

He was nice, quiet-like. I liked that. It gave me more time to think about what had happened earlier between Ms. Berenson and me. We sat at a picnic table across from one another as we waited for Tom and Sid.

I saw that his cell was right near me, next to the salt and pepper shakers. I wondered if I should call Mom to make sure she'd read my note. I was supposed to go to the dumb summer camp Science Fair today at 4:00, but I hadn't told her I'd already withdrawn my entry in the fair. My report and poster on buoyancy sucked anyway.

"Hey, Mr. Sumner, is there any chance I could use your cell to call my mom? It won't be long, just a quick check-in."

He picked it up and handed it to me, "Only if you call me David."

I nodded and moved just off the landing from where our table was. I turned my back to him and dialed. I moved even further away so I wasn't blocking his view of the harbor.

Mom picked up right away. "Hello?"

I realized she didn't know this number, probably thought it was a telemarketer. "Mom, don't hang up! It's me!"

"I got your note, but where are you exactly, Amy? And whose phone is this? It came up as Stamford, Connecticut." I glanced back at David. He gave me a little wave. I kind of waved back.

"I'm with Tommy and Sid like my note said. I don't know our exact location but we're on the water and it's real pretty. I forgot to mention — I pulled my entry from the fair. I don't like the camp at all, but I'll finish it, I promise." I said this in the nicest tone of voice I'd used with her in a long time. The change made a difference — she didn't even sound mad about the fair.

"Oh, I didn't know you'd dropped out, and your project didn't suck. Sidney told me last night she had something to do down in Connecticut. Isn't it a long drive for you just to tag along?"

"It's not so bad. Listen I got to go, we're eating seafood. Then we're heading home. If you call Tommy right now, he can tell you our exact location. Bye." I hung up and walked back to the table and sat down. I slid the phone over to Mr. Sumner and said, "Thanks."

We both settled in again, waiting for our seafood.

He finally broke the silence and said, "I thought you'd be like five six, five seven, but you're actually quite small, aren't you?"

"The scout's uniform makes me look younger, you know. But yeah, I am small. I haven't had my growth spurt yet." I felt my skirt; it was finally all dry.

"I remember you as a baby; you were pretty big. I just assumed that big babies grow into big people."

"Well, I'm only eleven — closer to twelve, so there's still hope." I swung my bare feet back and forth under the table. It felt good to kick off those shoes.

After the delivery to Ms. Berenson, we'd arranged to meet David in Stamford for lunch on the water. He was doing painting stuff, meetings nearby with some important people from New York. Sidney said he had painted us, me. I just knew somehow that it was the thing that got the ball rolling on what we were doing today.

"I'm sorry if I offended you by saying that." He smiled at me.

"Nah, it's okay. I'm used to being short."

"So, it went pretty smoothly today? With Hannah Berenson?" he asked.

"Yes," I said, then shifted on the bench towards him. "Can I ask you a question?"

He smiled. "Sure."

"Do you believe in reincarnation?"

He shook his head, bewildered-like. "Of all the things I imagined you were going to ask me, that was never, ever going to be one of them."

I stayed serious and he looked at me, now growing serious too. "I don't know. I've never given it any thought," he replied.

"When Ms. Berenson touched me, I saw and felt something. It was like a current ran from her to me. It was really powerful and lasted just a second."

He stared at me and then slowly said, "I don't know what to say."

I knew right then that he was a good guy, for real. He wasn't going to treat me like a baby or downplay what I'd just shared. I understood why Tom and Sid liked him.

Encouraged, I said, "I've been reading that we're all reincarnated to different time periods, but many times we're with the same group of people. We can be in different roles, but we're all together again. And in each of these lives, we're supposed to learn a valuable lesson. Then we die, get reincarnated again in a different body and a different time with a whole different life, and we meet again. We keep going and going until we've learned all the lessons we're supposed to."

David didn't say anything, but he didn't look annoyed or uncomfortable. He crossed his legs and seemed thoughtful.

"I think I've been with my parents before," I said, "and I think I'll be with them again. Maybe not as their daughter, but as someone close to them."

"That must make you feel good," he replied. He picked up the salt and pepper shakers on the picnic table and started to move them around.

"I didn't know my mom beyond the age of seven," he said. "She was seventeen when she had me. Never said who my father was. She abandoned me, at the farm. Took off and never came back. My grandparents brought me up."

I raised my eyebrows and in a kind of surprised voice said, "Wow, seventeen. That's only like six years older than me now. I can't imagine having a baby." I paused. "Sounds to me like she didn't quite abandon you, you know, since she left you with good people." I added in a confidential tone, "You'll meet up with her again."

David looked at me strangely but made no comment.

Just then Tom and Sid came out, carrying two big trays of fresh seafood. Sid gave David his credit card and thanked him, and they sat down to join us. David looked over at me just as I was picking up my lobster roll.

"Humility's mine," he said as he patted his chest.

"Ah…that's a good lesson, for sure," I replied back.

Rachel

His face was dirty and his hair was matted. I looked over at Kaitlyn and said, "I'm taking Isaac to the bathroom — we may be a minute or two."

Kaitlyn gave me a nod and started circle time with, "Today is Thursday, July eighteenth, and it's warm outside. Let's all make pretend little fans with our hands. Later today we'll make our own real fans."

Isaac walked slowly, looking back at the circle. He was always present and engaged, no matter what we did. Kaitlyn said it best: "It's like whenever he's in school, he's soaking us all up and in."

In the bathroom, I washed his face, first making a big heart around his hairline, down around his ears and past his chin. Then I started an inner heart, taking in his eyebrows, and looping around his mouth. The third heart was over his eyes and down his nose. Isaac liked this ritual of ours, jutting his face out to me, enjoying the feel of the warm washcloth and the smell of soap. I quickly rinsed his face.

His hair wasn't as bad as I first thought. I combed it quickly, looking for any nits. Not seeing any, I smiled and hugged him, exclaiming, "Isaac, you're all ready for school now!" He returned the hug, giving me my first sweet moment of the day. Teaching preschool was full of moments and feelings. Our Isaac was a giver.

At my break, I ran to the bank. Amy was going to Boston with Tommy and Sidney in two days. I think their time to Stamford and back had been good for her. She was getting out of the house more, not holed up in her room with her head in a book. I wanted to give her enough spending money to get what she wanted. She hardly ever asked me for anything these days. I also had an alumni committee meeting at a restaurant later and needed cash for dinner.

SOMETIMES AT NIGHT, as we watched television or read our own books in our separate bedrooms, I'd try to engage Amy. I'd encourage her to come down the hallway to my room to curl up and read with me or to sit in the den to watch a show that looked promising. Standing at her door, I'd begin, "Remember when Daddy…" and it'd be a memory of something simple, like how he would lick all of our ice cream cones up when they were melting or throw the softball up off of the roof for her to catch. Then I'd suggest we hang together, but she'd usually declined and I'd give up. *How does that void of no father and no desire to be with her mother ever change?* I wondered.

"I think the void of no father is, unfortunately, permanent," my mother had replied sadly after I'd asked her the same question. "But she'll find her way back to you, Rach — I know it."

When I came back from the bank, Isaac and two other little boys were playing under the awning in the sandbox. I walked by and he looked up at me and said, "Miss Rachel, I think you gots to take Sammy in to do the heart wash, okay?"

I looked at Sammy; he wasn't dirty, or at least not dirtier than any of the other children at playtime. Isaac seemed to understand my thoughts because he said, "Sammy's sad about his grandma, and a heart wash would make him feel better."

Sammy's grandmother had died recently, and she'd been a big part of his life. He'd spent many nights at her home, and she'd often bring him to preschool.

I looked at the little redheaded boy with a layer of sunscreen on and said, "Sammy, do you want to come into the classroom and have a little time by yourself? That's okay if you do."

He stood up and followed me while Isaac and the other boy went back to playing.

As we went into the classroom, I thought, *"We're all missing somebody."*

Sammy climbed onto my lap and I began to share the humongous chocolate chip cookie I'd bought at the Co-op with him. I held him to me and hoped his big gap of infinite loss would grow a little smaller with each passing day. I hoped that for my own children as well.

I didn't want to believe Pat had done this deliberately, but I wasn't so sure. John sat across from me, appearing to be equally embarrassed. I glanced at him and smiled. He returned my smile.

"Rachel, I'm really sorry. I thought you and about six other classmates were going to be here, you know? Pat said this was Class of Eighty-One planning committee. She mentioned you and Tina, Jackie, Paul, and Leo. Maybe a couple of others."

"Same for me." I looked at the line of people at the door and then back at John. "Actually, I do think she did this on purpose, and I'll tell you why. A few weekends ago we cleaned her cottage and we, um, you know, got drinking and I mentioned I was starting to 'live life again' or something like that after Tom's death. You've been divorced for a little bit, and Pat's a schemer. I'm going to kill her."

Just then the server came by and asked if we were ready to order. John shrugged and said quietly, "Please, please don't think I'm anything other than hungry, Rachel. I'm ordering. I drove down from a work meeting in Burlington and I ate a very light lunch. Plus, I've got nothing at my place. Stay or go. I'll take no offense if you leave."

I nodded. "Okay, if you're staying, I'm staying." We ordered our dinners and when the waitress left, I said to John, "I remember you were always the most level-headed guy in our group, weren't you? Like the time we all went to the movie theatre down in Peddan to see *Arthur* when it first came out and we were too loud and got yelled at. You stood up and moved to the other section to sit, telling me, 'I paid, I'm watching the movie.' I was impressed."

Our drinks arrived and we settled in, reminiscing. The years since high school had been good to him and I told him so.

He responded by running his hand through his hair. "At least I've kept my hair, haven't I? You look good too, Rachel. I know it must have been terribly hard with Tom's cancer and his passing."

Soon our dinners came and our talk turned even more personal. I ventured into his marriage ending; he asked me about Tom's final days. His two girls were Tommy's age and just out of college. His ex-wife, a girl from a class a few years after ours, was a nurse in Amy's Pediatric Care Office. I always enjoyed seeing her. Their divorce had been amicable, or as John clarified, "As amicable as a divorce can be, I guess."

It was nice and natural, and I enjoyed catching up. When the bill arrived, I said quickly, "We're splitting it John, if not, I'll take offense."

"Agreed, Rachel." He chuckled.

Just as we were going out the door, my cell rang. "Where the hell are you?" It was Pat. I motioned to John and put it on speaker.

"What do you mean?" I asked her. John leaned in to hear.

"We're at Josie's on Main and having a mighty fine time — right guys?" Pat must have held the phone out because I heard people yelling my name.

"Wait, you said the Italian place in Woodstock, Pat. I'm sure of it."

"No, Rachel, sorry, I didn't."

I started to say, "Then why is John here?" but she quickly hung up.

John was shaking his head as he started to walk to his car. I was parked two spots away. He called out, "This was nice. I didn't mind it so much, hope you didn't either."

But I was totally distracted. I had just seen a man who looked exactly like David Sumner walk past us with a bag of to-go food. I could have reached out and touched him, he was that close. He wasn't as polished as I remembered: his hair had bits of gray and was longer, curling up over his ears. He wore faded blue jeans and his shirt was untucked with the sleeves rolled up. He was still handsome but different. I stood on my tippy toes to see beyond the cab of a truck blocking my line of vision. I watched him get into a silver Jeep with Vermont plates. I wondered what he was doing back in Vermont.

Just then John drove past me and waved. I smiled and waved back, but I was bummed. I'd missed the direction the Jeep had turned once it left the parking lot. I got into my car and sat, thinking about Pat's plan to set me up tonight. I had absolutely no interest in starting something with John — none. Mostly, though, I sat and wondered about seeing David so randomly like that, just minutes ago.

If he had seen me, would the two of us have stopped and talked? *Would he have even wanted to?* I started the car and pulled out, heading back to Langdon.

BY THE TIME I REACHED HOME, doubt was setting in and I wasn't so sure it had been David. He'd been adamant about selling his grandparents' place and with land like that, I was certain it would have sold fast. Besides, he loved the city. *This is definitely not the city,* I thought as I drove around the cul-de-sac and into our driveway. Walking up to the porch, the only sound I heard was the beep from my key chain as I locked the car. The moonlight was muted by clouds, and I couldn't see any stars. A few lights were on in the neighboring houses and, of course, in Amy's bedroom window above me.

Minutes later I said goodnight to her. She looked up from her book.

"How was dinner at Meg's?" I asked.

"She made tacos — big ones. Brian ate three. Then we watched reruns of *Mad About You*. It's Meg's favorite show."

I nodded and started to close her door.

"You would like it, I think. Helen Hunt is good." Amy turned back to her book.

Well, that's something, I thought. She'd actually strung more than two sentences together on my behalf. I went back downstairs to lock up the house. When I passed the kitchen phone, I decided to give Pat a quick call. I wanted to let her know that I was on to her and that I might have just seen David Sumner. Even though I knew it was a crazy notion.

Sidney

aneuil Hall was busy with tourists shopping and eating lunch at the many different vendor stalls. People were milling about outside, pigeons weaving in and around benches and their feet. A magician was entertaining a circle of children and adults not far from our meeting place outside the bar, Magoon's. It was located at the very end of one of the brick buildings.

After the near debacle of Amy's 'drop' — our new word for delivering what we'd found — we decided that it would be best for those of us who weren't directly involved to stay close by with 'eyes on.' While Amy had been successful, she'd had to run like hell to get back to us. Tom felt that if one of us had been nearby, we could have somehow thwarted, distracted, or interrupted Sasquatch before the panicked sprint. I agreed. We both praised Amy; she'd managed to accomplish what we'd failed to do.

Our next name on the list was Mr. and Mrs. Adam Arenberg of Chestnut Hill, just outside of Boston. I decided to call on the pretense that I had 'bought' a lovely purse at a secondhand store in Newton and found a personal note inside that was addressed to Elisabeth Arenberg, Adam's wife. It was our chance to deliver the ancient sugar caster,

2010

or spice box, the pair of baluster-shaped Chinese porcelain jars, and the water pitcher. All were in excellent shape, and David, the art handler extraordinaire, had packed them carefully. I had a large Vera Bradley bag that he'd placed them in.

When I'd called, I'd learned that both Adam and Elisabeth had passed, but Elisabeth's sister, Leah, was very happy to meet and get the purse and the letter. "I'll pay you nicely for the chance to have something of my sister Elisabeth's. She was more like a mother to me than a sister."

I'd commented that the purse had only cost ten dollars, so not to worry. We were meeting at an open bench as close to Magoon's as possible. I'd told her I'd be wearing a red shirt and she'd laughed. "Then I will too."

All four of us had driven down in David's Jeep and enjoyed the festivities of a Saturday in Faneuil Hall. David then scooted across the square to an office at 60 State Street. He was meeting a family who was interested in having him paint their portrait. He knew my meeting place and time and would meet up with us after.

Amy and Tom had already landed a prime bench spot not far from me. Amy could actually see the magician, and I watched her trying not to smile. Maybe it was just me, but she seemed happier lately, palling around with us. We'd told Rachel the truth — we were going to Boston for the day. Thankfully, she had a function connected to the Children's Center and had told us she couldn't come. But she was happy Amy wanted to join us.

I'd asked Tom if he was okay keeping all of this from his mother. He'd basically said yes, for right now, but at some point he'd want to come clean. I thought he knew what was best.

I scanned the tree-lined square and shivered slightly. It was once more overcast, surprisingly cool for a July day.

Most of the tourists were wearing sweatshirts, many with the word *Boston* emblazoned across the front. Amy had a new hoodie on, one that was more colorful than I was used to seeing her wear. It was tie-dyed and had a big shamrock in the center. She'd just bought it.

Out of the corner of my eye, I watched a woman approach me. She wore a red tailored jacket and smiled. "Is this the bench for the Red Coats?"

I replied, "Yes, but I think about two-hundred and thirty years ago, Red Coats weren't very popular around here."

"Very true!" she said, sitting down next to me. I turned and looked at her. I thought she was in her late 60s. Her hair was colored and her makeup impeccable. She wore a silk paisley scarf around her neck. She was dressed casually and comfortably. *Like from Talbots,* I thought, *my mother's favorite store.*

"I'm Sidney, and you must be Leah." I extended my hand. She shook it warmly, glanced down at the Vera Bradley bag, then up at me. She looked unsure, and I knew I needed to get as much out as possible, so I began.

"Leah, I wasn't truthful. I do have something of your sister's, but it's not a secondhand store purse. That was a ruse to meet. I have some things, objects of your family's that were taken during the occupation of Germany. We came across these items and they have your sister's name as the rightful owner. I wish I could tell you the timeline of how these objects got in my possession, but I can't. I think they've been stored carefully and actually, possibly, lovingly by people who believed strongly in returning them to you. I'm just a cog in the wheel, and the wheel is done turning." I reached down, picked up the bag carefully, and handed it to her.

She took the bag from me and immediately opened it.

"All the items are packed carefully, as I said," I added. "There's a spice box, some Chinese porcelain jars, and a water pitcher. Your family's name and address were on each item. Please look, you'll see."

Leah turned to me. "Are you…Alex's great-granddaughter?"

My mouth dropped open. "No, but Alex had these. He died before he could return them to you. I'm so sorry it's taken this long to get them back to you."

Leah placed the bag carefully back down between her feet. "When and how did he die?"

"In ninety-nine, on his farm in Vermont. His tractor may have kicked out of gear and rolled over him. He was eighty-three. I didn't know him personally. His grandson, David Sumner, lives on the farm now."

Her eyes lit up. "Really, he came back? Oh, that must have pleased Alex so much."

I didn't say anything in response. We sat for a few minutes, quietly watching people pass by. At one point I looked over at Tom and made the 'okay' sign on my side of the bench, away from Leah's view. He nodded and whispered to Amy who then looked over and gave me a hint of a smile.

"Alex brought some other items to us, when Elisabeth was still alive," Leah said. "This was…oh many years ago, when he called and came to Boston. I was in the house at the time. Your call reminded me of his for some reason. Honestly, when I came here today, I wondered if it would be similar. Thank you so much."

I should check the ledger again, I thought. Had I missed an earlier entry? And if so, why then had Alex rewritten their names? I wanted to know more. "Leah, did you know Alex beyond him returning your family heirlooms?"

"Yes, you picked up on that, didn't you?" She quickly glanced at me and laid her hands across her lap. "Alex and I had a relationship — I'd guess you'd call it that. I was almost twenty years younger, but that's nothing. Only numbers, isn't it?'

I nodded and agreed, instantly thinking of the age difference between Tom and me.

"When Alex returned to Vermont after his trip to our home — I was also living at my sister's then — he called me. He was a widower and, well, he was interested in perhaps meeting up again. And we did. For about a year. He was such a sweet man."

"May I ask what happened? And please, tell me it's none of my business if you don't want to share this."

"Sidney, I'm an old lady, I'll be seventy-four in two days. If anyone is interested in my 'once upon a time' romantic life, I find it amusing."

I laughed and shifted, giving her my full attention.

"Alex was an old Vermonter, a good man as I said, but he was set in his ways. His farm was his world — well, except for the network. His wife's sudden death and David's departure years before had affected him greatly. I wanted him to move down to Boston, buy a place with me, and start a life together here — we weren't so old. I was divorced, no children, and he was alone too.

"He came down for a month and just about had a heart attack. The traffic, the noise, the choices, the people, the lack of space; it was all too much. I'd already been to the farm and knew it wasn't for me. So, we split up, like couples do when the differences are just too great. But we wrote to one another for several years; we still had affection for each other." She shrugged her shoulders and added, "His letters stopped coming."

I recalled the night we'd discovered the ledger and sat up in the kitchen till dawn. Tom and I had come out to see the sunrise across the fields, a frost covering everything in silver beads. David, leaning on the porch railing, told us he'd never appreciated the beauty of the farm until he'd left and then came back. "My grandfather loved this place, and sometimes I understand why," he'd said to us.

"It's my turn, what's your connection to Alex?" Leah asked.

I was about to tell her but said instead, "First, what do you know about the 'network?'" Suddenly people began clapping; the magician's final performance was over and the crowd was dispersing.

"Honestly, not much. I know Alex and his buddies devised ways to get art from people who shouldn't have it and then they delivered it to the right people."

"Did he ever tell you how they did that? How they retrieved it from people's homes?"

Leah was pensive before smiling. "He did share a few of the 'outings' with me."

Her eyes lit up while she watched the tourists moving about. "One time, someone posed as a piano tuner in New York City. The people who owned the Manhattan town-house were away and the housekeeper let the piano tuner in. He then shooed her into the kitchen and in no time, Alex and another man made off with certain 'objects' from the grand room where the piano was. Another person was in a van, double parked outside with flashers on, waiting. The maid, in the back kitchen, was foreign and watching day-time soaps with subtitles in her native language. Alex told me that the TV was loud and she never took her eyes off the screen.

"The schemes were creative, but some failed. Oh, another successful one was a trip to Fenway. They feigned that their car broke down. They asked to call a tow truck from a large home in Wellesley that reportedly had confiscated art. The homeowner was so charmed by the old men from Vermont, he drove them to Yawkey Way himself in his Maserati Quattroporte. Only thing was, a third man, one he didn't know about, stayed back, got inside the house, bundled up the objects, and then miraculously the car started. He picked the guys up after the second inning. Alex told me it was a great day: the Red Sox won, the art was stored in Vermont, and soon it was returned to the Jewish families it belonged to."

I sat dumbfounded. I knew Mr. Whittenback, who worked the farm's orchard, had told Tom and David that the stolen objects were never reported stolen because the provenance in the first place was highly suspect and could make things worse for the art owners.

"Now your connection, Sidney, to…" But she didn't finish her sentence because David strolled by and gave me a casual but curious look. He continued walking over to Tom and Amy's bench.

"That could have been Alex thirty years ago!" Leah exclaimed as she watched him go by.

"Well, Leah, that was David, Alex's grandson." She turned and looked back at him. David was unaware, chatting now with Amy. She was showing him what she'd bought in the many stalls and stores throughout Faneuil Hall. Tom looked at me quizzically. I smiled back, letting him know all was well.

"I think the biggest reason Alex wouldn't move to Boston was because he wanted David to find him on the farm, if and when he ever came home," Leah said. "I'm so glad the two reconnected."

I couldn't spoil that happy thought, so I didn't correct her perception with the truth: *"Alex was already dead when David finally came home."*

Leah stood up and again glanced quickly at David before looking back at me. "Sidney, while your 'bench' has been watching you, I've had a friend at the corner table in Magoon's watching me."

I turned to where Leah indicated. I briefly waved to the woman who was watching us.

"Thank you, again, for these things that belonged to my family. I was born in nineteen thirty-six, much too young to remember any of them, but I still treasure what was and is ours. And the network's involvement in returning them to me."

She extended her hand. I didn't take it though. Instead, I hugged her tightly. "Shalom, Leah."

"Shalom," she replied, hugging me back. She picked up the bag and walked stoically through the door to Magoon's.

ON THE WAY HOME, I told everyone the gist of our conversation, including the part where she thought David could have been Alex from years before. David was driving and smiled at me in the rear view mirror. He wanted to know all about the later years and especially how they managed to get some of the looted art. He laughed out loud when I described them getting dropped off at the Red Sox game. But I held back the part about Alex waiting for his return to the farm. I didn't want to hurt David or make him feel bad. I could tell he had some misgivings about the past — why add more guilt to it?

I asked David how his 'greet and meet' went with the family he had been asked to paint. "Not bad, at all. They seem very loving. I think I'd enjoy doing it for them, along with the hefty check after. But I told them my portrait of

Mom and her children wasn't going to be the traditional kind of sitting that families are used to. I want to spend a day in their home, in and outside, and just watch, sketch, and then decide how best to paint them. The grandparents are paying for it. I assume their daughter — the mother, and her husband — are obliging the grandfather's wishes. Honestly, though, I think I could really capture her and her love for the two boys. It was very apparent in even the short time we met today."

Tom started to say, "If your opening is any indication…" but David shot him a quick glance and Tom stopped. It was a touchy subject, and Amy was in the car. She knew very little about David's art and he wanted to keep it that way.

As we headed up Route 2 past Fitchburg, I leaned my head against the window and thought about Leah Arenberg as a baby and what her parents and Elizabeth must have gone through. Then it occurred to me: she never mentioned her parents, not once. Only her sister and that Elisabeth was more like a mother to her than a sister. Was that because her parents never made it out of Germany alive? Had they paid a 'Departure Tax' — a bribe for their two daughters: one old enough to flee Nazi Germany with the second one on her hip and raise the child in a foreign country as her own? My heart felt heavy, and I closed my eyes.

Amy reached out and took my hand. It was only for a moment, but it was sweet.

Rachel

I sat in the car for a few minutes. I was nervous, but knew this was finally the time to do it. I was going to pursue a Bachelor of Science in Education and make the leap into an elementary school position. I needed insurance, seniority, a retirement plan, and more money as a single parent. The preschool spot had always been 'adequate' because Tom's income from Dad's fencing company was more than enough. But now, two years out since his death, I could see that my savings — the reserve from us selling the cottage and the money my mother had given me — was finite. I needed more security and income. I also had more time now to devote to a career. Amy didn't need me nearly as much — to her thinking, not at all — and Tommy was all grown up and out on his own. Since I'd always taught, this seemed like a natural step.

I glanced over at my transcript from my associate degree and the four-page paper I'd written up about my prior experience. The college gave credit in certain cases for 'field experience,' and the man from admissions said to definitely outline my years at the Children's Center as well as all the trainings I'd attended. I counted over 38 different ones, ranging from parental substance abuse to literacy, number sense, emotional and behavioral needs, ADHD, social and communication skills, and children living in poverty. Twenty-one years was a long time to learn.

I was meeting an advisor in six minutes. I looked at myself in the mirror. While I felt nervous, I was also excited. "Here I go."

I opened the car door and walked down the path to the red brick building. A group of young people were gathered under the overhang and animatedly discussing something. When I walked by, one of the girls said, in a friendly way, "Hey, when's the rain going to stop?"

I shook my head, and replied, "Ah, maybe when the ark's ready." She looked blankly at me and I smiled. I felt good, hopeful that this was the right move for me. I also realized, at 47, that I'd been teaching pre-school longer than these college kids had been alive.

Todd Linden was friendly and knowledgeable. We were in his office and I could hear the rain continuing, now hitting the window. *Funny how it goes in cycles,* I thought. The significant drought the summer of Tommy's near drowning was now followed in the record books by this daily deluge through May-June-July; the greatest amount of rain in a three-month period in over 80 years.

I waited patiently while he read over my transcript, trainings, and then the short write-up I'd completed on my prior experience. He finally looked up at me and said, "Well, you certainly have been in the trenches, haven't you? I dare say you may know more than some of the professors teaching our future teachers." I laughed at that, but he just looked at me. "Seriously, there's a load of experience here."

I heard some voices down the hall and Todd called out, "Hey guys, keep it down, will you? I'm trying to recruit new faculty here."

There was a quick burst of laughter and then it was quiet again. I shifted in the chair and glanced at the family pictures behind his desk. He had young children, two girls. There was also artwork, handprints, and my favorite — bright, colored maple leaves that had been pressed and preserved.

"So, you want your bachelor's degree in order to make the jump into public education. Makes perfect sense and I'm sure when we really go through this all — " he pointed to what I'd brought — "we'll be able to determine exactly what you need. What's good is that Castleton has a professional development strand and a schedule of classes that are conducive to working folks. A few weeks in the summer, a class or two each semester, student teaching…it's doable."

I replied, "That's great, thanks. Can you call me once you've done the transcript review?"

"Yes. It'll probably be in an email, outlining my recommendations and a timeline."

I stood up and thanked him. He smiled and said, "Preschool teachers don't get much respect as far as salary or benefits. It's really a shame because we trust them with our most precious commodities. I have two small children, one in day care and one in preschool. I'm always appalled when I learn what the preschool teacher makes, or rather, doesn't make. And honestly, public school teachers are paid way less than what other comparable degrees are paid in the private sector."

At the door, I hesitated and then said, "That's the truth. I think, if I had a chance to do it all over again, I'd hound our lawmakers and work tirelessly to change this inequity. I'd educate everyone on the value of early education and not rest until my efforts paid off. I'd write grants, get on committees, ram it through the state legislature. It's the area where our state should be investing the most focus, money, and energy. Our kids are our greatest resource." I stopped and said, "I'm sorry. I'll get off my soapbox — I've been at it for years."

Todd Linden stood there, looking at me. Then he slowly said, "Rachel, you started with, 'If I had a chance to do it all over again…' That's kind of a cop-out statement, isn't it?"

I looked at him questioningly. "What do you mean?"

"Come back, sit down for a minute, and please, excuse my yelling." I went back to the table, not quite sure what was going on. I sat back down in the chair I'd just left.

Todd stuck his head out of the door and called down the hallway, "Samantha, are you available? I need you!"

Within seconds, a woman arrived, smiling. I presumed this was Samantha. Todd made our introductions. She was the head of the Sociology Department. I thought she looked my mother's age, early 70s, but I wasn't sure.

"Rachel, is it all right if I share with Samantha why you're interested in Castleton?"

I nodded and said, "Of course."

I listened to Todd explain my reasons for our meeting. Samantha nodded many times, glancing at me with a warm smile. When Todd got to the lawmaker stuff I'd said, he slowed down and asked me to clarify anything he may have misrepresented. There was nothing he said that wasn't true.

"No, I'm good with everything you just told her." I looked at Samantha. "I'm not quite sure though why, well, Samantha should care." I quickly added, "Please, no offense."

Samantha leaned into me and replied, "Quite frankly, Rachel, you may be applying for the wrong degree. It sounds to me that you might want to head in a different direction instead of education — though certainly something connected to education. Have you ever thought of majoring in Sociology with a concentration in Community Studies?"

I sat there, somewhat baffled. Samantha saw my expression and continued talking.

"You want to 'elevate' the preschool field? Do you know Obama has pledged to make early childhood education one of the federal government's greatest investments? It looks like there may be as much as eight billion dollars in federal grants available soon. We're on the cusp of incredible things happening. We offer courses in civil leadership training and grant writing in this field. Sure, you can teach, just like you've been teaching for the past two decades, or you can take all that rich experience, along with a new degree, and help change the world of early childhood education."

I looked down at my nails and heard my father say, *"You solving all the problems of the world?"*

"But how does that translate into a career?" I asked. "One that supports a child, a mortgage, insurance?"

Samantha replied, "Oh, I'll tell you exactly. One of the many careers you could choose from is to become a Public Relations Specialist, delving into the field of early education. Speeches, press releases, information presentations, a multitude of ways to press for reform. Things are going to happen at the state level as Obama moves forward. They'll need people like you."

I looked at her and shook my head. "It seems too wide open. I just don't know."

Samantha smiled at Todd and then looked at me. "I think someone your age is brave doing anything that involves going back to school. I commend you for that. But I also think you have plenty of time to 'do it all over' from this point on, because you're still relatively young, with invaluable past experiences and a passion. Your starting point is already ahead of anyone entering this degree program, trust me."

Samantha quickly went back to her office and returned with information she wanted me to read. We talked a little bit more and I thanked them both.

I left feeling drained but also excited in a totally different, kind of new, scary way. As Samantha said, starting school again, for anyone at my age, was commendable. I needed to think.

Tom Jr.

T he two paintings we had left were so significant that we wanted David to deliver them with just one of us present to make sure we didn't screw it up.

Nodding, he said, "Yes, I agree. Not because I'm worried you'll mess up, but because if this goes bad, it was my grandfather's deal and found on his property. I'll take full responsibility."

"What do you mean?" Amy asked.

"Some unscrupulous people traffic in art. They steal, forge pieces, and even use it to launder money — that means hiding money they've made through illegal means by buying art. To some extent, the art world has looked the other way and emboldened the crooks and dictators of the world. It's totally unregulated."

Amy frowned. "You mean crooks have a way to, like, appear high society but they're really scumbags?"

"Yes, exactly, Amy. In our case, other than Jacob Geller's name and his address on the paintings' tags written by my grandfather, we have nothing else to prove ownership. We hold no documents, whatsoever. I have to believe Mr. Geller does, however, since the network matched it with him…"

Sidney interjected, "These paintings by Jan Both are masterpieces. One could argue that they belong in a museum for all to see, not in someone's sitting room." She paused, then added, "We have to deliver them without compromising the network."

"Agreed, and as for their ultimate destination, it's all the more reason to return them directly into Mr. Geller's hands so he can decide what to do," David said.

I hadn't had the opportunity yet to participate. I raised my hand. "I'll be in on this drop." Amy smiled. She was different these days — *happier,* I thought.

Right before she'd climbed out of Sidney's car in the circle of the Sunrise Terrace Nursing Home, she'd said aloud, "Be still my thoughts." Sidney had touched Amy's hand and held it for a few seconds. I thought it was kind of weird — isn't the phrase something like 'be still my heart?' But now it seemed to fit. I looked at David, waiting for his thoughts.

"Okay then…because the two paintings are definitely worth a lot of money, we have to come up with an air-tight plan. I can't stress to you the importance of this. Anyone along the 'drop' could see the two paintings' worth and, well, act in a manner that…" David didn't finish his sentence.

Sidney piped up, "Could it simply be a UPS delivery that needs a signature? Do we want to use a system already in place that what…puts a package in the hands of a consumer, a homeowner ten-thousand times a day?" She paused. "That's a random number, by the way." She looked over at David.

"How do we manage that?" he asked.

"I can check out the uniforms, you can check out some sort of truck. And let's picture this handsome man as the

UPS guy…" She nodded at me and smiled, then quipped, "Unless, David, that's been your secret fantasy?"

He burst out laughing, and we all relaxed. We were at one of David's favorite places, a busy Italian bistro in Woodstock. A singing duo was warming up, tuning their guitars. Our early bird specials arrived and we began eating. By the time we left, it was raining again.

W e'd rented the box truck and I had a spiffy uniform: a hat, shirt, and shorts that were definitely the right brown color, with the UPS logo above the pocket on the shirt. Sidney had found the uniform on Amazon.

I'd driven David's Jeep down to a pull off near Westminster to meet him in the box truck. The place wouldn't rent the truck to me, said I had to be 25 years old and carry proof of insurance. I'd called David and we'd changed places.

The plan was to drive to Jacob Geller's house in Walpole, just over the New Hampshire state line. I'd looked at David and asked, "Is it okay that you got a white truck?"

He'd responded with concern, "Only one that wasn't enormous. Let's hope it's okay."

The Jeep was parked at the gas station up in the corner, locked. In the truck were the two paintings that David had carefully packaged in used, recycled Amazon boxes. Sidney had typed up labels with Mr. Geller's address and placed new return addresses she'd recently ordered from B&H Office Solutions and Bath & Body Works.

I was feeling confident until I read the second painting's return address. "What the fuck? Bath and Body Works?" I held it up to David and said, "This won't fly, will it?"

He ran his hand through his hair, looking stressed again. "He's old, let's hope his eyesight is shot."

I started to drive and it seemed we were both holding our breath. I glanced at him. "Well, it's not like we're posing as police officers. Right?"

"That's true," he said as we pulled down into the Walpole Square. Mr. Geller's home was the last white house at the northern end of the square. We pulled up, and I put the truck in park.

"Just be as natural as you can be," David said. "You definitely look the part."

"Okay," I said and jumped down with the two Amazon boxes. All I could think about was what David had told Sidney and me — they were definitely worth thousands, possibly even millions each.

As I walked down the sidewalk, an elderly woman passed me with a little white fluff ball on a leash. I smiled and she said, "Good day."

The number on the column of the porch matched the package's address: 6 Whiting Avenue. I started to walk up onto the porch, down to the door. It was a big house with a small yard. *Not too bad to mow.*

Just then I heard a woman's voice and turned. It was the same woman with the dog. "Mr. Geller just left, not more than three minutes ago. His daughter picked him up. They're going to Hanover to see his son. He's a big professor at Dartmouth. You must have passed the car coming around the square."

I paused and looked back at the boxed truck. David was in the driver's seat now and did a *'What's up?'* gesture. I immediately walked down the stairs to the truck.

"We have to drive up to Hanover. Mr. Geller just left for his son's house."

I got in and placed the two paintings carefully on the floor directly behind us. "That lady said we passed them coming around the square. I can google the Geller address in Hanover. I think this is still doable."

David hesitated, then started up the truck. "Okay, text the girls. They were going to meet us at Burdick's for lunch. Now make it Molly's in, let's say two hours."

We started to drive, taking the on-ramp for 91 North. David settled in at 60 miles per hour — anything higher and the box truck began to rattle and shimmy to the right.

I was hoping we made the right decision to head north, but I was nervous. "What if we get stopped and the cops search the truck? You know this is a drug corridor, from Springfield, Mass, up to Burlington and Canada. Lot of opiates and schmucks looking like us running the road."

David glanced over. "We've got over a hundred thousand dollars' worth of art in this truck, with questionable ownership. Let's hope the state troopers aren't so curious today."

WE DROVE A BIT IN SILENCE. Once David looked like he was going to say something, but he didn't. I thought about the network and how Alex and his buddies had done this after serving in Europe, after seeing the carnage up close, the destruction and the devastation. Somehow, driving in the north-bound lane with rain clouds cloaking the beautiful trees, the rolling hills, and the Green Mountains in the distance, the Nazis and their rampage didn't feel real.

The sirens came up on us quickly. "Ah, shit!" David exclaimed. I was in the passenger seat and could barely see the highway out of David's side.

"Take off your shirt and hat fast — do you have another shirt, Tommy? Quick!" I had my backpack behind my seat full of dirty laundry from Sid's place. I unzipped it and reached in, grabbing a blue t-shirt that reeked.

"Man, oh man, I can smell it — turn the UPS shirt inside out, hurry, hurry, and put it in the backpack. The hat too. That's good, now let me do all the talking, okay? You're you, and I'm me…and we're going up to move Sid from her…Dartmouth place, okay? I'm just a family friend."

"Got it."

The state trooper was middle-aged and all business-like. He took the rental's registration, insurance card, and our licenses back to his car. When he finally came back, he stood outside David's driver's side window.

"I'd like to ask you to give me consent to search the vehicle. This is voluntary; you do not have to give me consent."

David paused briefly and replied, "Yes, of course, it's basically empty — we're going up to move Tommy's girlfriend out of her apartment."

The officer took out his cell phone and asked David to once again give voluntary consent but to speak slowly so he could record his voice.

The emptiness of the truck was pretty straight forward and the officer quickly closed the back doors. The paintings were up further, towards the driver's seat. He walked up to the door. We were on the shoulder of the road where he'd asked us to stand while he searched.

David called out, "The packages are for Tommy's girlfriend's grandfather. She's planning on seeing him this weekend."

The officer looked over at us and then reached into the back of the truck. He pulled out both packages and the backpack. He walked towards us.

"I'd like to search these as well. Do I have your consent?"

Again, David paused. I didn't know how we'd be regarded if he said 'No.' I could tell he was weighing that too.

"Yes, officer, you can." David glanced at me and raised his eyebrows ever so slightly. I held my breath.

My clothes reeked. My toothbrush was in a baggie in a side pocket. He zipped the backpack up pretty quickly after thumbing through it.

"Now the Amazon boxes." The officer handed them over for David to open.

David carefully ran his fingers along the edge of each package, pulling up on the packing tape. He held the paintings up to the officer one at a time. The trooper took them from David and slowly turned them over, feeling all along the back matting. He shook them, then looked at us. Again, I held my breath.

"Nothing much to look at, are they?" he said.

I quickly glanced at David. He looked like he was going to bust out singing.

I helped put each painting back in the bubble wrap, then in its Amazon box. I held them, placing my hands strategically over the return address labels.

The trooper pushed his hat back on his head and said, "I played men's league softball with your father for years; I'm sorry for your loss."

I nodded and replied back, "Thank you, sir."

David reached out and patted my arm. "He raised a good guy, that's for sure."

Just then a second state trooper pulled up. The first officer walked to the second car.

David whispered, "Damn it."

After a brief exchange, he came back to us.

"You're free to go. Have a good day." He added, "Don't pull a muscle."

David called out, "Exactly, thanks!"

I looked over at David. I was perplexed. As we climbed into the truck, he explained, "He's referring to when we're moving Sidney. Guys our age have to watch it, make sure our backs don't give out."

"Ah, middle age, uh?" The rain started and soon became a downpour. The box truck's wipers were the best thing about it.

I FOUND THE ADDRESS easily enough. There were four Gellers in Hanover, but the only one listed on Dartmouth's faculty page was Sebastian Geller. Sebastian lived close to the campus on a quiet side street. We pulled up 72 minutes after leaving Walpole. *Not bad,* I thought, for getting stopped and searched. Maybe we even beat Jacob Geller and his daughter there.

Just as I thought this, a dark blue Volvo slowly came down Lincoln Street and pulled into Sebastian Geller's driveway. I looked over at David and smiled.

"Bingo," David said, and then added, "Try and get him before he goes into the house, catch both of them off guard. Also, there's a break in the rain right now…hurry with the shirt and hat."

"Oh, right." I quickly retrieved the shirt, put it on, and tucked it in. David handed me the hat. Then I reached for the paintings in the Amazon boxes — being even more careful as they were now opened on one end — and climbed out of the truck. I scooted across the street and met both Jacob Geller and his daughter as they came around to the front of the house.

"Excuse me, sir, but I have two packages for Mr. Jacob Geller. Would that be you? I need a signature." Shit, in my haste I'd forgotten the fake clipboard thing Amy had devised; it was in the glove compartment.

Mr. Geller was elderly and bent over a walker. His daughter didn't look much younger, or at least I didn't think so initially. In one hand she carried a plastic bag from Target. She put her other hand on her father's arm protectively and said, "Why would Amazon be delivering to my father up here in Hanover?" Her eyes were sharp, and she looked at me questioningly.

I wanted to say, "Good point!" but instead I bluffed by saying, "We were given an address for Sebastian Geller, but both packages say to the attention of Mr. Jacob Geller. Is that you, sir?"

The old man stopped moving and looked up at me. His eyes told me his mind was alert despite his body's slow shuffle from the car.

"I haven't ordered a thing from Amazon. I don't need anything besides a new body. Tell me, can Amazon send me a new body?"

I smiled and said, "No, I guess not. I can give you these two packages, sir, and be on my way." I held them out to him. He glanced over, then shook his head.

"Why would I take them if I know I haven't ordered anything?"

I hesitated. "Perhaps they're gifts from family?" My voice sounded lame, even to me.

"What are the return labels, *Foter*?" his daughter said. "Look and see, maybe you'll remember something."

Oh shit, I thought. I held out the two packages, giving him time to read the returns. "No Clarissa, they're not for me," he said. "And this boy isn't being truthful — Sebastian's name is nowhere on these boxes."

She looked at me warily and said, "So, bitte, take them back to your facility, do whatever you have to do. My father didn't order anything."

Just then a man walked out of the front door. He was younger than the woman and definitely curious. "Vos tut zich, Clarissa?" He walked down the steps and up to Mr. Geller. "Hello, Foter, what have we here?"

"Two packages, but I didn't order anything. I don't want to take them. They're not mine."

Sebastian Geller looked up at me and said, in a kind voice, "Could you do us a favor and take them back? My father is still very much with it and…" He looked at one of the packages. "I don't think, at ninety-six, he's ordering from Bath and Body Works."

I quickly looked back at the truck. David opened the door and climbed down. Jacob, Clarissa, Sebastian, and I stared at him as he crossed the small patch of grass and met us on the sidewalk.

"And who are you, may I ask?" Clarissa said. She placed herself in front of Jacob.

"Hello folks, I'm David Sumner and this young man is Tom Dunne. We're actually here to deliver two family art pieces that were taken some time ago from Mr. Jacob Geller's home in, well, I'm not exactly sure where or when. It was during the Nazi occupation."

Mr. Geller looked up at David, clearly startled. "What do you know about me? About the Nazis, the filth, the hunger, and all of the death?" He said this with vehemence, his eyes shooting daggers at David.

In a kind and respectful voice, David answered, "Sir, I know nothing. But my grandfather, Alex Sumner — who would be your age if he was still alive — was in Western Europe during the war. He was an American who saw what the Nazis did. Before he died, he retrieved some artwork. These two boxes contain your family's paintings by Jan Both. My grandfather stored them until we could deliver them to you and place them personally in your hands."

David briefly glanced up at the sky, then took one of the boxes from me, carefully pulling out the painting. Standing on the sidewalk in front of Professor Sebastian Geller's house, he held it up in front of the old man. Jacob Geller stepped back and brought his hands up to his mouth.

Clarissa reached out and steadied her father. In an authoritative voice, she said, "Let's go inside, please. My father needs to sit."

Sebastian stepped forward. "I've got you, Foter, please, put your arms around my neck." He gently lifted the old man up into his arms and climbed the three steps onto the porch. He turned to us. "Come, both of you, into the house." He carried him in.

David, holding both paintings, followed. I picked up Mr. Geller's walker and brought it into the small vestibule.

David whispered to me, "We need to hear him speak, hear him process what this means to him." I was self-conscious about my size in the small area but nodded.

On Mr. Geller's left forearm were tattooed numbers. I'd noticed them when his sleeves dropped back as he draped his arms around his son's neck. Auschwitz, the biggest death camp in Hitler's "Final Solution" marked the Jews as they came in. Now, less than 200,000 survivors of Auschwitz-Birkenau still lived. *Mr. Geller is one of them,* I thought. *He survived unspeakable horror.*

Clarissa called to us from down the hallway, "Into the living room, please."

MR. GELLER HELD THE FIRST PAINTING on his lap. He wiped away his tears with a white handkerchief. "This was one of two paintings in our dining room in Berlin. My sister and I would walk by them every day. Let me have the second one, please."

David quickly unpacked it and stood up. He walked over and placed it gently in the old man's lap. Again, Mr. Geller held it, crying. Clarissa took the first painting and set it carefully along the side of a chair where her father could still see it.

We remained quiet. I could hear children walking past the house and a truck go by, maybe a real UPS delivery. Sebastian moved to his father and said, gently, "Do you want to talk about the paintings further?"

The old man looked up, as if surprised he still had an audience. He looked directly at me. "I will tell you it all. Only my children know — no one else. You brought me these lost paintings. I feel you are entitled to know." He looked over at David. "I speak to you now as a man who barely survived and was given a second chance."

His daughter came over and sat on the arm of his chair. Mr. Geller reached up and took her hand. He began to speak. "The SS, Himmler's elite brutes, came to our house and took my parents. They were professors and had spoken out against the Nazi Party. And of course, they were Jews.

"They removed much of our artwork and all of my parents' books, documents, and writings. They were both published scholars. They would be back, they told me. My sister, at the time, was fourteen, while I was almost twenty-four. I hid her upstairs in a small linen closet. I didn't ever want them to know she was in the house when they were there.

"They returned a second time and confiscated more art. They heard her upstairs. She had a terrible cold and coughed too loudly. Three officers brutally raped her. They made me stand and watch. When it was over, I heard one of them say, 'Let's come back tomorrow. Virgins are hard to find.' They laughed as they left our house.

"There were strict laws in place, racial laws and military rules that no interactions between Jews and non-Jews were allowed. But the SS raped Jewish women frequently despite the fear of babies with Jewish blood. Racial defilement could result in jail or even death. Family members were forced to watch. It was a way to exert their power over us, and often the women were killed after being raped.

"Abagail bled from her injuries: bruising closed one of her eyes, her lip was split, and she could barely walk. The next day we waited in fear, but the officers never came. She pleaded with me to run, to go before they came back. But I cowered in fear, shaking my head. 'There is no place to run,' I cried. It was true, the awful truth.

"On the morning of the third day, I heard their boots on our stairs and ran to Abagail's room. My beautiful baby sister had hanged herself. She'd wrapped the cord to the lamp around her neck and jumped from the second story window. The officers laughed again when they saw her hanging. They cut her down and she fell the rest of the way to the street below.

"She was nine years younger than me. I loved her, would take her around the house on my hip, letting her touch everything. Her favorite stop — these two paintings of the golden Italian countryside."

I abruptly stood up and said, "I'm sorry, I have to go." I stumbled blindly out of the room and down the hallway. I couldn't breathe. I opened the door, escaping to the porch. Leaning against the railing, I started to sob. *This is too much,* I thought. *It's too much.*

Suddenly, I felt David's arm around my shoulder and I turned to him. I wiped the snot from my nose. "I can't, I can't hear anymore, David. All I see is Amy. I want to go."

"Okay, Tommy, we'll go." He turned and went back into the house. A moment later, he opened the front door and we left.

I walked into Molly's Restaurant and looked for them. I wasn't hungry. I was still affected by what I'd heard Mr. Geller recount to us.

I described who I was looking for to the hostess and she took me to the back deck under the awning. The place was crowded. I'd have to be careful with what I said. I did kind of a subtle thumbs up as soon as I saw them. Sidney hugged me when I sat down and Amy leaned into me, asking, "Wasn't it an awesome feeling to do it?"

We were too close to the other tables for my comfort, but I nodded my head and, looking at both of them, said, "It was, well, emotional. For David too, I think."

"Was Mr. Geller happy to get his paintings?" Amy asked.

I looked over at her and smiled, but I felt drained. The brutality of the Holocaust had never been clearer to me than it was now.

"Yeah, I think it reminded him of a happier time in his life. But he was sad too, because it reminded him of all he lost." I paused then added, "David would have joined us here, but he's returning the truck." Like me, he wasn't in much of a celebratory mood.

Sidney grabbed my hand and held it, perhaps sensing I wasn't myself. They were already eating but had told the server that more people would be joining them shortly.

Sidney took a bite of her wrap, chewed, and then hesitantly said, "Guys, I've been thinking. I'm ready to continue where Alex left off."

"What do you mean, Sidney?" Amy whispered, no longer twirling the cheese from her pizza slice into her mouth.

"Kind of like, start a new ledger?" I asked, raising my eyebrows. "But that would mean we'd have to find the pieces first."

Amy quickly looked over at Sidney and sputtered, "Is that, um, do you, um, actually mean that?"

Sidney nodded slowly and said, "Yes."

Amy seemed pensive and then responded, "It's important work. I think I'm an asset and I'd like to be included." She sat back and looked at me.

I wasn't sure how I felt. I said nothing.

"Well, I've got to do some research first," Sidney replied just as the server saw me sitting there and started to make her way towards our table. "One thing though. We need to get that phone number Alex gave his lawyer to call if something happened to him. Remember, the lawyer told David that no one ever picked up? It just kept ringing and ringing. I bet the lawyer was calling Alex's contact in the network. But the calls were coming from his office phone. So, wouldn't the caller id be an unknown number? We need to call that same number from David's house phone, you know, from the phone Alex always used at the farm. That way whoever is on the other end will recognize it and pick up."

Amy

The very next Sunday, David invited us to have bagels at his farm. Mom had planned for all of us to go to Grammie's for brunch, but Tommy told her Sidney wanted to check out a couple of places around the lake to shop for Vermont-made stuff. The brunch was moved to Sunday dinner and the three of us breathed a sigh of relief — we were free to go to David's. Grammie was always easygoing and said it worked with her. Mom seemed hesitant with the change, then maybe a little hurt that she wasn't invited to go around the lake with us.

As I slammed the porch door behind me on the way to Sid's car, I looked over at Mom.

"We won't be too long, okay?" I quickly said, sidestepping the perennials.

She was just starting to line the wicker furniture from the porch up along one side of the driveway. She was going to give them a fresh coat of paint. It had taken her weeks to decide what color to spray paint them — after asking me which color samples I liked. I had shrugged and said, "It doesn't really matter to me — you pick." She'd decided on a funky coral green, so different than the white I'd been used to all of my life. She'd also picked out a new tan rug for the floor of the porch. The design was kind of wild, like swirls of sand. I wondered if she was craving the ocean. I wanted to ask her, but I kept quiet.

Mom looked our way, shaking the can of spray paint back and forth, getting ready to start. I could hear the rattle of the can and wondered how many she'd needed to buy. "Have fun," she called out and turned away from us.

Tom and Sidney were already in the car waiting for me.

"Hey guys, should we invite Mom?" I asked suddenly as I climbed in. "Her and David could meet, or I guess, re-meet, whatever it's called. I feel kind of bad that we didn't ask her."

Tommy replied, "No, Amy. She needs to hear about our summer escapades in a more private way." He pulled out of the driveway, and, as we headed through Langdon, he looked at me in the rear view mirror. "She could be really pissed, and since she's starting to go out and do more things, I don't want to do anything to upset that momentum. I remember, as a kid, how tough her miscarriages were, and Dad telling me it takes time to heal from something like that. So, in a little while, I'll figure out how and when to tell her. Trust me, 'kay?"

"Wait. Mom had other babies that died?" I asked in disbelief. Never had anyone told me this before.

"Yeah, a couple, I think. Then voila, there you were in living color," he replied.

Sidney looked back at me. "Maybe, sometime when you're ready, you could ask her about them."

I nodded. Sidney was usually right about everything. I leaned back and wondered how this all figured into who I was — like my personality and sometimes my just knowing things. I'd have to think.

All the pieces had been returned, and we were feeling 'pretty accomplished,' as my 5th grade teacher, Mrs. Silverman, used to say. We had just about everything out: bagels, cream cheese, coffee, orange juice, and butter. We were taking a chance and eating outdoors in the chairs under the big tree. The sky looked iffy, but we'd all had enough rain to last a lifetime.

"Oh wait, I've got homemade jam in the house," David remarked.

I volunteered to go get one and skipped into the pantry. Grabbing a jelly jar — there were seven of them, lined up on the shelf next to the cans of corn, beans, and diced tomatoes — I sang out, *"David's got a crush on The Jelly Lady!"* I looked up and saw big jars of pickles, maybe a dozen of them, along the shelf. I *loved* pickles.

I moved the step stool over, climbed up, and reached for a pickle jar. Then I stepped off the stool. The jar was heavy and rusty on top. *Nope, too old.*

I'd seen something else up there too, though, hadn't I? I climbed back up and looked. Behind where the pickle jar had been, there was a panel of wood, yellow too, but the color didn't quite match the rest of the pantry. It was like someone tried to match it but missed it by just a smidge. I stepped off the step stool and onto the counter. I moved the rest of the pickle jars down and walked along the shelf, seeing how far this one, slightly off-yellow board ran. It stopped about four feet down.

It wasn't wide, maybe ten inches or so. I could see a slight gap where it was supposed to be flush against the pantry wall, but wasn't. I scooted down and went to the kitchen drawer to grab a plain butter knife. I looked out the kitchen window above the sink and saw them all in the chairs outside gabbing. I had time.

I climbed back up and started to wedge the knife into where the gap was. I went all the way down the length of the board, working it like a can of paint when you want the top off. I did it twice. The board gave way.

I hesitated and then reached in, hoping no mouse would bite my hand. I felt a box and pulled it out. It was a long, wooden box — not very big and with no noticeable markings. I placed my hand in again, making sure nothing else was there. The space was empty. I climbed down, grabbed the jelly jar, and went out the kitchen door.

"Hey guys, who covered the pantry when you searched the house?" I asked as I approached them.

Tom raised his hand, then looked at the box. "Whoops. I was the last one after we switched places. Did I screw up?"

I brought the box to David. He glanced up at me questioningly. "It was behind the large jars of pickles in the pantry," I said. "I noticed the board behind the jars was a little off in color, and I got a funny feeling. You'll see where it was when you go in."

Tommy said, hesitantly, "Amy, you kind of have a sixth sense, don't ya?"

Sidney moved over to David's chair. "Are you going to open it?"

Forgetting our bagels, we gathered around him.

David opened the box. He turned it our way and lifted up some of the items. In his hands he held jewelry, mostly women's gold and silver wedding bands, some earrings, and three watches. There was one locket. He opened it, and a woman's face stared out at us.

David reached in further and brought out a piece of paper. He unfolded it and read it first silently and then aloud: "*Alex, here's what I can't deliver. Ownership unknown. It's been good these past years. I like to think we made a difference, settled a score. Who am I kidding? It can't ever be settled, but we kept on doing our part, didn't we? Fuck the bastards, Goddamn Nazis. MaryBeth is buried up in our family plot, I'm heading there soon. The cancer ain't stopping. Yours truly — Zeke.*" David turned the note over for us to see. At the top of the page was printed: '*Zeke's Full-Service Mobil Station, Colebrook, New Hampshire.*' It was dated March, 1992.

We all sat quietly. The farmer across the way was cutting his fields, the big round balls of hay looking like spools from Mom's sewing basket. We could hear crows 'cawing' further down in the meadow. I wondered if a fox might be in the tall grass stalking something and the crows were sounding the alarm.

David closed the box, stood up, and gently placed it in Sidney's hands. Then he started to walk towards the shed. I got up and followed him. Tom stayed put, with his arms around Sidney because I could tell she was pretty emotional.

As I walked behind David, I thought about those ladies dying awful deaths without any relative being able to save their wedding bands in a drawer, tucked safely away but still close enough to see, to remember. I knew right where Mommy put Daddy's wedding band. It was in her top right dresser drawer, next to his Senior class ring.

David opened the shed door and splattered across one side of the wall was the same yellow color as the board. "That the color?"

"Yes," I answered.

He nodded, then said, "You ever throw stuff, break things in a fit of self-pity?" He didn't wait for me to answer. "It took me all my life to realize that my self-pity was bullshit. My mom took off, but I still had family, still had a life. So many other people lost everything."

He was pretty serious, and I wasn't sure what to say, so I said nothing.

He put his arm around my shoulder, and we walked back to the chairs. Sidney glanced at Tom and then turned to David. "The three of us have been talking, David, and we'd like to continue in your grandfather's footsteps." She looked over at me and smiled.

"That's something you really need to think on," David replied. "First, let's decide what to do with this box."

Sidney stood up, still holding it. "The Holocaust Memorial Museum in D.C. has a way to search through their collection online. There are pictures of items like this jewelry and a brief description of the circumstances surrounding each piece. While we don't know the particulars of each of these pieces, I think they would accept them into their collection."

"It'd be nice for the family of the woman in the locket to see her and get her back, wouldn't it?" I asked no one in particular.

"Yes, Amos," Tommy replied. He sounded just like Daddy as he leaned down to hug me. He added, "We should get going, Mom expects us back soon."

I ran over to the unopened jelly jar on the tray near one of the chairs and picked it up. I turned to David and asked, "Can I take this for my mom? She loves raspberry jam."

He nodded, looking kind of wistful. "Of course you can."

As we started down the hill, I waved goodbye. David stood watching us from the top of the driveway. When I turned back around in my seat, I smiled. I saw myself standing right there next to him, only taller, older.

Tom Jr.

I t was the seventh dock in, right?
That's what you wrote here.
I'm sure it's this one."

Sidney and Amy pulled their kayaks up to mine. We were on Keuka Lake in upstate New York. It's where Sidney's research had brought us. That phone number Alex wanted his lawyer to call had worked when we tried it from the farm — an elderly man picked up on the fourth ring. The directions he'd given Sidney were pretty specific.

THE NIGHT BEFORE, we'd swung by the Langdon library's back entrance and there was Amy looking quite jovial. Climbing into Sid's Toyota, she'd said, "Mom thinks I'm at a sleepover at Bella's house. I've been reading here under the security light for a while. It's been fun." She'd stretched out with a pillow and what looked like her sleeping bag.

Ever since Amy had mentioned that she felt bad about excluding Mom, I'd felt the same way. "It's time to tell Mom everything, I'll do it when we get back."

Amy had nodded and said, "Good."

We'd driven down Main Street and picked up speed
once we were out of Langdon. Seven hours later, after pit
stops and winding through Vermont on Route 7, then on to
the New York State Thruway, we'd entered the Finger
Lakes region. Keuka Lake was long, almost 19 miles.

We'd made it to the exact rental place Sid was told to go.
The place opened at 6:30 a.m.

"SID, HOW DID YOU LEAVE IT?"

"Just that we'd be here, at their dock, as close to seven as
possible. So, let's just chill for a little while. Someone will
come."

The dock looked brand new and the floating raft equally
new with a tall, curvy slide — it was inviting. A sleek
speedboat and two jet skis were tied to it, the dark water
lapping up around the bumpers, keeping them in place. I
looked up the sloping yard to the cottage. Really not a
cottage, rather a home with a long, wraparound deck. The
flower boxes were overflowing with pink and purple petu-
nias. Unicorn and dolphin floats were hanging from a
corner post. A tire swing was tied to a big willow tree and a
croquet set was leaning against it. It was quite a spread. I
guess I was expecting it to be a kind of a rundown place,
like David's grandfather's farm in Plymouth.

Sidney looked nervous, despite clearly trying not to be. I
was nervous too. Amy sat moving her fingers through the
water, ripples spreading out. I couldn't tell what she was
thinking, but she seemed patient enough.

I heard voices and looked up. A man was pushing
another, much older man, down the slope in a wheelchair. I
thought of Joe and realized this old man and Joe may have
known each other at one time. He'd definitely known Alex.
The man behind him steered the chair down slowly and
carefully.

We paddled closer to the dock. It was very quiet since it was so early. It was overcast like it had been for most of the summer. It was strange to be out on a lake none of us knew.

They made their way up onto the dock, then down it towards us. The wheelchair made no noise. *It must be the Cadillac model,* I thought. The old man put up his hand and waved at us. He'd been a tall man once, I could tell. His hands were large, the bony fingers long.

"Good morning," I said, maybe a little too loudly.

The old man said affably, "Why it is, isn't it?"

The man behind him was younger than I first thought, definitely older than me but still young. He bent down and put the brake on the wheelchair. "They're all good mornings, aren't they, Grandpa." It was more of a statement than a question. The old man was holding a thick manila folder, a rubber band around it.

"This is Sidney, who you spoke with on the phone. I'm Tom Dunne and that's Amy, my sister." Amy responded with a quick wave.

"Nice to meet you all…This is Ryan, my great-grandson. He knows all about why you're here. In fact, he's been involved to a certain extent. Right, Ryan?"

Ryan affectionately placed both hands on his great-grandfather's shoulders and replied, "Definitely." Then he reached down and took the folder from the old man's lap.

"In this, you'll find a lot of the northeast network's past dealings dating back to the early sixties when it first started," Ryan said. "It'll give you some perspective. Some of the younger players involved have made it digital. There's a secure site, and I included log-in information for how to access it, now that you've been cleared. A lot of us are relatives of the first wave or two." He started to come towards me with the folder.

"I'll take that," Sidney replied. "David, Alex Sumner's grandson, has given us the green light to do what we can in his name. We really thank you for this honor." The old man smiled while his great-grandson reached down and handed the folder to Sidney.

"Alex was a good man. Always gave us full use of his farm — pretty spot in Vermont," the older man said. "The missus made the best cherry pies every time we'd come. I think that's why we all decided on meeting in late June — so the cherries were ripe. I'm glad to know it's stayed in his family."

He looked out over the lake. "We had some memorable times, that's for sure." He hesitated and then added, "The years go by and the mind dulls and the body doesn't work anymore, but we must stay vigilant. Giving back the art is but a small part of the bigger picture. Atrocities committed in the name of racial cleansing, well, they go on to this day in other parts of the world. It's up to your generation and the next to stop it, finally." He reached up behind him, looking for Ryan's hand. Finding it, he held on.

As the old man sat back, he continued to take us in.

Ryan spoke now. "My great-grandfather helped liberate Dachau. He's described the inhumane conditions he and his fellow soldiers witnessed. His experiences affected me and I got involved. We're glad to have you on board. Especially you, Sidney, with your education and credentials. If you have questions about the folder's contents or the website, please contact me. I've included my own secure email and private number."

He now squatted down on the dock, leaning towards Sidney and me. "That's one thing I insist you do — set up an email and a phone contact totally separate from your present means of communication. It's imperative that there's no trail, that security measures are tighter than when our great-grandparents and grandparents did this. What we're doing is the right thing, but it's a really gray area in acting on our own. You understand?"

Sidney said clearly, "Yes, we understand. And this — " she held up the folder — "will be kept safe, I assure you."

Ryan continued, "We only go in if families have irrefutable proof of provenance and have lost in mediation or litigation. In other words, when diplomacy has not worked to bring about justice. We have a European counterpart group and they're extremely helpful. Very few people know of the existence of the network; we can go a year, even two, without being contacted."

Sidney placed the folder in her backpack and stowed it in the kayak's front water-tight compartment. Ryan stood up and again placed his hands on his great-grandfather's shoulders. I thought about my own father and how much I had loved to touch him, lean into him, climb up into his lap. *I'll never have a chance to see him this old, nor will my children,* I thought.

Amy surprised me by suddenly asking Ryan, "I have a feeling you might be an insurance guy? Am I right?"

The old man pointed at Amy. "That's a smart one, right there."

We said our goodbyes and started to paddle away. I could see rolling hills, farms, and several vineyards in the distance as I turned towards the boat launch to where our car was parked. But Amy called out, "Hey, let's paddle a little further down the lake, it'd be fun, get our money's worth."

I looked at Sidney and she shrugged her shoulders in a *'Why not?'* kind of way. I made a loop back around and came up alongside Amy. "How the hell did you know what line of work he was in?"

Amy smiled and said, "Duh, the speedboat's name is 'Be Sure-Insure!'

                    2010

Amy

It was Bella's number. I was surprised it was her. How could she like me anymore? I turned from the kitchen window and held my breath.

"Hi Amy. Can we talk?"

I didn't say anything for a second, because I didn't know what to say.

"Please?"

"You're not mad at me?" I asked, leaning against the door to the den.

"Mad? I wasn't ever mad at you. I felt bad because of, you know, your dad, but no, I wasn't mad." She paused, "I didn't understand why you pushed me and called me that but then my mom kind of told me that being sad sometimes comes out as being pissed off."

It got real quiet and then I said, "It's been hard. Sorry I broke your statue."

"That thing…it was pathetic," Bella replied. She was eating something crunchy.

I didn't mean to laugh, but I did. Then I changed the subject because I still felt bad. "I can't believe we're going to be in seventh grade, can you?"

"For real, it's crazy. Did you get your schedule?" she asked.

"I did. We've got more classes than we had in sixth grade. I hope we get lockers or we'll have to lug around all our stuff." I walked to the refrigerator and grabbed a bottle of soda.

Bella replied, "I found out we have the same homeroom. That's, um, why I called. I guess they're called advisories. We have Mr. Latimore. I know because I helped Mrs. Anders make signs for opening day. She wondered if maybe I felt like calling you to…like, fix things between us."

"Really? We start every day together? Wait, I'm gonna run and grab my schedule."

I was skipping up the stairs towards my room. Mom passed me and asked, "Who's that?"

"Bella," I answered and kept on going.

I moved to my dresser. "Here's my schedule. Give me a sec…You're right, I've got Mr. Latimore too."

"Memories of us terrorizing Mr. Chase in fourth grade just hit me. 'Member the time we put all those things in his room upside down — the clock, every book in the shelves and all the posters on classroom expectations!" Bella replied, giggling.

"Yep, Mr. Chase blamed it on Jackson at first. He couldn't believe it was us." In a deep, slow voice I imitated Mr. Chase, "Now girls, I'm very disappointed in you."

"Didn't we buy Jackson ice cream like every day 'cause we felt so bad?" asked Bella.

"Uh-huh," I replied. I walked over to my bedroom window and looked out. Meg was weeding in her side yard and Brian was picking up the clippings. Mom had the radio on out on the porch and was starting to shuck the corn we'd bought at the vegetable stand. I could hear Meg telling her they'd eaten the best corn from Shaw's: "Imagine that!"

"So, what have you been up to this summer?" I asked.

"Not much, the friggin' rain has been awful. But tomorrow I want to go to the lake. It's supposed to be sunny and warm."

I put my schedule on my bed. "Yeah, I heard — I mean about the weather."

"If I go, you want to come? Just me and you? Maybe sit up by the snack bar so we don't have to walk too far?"

I thought it'd be nice to finally feel the sun, even swim if the water wasn't too cold. "Hold on, I have to ask my mom."

From the landing upstairs, I yelled down to my mother. She came into the house and to the bottom of the stairs. When I asked her about the lake, she nodded and said, "Of course you can go."

Bella was waiting when I got back to the phone. After I said I could go, she replied, "Get dropped off at the gate, at like noon. My mom can give you a ride home. Okay?"

"Yes. See you tomorrow."

WHILE I WAS SURPRISED about Bella calling, I was excited about hanging with her tomorrow. We'd been buddies for more than half our lives. I stretched out on my bed and looked at my schedule again. I had a lot of different classes each day besides lunch. Seventh grade was going to be a huge change and kind of scary, too.

This summer had been something I'd never expected. Instead of being bored out of my mind, I'd had a lot of chances to hang with Tommy and Sidney. We'd done some pretty cool things, good things.

Ms. Berenson's face popped up suddenly and I replayed her reaching out to grab hold of me. She'd called me 'little sister.' What was her sister's name and how old was she? Did she survive, I wondered. I hoped Ms. Berenson was still alive and still sitting in front of the picture window in her room having good memories, not those bad feeling ones.

I was going to miss David. I liked the way he talked to me, always making sure I was included. I asked him once if he had kids of his own and he told me he'd never gotten that lucky.

I decided to bake him cookies — he liked sweets and Sidney could give them to him. I'd write him a note and tell him to have a good year and that…I sat for a couple of quiet minutes thinking, but nothing else came to me.

I reached into my desk drawer and pulled out my new package of sticky notes instead. Mom and me had gone school supply shopping and all my notebooks, folders, pens, and mechanical pencils were still in their packaging. I chose the bright green ones and tore them open. I'd make a smiley face on the sticky note, sign it, and put it on top of the cookie tin. David would know it was my way of saying 'thanks.'

But first, I went back to the landing and yelled down to Mom, "I've got to make cookies."

She came back to the stairs and said, "Okay, sweetie. We've got everything for chocolate chip ones."

Just the right kind, I thought, *David will love them.*

Rachel

The café owner leaned in and asked, "Are you all right?"

"Did he just bang into me?" I opened my car door and climbed out.

"Yes, the elderly guy was driving. He meant to put the car in first when the light changed, but he hit reverse instead." The café owner stood at the curb with his hands on his hips. He'd just put the awning up on the picnic table out front.

We could hear the police sirens coming. "Oh God, really? Are sirens necessary?" I said out loud, turning beet red.

Soon I was exchanging insurance card information with the Batemans of Charleston, South Carolina. The woman was lovely while the man seemed somewhat befuddled. I kept reassuring them that I was fine, my car was fine, and we all agreed that finally the weather was fine. The policeman was young. I think it may have been his first week on the job.

I got curious looks as traffic inched through the stop-light. Once we were done, I pulled into the Café's parking lot. I wanted an iced coffee.

I paid for the drink and walked out to the table in front of the café. The deli down the street had a picnic table out front too, but I liked this one here because of all the action of the intersection. I guess today I became a part of all that action.

Langdon was a tourist town and growing, with second homes being built everywhere and 'townies' cashing in on the value of their houses and leaving. Each year it seemed a new restaurant had opened or a new specialty shop was popping up on Main Street. I'd seen a flyer for a new boutique just up the street that was having a sidewalk sale today.

So many people in Langdon had extended kindness to me and my mother when our husbands had died. I never thought we'd both be widows together, ever, in a million years.

I took a sip of the iced coffee. I wondered what it would be like right now if my father and Tom were still alive. Sometimes I played this mind game on days I didn't have to work and rush from one place to the next.

Immediately, I imagined that Amy and I wouldn't be having such a hard time connecting, like today when I'd dropped her off at the lake and she'd hurried me away as if she was embarrassed. And Bella acting like they hadn't seen each other in ages, even though they'd had that sleepover not so long ago. Then when I'd asked her where the tin of cookies was, she'd gotten impatient and replied, "It's no big deal, I forgot them." Yet the night before she'd burned the first batch and had almost cried. I'd made the second and third batches for her.

Tommy was home, mowing the yard and thinning out two of my perennial beds. Tom would be doing that, and maybe we'd have a new puppy too — another beagle after Jelly Beanie, or maybe a shepherd or even a rescue.

Dad and Mom would be deciding where to go for dinner tonight. It'd either be the club or maybe the new place out on the lake. We'd still have the cottage, and I wouldn't have ever decided to get a degree at Castleton because I wouldn't be worried about money, at least I didn't think so.

My thoughts drifted over to the meeting I'd had with the two staff members at the college. I'd never been comfortable taking a chance or doing something new or different. I always chose the safest path, the one I was most familiar with. Sometimes that had bothered Tom. There'd been a year, after Tommy was born, when he'd had a chance to coach at a big high school in Connecticut. He'd been offered the position, but I'd discouraged him, said I wasn't comfortable starting out in a new town, a place where I didn't know anyone. We'd stayed put. *I've still stayed put,* I thought, even when two of the three men I loved most were dead and in the ground.

I scooted further down the picnic bench into the sunshine, feeling its warmth. It suddenly occurred to me; Tommy doesn't have that cautiousness or fear of the new or unknown. His desire to spend so much of his time with Sidney was proof of that. She was about the furthest thing from the girls he'd dated in high school.

I finished the iced coffee and stood up to go in and return the glass. As I turned towards the Café, I wondered what desire looked like for me at my age. Tom had been the sum total of mine. But that wasn't exactly true — there'd been that very brief time with David. *More like a moment or two,* I thought.

I stepped back out onto the sidewalk, looking at the cars now moving through the light. I glanced at my watch. I wanted to get home in time to call my mother. She had a hair appointment, and I wondered if she wanted my company on the drive to Peddan.

I hesitated, then turned away from where my car was parked. I decided to check out the boutique's outdoor sale first. I had plenty of time.

Sidney

Imoved to the picnic table, carrying the two iced teas. David had parked his Jeep and was walking across the small parking lot to me. He wore jeans, a black t-shirt, and old sneakers. He moved confidently, like he owned the ground he walked on. It was hard to explain, and then I quickly thought, *Every woman sees what I see, there's no need to analyze it.*

"Sorry I'm late, Sidney. There was a fender bender at the lights in front of the Café. An elderly couple with Carolina plates hit an SUV. It just happened. Here come the sirens."

"You okay if we sit outside and soak up the rays?" I asked, believing he'd agree. "I'm going to be stuck in the lecture hall soon, once the semester starts."

"Yes, this is great. I love the deli, but I usually grab a sandwich and go. The weather couldn't be better after all the rain we've had."

He sat down and thanked me for the iced tea. I pushed a chocolate thin mint towards him too. The deli had a dish filled with them at the register.

"Thanks. You know I have a sweet tooth, huh?"

I smiled and got down to why I'd asked him to meet me here. "David, we met with someone from the network, actually two people — an old man and his great-grandson, in upstate New York. They gave me this thick folder covering the activities of the network in this region, definitely through your grandfather's years."

The traffic in front of us started to move again. We both took sips of our drinks.

"I think the network may have provided restitution for several Jewish families throughout the country. I get the strong impression that the members worked together — no one person was in charge calling the shots. A case of true collaboration. There's a similar network in Europe. I'd love to study and write about their incredible deeds, but, of course, that can never happen."

Suddenly, a kid stopped not far from the picnic table. The chain to his bike had come off and he put down the kickstand.

"Sid, I'll be right back." David walked up to the boy and knelt down. I couldn't quite hear what they were saying, but the boy smiled and stepped back while David leaned in to work on the bike's chain.

Two women reached the boy and David. I stood up and walked over with my iced tea, but kept an eye on the folder on the picnic table. They were women a little bit older than me, in yoga pants and carrying hand weights. It appeared that one might be the boy's mother.

"I feel that I may know you," David was saying, and the boy's mother replied, "I get that feeling too!"

David stood up — the chain was on and the boy was smiling. David's hands were greasy and the second woman quickly said, "Oh wait, I have wipes, let me get you one." She reached into her fanny pack and handed him one.

David started to laugh. "The Jelly Lady — Annie! That's how I recognized you!"

                                                    2010

The boy's mother smiled. "Yes, of course. We met in Bridgewater too, at one of the parties. Please give Annie my best."

"Oh, we're, um, we aren't together anymore, haven't been for a while."

"That's too bad," she said as her boy leaned into her.

"Mom, tell him about Annie," he said.

"What's that?" David asked.

"Michael wants you to know that he's the one who gave Annie her 'Jelly Lady' name. She started out with 'The Jam M'am' but..."

David made a face and the woman laughed. "I know, it's bad, isn't it? Every time we'd drive by her, Michael would yell out, 'The Jelly Lady,' and she changed it."

"Ah, you're destined for a career in marketing, Michael — or is it Mike?" David asked.

The boy nodded and said, "It's Michael," and then pointed to his mother. "And that's my mom, Sara, and my Aunt Jeannie."

David smiled. I watched the boy's Aunt Jeannie just about devour him with her eyes.

"Well, Michael, I'm David, and this is Sidney, a good friend of mine. I'm a painter who lives on a farm. So, what name would you give me?"

The kid thought a moment and said, "The Painter in the Dell?"

David laughed. "Hey, that's not bad, not bad at all." He ruffled the boy's hair.

"Thanks for fixing my chain."

David gave him a thumbs up and we returned to the picnic table.

"If ever you eat at Shay's ask for me — Jeannie. I'm the dining room manager!"

David smiled and we sat back down. I asked him if he ever got tired of women fawning all over him, like 'Aunt Jeannie' just had.

"There was a time when that's all I thought about." He looked out across the street at the sidewalk sale. It was doing a brisk business.

"What do you mean?" I asked. But David suddenly seemed elsewhere, kind of frozen-like. I turned to where he was looking, then slowly repeated my question, "David, can you tell me what you mean?"

Reluctantly, he pulled his eyes away from the boutique and responded, "Oh, let's just say, I cashed in on all that fawning…It's not something I'm proud of."

I started to gather up the folder. David reached over and placed his hand on my arm. "Sidney, you make absolutely sure that you never put Amy in harm's way. Please, promise me that. And you and Tommy have to be careful, too. Art is stolen all the time by people looking to flip the work, and there are too many unscrupulous dealers out there. I'd say ninety-five percent of thefts are from private residences, with the art valued in the thousands. It's hard to trace and easy to transport. Rarely is it ever recovered. Please, do not do anything rash. Let other people take the risk."

I was moved by how much he cared. We'd all spent meaningful time together since the spring. I wanted to alleviate any worries he had and replied, "I promise you, we'll never put ourselves in any situation that is the least bit questionable or dangerous. I'm not even sure to what extent I'll be involved, let alone Tom. The network is not anywhere near as active as it once was. And as for Amy — she's going to forget all about this. Today she's at Echo Lake with a friend enjoying the end of summer."

He smiled and said, "I mean it, be careful."

I got up, walked around the picnic table, and gave David a big hug. "That's from Tom and Amy too. Oh wait, I almost forgot…" I quickly reached over to the bench and picked up the tin of cookies. "Amy made you these. We love you."

When I left, I glanced back at David still sitting at the table. He seemed deep in thought.

David

Three days after meeting Sidney, I crossed the road to get to the mailbox. I waited for a semi-trailer to go clamoring by before I quickly scooted back over. Leaving the main road, I started to walk up the long driveway while I thumbed through the mail. It was a whole lot of junk, although I liked the advertisement from the deli down in Langdon where Sid and I had met. I loved their reubens, and now I loved the picnic table out front.

I hadn't said a thing to Sidney at the time, but I'd seen Rachel across the way at the boutique. A tall woman had turned toward the street holding up a long, turquoise, flared skirt. I'd felt a jolt and held my breath. Rachel had been shaking her head 'no' as she'd placed the skirt at her waist and then put it back on the rack. She'd been smiling and talking to someone, but I couldn't see who.

She was exactly how I remembered her — *but even more beautiful,* I thought. She was older, yes, and pale, with darker hair than that summer, but she was still graceful and poised. For a split second, I imagined I'd heard her laughter, but then she'd moved from my line of vision. After Sidney had pulled out of the deli's lot, I'd sat at the picnic table for a little while longer. I'd liked being somewhere close to her, even though she was already gone. I'd toyed with the idea of calling her right from there — just to hear her voice. I still had her number from the time Amy had used my cell in Stamford. But I didn't, just like I never did all the other times I'd thought about it. *What if she picked up?* Eventually I did what I always did — I filed her away. But this time it had been harder.

HALFWAY UP THE DRIVE, I realized I'd missed one small envelope. Latara's return address was up in the corner. I opened it and read: *"Dear David, I wanted you to know my granddaddy passed away at the start of the month. He died peacefully, in his sleep. He was seventy-nine. Your visit was certainly the highlight of his spring, actually of many springs he spent with you. In going through his things, I came across a few pictures I thought you'd like to have. All my love, your running buddy — Latara."*

There were four black and white photos, a little grainy and not in the best condition. The first one was of me and Joe in an old Ford truck going to market to have the cherries weighed. We both looked purposeful. I smiled, remembering those trips. The second photo was of Nana hanging out sheets to dry and me wrapped up in one of them. She had a smile on her face, and I was sticking my tongue out at whoever was taking the picture. The next one was me and Latara, sitting on the steps of the porch eating popsicles. My grandfather was leaning against the railing, looking at the two of us. He had an amused expression, kind of like, 'Will you look at these two.' The last one was of a young woman, a girl really, cradling a baby in her arms on the living room sofa. I turned it over. Written on the back was, *'David, three months old, 1959.'* I studied the girl. *She looks like a deer caught in the headlights of motherhood*, I thought.

I carefully put them back in the envelope and went up to the house. It was time to look at the diary Tommy had found in my grandparents' closet. I'd placed it in the junk drawer in the kitchen and had been sidestepping it ever since.

I put a pot of coffee on and went into the pantry. I grabbed the tin of chocolate chip cookies Amy had made me and brought them out. I took her sticky note with the smiley face off of the top of the tin and stuck it up on the refrigerator. I was going to miss seeing her, being around her.

I placed Latara's envelope on the old, chipped Formica table. I only used a tablecloth when I had company, which was now probably going to be never since the kids were all tied up and going back to school. I opened the junk drawer and took out the diary. I poured the coffee and sat down.

It had a little clasp with a lock, but it wasn't necessary to find the key; it wasn't locked. I took a bite of a cookie and opened it. Written on the inside cover, in sprawling, large cursive handwriting was the name *Jenny Sumner* with a pronounced period at the end. The year *1956* was written equally large and she had drawn rays shooting out from the numbers. I took a moment to figure out her age — she had been 14, maybe in 9th grade, just starting high school at Plymouth.

I was instantly disappointed. I had hoped to learn who my father was from her entries. During the weeks since Tommy had handed it off to me, I'd imagined all sorts of things. I would not only discover who my father was but would finally read why she left and what she thought of me. But this year, 1956, was way too early.

"What a fucking joke, as usual." My heart sank. I turned the page and was flooded by a series of charcoal drawings. She'd used the lines on the pages as a guide for positioning the eyes, nose, mouth, ears, and chin. I quickly realized that most of them were selfies — I was looking at her face, page after page. But then I recognized my grandmother and, further along, two drawings of my grandfather, though younger, much younger than I ever recalled him being.

She hadn't torn out her early attempts, instead she'd written the date on each. She'd been patient and persistent; the self -portraits getting better in her ability to define features, blend out layers, and darken areas of the skin.

Finally, the last drawing of herself was quite good. She'd added even more detail, like the way her bangs fell down along her forehead and her hair on each side of her face curling slightly up on the ends. There was a mole above her mouth, and on the bridge of her nose she'd lightly placed freckles. She wore little earrings and a chain with a tiny cross around her neck. She wasn't smiling, but she wasn't frowning either, her lips full and feminine. Her eyes were especially impressive: the thick lash lines and the pupils and the shadowed brows above that were drawn in with perfect arches. She'd used shading with highlights and varying degrees of pencil strokes to render what I'd imagined was a decent likeness. *My mother was an artist.*

I stood up and moved over to the sink. This time I said it out loud, "My mother was an artist." This knowledge, this realization was mind blowing. I'd never once, in all of my fantasies growing up, and then in the early, waking moments of so many years as an adult, played out this scenario, this possibility. Not once. I reached into the cupboard and took down a glass, filling it up with cold water. I drank it all down.

I turned around and returned to the table. I tried to remember her. The sad thing was I only had a few, shitty memories — waiting in the van, different men's voices, and being hungry. Then living here without her.

As the days and months and finally the years had ticked by, I'd grown to hate her. Yet that hate of mine had been laced with longing, so much longing for her to come back, to fetch me, to take me with her.

I combed through the other pages in the diary — she was mastering her signature, practicing different styles. Big loops like her opening page versus small, tightly controlled ones. She seemed to want the more controlled style, but I gleaned her natural tendency leaned toward the big and flowery. I noticed she never included her middle name, my grandmother's — Mildred. I could understand why.

I came upon a Christmas list, complete with doodles of stockings, candy canes, and snowmen. She'd wanted records, Elvis Presley and The Planters, new shoes, art supplies, and a house kitty (the word house was under-lined). Then came a series of pictures of dresses cut from catalogs and magazines taped onto the pages. Below them were different comments: *"Mom, can you make this for me?"* or *"I think this is nice, do you?"* And *"Get a look at this pattern!"* Nana had written below each one, tender replies from a mother to her daughter. *"I can try, Jenny!" "Yes, I like this, too!"* and *"It's awful, isn't it! Did you show Daddy?"*

The last page was a poem written in the smaller, tightly controlled cursive she'd worked so hard on in earlier pages: *My little kitty and I play down in the meadow. She wants to go to the barn. She wants to see the others. No, I say loudly, they aren't loved like you. They can't cuddle with me on the bed like you. They aren't clean and brushed like you. You are mine! She still wants to go to the barn. I'll never let her. By Jenny Sumner.* On the corresponding page she'd drawn a kitten with big, sad eyes. It was rather good, but lacked the great detail of her final self-portrait.

I closed the diary. I looked up at the sticky note from Amy. It struck me that my mother seemed and felt young to me in this diary, closer to Amy's age than what I imagined a girl of 14 to be like. Maybe it was due to the times, the 1950s, or living isolated out on the farm, as opposed to living in a town or a city. *It could be a combination of both*, I thought.

I sat for minutes watching the afternoon sun fade. I thumbed back through the diary. How did she become someone so totally different than this girl in these pages? As the old neighbor had implied, she'd gotten around.

In three short years, she'd be pregnant, then waking to feed a baby in the middle of the night. Had she been shamed, ostracized for being an unwed mother? And how had my grandparents reacted to the pregnancy? I didn't know the answers to any of these questions, but it seemed important for me to know, especially now that I saw her here so childlike, so young.

I GOT UP AND DECIDED TO head out to the shed and start to get it cleaned up and organized. Besides, I needed to get physical, to expend some energy.

I walked across the driveway, past the barn, and thought about what needed to get done this fall in order to get the place ready for winter. Cleaning a spot for the tractor was imperative. I had a lead on a used plow attachment — I didn't want to keep paying for plowing since the cost was a financial drain.

It didn't take me long to turn my focus in on myself and how I'd been at the age of 14, living here. I remembered a trip to Maine and how I'd berated my grandparents for miles and miles on the way home because we didn't live on the water. "The farm is boring, I hate it."

Leaning on the broom, I knew I'd made both of them give up their daughter for me. I had demanded loyalty only to me and they had acquiesced. Any talk, any memories of her in my presence had been forbidden — all those times I'd insisted, "Make sure, Nana, make sure Papa."

I realized, vigorously sweeping the floor of the shed, that the monster I had created out of her was crumbling, but what remained was me, another kind of monster.

LATER THAT EVENING, I walked through the living room and dining room to get to the sewing room. I passed my paintings, all returned and in two neat rows, leaning against the faded wallpaper. I sat at my grandmother's sewing machine. I discovered that if I held the diary in a certain way, I could flip the pages fast and see my mother's young face move. I did that several times.

By bedtime I thought it might be a good idea to contact Everett, my therapist, and ask if I could check in with him sometime soon.

Just before sleep came, I replayed Rachel holding up the skirt and the way her thick dark hair met the curve of her shoulders.

Rachel

Tommy came in and sat on my bed, the weight of him causing all my markers to roll towards him and almost off the bed. He caught them.

"Nice save! What's going on, sweetie?" I asked him.

Looking up at him, I thought how much he looked like his dad. I thought this every time he'd been away, even for just a day. He wasn't smiling at me, and I immediately wondered if Sidney had broken up with him. I worried he'd fallen hard for her and, while I liked her, I couldn't quite figure her out. I moved the construction paper and cut-out pictures off to the side. My pre-k prep could wait.

"Hey really, what's up?" I said this gently, taking in his own look of concern.

"Oh, I really don't know how to tell you, but it's time I did and please, promise me you'll hear me out before you, like, blow a gasket, okay? You promise?"

Was Sidney pregnant? Had he gotten a DUI? My mind was racing. Tom reached over and took my hand. "Still your thoughts, Mom, as Amy would say."

"She does? She says that?" I asked. I had never once, in her eleven years of living, heard her say this.

"Yes, sometimes when she was hanging out with Sid and me this summer."

I sat up and crossed my legs. I had no idea where this was going, but Tom was serious and I needed to give him the attention he was asking me for.

"Okay, thanks, Mom. I like your eye contact and your body language looks good. Stay that way, okay?"

When did he learn how to run circle time? I thought.

THEN HE TOLD ME EVERYTHING, beginning with the gallery opening this spring and what had ensued. He slowed down and gauged my reaction when he mentioned getting Amy involved. He described how Amy had sprinted across the lawn at the nursing home, tripping the sprinklers. "Like a running back in training — dodging here, dodging there!"

He grew somber when he described how the old man stepped back when David carefully opened up the box and he saw the painting. Tommy started to say more, hesitated, and then fell silent.

He looked at me closely. "What are you thinking, Mom?"

I was at a loss and shook my head. "I don't know what to think. I need a minute to process this."

Before he left my room, I asked, "Why didn't David Sumner ever sell his grandfather's farm? And what's he like now?"

He came back to the bed and replied, "He's an awesome guy, and not just because he saved me. His art opening was incredible. He's a really good painter now. His paintings are all of you and us."

I heard him going down the stairs and soon he and Amy were playing basketball out in the driveway.

I sat, stunned, still not knowing what to think. Amy and Tommy were involved in returning stolen art? David had painted us? I'd never bothered opening the certified letter addressed to 'Mrs. Thomas Dunne' from that Williamstown gallery. *What would the Jonathan Taylor Gallery ever want with me?* I remembered thinking at the time.

I looked up and smiled. I still didn't quite know what to make of her. She was brainy and cold, just so different from what I thought Tommy would have been attracted to. I felt like we were both always trying to size each other up, especially this latest trip home.

"You sleep, okay?" she asked and now I did look straight at her. It was more than a simple question of how I slept.

"Tommy told you about the art we returned?" She reached up into the cupboard and took down a glass. She moved to the refrigerator, seeming very at home in our house.

I cleared my throat and replied, "Yes, he did. I don't really know what to make of it all. I'm still trying to figure out if you three were in any danger."

Sidney paused and turned towards me. "I don't think we were in danger at any time, per se…except for the Jan Both paintings Tom delivered to the professor's father. Those pieces of art may be worth over a hundred thousand each, or even more. We needed to be extremely careful with how we handled them."

After pouring a glass of juice, Sidney came over to me and sat. "And your thoughts on the paintings?" I made no comment. "I mean the paintings that David painted?"

Sidney shifted in her seat and looked at me directly. She hadn't touched her glass yet. "Rachel, the paintings are of the near drowning: Tommy poised to hit the water, and you and Amy, you know…you nursing Amy and…"

I heard Meg's husband in the driveway, wheeling the garbage can to the curb. The upstairs toilet flushed. Sidney surprised me and reached over, placing her hand on top of mine. It was a gesture of kindness, and it touched me.

I smiled at her and said, "That summer — it was such an emotional summer. Almost losing Tommy the way we did and David's involvement, how he ran in to save him. I think it changed us. The feeling that we take everything and everyone for granted. It definitely gave us, you know, the awareness to really make time for each other."

"I can imagine that. And I think David was greatly affected by Tommy's rescue too."

I was struck by the way Tommy and David's names rolled so easily off her tongue.

Sidney continued, "The paintings are definitely a testament to that. But, Rachel, there's something, um…I'm not sure if Tom went there, but I'm going to because I think you should know. There are many paintings, but some are of just you and…" She looked down at the floor and then back at me. "They're breathtaking, and it's clear to me he was in love with you — still *is* in love with you."

This was awkward, and something I didn't feel comfortable talking about. I felt old and tired and stuck and not sure I believed her words. I still hadn't made up my mind about going back to school; the decision had become complicated and I had left the emails from the admission's department unanswered. My God, just the porch redo had been overwhelming for me. *Is it normal, at 47, to feel this way?*

Sidney sipped her juice, but gave no indication that she was growing impatient with me. In fact, her patience and overall demeanor was welcoming. Maybe I did want to talk about it, after all.

"I've thought a lot about those days," I began. "The morning of the near drowning and then later, at David's grandfather's farm. That day, especially — how we talked with one another, the way he looked at me. I think I was so different from the women he knew, had relationships with. He told me about his own mother leaving him and then finding her death certificate. I think he was trying to make sense of me as a mother too, figure out how mothers act. It's hard to explain.

"Tom and I were kids, really, when we met and then when we got married. And we loved each other, grew with each other, knew each other to the core. David, he was unlike anyone I'd ever known. He was smooth and classy and, I think, very rich. But he was sad, too, and lonely and kind of demanding, especially with the way he called me after that day. Like he could beckon me and I was just supposed to leave everything and go to him."

"Wait, he asked you to leave Tom and the kids?" Sidney's face was incredulous.

"No, no, nothing that drastic, but he definitely wanted us to go further, like have an affair. He stalked me at the Children's Center. I told him to stop. And he did."

Sidney stared at me. She started to say something and then stopped. Finally, she replied, "Well, I think he may have changed from that demanding, kind of 'this is what I want, this is what I get' arrogant guy. It's been what, eleven years? I think — no, I know, Rachel, that this David is humble, less full of himself."

I got up and walked to the sink. I turned around. "I'd be lying if I told you that I wasn't attracted to him back then. He was like a movie star in our midst. But I never would have gone any further, ever."

Sidney came up to the counter next to where I was standing. She was pensive, then hesitantly said, "Rachel, if ever you want to be loved again, I know a wonderful painter who's waiting for you."

She walked out of the kitchen. I heard her climbing the stairs. Tommy was calling her name.

Amy

Tom and Sidney beeping their goodbye woke me up. It was early, but I was ready to get up and go down to see Mom. It was the fourth day in a row without rain. It was like somebody suddenly turned on the switch for hot, sunny weather.

The sun was streaming in through the kitchen windows. Mom was sitting there with her coffee, and I think an apple cinnamon muffin — my favorite.

She looked up at me and, for once, I smiled. I smiled big and pretty because today I was going to confirm why I was so different. Oh, I knew why ever since Tommy let it slip on the way to David's farm. But today, here, was where I was gonna solidify my theory. Mom smiled back — her smile was always big and pretty — and motioned to the kitchen chair across from her.

"Come sit, I made muffins," she said.

The kitchen smelled good. As I passed the fridge, I instantly thought of the time Daddy put me up on top of it. He wouldn't come get me down until I sang *Itsy Bitsy Spider* to him. I was 3, maybe 4, and in Mommy's pre-K class. I liked all the attention then. It was a happy memory.

I sat down and reached for the plate of muffins. Mom got up and poured me a glass of juice. I wanted milk instead, but I didn't tell her that. I nodded and said, "Thanks," as she set the juice down. She took up her seat again and smiled at me. It'd been a while since I'd joined her in the morning. I thought, *Why not say it now?*

"Mom, how come you never told me about all those babies you had who died?" Boom! Her whole face changed. It was like she'd been slapped, and I felt so bad. But my need to know was greater. I sat, staring at her.

She turned away and stood up to refill her coffee cup. She turned back to face me, leaning with her back against the counter. I waited and then raised my eyebrows in a questioning kind of way. In my mind I said, *Go on, Mom, you can tell her the truth.*

"Oh, Amy, that was such a hard time, and I mean a really hard time for me, and for Daddy too. I try not to think about it. We struggled through it and then you came along and surprised us. You were our miracle baby."

I took a bite of the apple cinnamon muffin then looked back up at her. "Is that why there's so many years between Tommy and me? And were you kind of worried I wouldn't make it too?"

She didn't answer me right away. She came back to sit down across from me at the table.

"But I did make it and I was a big baby, wasn't I?"

Looking very serious, Mom replied, "I held my breath the whole time I carried you. You were, as Daddy liked to say, 'Tough as nails.' In fact, I ended up being induced with you — you didn't want to come out."

I looked at her tentatively and whispered, "I'm an old soul. I know you probably don't like that phrase, but that's what I am. I think I came to you and Daddy and Tommy from some" — I moved my arms around — "some place that's out there in another dimension." I thought of the reincarnation book that was under my mattress. I had found it in the 'discard bin' at the public library and read it like three times.

I could tell she was not okay with the direction our discussion was going, but I kept her in it. That's when I asked, "Tommy told you about us getting some heirlooms back to the Jewish families who, well, who lived and died during the Holocaust?"

"Yes, he did, Amy. I'm glad that worked out, that you're safe. Were you scared?"

I took a big gulp of air and said, clear as day, "Mommy, I was there — I lived during that horrible time, I'm sure of it. I felt the suffering, and the fear. The old woman at the nursing home — Ms. Berenson? She and I connected. It was like a shock passed through us, like we crossed through time."

As soon as I said all this, I realized I didn't need her or anyone else to believe me. I knew it deep in that dark place of my being.

I got up and came over. I leaned down from behind and wrapped my arms tightly around her. She reached up and covered my arms with her hands. It was nice feeling her with the sun streaming in. I didn't hurry from our hug like I usually did.

Rachel

The upstairs was warm. I should have closed the windows this morning and pulled the blinds. That was something Tom always did — took care of the house, knowing how to make the heat of the day bearable by just maneuvering what stayed open, what got closed. I was glad my mother was in the den downstairs where it was cooler. I could hear the TV on and imagined her comfortable on the futon.

She'd asked earlier, "Would it be okay If I spent the night? Meg and I are going to the Senior Center really early to set up for the tag sale."

"Of course! I love having you." We were talking openly now about her development with the gentleman friend and her possible move.

"It's not really that serious, at least not yet," she'd told me, laughing as she said it, her voice full of hope.

As I came down the upstairs hallway, I stopped at Amy's bedroom door. I called to her, "Is it too hot for you?"

There was no reply. I opened her door and looked in. She was sound asleep with headphones on. Her windows were wide open and the oscillating fan was on high. The room wasn't bad. Maybe she'd known about Tom's system and had done it today in her own room. I didn't dare take off her headphones, worried it might wake her.

Her looks were changing — she was starting to morph into a teenager. While the fake nose ring was gone, she still wore the black eyeliner with a little mascara. Both were now smudged. She'd written on her hands and a little bit on her legs with a sharpie. I turned my head — I couldn't quite make out what she'd written. *I was slow to develop,* I thought, *I don't want to hurry her.*

The hug she'd given me this morning meant something. Was it a shift? A start for us to begin to reckon with the distance between us? I'd felt it deeply in the moment and then all day I'd tried to make sense of it. I wasn't sure, but I hoped.

Amy had called me out onto the porch just before dinner. She'd seemed pensive at first, reluctant to say want she wanted to say. I'd waited. "I saw your confusion with Bella about the sleepover. I'm sorry. I was really with Tommy and Sidney that night."

"Okay, sweetheart. Is there anything else you want to tell me?" I wasn't angry and I'd wanted her to know that.

She'd put down the book she'd been holding and patted the chair's armrest. "Well, I really like the new look of the porch. It's awesome. It reminds me of Maine and the ocean."

"It's different, isn't it? It took me so long to decide." I'd moved to the table and picked up a dirty glass. "Maybe you and I could scoot to the beach for a day before school starts."

"There's one more thing Mom — the cookies I made…I mean you made…They weren't for Bella and me. They were for David, David Sumner. He's been nice to me all summer. Him and I have even talked about past lives."

That had shocked me, but I'd downplayed my surprise.

NOW, I CLOSED HER BEDROOM DOOR carefully. Walking further down the hallway, I realized I needed to keep an open mind about her odd beliefs and read what she'd been reading in order to get a better understanding of where her head was at.

My room was the warmest place in the house. I turned the fan on, blowing the hot air out the window. I walked to the mirror.

"Forty-seven doesn't look so good on me, does it?" I asked aloud. My hair was dull, my shoulders slumped, and the summer's rain had left me woefully pale.

"What's my problem?" I asked myself. "How did all these things happen while I was so oblivious?"

I sat on the edge of the bed and ran my hand across the bedspread. A kaleidoscope of images flooded me: the French woman with the long silver hair, asking me how it felt to be a 'muse' as the cold air enveloped us; the farm's familiar cherry trees twisting in the glow of the light above the easel; the formal letter addressed to 'Mrs. Thomas Dunne' in fancy, cursive writing; David leaving the restaurant in that self-assured way; and Amy carefully layering the chocolate chip cookies into the tin for him.

I stood and turned the fan on higher. I moved the curtains aside and looked out at the cul-de-sac. It was almost dark, the light of the streetlamps illuminating the circle. I remembered Meg's tiki lanterns lit up at the party years ago and Tommy sitting in the back of our pick-up. I heard Tom's big, sweet voice bellowing above everyone else's, "Here's the guy who saved our kid!"

"What should I do, baby, tell me?" I whispered. Then I heard Pat's words, "You're going about living. Tom would want you to."

Sidney told me David was different and still in love with me. *Eleven years is a long time*, I thought. *But so is the rest of my life.*

I looked at my reflection once more. "If ever you want to be loved again, I know a wonderful painter waiting for you."

I wasn't tired. I turned and left the room.

David

I took a drag of the joint. It burned quickly, but I could tell it was really good shit, its sweet pungent odor strong. Sitting in one of the Adirondack chairs, I looked out over the meadow and across to the orchard as the sun was setting. The mowing I'd done earlier made everything greener now with the clover cut down. The sky was turning pink with hints of purple, some yellow. The lighting was amazing. I tried to identify all the colors I was seeing, what I'd choose from my paints to capture the evening's hues. The big maple stood tall, its leafy branches a silver green. A fleeting image of Latara as a girl came to me.

I heard a rustling to my right, at the end of the porch, coming from where I suspected he'd been during the heat of the day. The first time I'd caught wind of him was about three nights ago. I'd turned off the kitchen light by the sink and spotted him sitting on the porch. The next morning, I'd set out a bowl of water and my morning scraps of eggs and bacon.

I turned slowly and saw him stretching. He was skinny, his tail broken or maybe just crooked. His fur was black, but I could see scarring, a healed-over gouge up on his front shoulder. There was no white in his muzzle; he was younger than I first thought. He stood, looking at me pensively.

"Hey fella, come on over, sit awhile." I reached into my blue jeans and took out the handful of dry dog food I'd put in my pocket right before I'd grabbed the joint, the lighter, and a bottle of beer.

His nose started to twitch and he moved slowly to me, not quite cowering but definitely not trotting, either. I put the pieces of food on the arm of the chair but kept one piece in my hand. Now, I leaned forward, holding it out. "Come on, come get this."

The dog kept moving slowly toward me, closing in on the distance between us. I stayed very still, the one tiny bit of food still in my outstretched hand. He gently scooped it up and chewed. I took a sip of beer and started to feed him slowly, making sure I made no sudden moves. The peepers were out, and dusk was falling. I took another drag and the dog laid down at my feet. *I should go get him more food,* I thought, but I didn't get up. I sat there enjoying his company, his acceptance of me.

I looked down the driveway and watched a car go whizzing by. How many times did I sit on that front porch and watch those cars? Nana calling to me to come in and have dessert, Papa telling me the game was starting. Many nights I didn't go in though, at least not the first time they'd call. I remember with each new car passing, I'd whisper, "Maybe the next one will be my mother."

I started to move one hand down the dog's back, slowly, gingerly, all the way to his tail. "Fella, you've had some hard times in this young life of yours, haven't you?"

Today I turned 51. I'd almost forgotten until I saw the calendar hanging up on the Agway wall when I went in to get some new blades for the mower. It was a surprise discovering that today was my birthday. For once in my life,

I hadn't thought of what I wanted, or more, what I felt I deserved. That's when I grabbed the small bag of dog food. I was thinking of something other than myself for a change.

The dog shifted and now laid completely out on the grass. "You've got some lab in you, maybe?" He raised his head and looked at me.

Fifty-one, I thought, about the same age my grandfather was when he took me in after my mother snuck out in the middle of the night, popping the clutch to her hippie van and rolling down the driveway. He and my grandmother never saw their daughter again. But in her wake, she'd left a boy, me, almost 7 years old.

I wonder what my mother thought when she left — *Good riddance,* or maybe, *Finally, I'm free of the little fucker, that albatross.*

Tears fell and I slowly wiped them away. *She was just a kid herself, wanting to be free.*

I TURNED AND LOOKED BACK at the old farmhouse. Its railing was rotting, the roof needed to be replaced, and the curtains that my grandmother hung decades ago looked faded and sad. I swished the beer bottle around and took the last sip. I put out the joint, carefully saving the rest for another time. I started to get up but thought better of it and sat back down. The evening air was a relief from the heat of the past few days. We'd traded the rain for high temperatures. I reached over to pat the dog again. His tail thumped.

At 29, my grandfather was driving across Germany, reclaiming stolen art. At 29, I was screwing and snorting my way through Soho's art scene. At 50, he was meeting people in the dead of the night, still returning stolen art. Near that age, I was trashing his house, furious at the world. What a joke I was compared to him.

Finally, though, I'd understood that anger and had let it go. Then along came a couple of college kids and a quirky 11-year-old. It was their moral compass that helped me see that my self-worth hinged on my own actions — and nobody else's.

I stretched my legs out in front of me. My pants were grass-stained like when I used to roll down the hill, finally drifting to the right or to the left and stopping. My grandmother would complain about the stains, but I knew she wasn't really mad. My grandfather sometimes winked when she'd go off on me like that. Those winks were gestures of endearment, like 'we're in this together.'

I replayed my early morning session with Everett and what I'd come to see: My grandparents loved me as much as a child could possibly be loved. But I'd seen that love as a consolation prize, never the real thing because it wasn't my mother's love. All these years, I couldn't see that they'd given me everything I needed.

I wished for one more chance to redeem myself, to sit with them and listen to our lives and let myself be happy.

Looking up at the stars coming out, I whispered, "I love you, Nana and Papa. I'm sorry I treated you like shit. You were enough."

I HEARD A BARN OWL HOOT and the dog sat up and cocked its head towards the brook. It was getting late, nearing 9:00 p.m. I stood up, grabbing the beer bottle and the joint. I started to walk towards the house and he followed. I hadn't gotten that far in my thinking about the dog. I looked down at him and said, "Okay, fella, you and me are gonna watch a little bit of the Red Sox. They're playing on the West Coast. Then we'll hit the sack." This time his tail definitely wagged.

As I stepped up onto the porch, I heard the sound of a car turning in, its tires crunching on the gravel driveway. I turned back and watched it make its way up to the house, its lights switching from hi-beams to low. "You know who this is, fella? 'Cause I sure as hell don't."

The car pulled up to the porch and stopped. I came back down the stairs.

A woman, sitting in the driver's seat, turned off the engine and looked at me. "Hello David," she said and smiled.

"Hey, Rachel." My heart quickened as she started to climb out. The dog's tail went crazy.

"I've come to see the paintings."

2021

Amy

I brought the quilt out and laid it down between the chairs. Mom and David were in the kitchen, getting lunch ready.

It'd been almost two years since we'd last seen Tommy and Sidney in person. Even before the whole world went mad with COVID. Then it was all masks, borders closed, no traveling, Mom doing her state work remotely, and me taking my courses in gerontology online. Turns out, I do like nursing homes, after all.

Now things were starting up again, and we were all vaccinated.

I looked down at the road, past the wooden sign that read, *The Painter in the Dell — Family Portraits — Oil Paintings*. I was hoping the next car would be them. And it was!

I quickly ran to the porch and yelled, "It's them, they're here, they're here!"

Tommy parked right near the arrow pointing to the studio out back in the little house by the orchard. He climbed from the rental, stretched, and turned to where Mom was coming down off the steps.

The joy on her face was indescribable. David winked at me. Old Fella came out from his shady spot under the porch.

"Wow, the place looks fantastic!" Tommy called out.

"Thanks, we're almost there." Mom replied, grinning at David. He nodded, clearly pleased.

Sidney, emerging from the back seat, lifted the baby up. She turned to us, smiling.

"That's how I remember you the first time we met," David said from behind.

I beamed a hundred-watt smile as he moved to stand beside me.

I'm one happy ole' soul, I am, I am — and Daddy, I know you're right here, too.

We moved closer to see baby Alexandra as the sun and clouds took turns on this beauty of a Vermont day.

With Gratitude

*To my team — Rachel Carter, editor and
Jen Payne of Words by Jen, graphic designer
and book builder: your professionalism, expertise
and honesty continue to amaze me.*

*Thank you to Rabbi Avremy Raskin
for your time and feedback.*

*To my cousin, Matthew Blackwell, an incredible
painter in New York — thank you for your knowledge
and insight. Those beautiful sisters, our mothers, will
always be the women I most admire. I love you, Matty.*

*Thank you, Tricia and Michael. You allowed
me in at a time when the moments left were precious
and filled with whispered words of love.*

*Thanks, Andy, for your continued patience,
support and love. Also, to Calli, our big, shaggy
sugar doodle, for waiting those extra few minutes
for our walks each and every time.*

*Much appreciation to all the people who read my first
novel, Rectified, and encouraged me to write a second
one. Your vote of confidence spurred me on. Retirement
certainly is a new chapter in one's life, or, as the case
may be in mine, a new book or two.*

*Finally, to Vermont, my adoptive state — your beauty
and sense of community for the past 30 years has
warmed my heart. I love this place I call home.*